More praise for

THE SNOW FOX

"[Readers] will be swept up in Schaeffer's passionate evocation of the war between the sexes."   —Joanne Wilkinson, *Booklist*

"Schaeffer is known for writing passionate novels . . . that evoke widely different worlds in intimate detail. . . . The underlying theme of [*The Snow Fox*] is timeless—the endless complications of the relations between men and women."
    —Lesley Downer, *New York Times Book Review*

"Love, poetry and severed heads on pikes: A novel with some of the majesty of *Cold Mountain* immerses you in the complex social world—and heinous cruelty—of medieval Japan."   —Laura Miller, *Salon.com*

"[An] engaging tale of honor, loyalty, and discovery. . . Schaeffer creates in *The Snow Fox* a world long passed yet familiar to modern day audiences—replete with scenarios of love, betrayal and violence."
    —Angela Roberts, *The Virginia-Pilot*

"[*The Snow Fox*] beautifully evokes a lost time, when nature was pure, heroes had values and allegiances which they could not discard, and poetry was a natural part of everyone's life—it is certainly part of this novel."   —Mary Whipple, www.desijournal.com

"Its evocation of a magnificent but brutal society in which, against all odds, a great love manages to survive makes *The Snow Fox* a truly unforgettable book."
    —Rosemary M. Canfield Reisman, *Magill Book Reviews*

"Susan Fromberg Schaeffer has painted an elegant, intricate portrait of 12th century Japan, a world of noble lords, samurai and their beautiful ladies whose faces are always hidden from view."
    —Luan Gaines, *Curled Up with a Good Book*

ALSO BY SUSAN FROMBERG SCHAEFFER

Fiction

Falling (1973)
Anya (1974)
Time in Its Flight (1978)
The Queen of Egypt (1979)
Love (1980)
The Madness of a Seduced Woman (1983)
Mainland (1985)
The Injured Party (1986)
Buffalo Afternoon (1989)
First Nights (1993)
The Golden Rope (1996)
The Autobiography of Foudini M. Cat (1998)

Poetry

The Witch and the Weather Report (1972)
Granite Lady (1974)
The Rhymes and Runes of the Toad (1976)
Alphabet for the Lost Years (1977)
The Bible of the Beats of the Little Field (1979)

Books for Children

The Dragons of North Chittendon (1986)
The Four Hoods and Great Dog (1988)

THE SNOW FOX

A NOVEL

Susan Fromberg Schaeffer

W. W. NORTON & COMPANY

NEW YORK LONDON

For information about permission to reproduce selections from this book, write to
Permissions, W. W. Norton & Company, Inc., 500 Fifth Avenue, New York, NY 10110

Manufacturing by Maple-Vail Book Manufacturing Group
Book design by Mary A. Wirth
Production manager: Julia Druskin

LIBRARY OF CONGRESS CATALOGING-IN-PUBLICATION DATA

Schaeffer, Susan Fromberg.
The snow fox : a novel / Susan Fromberg Schaeffer.— 1st ed.
p. cm.
ISBN 0-393-05814-X
1. Japan—History—To 1185—Fiction. 2. Triangles (Interpersonal relations)—
Fiction. 3. Wilderness areas—Fiction. 4. Women poets—Fiction. 5. Samurai—
Fiction. I. Title.
PS3569.C35 S66 2004
813'.54—dc22

2003021067

ISBN 0-393-32652-7 pbk.

W. W. Norton & Company, Inc., 500 Fifth Avenue, New York, N.Y. 10110
www.wwnorton.com

W. W. Norton & Company Ltd., Castle House, 75/76 Wells Street, London W1T 3QT

3 4 5 6 7 8 9 0

For

OLWYN HUGHES

Maple leaves fall
Into the winding Shirokawa river.
Truly it is brocade.
If it were not for my obligations
I should sink into those robes
Forever.

—UTSU NO YUKIKUNI

PROLOGUE

WERE YOU NOT TOLD the story of the four children?

I myself told it again and again when I had children of my own. By then everyone knew the story of the four children, mixed up after a battle, a story to make ungrateful children behave well, to frighten them into obeying their parents because at least they knew who their parents were, or to remind people of the perils of war. And because children liked the story, and still do, it may well be handed down for some time.

When I first heard the story of the four children, and when I began to recite it to my children, I had no inkling that the story concerned me in any way. Yet I am the daughter of Lady Utsu, one of the four children, Lady Utsu, the famous beauty and the even more famous poet. And I am undoubtedly also the daughter of the second of the four children, Lord Matsuhito, the famous samurai who fought at the Battle of Sanomi. He is my father. The third of the four children was a monk who abandoned the ways of this world to study the sutras and live in isolation in his mountain hut. The last of the four was a young girl who as a child exactly resembled my mother, Lady Utsu, and has been lost to history. No one can discover anything about her. How strange it was to learn that my life had, in many respects, followed my mother's, that I, too, grew to maturity not knowing who my real mother or father was, and that I, who had been so sure of my place, was little more than an abandoned child.

I discovered all this from a man named Shinda, a peddler and also a bandit, who came upon me in his travels. He saw to it that the monk, the third of the four children, was informed of my existence and where and how I lived. When the monk died, Shinda did as the monk instructed and sent me every scroll on which the monk had written the true story of the four children.

FOR YEARS AFTERWARD, I was furious. When I read the scrolls, I learned I had been abandoned and then deceived.

When I married the governor of a northern province far from the capital, I missed the palace and all its doings. I missed the poetry competitions, the competitions to see who was the best archer, the horse races, the dramas created by the competitive women of the palace. But I soon came to love the isolation in which we lived, and the freedom we would have had nowhere else. In the north, I saw a clear sky. In the capital, the sky always appeared full of the faces of courtiers and court ladies, all looking down at me and deciding if they approved or disapproved of my slightest gesture. Here it is enough for me to simply exist. I am happy here along with my husband and children. I know they belong to me and I to them. We are happy, although I often find myself thinking, What would Lady Utsu, my mother, have thought of me?

Although I was told a great deal about her, what I most wished for was to have seen her, even once. Finally, I asked Lord Norimasa to describe her. "Oh, that is not difficult," he said. "What you must do is find an excellent mirror and you will see her image looking back at you. She was taller than you are, and her voice was deeper, but otherwise I would defy anyone to tell you apart if you were both kneeling on a mat."

"I am sure the resemblance between us is not so strong," I said.

"It is not a question of resemblance," said Lord Norimasa. "It is a matter of absolute duplication. I have often thought that Lady Utsu must have died and was immediately reborn, and her will was so strong that she returned in your body as she once was."

I asked him if she was truly no longer alive.

"Who can know?" he answered. "But I swear to you that your face is her face. Even your bodies are the same. But, as I said, she was taller."

So I see that if I must describe Lady Utsu, I must describe myself.

I wear my hair as all the ladies of the palace did and still do. Our hair is not cut after it begins to grow. My hair reaches almost to the back of my ankles, and is parted in the middle and then falls unencumbered. It grows quickly, and soon my hair will be longer than my body. I have unusually high cheekbones, which are not favored, but many people say they are beautiful. My eyes are very round and large, and one of the older women who knew my mother said that, if she stared at you long enough, her stare would hypnotize you. Perhaps, she said, that was one of the reasons some people of the palace believed she was a fox in human form.

I have small, very red lips, and when I whiten my face, I believe my lips look startling and foolish and frightful, like blood on snow, but the women of the palace seem to envy me everything. They say I am very graceful, just as Lady Utsu was, and that I am as indifferent as she was to what other people think, although I try to please. She had about her, some said, a remarkable stillness and could go for days without saying anything. In that way, too, I am like her.

I do not think of myself as beautiful, but I have been told that Lady Utsu knew very well how beautiful she was, and as a consequence she was unhappy. She believed that all men who loved her came to harm, and often said that she would have been happier if she had been born ugly because then she would not have been the author of so many tragedies. "I never knew if she spoke the truth," said the woman who told me this.

It is said that she was remarkable for creating her own incense, and excelled in creating pleasurable, if unusual, color combinations when she layered her twelve robes. Many have praised her for her courage. I, on the other hand, was a hapless thing.

One afternoon Lady Kitsu, who was once close to my mother, said she was going to see me dressed properly, and all of the ladies would assist me and teach me, and when they were finished with me, they, too, would dress in their most beautiful robes and demand to be taken outside the palace walls for a picnic in the country. Eventually, the excitement proved contagious and I found myself turning this way and that in the dim mirrors to see what I looked like, and my face ceased to turn the color of a red sunset when people complimented me or stared at me too long.

One day in the palanquin, I let my layered sleeves spill from the closed blind of the carriage, and for once I imagined great lords and ladies envying me. But when the elation wore off, I was sick at heart, and my ambition was to retire behind my dark screen in the dim room and hide from everyone's eyes.

"Really, you are hopeless," Lady Kitsu said. "There was a woman who was your precise image when she was young, and she would have gloried in a chance to show herself." Naturally, I began to cry.

"I am unaffected by tears," Lady Kitsu said. "I have no more to shed. I have cried them all in my time. I do not understand you."

And I did not understand Lady Kitsu or any of the women of the palace. Lady Kitsu often said that I had the disposition of a peasant, although she herself had never encountered one. "And you do not write poems and you do not keep us amused," Lady Kitsu went on. "I cannot understand why you have been chosen in an assemblage like this. If looking at you were not Lord Norimasa's greatest comfort, there would be no reason to keep you here."

"Send me home!" I said.

"Lord Norimasa will never let you leave," she said. She paused and then said, "Perhaps someday he will. He let the original leave. It is as if someone had painted her face onto yours."

"I wish she had never existed!" I exclaimed.

"Do not say that," said Lady Kitsu. "You do not know the nature of your connection to her. The gods will hear you and they will not approve. She had enough trouble when she lived in Lord Norimasa's palace. No one could ever match her. The Empress herself loved her and once visited here to see her. The other women envied her dreadfully. No one could surpass her in poetry. Only once did someone else win a poetry competition, and I believe she persuaded Lord Norimasa to let someone else win. And, as you know, she was so beautiful! And on top of that, Lord Norimasa favored her above all others. When all the women were given new silk robes for a festival, hers was always more splendid. The excuse the lord gave us was Lady Utsu's unusual height. Special robes had to be made up for her. Everyone knew that was not true. They envied her and now they envy you because they believe she has come back in your body. They believe that you are a fox who has made itself human and thus are capable of many magical doings, and so they behave and do not torment you. It would have been folly to torment Lady Utsu, because if one of us had done so, the lord would have expelled that woman from the mansion.

"Every woman in the pavilion was entranced by Lord Norimasa, so elegant was his demeanor and his dress, and his sharp beard and upturned moustache. And he was also renowned for writing poetry. His sensibility was much admired. But his principal wife, the Lady Tsukie, was a terror, and everyone feared her. He used to say that he feared two things: the sun falling from the sky and Lady Tsukie rising from her bed. When Lady Utsu came to the palace, it was soon clear that Lady Tsukie's character was not the only reason Lord Norimasa's attention strayed. Lady Utsu had a great many difficulties. I believe you were one of them."

"What are you telling me now?" I demanded, but the lady refused to answer.

Such was my life in the palace. To tell the truth, I was like a mouse among tigresses. My greatest pleasure was tending to anyone who fell ill. I myself never fell ill, and it was predicted that the first illness I had would sweep me away. But even now I have never succumbed to an illness, and so I am still here.

Once, when Lady Kitsu was suffering from a dangerous fever, I insisted on taking charge of her. Day and night I stood by her bed, coaxing her to drink sips of water and pressing cold clothes to her face and neck. The people in the palace shook their heads and said, "This is the end of Lady Kitsu." I knelt at her mat and watched. I no longer remember how long this continued. One night, I fell asleep while I was kneeling and I was awakened by Lady Kitsu's hot hand stroking my cheek.

"You are just like the Lady Utsu," she said, her voice hoarse. "Once, when I fell ill, she tended to me as you are tending to me now. People speak of how cruel she was. People go so far as to say she was murderous, but she had a side not often seen. She was kind and good. If it were not for her tenderness, I would not be alive today. Please remember that when other people speak of her. She had reason to grow cruel. Even I sometimes forget how kind and sweet she could be. Say you will remember!"

I said, "I will remember."

"And there are so many more instances of her generosity," she said, sighing. "But it is easier to remember the cruelty and the heartlessness, if indeed that was what it was."

Many years have gone by since then, but I remember Lady Kitsu's words vividly.

While I was still in the palace, I took up painting and was good at that. I painted hell screens. Lady Kitsu would look at them and say, "Something of her remains in you," but if I questioned her, she refused to elaborate.

My life changed radically one day when we were to be taken into the country for a diversion. Lord Norimasa had built more pavilions for some of us, but he reserved some of the old, rustic ones for his special favorites. There was also a beautiful little house that resembled a palace, and I was put in this. The house was not tiled but thatched. When I first entered the house, I could not stop staring, it was so beautiful in its proportions and its decorations. I remember there was a suit of armor suspended from a rack and I recall Lord Norimasa telling me that often he and the other samurai kept their armor in this way so that, when there was an emergency, they could simply step into it from below. The wood floors were polished cypress, and the endless polishing gave them a beautiful color and sheen. The placement of the sliding screens was perfection itself, and the shadows of the leaves cast by the trees outside played on the white walls and on the floors in the most beautiful designs. Except for a few mats, the room was almost empty.

"I shall like sleeping in this room," I told Lord Norimasa.

"Good," he said. "Lately you have not looked well."

We picked persimmons and berries and ate the lunch packed in buckets for us, and then we were exhausted and ready to sleep. But I stayed awake in the beautiful room so that I could continue looking at it. In short order, my companion, Lady Kitsu, was asleep. By then, she was half deaf and heard very little, and so she did not hear the scurrying begin in the roof above. Rats, I thought. We had rats in the thatched roofs above my rooms in the palace. But as I watched, one rat began to climb down, and then another followed, and soon there were ten or more standing in the corner of the room. One began to approach Lady Kitsu, whom sleep had rendered insensible, and the rat climbed onto her arm and moved up to her face, and I knew the rat's intention. He was going to bite her cheek and the beast would eat to its heart's content. I screamed and continued screaming. The rats scurried up the wall and back into the roof. Almost at once, Lord Norimasa was at the door of the little house.

When he calmed me down, and when I explained what had happened to Lady Kitsu, who had finally heard my screams, the lord thought a moment and then said, "I should have remembered. There was a terrible murder here, and afterward, all the rats took up residence in this house and its roof. There are no rats in the other houses."

I was shaking and trembling and refused to look at him.

"Perhaps you would be happier returning to the palace," he said.

"No, she will not be, my lord," Lady Kitsu said. "We will move to one of the huts, and if you can spare one of the samurai to guard us, all will still be well."

And so it was done.

As I said, that incident was decisive in forming my inner image of the palace and its inhabitants. It appeared beautiful, so beautiful that one was loath to close one's eyes and fall asleep, but when you did, the rats descended, intending to eat you alive. I thought, This is the nature of life. You live in the palace, or in the days of your youth, and then one day the rats descend. From that day forward, I wanted to leave the palace. Lord Norimasa knew it, and when I was old enough, and found a man I thought I could admire and stay with for the rest of my days, he let me go. He sent us far away, into one of the northern provinces, where I live now. He must have been unhappy about my leaving, or he would not have sent me so far.

After that, my life remained untroubled until the scrolls arrived. The monk, third of the four children, who survived longest, had retreated into the mountains, where he built himself a hut and devoted himself to studying the sutras. However, I think he pondered his own life a great deal of the time, reflected on his own destiny and those of the three other children, and so he was finally driven to write down the story of all their lives.

In his scrolls, he lamented the fact that he had had to spend so much time learning the art of the bow, shooting arrows from horseback, treading water in the lake in full armor, coaxing secrets from ancient women who taught him the use of poisons, learning from them their ability to hide in plain sight, and how it was, in the end, all for nothing. He was trained to take over his clan should the two leaders of the clan, Lord Norimasa and Lord Matsuhito, die and leave the clan rudderless, but when those two were indeed gone, the clan itself was destroyed in battle and so all his training proved useless.

When he found his mountain, he said he saw only deer and monkeys, and he thought, This is what I want. He thought he could live in absolute isolation, but he forgot Lord Norimasa's maxim. You cannot see both sides of the mountain at once. At certain times, he saw smoke rising above the mountain and believed he smelled wood burning. He wondered if there was a burial place on the other side of the mountain. Or if someone else lived there. He decided that if there was another, it was best to leave him alone. "Two people together," he wrote, "and one is likely to kill the other."

I should like to have known him.

He wrote that the stories of the four children had remained locked more securely than any storehouse, but that time was breaking down the walls and the doors that held them, and rumors escaped like birds nesting in a rotting roof. "*Mukashi, mukashi,* a long time ago, there were four children and no one knows who any of them were. No one could say for certain who the parents of those four children were."

To this day, that is how the story begins.

Once, he heard an old woman telling her grandchildren this tale. He was on a pilgrimage and when night fell he stopped at a hut. One of the children played with his traveler's bells, and the old woman took them away and sent the children to bed.

"Please continue the story," he asked.

"Oh, it is more nonsense," said the *obaasan,* the grandmother.

He asked her if she had invented the story herself.

The old lady cackled at the very idea. She said, "A peddler told it to me while he was mending my pot. It was a long story and a badly broken pot.

Mukashi, mukashi. Already his life and those of the three children were turning into stories. He wondered if the other three children would recognize themselves in the events and people in those tales.

He asked the old woman if the peddler had spoken of Lord Norimasa.

She said she no longer remembered things well. The peddler might have mentioned Lord Norimasa, but then again, he might not. She said again that it was a long story, but shorter than fixing that pot, and probably she did not hear all that she had been told.

He said he understood.

"So it goes," the old woman told him. "Nothing remains whole. There are moths even in our brains."

It is true. Today, my children will ask me, "Do you remember when you jumped from the boat into the pond lilies because you thought they were so beautiful?" and I have no idea what they are talking about. My daughter, who so resembles me, asked if I remembered the day of the picnic when we all went into the river and my daughter refused to stay with the rest of us and swam back to the riverbank. I told my daughter, "Go to your room!" and she answered me, saying, "It's not here!" I do not remember that incident, although it must have happened. If I had told her to go to her room when we were outdoors and a great distance from our home, she would have answered in that way. She has always been terribly literal-minded, and to this day she has no patience with flights of fancy. She resembles, I think, her husband. So time changes us, and our memory changes what we believe truly happened. Our minds are not reliable, some less reliable than others.

Lord Norimasa, who everyone knows, was one of the greatest and most famous of the warlords. He intended to unify the province of Kai and then march on the capital. He said he would not rest until he restored order to the country. But a raging fever put an end to his dreams, and when Lord Norimasa died, Lord Matsuhito, as he had come to be called, left the palace and did not return. Some years before he died, Lord Norimasa had accidentally found me and persuaded my parents to let him make me his ward, just as he had made the monk, Lady Utsu and Matsuhito his wards so long before.

After Lord Norimasa died, the monk, the third of the four children, settled in with his inkstone and ink sticks and brushes made of fox fur. Some years passed. One day, he noticed a brush he had carelessly left out, and a rat had chewed through most of the hairs. He had scrolls of paper and stacks of michinoku paper. Often when the rain kept him inside his hut, he would think, I am doubtless the last of the four who still lives, and I should write the truth of all of our lives, as far as I know them. There were also mornings when he woke up and was on the verge of filling the scrolls with long lines of characters, but he did not begin. Like a strong hand, something stopped him.

Like a strong hand, something stopped me from attempting to write poetry. Something stopped me from asking questions, as if I knew I would not like the answers. I understand the monk and his thoughts.

It does not matter where you begin a story, or in what sequence you tell it—provided you get to the end, even if that end is the smoke sent up by a funeral pyre. All stories end in that way, although I believe my life will not end when my heart stops beating because my spirit will continue in my children. And yet it does not seem as if my mother's spirit somehow continues in me.

The monk was so absurdly comforted by the thought that all lives and all stories ended in the same way that he took up his ink stone and stick, unrolled his scroll and began to write. He was going to begin with Lady Utsu and Lord Matsuhito at the time of the plague, but he saw that to tell the story of their lives properly, he had to begin earlier.

This is a story of great passions, ambition, loyalty and love. It is also a story of how all such human things can be distorted and twisted like the pines near the tops of mountains. The monk wrote that he, who had always wanted peace, was perhaps not the best person to tell this story. I am not the right one to do so, either. I value peace and do not look deeply into things. I fear what I would see if I did. Still, there is now no one who knows as much as I do. I have Lady Utsu's—my mother's—diaries. In his scrolls, the monk summoned her up as she sprawled on the floor of the palace, her roll of writing paper unfurled the length of the room, writing furiously as she moved down the paper, poem upon poem. He remembered one of the other ladies of the palace watching her and saying, "And all of it will be good," as she shook her head in disbelief. "To be so beautiful and so talented."

I have not inherited my mother's talent, and I have no desire to have it. As for my beauty, who sees it but my husband? What trouble can my beauty cause?

Then, said the monk, there was gossip, the sort a woman will tell a man in incredible detail if the man will only listen. For a long time, the monk visited one of Lady Utsu's companions at night, and in her appetite for gossip she did not differ from other women he had known. As for Matsuhito, the monk knew him inside out. The monk had set spies to watch him and tell him what Matsuhito said and did. Yet the best spy would have been any woman in Lady Utsu's entourage.

At times, I believe I have inherited the monk's obsession with both Lady Utsu and Lord Matsuhito. On my shelf are two things I cannot live without, both of them sent to me by the same Shinda who brought me the scrolls. One is Matsuhito's helmet and face mask, the one he wore into battle, the one of which everyone has heard.

"This mask," Lady Utsu had said, "must be the most terrifying, the most hideous, the most gruesome mask. I want it to inspire terror even when it is motionless and silent on its frame. The deep red holes of that black mask, the gaping hole of its mouth, its red whiskers. The red, insolent horns of the helmet." She had them sharpened along the edges. The long, thick red strands were like hair, protruding beneath the neck of the helmet—the very image of a devil.

How can my mother have given birth to something like me and have had such violent passions?

The second is the image of a woman, carved out of wood, meticulously painted, an object of adoration. Can anyone believe that her face, hidden as it is, is less beautiful than any other face? She is wearing six robes. At the neck, you can see the red of her undergarment. The topmost robe is speckled with silver. Below that, there is a blue robe patterned with gold chrysanthemums and splashed with orange flowers and occasional tiny indigo flowers. Her black hair reaches the back of her knees. She is a goddess. Lord Matsuhito must have worshiped her. How else could he have brought a block of wood to life? I am reminded of the screen Lord Norimasa had a great artist paint for me, a hell screen, and on one panel, three horses so alive that people swore they escaped from their panel at night, smashing and trampling fences and rice plants growing in the paddies as well as anything else they came upon. Lord Norimasa had to find the painter and have him paint in a post and a rope for the horses so that they could not gallop out in darkness and wreak havoc.

She is loose in the night, too, Lady Utsu, this figure of a woman. At night, I see her moving behind the trees beyond my pavilion. The moonlight seeks her out. And there are times when I can smell incense, a strange incense, and I believe Lady Utsu perfumed her robe with it.

Why do I hesitate before beginning, as the monk did?

I think, A story is like a battle. You can decide against beginning, but once you begin, you cannot stop. I shall begin with what I found most shocking.

BOOK ONE

CHAPTER ONE

LADY UTSU WAS SUMMONED to Lord Norimasa's quarters. She had been brought to his palace as a child, but over the years, she became indispensable to him. At the end of a difficult day, he would go to the ladies' pavilion and sit on the veranda and Lady Utsu would move to the window where she sat concealed behind a screen. He tended to arrive at twilight, and the distinctive sound of his footsteps coming over the bridge that crossed the artificial pond alerted the women to his coming. Anyone who was on the veranda fled inside and no one in the dim rooms would have dared to come out. He would climb the three steps onto the veranda.

"Play a song for me," he would say, and Lady Utsu would answer, "I sing like a crow, but I can read a new poem. It is not good."

"Do it, then," he would say, leaning back against one of the heavy wooden lattices. She would recite a poem she had just written, chanting it as poems were chanted, or she would invent one on the spot, always a poem about the lord's fame or bravery.

> *The many-bladed Muzashino plain.*
> *Surely your reign will last longer*
> *Than there are blades of grass.*

Then he would laugh at her and ask her if that was the best she could do. Often, he would ask her to recite other poems. At other times, he simply sat on the veranda, staring out over the bridge surmounting the ornamental pond. After a while, he would get back on his horse and return to his own quarters. Often, he called her to him. When she grew old enough, he summoned her for another reason. Even as a very young woman, Lady Utsu was something of a seductress.

Aki, who had been Lady Utsu's nurse and then her companion, disapproved of the many summonses Lady Utsu received requiring her to come to Lord Norimasa's quarters. When she and Aki arrived, Lady Utsu was brought to the room reserved for important nobles and officials, while Aki was left outside to wait in the palanquin which had brought them. Long ago, Lord Norimasa insisted that when they were alone together there was no need for Lady Utsu to hide behind a screen. After all, he said, had he not brought her up as he had his own daughters? The real reason for his decree, however, was his desire to look at her and to watch her fleeting expressions. Long ago, he learned to read her face, although even Lord Norimasa could not see into her thoughts when she drew a black curtain over them.

All this Aki found disgraceful. "What will the other women think?" she asked. "What will his wife, Lady Tsukie, think?"

"She cannot hate me more than she already does," said Lady Utsu.

"He is not happy unless he is breaking rules!" Aki said angrily.

"I, too, like to break them," Lady Utsu said softly.

"And you will pay for every one you break!" Aki retorted.

"For some things it is worth paying," said Lady Utsu. "I cannot live behind screens."

"Every lady in the world manages it!" Aki said.

"I know I am a trial."

"You put him up to it! At least you do not discourage it!"

"If you must blame, blame my own nature."

"And he consults you, a woman, on affairs of state! I know he does! If anyone knew! Consulting a mere woman!"

"Tread carefully here," said Lady Utsu, her eyes narrowing.

Aki assumed a mutinous silence.

"You do not know what we discuss," Lady Utsu said. "You must not say such fanciful things again."

"And can I not say what I think?" Aki asked.

"You can. But you are not to speak of this again. I should not like to lose you as my companion."

At this, Aki's eyes teared and her throat seemed to close. "I understand," she said.

INSIDE THE COUNCIL ROOM, Lord Norimasa stood on his elevated platform. Lady Utsu approached and prostrated herself, her forehead touching the floor.

"Get up, get up," the lord said impatiently. "There are things to discuss. Stop this ridiculous prostration. You know how unnecessary it is. Kneel on that cushion. I provide it for your comfort."

When she was seated, they sat in silence. "It is a delight simply to look at you," he said. She inclined her head slightly. How tired she was of hearing such things.

"Lord Tsurunosuke has been visiting you at night," Lord Norimasa said.

"Yes," she said.

"And he is very important to you?"

"As important as anyone can be to me," she said.

"You must kill him," said Lord Norimasa.

"My lord?" she said.

"You know very well that enemies are working against me. We are preparing for a decisive campaign. For quite a while, we have known that someone conveys our plans to the enemy. We cannot afford to be anticipated this time. Lord Tsurunosuke is a traitor and a spy. He must be killed. But if we order one of my generals to do so, we would enrage several clans we cannot afford to turn against us. He must be killed, but no one must know who killed him. I have considered this carefully. It must be you who kills him."

Lady Utsu said nothing. She had never before considered marrying, but she had begun to wonder if she might be happy with Lord Tsurunosuke. Lately, she found herself saying aloud what she was thinking, something she had never done before. Now she was to kill him.

The lady often sat without moving, as if she were made of stone, but now she was toying with the edge of her sleeve.

"Something is troubling you," Lord Norimasa said.

"I thought I had discovered a moth hole in the fabric," she replied.

"And is there such a hole?" he asked.

"No," she said. "But a poem has just drifted into my head."
He asked her to recite it.

> *Spring.*
> *Fans and green leaves rustle*
> *But I can see*
> *Only the bare, dead tree of winter,*
> *Its roots deep in my heart.*

"And whose poem is that?" Lord Norimasa asked.

"Mine," she said. "It is not good."

"But through your poems, you say what you mean."

She did not answer.

"When did you compose that poem?" he asked her. "In your quarters? Or did it just drift through your mind?"

"It simply drifted across my mind as I sat here," answered Lady Utsu.

"I am sorry to ask this of you," he said. "I had not realized how deeply your feelings went."

"I thought that, through him, I could learn to become human once again," she said at last.

Now Lord Norimasa said nothing. "You have survived many plots against you," he said at last. "I endangered you, taking you into my bed when you were still too young. Now even my own wife schemes against you. I never thought she would know of what happened between us. Your beauty and your talent make you powerful, and so you make powerful enemies. Yet you have always put my concerns above your own. I know you would die for me."

"Yes," said Lady Utsu. "I am bound to you by loyalty. All the members of our clan are so bound."

"But to kill for me, that is another matter?" Lord Norimasa said.

"Yes," Lady Utsu said, her voice barely audible.

"Will you do it?" he asked her.

"What will you make of me?" she said. "I see I am meant to be a monster."

"I would not ask if there were another way," he said.

"And cannot bandits set upon him one night when he rides?" she asked.

"Who would not see through that?"

"But such things happen." He heard the note of desperation in her voice.

"It must be something no one will trace back to any of us, especially not to you," he said. "Have you not been taught such tricks?"

"Yes," she said. "You know how curious I am."

"And would such a trick work?"

"Yes," she said. "But afterward, I would not be the same. Already I am turning to stone."

"It is a pity to ask this of you," he said. "Do you believe I ask this of you because someone else has taken my place in your heart?"

"No," she said. "When it comes to the safety of the clan, you would do or command anything."

"Perhaps there is some jealousy in my request," he said, considering.

"Do not trouble yourself," said Lady Utsu. "I myself cannot think of someone who would do as well."

Then she said nothing. He watched as one lone tear made its way down her cheek. He would not have thought her capable of crying if someone was watching her.

"Will you do it?" he asked finally.

"Yes, my lord," she said. Her voice was flat and expressionless. "If you command me, you know I must. I swore an oath. I must obey you as absolutely as any samurai."

"Do you remember?" he asked. "I gave you blue leather gloves painted with flowers for the occasion."

It was as if she did not hear him.

"I have to ask this of you," he said. "You know more about my mind than any general. And there is one more thing I must ask. You must never tell another soul. Aki will know, but even if the memory burns you like fire, you must not divulge what I have done or what I have asked you to do. It will be hard to keep that promise. Do you swear it?"

"I do swear it," she said, her voice low.

"And will you tell me what you will do? I should like to know."

"I know you do," she said, her voice low. "It is an intimate thing to kill someone. No, I shall not tell you."

"When will you do it?" he asked her.

"When must it be done?"

"In three days," he said. "He will have time to convey false plans to our enemies but no time to learn of our true designs. If he dies in three days."

"I will need a special dinner for tomorrow night," she said.

"Ah, so you will poison him," he said, flushing with excitement.

"That would be too simple," said Lady Utsu. "Leave it to me. He particularly likes smoked eel."

"I am not sure it is the right season for it."

"I will not sit here discussing menus!" Lady Utsu burst out.

They sat in silence.

"I will need a secret place to work tomorrow. Aki will help me," she said. "If I know you are peeping about, I will stop and I will not do as you wish. I will send Aki with a list of what I will need."

"Insolent!" said Lord Norimasa.

"You dare to call me insolent!" she shot back. "Have me killed instead!"

"Yes," he said, "I am sure you would prefer that. I have felt the same thing many times. These are terrible burdens to take on. They eat at the soul until a cobweb is all that remains."

"I shall not have even so much!" she said.

"Would I ask were it not necessary?" said Lord Norimasa.

There was a long silence. "A world cannot be overturned for one person," she said. "If what you say is true, he must be killed."

"That," he answered, "was the most bitter lesson of all to learn."

"Must it be me?" she asked desperately.

"I know no one else I can trust," he said.

"Then are we finished?" she asked.

"Yes, you rude and arrogant and audacious and impertinent and outrageous being. I will find you a secure place for tomorrow."

She stood up and left the chamber as if she were leaving a servant.

THE NEXT DAY, Lady Utsu and Aki followed a servant at a distance through a maze of streets until they reached a storehouse hidden behind the palace laundry. When the door was opened, they saw that Lord Norimasa had had the chamber was fitted out with new tatami mats, white sheets over them, and white robes for the two women to put on. Lady Utsu staggered slightly and Aki steadied her.

"It looks like a room readied for *seppuku*," Lady Utsu said. Her voice shook. I might as well hold a sword and cut off Lord Tsuruno-suke's head myself." The two women sat still, not looking at one another.

"Well, we have work to do," Aki said at last.

Lady Utsu took out a small package she had hidden in her sleeve.

"I don't like you fooling with poison," Aki said.

"It's not poison," said Lady Utsu. "It's worse."

She unwrapped the package, and in it were two very thin, transparent glasses. "The Chinese man who was my teacher while I still lived at home," she said. "He gave me these."

"You will commit murder with these?" Aki asked incredulously. "Will Lord Tsurunosuke sit there while you saw your way through the large vein in his throat?"

"Do you see that stone pestle?" Lady Utsu asked. "And the grind-stone? We are going to grind these glasses finer than grains of salt."

"And what will that do?"

"You do not need to know everything," Lady Utsu said. "We will take turns grinding." She wrapped the glasses back up in the fabric with which they had been concealed. "Check and see that the sliding doors and shutters are tightly closed."

"They are," said Aki.

"Put on those high wooden clogs and pound the glasses inside the cloth."

Aki did as she was told. "Now what?" she asked.

"We start reducing the glass to an almost invisible powder," she said. "I'll begin. We start with one small piece of glass and grind it thoroughly, and when we're finished, we begin another piece. This must be done with great care."

Aki was staring at the white robes. "Must we put them on?" she asked.

"Unless you want little bits of glass in your own robe."

They put the robes on.

"How innocent you look," said Aki, regarding her. "Like a *tennin,* a heavenly creature." Lady Utsu ignored this.

"Now," said Lady Utsu, "when we grind, we wrap our faces with two layers of thin veiling to prevent splinters. I will begin." She put on her blue leather gloves.

She selected a piece of glass, put it in the mortar and began to smash it with the pestle. When the glass was in small pieces, she began the grinding. Soon her face was shiny with sweat. "It is hard work," she said.

"Let me do it," said Aki.

"No. This is my work," she said. "It will take two of us. You'll see."

"How much powdered glass do we need?"

"Enough to fill this vial," Lady Utsu said. "It's there, standing behind me."

Aki got up to inspect it. "It's not very big," she said.

"You won't think that in three hours," Lady Utsu said.

Lady Utsu pounded and ground, finally moving the pestle in a circle, and Aki, watching her, began to fall into a kind of trance. The repetitiveness of the motion was creating the same result in Lady Utsu.

"Do you remember," Aki said dreamily, "the four-paneled screen your mother ordered for us? So you would not forget the home you came from?"

"I remember. I have forgotten nothing. That is my trouble. If it is true that we are reincarnated, I want to come back as a mouse. Their memories are not long."

"We don't know that," Aki said.

"Or a tree," said Lady Utsu. "But they last a long time. Who is to say they do not remember and dream and even speak? I have seen leaves rustle and stir when there is no wind anywhere."

"The pavilions there were so beautiful," Aki said. "But what I liked best was the artificial lake and how it was made to look like a sea, and farther out, the foam of waves breaking on the rocks, and you, sitting in a golden boat, farther out than you were permitted to go."

"Such beautiful colors," Utsu said, pounding again. "How she loved orange and gold and dark green—when the dyers could get it right."

"I think it was more beautiful there than here," Aki said.

"It was mine. It was ours."

"Yes," said Aki. "It was. Someday you may go back."

Lady Utsu looked up, regarded her speculatively and then returned to her pounding. "You never think of the bough that shades you until something strikes it down," she said.

How my mother used to promise me, Lady Utsu thought. She swore she would never let anyone take me away from the pavilion and my family. How good she was about letting me run wild even though I was not a boy. How she insisted that I be taught as carefully as my brothers. How she insisted on that, saying no one on this earth knew if she would have to earn a living or make use of a talent that might keep her alive. And the way she combed my hair, so gently, no matter how tangled it became. Yet when it came to it, she gave me away and I was sent to Lord Norimasa's. How bitter I became! How betrayed I felt! What a nuisance I was on the journey. "Stop the carriage! Stop!" And I would pretend nausea and come down from my carriage and pretend to retch at the side of the road.

My mother did not overlook my little cruelties. I think, in time, she would have rooted them out. One day, I said, "I wish all the people in the palace would die and we could live in it alone. And she said, "How would you feel if everyone in the palace was wishing the same thing? Would you like to die so they could be left alone?"

I heard her speaking to Aki one day. "My way of dealing with Utsu is not to oppose her or to order," my mother said. "That would be to go against her nature. It would be useless. She would grow more extreme. But I can teach her what it means to be human."

And she would have succeeded, my mother, I feel sure, if she had lived long enough. But when she died, I was still not quite human, and as time has passed, I have become less so. Lord Norimasa teaches me loyalty and strategy and encourages my poems, but he also makes me do what I am doing now. He would not ask if it were not in me to do it.

"I have thought of a poem," Lady Utsu said. "I will tell it.

Winter.
The thick snow forces the black branches
Into blossom.
Why, then, will my body, which yet lives,
Refuse to blossom?

"Is it a good poem? Or is it a premonition?"

"I do not believe in premonitions," Aki said. "Let me take over. You are tired and upset."

Lady Utsu nodded, stood up, and she and Aki exchanged places.

"Am I inhuman?" Lady Utsu asked her.

"Sometimes. A little."

"Do people who are inhuman feel as if they are dying when they must do something like this?"

"Do you feel so?"

"Yes," said Lady Utsu.

"Then you are not inhuman. In any case, I know that you care for this man above all others you have known."

"And I must be the one to do this!"

"Perhaps the lord is jealous," Aki suggested.

"He would not kill out of jealousy," Lady Utsu said. "The good of the country is all he cares for. One man counts for nothing. Even his own life counts for nothing. That is why he is so brave."

"This powder grows very fine," Aki said.

On her knees, Lady Utsu crept forward and looked at the mortar. "That piece is almost finished," she said. "Perhaps five more minutes. Always stop and pound before grinding," she said wearily. How many times had the Chinese man told her that?

"But I will never need to learn this!" Lady Utsu had protested to the Chinese man, who only said, "You must learn these characters all the same," and so she wrote them and rewrote them. What kind of destiny had he foreseen for her? Yes, to be truthful, she wished everyone in the world would die and leave her alone with Aki. Her mother's work had gone unfinished, interrupted.

"Do you remember the crucified man we went to see on the road?" Lady Utsu asked in a low voice. "A thief. I should rather be crucified than do this. And the terrible thing is, I will not be punished, but rewarded."

"Yes, after this, the lord will send you many extravagant robes."

"I will throw them in the fire!"

"You will do no such thing!"

"How you speak to me! I am not a small child any longer!"

Aki continued her grinding.

"I think that is finished," Lady Utsu said, coming over to inspect the ground glass. "You cannot tell what that dust is," she said. "It is done. Now for this piece," and she selected another piece of glass. "We have a little funnel to let us pour the powder into the vial. You do it, Aki. I am afraid I will spill it out."

Aki carefully poured the powder into the vial. "It is only one-third full," she said wearily.

Lady Utsu lifted her veiling up over her eyes. "I will begin again with this one," she said.

She is taking it well, Aki thought, better than I expected. Then she saw that Lady Utsu was shuddering as if she were weeping violently, but without making a sound.

"He means so much to you," Aki said.

"Lord Norimasa?"

"No. Lord Tsurunosuke."

"Don't speak of him!" Lady Utsu said furiously.

By late afternoon, the vial was full.

"He wanted it to look like a *seppuku*," Lady Utsu said. "If anyone happened to look in here through a crack. No one wants to be near a place prepared for *seppuku*. He anticipates everything, even the most remote possibilities. But I have thought of a poem. I must write it down when we go back. Do you want to hear it?"

"Please," said Aki.

> *The pine, the crane, the turtle*
> *Last forever.*
> *The sun is inconstant.*
> *After one season, people and leaves fall.*
> *I should have loved*
> *None but the first three.*

"It is too long, I think. The rhythm is not right and there are too many words. What do we do now?"

"You will fix the poem and it will be fine," Aki said.

"We go back and give this powder to Lord Tsurunosuke. He will never know what caused his death."

"But," said Aki, "how can this powder hurt anyone?"

"Every little grain is like a little sword. When he swallows his food, the grains will do their work. They will make tiny slices in his organs and the veins of his blood. He will not feel anything or suspect anything. But in three days, or five at worst, he will be dead."

"How will we know if the glass has destroyed him?"

"His fingernails. See how pale and pink ours are? His will grow a very rosy pink. The bleeding betrays itself through his fingernails. Even if anyone understands what has happened, he will not be able to stop it. But almost no one in this world knows this method, this poisoning by glass. Who can trace what happens back after so much time? Who would think to suspect me?"

Aki sat back on her heels, saying nothing.

"What are you thinking?" Lady Utsu asked.

"You will suspect yourself," she said.

"I already do."

"No," said Aki. "After this, you will suspect yourself of everything, every thought, every feeling. I do not envy you."

Now Lady Utsu sat, silent. "It must be done," she said in a low voice.

Aki stood up, picked up the vial, put it in her sleeve, and the two women made their way back to the pavilion. It is terrible that a *daimyo*, a clan leader, must be obeyed in everything, Aki thought. "It is said that he killed his father and brother," Aki said aloud.

Lady Utsu said nothing.

"The ducks on the pond are lovely," Aki said, as they crossed the arched bridge.

"Lovely," said Lady Utsu.

CHAPTER TWO

EVERYTHING WAS ARRANGED. Most of the women were in another pavilion, reciting poems in honor of Lord Norimasa's uncle. Two women who felt ill remained behind their screens, but Lord Norimasa sent palanquins for them and had them taken to another part of the palace, saying that he feared their illness might prove contagious. The cook was preparing dishes all day; she planned on creating at least fifteen. On a high shelf, she discovered pickled smoked eel and took it down. The rice was flavored with the cook's special recipe. It was Aki who would mix the glass grains into everything but the soup and smoked eel.

As the sun began to sink, the colors of the sky became ever more beautiful. Light purple and pale yellow seemed to swirl together and streaks of deep rose glowing brilliantly cut across the other colors.

"If the colors were a little darker," Lady Utsu said, "the purple and yellow sky would be the colors of a bruise."

"A bruise!" Aki said. "If only such a fabric existed!"

The two women sat in silence as time passed.

"There is the moon," Aki said.

"Where?" asked Lady Utsu.

"Over the north fire tower," she said.

"Then he will be here soon," Lady Utsu said.

"It is a full moon," Aki said.

"Ideal for moon viewing," Lady Utsu murmured. "Lord Norimasa will take the women and the guests to the viewing platform. Is my makeup smoothly applied?" she asked. "I hate it when patches of plain skin show through the makeup."

"You are perfect," said Aki.

"To choose my robes so carefully for such a reason!" Lady Utsu said violently.

Minutes passed while they waited for the tapping at the lattice. In the room, the gold screens glowed in the perfumed air. The room was warm. All the braziers were lit. Lady Utsu's four-paneled screen had been brought in early that afternoon and she had spent some bitter hours staring at it. Why was it here? Of course. It was here to remind her of her home and family and how she would disgrace not only herself but them if she failed in this task. Would Lord Norimasa be capable of harming her family? She knew he would.

"He is here," Lady Utsu said. "Show him in."

LORD TSURUNOSUKE WAS NOT A HANDSOME MAN, nor was he tall. Still, there was something hypnotic about him, it was difficult to say what, but Lady Utsu thought it might be wisdom. His feelings were strong, like the winds that could uproot trees and cause rooftops to fly from their houses, but even at their stormiest, they were not easily evident to others. She often thought of him as a violent wind that somehow did not cause the leaves to shake.

Lady Utsu stood up when he came in. Both of them were smiling. He moved toward her and touched her cheek with his hand. "You are well?" he asked her.

"Very well," she said.

"Please be seated," she said. "The cook has prepared quite a feast. Fifteen dishes. And there will be smoked eel!"

"Ah, smoked eel," he said. "It is what I love best."

"I know."

"And there is a full moon tonight," she said. "Everything cooperates with us."

"When we have eaten," he said, "we can walk outside and enjoy it. Before we go behind your screen. That is the screen displaying your home, is it not?"

"Yes," she said.

"Yet another beautiful thing to contemplate," he said.

They conversed, speaking of this and that. He asked her to read the poem she had written for Lord Norimasa's birthday. "May there be many more," he said. Aki, listening, could detect nothing unusual in her voice. Lady Utsu laughed often, and her conversation sparkled.

"Tonight," Lord Tsurunosuke said, "we could celebrate as if this were the ceremony of the third night we spent together. If it were, we would be sealing the marriage pact by eating three rice balls each and drinking three cups of saké. Would you like that?"

"More than words can say," she answered. "But must we eat the rice balls? Lately, rice has not been agreeing with me."

"We will pretend we ate them," he said.

"Yes, let us believe this is our 'third night,' and after that, we shall be forever joined."

Aki approached, moving slowly forward on her knees. "Shall I prepare the meal?" she asked.

"Yes, do," Lady Utsu said. To Lord Tsurunosuke, she said, "You must be very hungry."

"I was taught to eat something before visiting another's house," he said, "so that I would not eat and gruffle like a boar, but this time I could not eat, knowing I was coming. I could not swallow."

"Then I am very happy we have such fine dishes, and so many," Lady Utsu said serenely.

They had the clear soup and the little duck eggs that bobbed in them and the pinkish slices of ginger.

"It is very good," said Lord Tsurunosuke said. "If the rest of it is as good, I shall die of happiness."

"Please do no such thing," Lady Utsu said, laughing lightly.

Aki asked her if she should set out the other dishes at once, or several at a time.

"Oh, I think all at once," she said. "Will it not be more pleasurable to choose between so many delicious things?"

"By all means," he said.

Aki set about placing the covered dishes on the low table. As she opened each lid, she said, "These are quails' eggs. This is shrimp cooked in ginger; these are four different kinds of dumplings," and when she opened another lid, Lord Tsurunosuke said, "That is all meant for me, of course. You know how I am about smoked eel."

"I wouldn't dream of eating it," said Lady Utsu. "It is all for you."

"No, no," he said. "I know you love it also."

"And the saké is warmed just right," Aki said, "and the tea, so if you will excuse me, I will go into the room down the corridor, the first one on the left." Then she left them.

"We are alone," he said. "How strange it seems."

"It is our third night," she said, and began holding one dish after another up to her companion.

He ate wolfishly. "Won't you eat this?" he asked her. "What about this?"

"I have been tasting and tasting all day and now I find I am not hungry," she said. "But I will certainly eat some of the eel."

"Please," he said, ladling the eel into her bowl. "Eat."

He took a bite himself. "Exquisite," he said. "Please eat most of it. You are eating nothing else." He coughed suddenly. "Something is caught in my throat," he said. "This is what comes of eating too fast."

"Here," said Lady Utsu, handing him the cup. "Drink some saké."

"Ah, that's better," he said. "The eel was particularly delicious. I see you thought so, too." At last he surveyed the table and said, "I appear to have eaten everything. Shall we look at the moon? Or is it too cold?"

"It is not too cold," she said.

Outside, he said, "The moon seems much closer than usual tonight. As if you could shoot an arrow into it."

"The rabbit who lives in the moon would not approve."

"No," he said. "You are shivering. We should go in."

"After we look at the moon reflected in the pond," she said. "I don't know why, but I always find it soothing."

They walked up onto the arched bridge. "Two moons," he said. "If only nature arranged things this way. It would be good to have a spare moon, a spare persimmon tree, a spare Lady Utsu. How much safer it would be."

"Yes," she said. Her voice was muffled.

"Such wind," he said. "How it howls."

"It howls for those who must keep silent," she said.

"Does it?" he asked, turning to look at her.

"The moon, I think, brings on melancholy."

ONCE BACK BEHIND THE SCREEN, Lady Utsu struck her gong softly and Aki returned and removed the dishes and the low table. She spread out Lady Utsu's sleeping mat and covered it with several warm robes. "Good night, my lord, good night, my lady," she said, and disappeared.

"She would kill for you," he said, as he lay down beside her.

"I should not like her to have to do it."

"How you part your legs for me," he said.

"How happy I am to do so."

"Did I teach you so well, or is this also a talent?" he asked. Her body, how hot it always was, how smooth, how well it responded to his least touch.

Her laugh was low. "Do not ask so many questions," she said. "Push the robes away."

When they finished, Lady Utsu began to cry. "I cry because I am happy," she told him.

"I do not think so," he said. "You must tell me what you feel."

She was filled with horror at what she had done, and filled with sorrow for what must now become of them both. "If anything happened to me, what would you do?" she asked.

"If you died?" he asked.

"Yes."

"I would be inconsolable for the rest of my life."

"What would be the worst?"

He shook his head.

"If someone dies," she said, "the worst thing is this. There is only one person you want to speak to, and that is the one who has died."

"It's true," he said.

"We live in a terrible heartlessness," she said. "Why must we die at all? Why must we have bodies?"

"Our spirit may return in another form and our bodily form is inconsequential."

"And if you returned as an eel?" she said. "Would that make the world less heartless? Would I be happier?"

"I am not going to die," he said.

"My sister said that. She complained of her throat, but when her throat improved, she could not breathe or stand up. She died, of course."

"Why this sudden terror of death?" he asked. "I have never seen you show the slightest fear of anything."

"Perhaps I am old," she said.

He burst out laughing. "Old!" he said. "Some would think you are still a child."

"Do you think a person who is about to die senses what is happening? Even though he seems quite well?"

"Have you had a premonition?"

"No," she said. "Have you ever felt such a thing?"

"Only before a battle. At such times, everyone feels a shadow fall over him."

"But you feel no such premonition?" she asked. "Not now?"

"You have been speaking to a fortune-teller," he said. "Haven't you?"

"Yes," she said.

"You are disturbed because we have made tonight our third night. Who cannot be shaken by the enormity of what we have done?"

"No one," she said.

She took his hands and looked carefully at them. "Such beautiful hands," she said. His fingernails were just as they should be.

"Ah," he said. "There is nothing beautiful about me. But you are another story. Tell me a *monogatari*, a tale."

"*Mukashi, mukashi,*" she began, and commenced speaking of a man whose ship was driven against the cliffs, but she began to cry and could not stop.

"A tale is not a good idea," he said, stroking her forehead.

Finally she was quiet.

"You have killed in war," she said at last. "I should like to understand war."

"Yes. I have killed in war. Of course."

"And do they haunt you, those deaths?"

"For some time, they do. Often, you see their faces drifting by as you are falling asleep."

"And do they change you?" she asked. "Those deaths?"

"Yes," he said. "Once you have killed, you understand how fragile a human life is. You understand how your own hangs from a spider thread. You realize how much you destroy when you kill only one human being, noble or peasant. You ask yourself, Why did I survive when the man I killed did not? You begin to question why it is you who are alive and if there is a point to living. The palette turns darker. And then you are changed, you stop asking most of those questions, but you continue to ask yourself, Why do I live? Only a beast does not ask such questions."

"How do you forgive yourself?"

"As you forgive everything else. You tell yourself, It had to be done. You deny responsibility and continue denying it, and with time, you come to believe that what you have been told yourself is true. It is not forgiveness. It is survival."

"What will I do if anything happens to you!" she burst out.

"You will continue your life, and you will grow well again. Time will make your life happier, perhaps even more happy. You will forget the little patch sewn over the rent in the cloth."

To ask comfort from a man she had just set dying! Had she no shame? And yet she could not stop. Once he was dead, she could not ask such questions.

"Would you want me to remember you? If you died?" she asked.

"Of course. But I would not want you to spend your time trying to remember me even as my image grew dimmer and dimmer."

"Could you come back to me as an angry ghost?" she asked.

"If I died even today," he said, "what reason would I have to come back as an angry ghost? I have never been more content."

What have I done? Lady Utsu asked herself. Then she answered, I have done what I had to do. I have eaten the glass as surely as he has. I should have eaten all the dishes as well. A loyal woman would have done that.

"When I return, we will talk to Lord Norimasa, we will move into our own mansion and we shall have children. How many would you like?"

"Twelve," she said promptly. She was again smiling and laughing, but somewhere inside herself, she could hear temple bells tolling.

"When must you leave?" she asked him.

"Tomorrow, early."

"I will get up to send you off."

"No. Sleep. It is good to think of you sleeping. I will see your sleeping face every step of the journey."

"And you will send a messenger every day telling me of your progress?"

"I will," he said. "I often ask myself what good fortune brought me to you and caused you to care for me."

"There is no good or bad fortune," she said slowly. "There is only destiny, and the destiny that determines us is not always our own."

"I predict," he said, "that after two days, your spirits will be completely recovered."

"And will yours?"

"I am always happy when I am busy," he said.

"I see," Lady Utsu said, smiling.

The circumstances she found herself in loosed a storm of passion in Lady Utsu. Lord Tsurunosuke was astonished. When the two of them were entirely spent and were slipping toward sleep, he said, "I always thought there was something cold in you, or if not cold, something you kept back. I did not feel that tonight."

"It is a strange night," she said, "perhaps enchanted."

"Enchanted," he said. "Exactly." Then they were sound asleep. He awakened at the first hint of dawn and left quietly, the morning-after poem he wrote even before he arrived pinned to her topmost robe.

When she got up, she wrote her own, answering poem.

> Even in the long rains
> When the raindrops are nails hammering
> I will see your face
> And it will be the sun.

Then she began to weep and could not stop.

"I knew it," Aki said, sighing. "Move over a little and we will lie together on your mat."

CHAPTER THREE

"WELL?" Lord Norimasa asked.

"It is done," she said. She did not look at him, but stared at the floor.

"Your eyes are not red. You have not been weeping. If it will please you, I will have a courier come every day and tell you of his progress."

"It will not please me to receive such news," she said. "And if I were to weep, do you think I would give you the gratification of letting you discover it? I would rather you think I was made of stone."

"It did not gratify me to give you such a command," he said.

"No doubt you found some enjoyment in it," she said. "Do you remember how, when the severed heads of the enemy were brought back to the palace, and the women worked on them, washing them and then fixing the hair, you used to take me with you to watch? Do you remember how frightened I was? How young? And how you insisted it would be good for me because the ward of a samurai, a child who was born of a samurai, had to understand what it meant to be a samurai and not a peasant?"

"I remember," he said.

"What were your thoughts then?" she asked. "Since those days, I have learned how cruel a peasant can be. I have heard tales of men who steal food being buried alive in deep pits by the other villagers. I have heard of the villagers who send their old people to die on the mountain when they reach the age of seventy and the way the birds begin to rend their flesh before they have even died. Did you not think I would learn cruelty soon enough?"

"You are bitter," he said.

"I am not surprised by your character," she said. "Mine is no better. Have you ever heard of a woman who, as she is poisoning a man, looks to him for solace? Asks the man she is murdering how she will survive the mourning and the treachery? If he feels any premonition of death coming closer? That was worse than bringing me to see the heads— over again and over again, as you did."

"Those questions you asked," he said. "Did he suspect anything? Were you trying to warn him?"

"Why warn him when it was already too late?"

"Did he have any suspicions?" he asked. Lady Utsu looked at him and saw his eyes. They had narrowed to slits.

"None," she said. She repressed a smile. "It was a night of such passion there was no time for suspicions." She knew he would not like that. She understood that he himself would again like to sleep beside her behind her screen.

"That was an interesting touch," she said, "bringing my screen into the ladies' quarters."

"Indeed," he said, considering her as if she were an insect. "Did you appreciate it?"

"You know how happy I am to think of my home," she said.

"Tell me," he asked, "was the night of passion so intense because of what you had just done? Did the intensity of the cruelty become the intensity of the passion?"

"I do not know, my lord," she said.

"You do not know?"

"I am not as well schooled in cruelty as perhaps I should be," she said.

"You play cat and mouse with me!" he roared. "Who do you think you are?"

"I know very well who and what you are," she said.

"Yes," he said. "You do. I do not know you as well."

"Women will have their secrets," Lady Utsu said.

"The consequences for you will be terrible if you did not carry out your task successfully," he said.

"Then you can bury me alive," she said. "I have always loved the dark. It will be as if the dark sky itself were falling on me."

"You may go," Lord Norimasa said impatiently. Then he abruptly changed his mind. "You always ask me, as you ask yourself, how this or that has changed me. How has this changed you?"

"I shall never have children," she said.

He was startled. He asked her why.

"I shall never take such responsibility for another human being. I doubt if I will marry, for the same reason."

"You are not serious," Lord Norimasa said.

"I am."

Lord Norimasa contemplated her. "Do you mean what you say?" he asked.

"I do."

"Perhaps I have done wrong," he said softly. "I did not think you would be changed in this way."

"Many times," Lady Utsu said, "you have told me that no one knows how they will react to an event until it has happened."

Lord Norimasa's face went red. "Must you remember everything?"

"It is the nature of my memory," she said.

"Out!" Lord Norimasa thundered at her. He knew, as did she, that he was sorry for what he had done, and they both knew he was incapable of admitting it.

She was not sorry to leave his presence.

OUTSIDE, AKI WAS WAITING. "What did he say?" she asked.

"The predictable things. Had I done it? Had I done it right? Did I know I would be buried alive if I had not succeeded?"

"He did not say that!" Aki exclaimed.

"No. But he hinted at such things."

"We did do it right!" Aki said.

"He would be happy if he could spend his days severing enemy heads. If he were otherwise, he would not be the head of his clan."

Aki said, "They tell a story about how he killed his brother. He sent his brother on a campaign and the brother won. The snow that winter was terrible. They were half dead when they came nearer the palace.

But while they were gone, Lord Norimasa built a barrier across the road to the palace, and Lord Norimasa's men fell on his brother and their soldiers and killed them all. Some say Lord Norimasa had his own father killed."

"None of this is your concern," Lady Utsu said. "No one does you a favor when they tell you such tales."

"I doubt if they are tales."

"Whatever they are, they have nothing to do with you!" Lady Utsu said. "Do not ask for trouble." They reached the arched bridge. "Do not speak of this any longer," she said. "The bushes have ears."

"Am I not always careful?"

"No," said Lady Utsu. "Not careful enough." She paused, looking down at the pond. "I told him I would never have children, and probably I should never marry."

"You are calling evil spirits down upon yourself!" Aki said. She was deeply shocked.

"I will always be the creature I was born to be, but I will also be the creature he made me," Lady Utsu said. "He will have a courier here every day with news of Lord Tsurunosuke's progress," she said. "Truly, we are in hell."

LATE THAT AFTERNOON, a mounted courier raced up to Lord Norimasa's quarters, the flag attached to his back flying, leaped from his horse and was escorted from the stable to the lord's quarters where he disappeared inside. Shortly thereafter, one of the men of his household brought a sealed, rolled-up note to Lady Utsu. "Throw this in the brazier when you have read it," it said. It was written in Lord Norimasa's handwriting. "Lord Tsuronosuke is reported to be well and going about his duties. Perhaps you need not fear for him."

Idiot! Lady Utsu thought. Had she not told him that the poison took at least three days to take hold?

"Look," Aki said, coming in. "A messenger brought this," and she handed her a package.

Lady Utsu ripped it open. It was one of Lord Tsurunosuke's robes. "Wear it at night and my robe will touch you as if it were my own skin," he wrote. Lady Utsu sank down on the mat holding the robe and began to sob.

"Was I ever a child like any other?" she asked Aki, tears streaming down her face. "Was I ever innocent and soft? Did I know how to love?"

"Certainly you did," Aki said indignantly. "And you are still that child, deep inside."

"If I could think so," Lady Utsu said. "If I could."

"You must believe me," Aki said. "I always tell the truth. Is it not so?"

"Lie beside me, as you did when I was a child," Lady Utsu said.

Aki lay down. She sighed deeply. "You will always be as I once saw you," she said. "Always. When you doubt it, you must look into my eyes, and you will see yourself again as you really are."

"You must live as long as I do," Lady Utsu said at last.

"I will try," Aki said. "And you must stay alive for me."

A SHORT TIME LATER, both Aki's and Lord Norimasa's thoughts were running along the same lines.

I should have stopped this, Aki thought. I knew how she would take it.

But Aki thought, How could I have influenced Lord Norimasa? If he had been angry, and was made aware of how completely Lady Utsu confided in me, he might have turned on both of us, or worse, would have exiled me from the palace. Then how would Lady Utsu manage on her own?

She understood better than anyone else how Lady Utsu overestimated her own strength. Lady Utsu had fought against her parents and won. She had fought against Lord Norimasa and won, but the stakes had never before been so high as this. Underneath her arrogant and sometimes formidable behavior was the child Aki remembered, the one who cried when the cat was beaten (and what a horror that was), the one who cried out in the dark and saw strange people walking toward her while she herself could not move or say a word.

Perhaps if Lord Norimasa knew about the cat. Would that have made a difference?

A stray cat had appeared in Lady Utsu's mansion. The cat was covered with fleas and had a bad case of mange. Lady Utsu, who must have been nine years old, took up the cat as if it were her own child. After one of the servants told her how excellent such tea was for killing fleas, she ordered the cat washed with green tea. After that, she began combing the cat and feeding it from her own dishes. Lady Utsu carried her everywhere. The cat barely touched the ground.

One day the entire family went on an excursion to view the cherry blossoms. One of the new servants saw the cat, thought it was a stray, and beat it until he thought it was dead. When Lady Utsu was told, she screamed and cried until she fell down in a fit. For weeks after that, she lay on her mat with her back to the entrance to the room.

"She may not recover from the death of that cat," said Lady Utsu's mother.

But her father said, "She is a strong girl. I think she can withstand even an earthquake."

"You overestimate her," Lady Utsu's mother said.

More time passed and Lady Utsu did not get up or leave her room.

One afternoon, when it was very hot and almost everyone had fallen asleep, the child heard a cat's voice. Now I am dreaming, she thought. But the cat's voice became more distinct. It is only my imagination, Lady Utsu thought, when a small head pushed itself into her hair.

The cat had somehow managed to survive. Her bones showed through and so did the caked blood she had been unable to clean, but it was clearly Hotaru, Firefly. Lady Utsu finally got up, picked up the cat and almost killed her with hugs and nudgings and petting. Lady Utsu's parents were notified and they joyfully ordered the servants to wash the cat. The servant who had beaten Hotaru was himself badly beaten.

"Ask before you try to commit murder!" Lady Utsu said.

The child's father was proud of his daughter. "How like a little queen she looks, a vengeful little queen. What a spirit she has!"

"Spirits can be broken," said her mother in a low voice.

"Not hers. If only she had been born a man. What she could not have done!"

The cat was tied to a bell and carried a charm tied to a ribbon about its neck. Lady Utsu and her mother were not about to have someone else mistake the cat for a stray.

If the cat had not survived, if it hadn't been returned to her, Aki thought, as she had many times before, Lady Utsu would have been broken. But the cat had returned, and Lady Utsu changed and grew stronger. She also acquired a taste for vengeance and a lifelong terror of loss. When someone threatened anyone near her, she became worse than an angry ghost. "Do not make an enemy of her," people said as she grew older. Now she had been forced to bring about the most severe loss of her life. She would turn her hatred against herself. She would never forgive herself. She had been forced to become her own enemy. I thought Lord Norimasa understood her better than this, Aki thought.

She saw Lady Utsu as a child, eating persimmons and throwing the pits into the *koi* pond to frighten the fish. She saw her when she went outside refusing to wrap her hands against the cold and built a snow fort in front of her rooms and came in with scarlet cheeks and bright red hands so numb she could barely hold anything. And this, Aki thought, was the trusting, playful child Lord Norimasa had taken and changed.

In his own chamber, Lord Norimasa was remembering Lady Utsu as a child, her beauty, her grace, her fearlessness. She was like a little general, born to command. But evidently not to serve and obey. He suspected that she was incapable of deep feelings for men, whom she toyed with as if she were a cat and the man a mouse. She had been his lover, and he showed great passion for her. Now he saw that yet she had not been fully awakened to sexual love. Lord Tsurunosuke had done that for her. Now that she had given him the poison with her own hands, she said she would not have children and probably she would never marry. It was her nature to magnify the truth of any emotion. Still, she meant what she said. For the first time, he felt frightened for her, and once more asked himself what he had done.

He thought, I care for her more than anyone else in this world. At least, I cared for her as she was, before ordering the murder of Lord Tsurunosuke, before so many things I myself commanded her to do. I could almost hope that she had disobeyed orders or subverted their plan. I would give a great deal to have her returned to what she was only a few days ago.

In the middle of these reveries—visions in which Lady Utsu played with her *temari* ball or her spinning top—a horse dashed up to his quarters and came to an abrupt stop. A servant asked permission to enter and, when he did, told Lord Norimasa that there was a messenger who came from Lord Tsurunosuke carrying a letter.

"Lord Tsurunosuke is well, but he is a little tired," the message said. "Of course, it has been a long trip. The weather was cloudy as we traveled, and no one suffered sunburn. But Lord Tsurunosuke's face looks very red, as if he were burned by the sun or as if he had been drinking. Otherwise, there is nothing to report."

The glass is working on him, Lord Norimasa thought. Probably his fingernails are red, but if he is wearing gloves, no one will have noticed. Even if they do, they will not suspect anything.

The servant again appeared, saying Lady Utsu had asked for an audience.

"Bring her in," said Lord Norimasa.

"So the glass is doing its job," she said in a voice he had never before heard.

"How do you know? You have not seen the message."

"The sight of your face is message enough," Lady Utsu answered.

LADY UTSU BANISHED AKI to her own screen and now sat alone behind hers. It was a particularly brilliant day and the room was far brighter than usual. In this unusual light, everything appeared more garish. The gold screens and the women's robes draped upon them screamed out their colors. Really, she thought, it was a sickening sight, gaudy and vulgar. Her own screen, which she now hoped never to see again, mocked her, reminding her that her mother had tried to keep her at home, but failed when her father and Lord Norimasa would not hear of it.

So much to be a woman and bear a child, she thought. So much for thinking a woman had command of her own fate. They say one of the lords of Echizen took a peasant into his palace and had a child by her. As soon as the child was known to be safe, the mother was thrown out and sent home as if she were nothing but a peddler. In the end, men always won.

If only she had not done her job so well! If only she had not ground the glass so well, so a gleam, a splinter, would have warned Lord Tsurunosuke. But if she had not done her work thoroughly! If the grains of glass had been larger, and the lord ate his meal, he would have suffered far more. And, she thought, I became so absorbed in the task, as if it were important for me to do it perfectly, as if I had forgotten why I was grinding up the glass.

Horses carrying messengers would come pounding up to Lord Norimasa's stable every day now. I will see them and I will learn the outcome, she thought, but the outcome is certain. And the riders would soon stop bringing their news of Lord Tsurunosuke. Would it be two days? Three, at the most? She prayed repeatedly to Kannon, asking that Lord Tsurunosuke's blood be purged of the glass powder. But really, she told herself, I have no hope. In the end, he will be happy to die, as who would not, cut to pieces inside by the tiniest of swords? She thought, I must avoid men. I bring them no good fortune. My beauty entraps them as fatally as a wasp in a spider's web. And what do I have to offer them? A coldhearted woman, becoming colder with every hour that passes. She heard the watchman go by, clacking out the beginning of another hour. Time was slow now. Before, she thought, I used to think that every hour added another small treasure to my string, but now the string has been broken and the prizes have run everywhere, hiding themselves in every crack, and even if I searched and found many of them, I would never find them all. Yes, the string was broken. She was less than she had been.

She lay down on her sleeping mat and began to drift into something like sleep. If I could sleep forever and never wake, she thought. But people who wished for death were never granted it. If I could sleep through the next four days, or five, how good it would be.

And so thinking, she fell fast asleep.

The next morning, Lady Utsu was kneeling behind the lattice, looking out, when she heard a horse galloping up to Lord Norimasa's stable. She stood up and went back beside her screen, calling for Aki. "Find out what the message is," Lady Utsu ordered her.

"Lord Norimasa will not tell me," Aki said.

"You have your ways," Lady Utsu said. "That man you speak to in the stable, he knows everything."

"And so do you," Aki answered peevishly.

"Go!" said Lady Utsu.

But it was not necessary. Lord Norimasa himself soon appeared in front of the building. He sent in one of the women who worked in his pavilion and asked Lady Utsu to do him the favor of coming out.

"How quickly you came," he said, seeing her.

"What was the message?" she said impatiently.

"Apparently, he is not feeling well. He complains of exhaustion and pains. But no one believes it to be serious. What worries the others is how flushed he is. He has turned from a pinkish color to one almost red."

"It will not be long," Lady Utsu said softly.

"If you did your job correctly," he asked her, "how much more can he last?"

"One day, two at most," she said. "I hope it is only one, because the day after that will be terrible."

"You will feel better when it is over," Lord Norimasa said.

"Better?" Lady Utsu answered. "I shall not recover any more than he will."

"Do not say such things," he said.

"You are the one who insists on the truth," Lady Utsu said, turning back to the veranda.

"You treat me shamefully. You leave my presence most rudely and you speak impolitely. What am I to do with you?"

"Kill me," she said.

"I will not converse with you in such a mood," he said. "I will come when the next messenger arrives."

"How nice to receive good news," she said, again turning away. "But it is not my good news."

THE NEXT DAY, when the messenger arrived, Lord Norimasa again called Lady Utsu outside. "The news for Lord Tsurunosuke is not good," he said. "Last night, he had a nosebleed and no one could make him comfortable. They gave him saké, but he claimed it stung like vinegar in an open wound. He has little strength. How much longer can it go on?"

"Another day," said Lady Utsu. "I am surprised you dare to mention his name."

"I dare what I please," he said.

"The entire country knows that," she answered.

"I suppose you are praying?" he asked curiously.

She turned without answering and went back into the building.

THE NEXT AFTERNOON, she and Aki happened to be walking near the trail that led to Lord Norimasa's pavilion. The messenger's horse was about to pass them.

"You!" Aki called out. "Can you not stop to answer a woman's question?"

"What do you want, madam?" the messenger said, reining in the horse.

"Lady Utsu wishes to know how Lord Tsurunosuke is progressing," she said.

The messenger appeared nervous.

"Lord Norimasa will be angry if you do not tell her. Every day, he comes straight to her pavilion and repeats all the details of his illness. Can you not guess why?"

"It is not pleasant to hear," the messenger said.

"Speak and leave nothing out," ordered Lady Utsu, hiding her face with her sleeve.

"We fear for his life. He bleeds from his ears and his nose and he has coughed up a great deal of blood. He grows so red he is beginning to glow like the setting sun. When he needs to relieve himself, two men take him to the paddy, but the entire time, he shrieks with the pain of passing his water. There is an icy lake there and he pleads that he be taken to it and put into it. It is the only thing that gives him relief. He asks for you, Lady Utsu, and he cries when he thinks of you."

Now tears were streaming down Lady Utsu's cheeks. She lowered her sleeve so the messenger could see her face. "You must tell him how I cried for him," she said. "He knows that, until now, sadness could not make me cry."

"I will tell him, my lady," said the messenger.

"And please," she said, "tell Lord Norimasa not to come and report. I am miserable enough. Lord Tsurunosuke is dying. I doubt if he will last the night."

"Do not say so, my lady!" exclaimed the messenger.

"I do not say it," she said. "His body says it for us all."

"Go report to the lord," Aki said. "See how she sways? I must get her to her room."

The messenger urged the horse forward.

"At least we will be spared Lord Norimasa's gloating," Lady Utsu said. Her voice was hoarse.

"He did not do this out of anger," Aki reminded him. "He was protecting us all. He cannot allow anyone to endanger Lord Sugimasa. Lord Sugimasa helps keep us safe."

"He has enjoyed this all the same," Lady Utsu said.

It seemed to her that the trees were playing tricks, doubling themselves, and sometimes, when she looked down the path, the leaves were gone as if they had somehow been transported into winter.

"Hold on to me," Aki said. "You are weaving and next you will fall."

She held on to Aki, but her dizziness increased. When she next looked up, she was sitting on the ground, propped against a tree.

"You fainted, my lady," Aki said. "This is what happens when people do not eat."

"Are we far?" she asked.

"No."

"Do not summon help. I will get up and I will walk."

The two women reached the house. Aki had barely settled her on her mat when the summons came from Lord Norimasa. "I will speak to him," Aki said.

"She is not well," she told Lord Norimasa.

He went white. "She did not herself take any of that powder?" he asked.

"Yet it has had its effect," Aki said. "But she has great strength, and although she would prefer not to, she will rally."

"She thinks Lord Tsurunosuke will die tonight?" he asked.

"Yes," said Aki.

"Believe me," he said, "it is best for all of us. Would she be happy to see the palace a smoldering ruin? There is no question that he was a spy."

"I will tell her what you said, my lord."

"I should have liked to speak to her," he said.

"If Lord Tsurunosuke dies, I am sure you will speak together. But she cannot bear any more."

He said, "That is not like her," and Aki answered, "She is not as she was and she will never be as she was again."

"I hope that is not true," he said.

"Hope is a wonderful thing," Aki said.

THE NEXT DAY brought the expected tidings. Lord Tsurunosuke had died during the night. The men had been terrified. Blood poured from his mouth, his ears and even his eyes. He screamed in agony and no one could comfort him. One of the men whispered, "What can he have done to deserve such a death?"

"A spirit may have entered him," said another. "We have been remiss. We ought to have summoned an exorcist."

But in the end they all agreed that nothing could have been done. He would be carried back to his own mansion and he would be cremated there. "What acrid smoke it will be," said his second in command. "Will the smoke drift in the direction of Lady Utsu?" another asked. "He so wanted to see her."

"Lord Norimasa would never have exposed her to a dangerous illness," someone said.

"No, that is true. He guards her as if all his good fortune depended on her."

"We must send his body back with all honors, but with a small contingent of men. We must send a messenger to Lord Norimasa asking him who is to be in command."

Lord Tsurunosuke was gone, but within an hour, worldly affairs were making their demands, obliterating his life and his death. Behind her screen, Lady Utsu was thinking the same thing.

The next day, Lord Norimasa asked Lady Utsu for an audience. "You must let me make amends," he said.

"Then let me spend some time at my sister's house," she asked.

"I cannot do that," he said. "In your current state, you would never come back."

"And would that be a dreadful outcome?" she asked.

"It would."

"And what shall I do here?" she asked.

"You will write, as always, and go on excursions. You will continue your writing and painting."

"May I ask to have my sister brought to me?" she asked.

"Of course. I will make a wing ready for the two of you."

"And I must not see anyone I do not want to see."

"You mean me," he said.

"I mean anyone," she said.

"I give you my word," he said.

"Then shall I summon my sister?"

"Of course," Lord Norimasa said. As he watched her leave, he thought, It is like watching a stranger. A great deal of time will have to pass to restore her to what she was.

What a life we lead, Lady Utsu thought, walking silently with Aki. It is like walking on sword blades. And I myself have brought this about.

AT NIGHT, Lady Utsu did not sleep until exhaustion closed her eyes. As autumn began, she invented a litany that inevitably put her to sleep. As she said each thing, she pictured it, each an image of something she found indescribably lovely, until she began to smile. The curved green roof tiles of the palace, the metal fish with its tail upended on either end of the roof beam, the *koi* jumping up out of the water in the pond and splashing back down, the gardener sweeping the path removing fallen leaves, then artfully taking up the brightest fallen leaves and scattering them skillfully, the high arch of the bridge in the shape of a rainbow, the first heavy snow erasing all flaws and scars in the earth, snow falling like unexpected time, the slap, slap, slap of the little waves against the edge of the artificial pond.

She had stopped thinking of Lord Tsurunosuke and whether or not he had left a death poem and, even if he had not, what he would have said. She had composed many such imaginary poems, but she no longer did so. She was careful not to do so.

CHAPTER FOUR

"WHAT WOULD BE BEST for her?" Lord Norimasa asked Aki.

"If she could find someone else, my lord," she said.

"Does that seem likely?"

"No, my lord."

"What must I do?"

"It is not for me to advise you," Aki said, "but I think we must rely on passing time. She is beginning to write again."

"Poems?"

"I don't know," Aki said. "She does not let me see what she writes. She rarely has."

"I am grateful for your advice," said Lord Norimasa. "You may go."

When Aki left, a man who had been standing behind a tall screen stepped forward. He was Matsuhito, who, although young, was trusted and relied on by Lord Norimasa above everyone else.

"You heard it all, Matsuhito?" asked Lord Norimasa.

"I did," he said.

"And what is your opinion?"

"I am no expert in women," Matsuhito said. "But the woman was right. Passing time is the only medicine I am sure of."

"I am not happy to hear that," said the lord.

"Why is the lady so unhappy?" Matsuhito asked.

Lord Norimasa hesitated, and then told him everything that had happened.

"I see," said Matsuhito.

"What do you see?"

"Probably you have forgotten the first time you killed a man, and how you suffered afterward. Many men see the man they murdered drifting toward them in fogs. They grow afraid of cemeteries, especially when the stones are shrouded in mist. They consider finding the man's family and making reparation to them. Their own bodies feel like mist, and they look down at their feet to be sure they are visible and they themselves have not died. Some behave quite crazily. One man beat his horse to death and then lay on the beast, refusing to have it moved. It is no wonder there is trouble if a woman has such experiences, and since women are more emotional, probably the lady has experienced something worse than even you and I."

"I cannot remember such a reaction to the first time I killed a man," Lord Norimasa said. "Although it is true that everyone complained of my temper and it was around that time when I set fire to my wife's robe when she did something trivial."

"Perhaps you have forgotten even more," Matsuhito suggested.

"If I did," he said, "I do not want to remember it." Memories were beginning to lick at him like flames. "So I must give her time," Lord Norimasa said.

"Yes," said Matsuhito.

"And you?" he asked. "How far have you progressed with your thinking about our next campaign?"

"Quite far, my lord."

"Good," said Lord Norimasa.

LORD NORIMASA FIRST ENCOUNTERED MATSUHITO when the boy was twelve. The boy was audacious enough to demand an audience with him, saying that he wanted to become a warrior and a samurai, and, since Lord Norimasa was the best of all the warlords, he wanted to support his clan.

At twelve, Matsuhito was tall and very thin, almost emaciated, and the other nobles around him roared with laughter.

"I will fight any one of you," Matsuhito said desperately.

"That will be unnecessary," said Lord Norimasa. "But perhaps I should see what you can do." He signaled to one of the nobles. "Knock that man down," he told Matsuhito. "Use no weapons."

At that, Matsuhito ran away from the noble, and everyone screamed with laughter, and so no one was watching closely when Matsuhito suddenly appeared behind the noble, leaped on his back, and placed his hands over the noble's eyes. The noble tried to shake him off, but he was maddened by the pain in his eyes. At last, the noble lost his balance and began staggering. Meanwhile, the boy began to rock himself backward and then forward until the noble lost his balance altogether and fell.

"I win!" Matsuhito shouted.

"That was not a fair fight," Norimasa's old counselor said.

"When have we ever worried about fair fights?" asked Lord Norimasa.

"We do not disgrace our honor," said the old counselor, a revered and extremely old member of the Council of War.

"Neither did the boy," the lord said. "It was not a fair fight from the beginning. The boy was too young and inexperienced. Instead, he thought of a way to win. He is intelligent and brave." Everyone was silenced. "Come with me," he told Matsuhito. "You will keep me company during the long nights while we wait for the dawn."

"I see well in the dark," said the boy. "I can scout at night."

"I may ask you to," said the lord. "But before that, we will talk. I should like to know about your life."

"I will tell you anything you like," he said.

"You were not obedient. Is that true?"

"Yes, my lord, it is true. I caught a monkey when it was injured, and when it was again healthy, I taught it to steal fruit for me. Then, when I was accused of stealing the fruit, I swore on my ancestors' souls that I did not do it. And I did not. The monkey did the stealing," Matsuhito said, smiling, "but for some reason, they punished me."

Lord Norimasa laughed. "You would do well in the Imperial Palace where no one says what they mean."

"I should not like to live there," Matsuhito said. "They say everything is so stiff and formal."

"Not like your village?"

"In my village," Matsuhito said, "life was even more stiff and formal than any palace. There were rules for everything. I was hung from a tree by a rope overnight when I caught a *tanuki* and roasted it and did not bring the meat back to the village so it could be shared with those who had none."

"Hung by a rope?"

"For four hours. From a tree. I would have been there until daylight if the monkey had not worked as quickly as he did. He tried to undo the knots, but he gave up and gnawed through the rope and I fell to the ground."

"And were you punished? For getting loose?"

"I broke my left leg and my mother said that was punishment enough."

"And the village? Was it large or small?"

"Small, my lord. The villagers who lived near the beach, just before the woods began, were fishermen. The women were divers. The villagers who lived higher up the mountain were farmers, although they often sometimes fished. When I began to run away, they would look for me. After many times of searching for me, they threatened me with *mura hachibu,* complete banishment from the village. Even I was afraid of this, so when I next decided to run away, I knew I could not come back. I spent time as a beggar and then I became part of a gang of bandits. They took good care of me."

"What a trial to your parents you must have been," Lord Norimasa said.

"They adopted me. I am sure they came to regret it. And they did not like having to let me go to Lord Kuronosuke's castle for half of the year so that I could be educated. They agreed to this when they adopted me, but they never liked it. They never would explain why I had to go. They said I learned bad habits at the castle and that was why I ran away."

"Is it true?"

"No," Matsuhito said. "I was wild. If I had been interested in something—like fishing—I suppose all would have gone well."

"And will you lie to me?" Lord Norimasa asked. "Or bend the truth, telling tales of monkeys who stole fruit?"

"I will regard your will as my own. But," he said, after some hesitation, "if I disagree with your plans, I will surely tell you in spite of any resolve I make to keep quiet. I have learned that much about my character. I am afraid I speak plainly or not at all."

"I charge you to speak plainly to me at all times," Lord Norimasa said. "If you are unsure whether it is wise to speak in front of others, wait until everyone has left, and then tell me what you think to be the truth. Can you do that?"

"I can," said Matsuhito.

"And women?" asked Lord Norimasa. "If I set you to keep watch over a woman, will that woman be safe with you?"

"I know only of village women. The women here are so unreal as to be frightening."

Lord Norimasa laughed. "Do not forget that feeling," he said. "Many of the women are to be feared more than their men. At times, I think most intrigue begins with them. And they are often implacable when even the roughest man would relent."

"I only see evidence of them when they are in their carriages and they let the sleeves of their robes trail out of their doors. Sometimes I smell their incense. And once I saw a very beautiful woman walking with someone who appeared to be her maid. That woman often stands on a high, arched bridge and looks out over the pond, and then she does not bother concealing her face, although the other woman scolds her. I have heard her called Lady Utsu."

"Do you like women?" Lord Norimasa asked suddenly. "There are men who do not."

"In the village, I had a sister whom I loved. I would have done anything to protect her. My parents said that my love for her was my one virtue. I understood the village women. There they did not hide their faces or put on airs. If one of them became pregnant, she married the man who created the baby. So it was simple, dealing with the village women. Unless they all became angry at you, as they did when I ran away, and their men had to find me and could not fish or work in the fields, and the women were forced to work harder. Women bind themselves together with mortar."

Lord Norimasa laughed again. "You keep your eyes open," he said. "I was not a good child when I was a young boy. Once I burned our house down trying to find out how big a cooking fire pit could be without setting fire to the walls. I discovered that it could be quite large, but not as ample as I made it. The men whipped me until I could not stand up. There is a long, dark scar on my side that reminds me of that whipping. My mother used to say, 'I will be traveling home one day and see you crucified on the road.'"

"Yes," said Matsuhito. "I heard that many times."

"And she would say, 'You will end up in jail or burned at the stake. People do not survive long in jail.'"

"I heard such things many, many times," Matsuhito said.

"Yet here we are," said Lord Norimasa. "But I was always angry at someone, and a monk who took me in for some time said my anger had turned to cruelty. I believe he was right."

"That did not happen to me," Matsuhito answered. "If I was angry, I was angry at myself. And how long can you remain angry at yourself?"

"Very long," said the lord. "But you did not react in that way."

"I think I am a simple creature," Matsuhito said. "Because the monkey freed me, I broke my leg, but the monkey was trying to help, and it was my fault I was hung from a tree branch."

They continued talking through the night, and by morning, Lord Norimasa decided that Matsuhito was to sit in on his councils of war, although he was not to say anything unless the lord asked him for an opinion. And from that time, they grew ever more close. In Matsuhito, Lord Norimasa sensed a terrible loneliness not unlike his own, and in time, when the boy grew older and became a man, Norimasa came to rely on him both for advice and sympathy. He observed how Matsuhito managed to catch sight of Lady Utsu when she stood on the arched bridge and made note of his interest. He will be the one to protect her, he thought, if it becomes necessary. My wife hates her. Now there were two people, thought Lord Norimasa, whom I love without reserve: Matsuhito and Lady Utsu. I wonder if fate has brought them to this place for a reason, he thought. He asked himself that often.

CHAPTER FIVE

FOR THE THIRD YEAR in a row, the plague struck the capital. But this year, it was early. There was a saying, "The plague does not strike until the cherry blossoms fall." This third year, the blossoms had opened early and were beginning to fall, and red boils were opening on people's skin.

The people assumed that they were being punished. There was terrible unrest in the capital. Offerings were made to the gods; noblemen expended vast amounts to copy the sutras in gold ink. The twanging of bows meant to frighten off evil spirits made a prodigious din and many people died listening to it. Drums beat, bows twanged to ward off evil, exorcists wailed, priests chanted the sutras, half-crazed men and women roamed the streets, prophesying doom. They were the ones who fell first, who knows why. The Emperor decreed that all dreams were to be reported to the Bureau of Divination. The weather grew hot far ahead of its time. People began to say that these were indeed the Last Days of the Law. Food spoiled quickly and many died of food poisoning. The worst of it was the absolute certainty that, although there had only been minor outbreaks so far, the worst was yet to come.

There was a dreamlike air about the palace. Lord Norimasa went to great lengths to make it seem that nothing out of the ordinary was happening. Poetry competitions were announced with great excitement and elaborate preparations. The women were told to dress in their most splendid robes, and in the hot afternoons, in the dim, almost dark rooms, behind their screens, they sewed until their backs ached. Daily, bolts of brocade or newly dyed silk arrived, sent either by Lord Norimasa himself or by relatives of the women who served in the palace, and, of course, by the lovers of those women.

"Is it enough?" asked Lord Norimasa.

"The women are restless," said Matsuhito, who was quickly becoming Lord Norimasa's most trusted man.

"You hear them at night. They are uneasy. It is amazing," Lord Norimasa said, "how silly women will convey fear and danger to the samurai. How do the men know what the women feel?"

"I cannot guess," said Matsuhito. "Few of them visit the womens' quarters."

"You will continue to stand guard at night. I want you to guard Lady Utsu in particular. I will tell her you are to guard her. Listen to what the women say. No harm must come to them. There are spies who say that some of our men who died in the forest were missing their bows and arrows. The spies believe flaming arrows will be shot into the palace. Fear fire."

"I have always feared fire," Matsuhito said.

"Yes," said Lord Norimasa. "There are a thousand things to fear, but fire—I do not have to tell you."

The two fell silent.

"As things stand," Lord Norimasa said, "is another entertainment in order?"

"Perhaps one more," Matsuhito said. "Too many excursions, too many diversions, the women will become suspicious."

Lord Norimasa sighed. "Suspicion is in their nature. Once we had an excellent spy. A woman. Men trust too much in appearances. But women—never. You must realize that our sole purpose is amusing the women to reassure the men. If the men believe the women are content and secure, all will be well. There is never a straight path. Suggest an entertainment."

"They love the shell-matching game."

"They are forever playing it," Lord Norimasa said. "I myself am tired of it. I know all the poems by heart. When a poem is read out, it is only a question of how quickly I can find the shell painted with the right pictures illustrating the poem. Of course, they deliberately turn some shells upside down so you cannot see the pictures so easily. It is a tedious game. Always the same poems, the same pictures, the same etiquette. There are too many rules for everything!"

"Throw the rules out," Matsuhito said.

"The earth will tremble," Lord Norimasa said. "Everything must always be done one way. But," he said, considering, "why not throw out the rules?"

"Make it a contest within a contest," said Matsuhito. "The women will be given shells and on each they will paint a new image that stands for one of the poems. There will be artists who will judge the winning sets of shells, and after that, the women will play their game. It can be made even more interesting. Set a theme on which they must all write new poems and illustrate each with a matching shell. Then see who can match the new shells to the new poems."

"They will fuss in the beginning," Lord Norimasa said. "They hate change—unless it happens behind screens in the dark. But in the end, there will be hilarity. It is a good idea. I will order the contest to be announced. You will continue to protect Lady Utsu and her attendants. Be sure nine strong men also stand guard. Outside the rooms, not in them."

INSIDE LADY UTSU'S QUARTERS, the heat, even at night, was intolerable. The women moved closer to the lattices and raised their screens, but there was little relief. Most extinguished their lanterns. Some would soon take to lying on the roofed porches. Matsuhito and his men were positioned on the far side of the trees outside the pavilion so that the women could not see them. The men were very close to the veranda and spoke softly to one another.

"If times were different," said one of the women, "we could go down to the ponds and sit on stones and dangle our feet in the water."

"Take my moon-shaped fan," one said.

"Even the fan exhausts me," said the first woman. "It does not help."

"In such heat, the plague will move on swift wheels," said someone else.

"We were spared for two seasons."

"But many were not."

"Do not speak of them."

"Yet we could read out their names."

"When do you think they will move us? They keep us here so the people in the capital will think it is safe to stay."

"They have made no preparations."

"On the day they announce an expedition to view the fallen cherry blossoms, that will be the day."

"No, not the fallen blossoms. The weather is peculiar and so is all of nature. But the full moon will arrive in its time. Then they will take us. That will be the pretext. They will say, 'We will take the best carriages, and even if it rains, we will go.' It may be pouring down, but they will say, 'It is a rain that will soon stop falling.'"

The woman who said this had an unusual voice, deeper, more serious. If a bottomless lake could speak, thought Matsuhito, it would sound as she did. To what face did that voice belong? Lord Norimasa often told him, "Matsuhito, you do not know women. Sometimes it is a blessing. But in their words are often the answer to riddles. How can you know of women, given the strange experiences of your early life?"

"I cannot endure the heat, and I do not care who sees me!" someone said.

The women fell silent.

"I am taking off my robe."

Matsuhito moved silently so that he could see the women's quarters. A woman shed her robe and was standing completely naked. Because the moon was obscured by clouds, and because outside the night was so dark, the shapes of the women inside the room were clearly illuminated by a lantern. Fear fire, thought Matsuhito.

"Sit down at once!" said the woman whose voice was like a deep lake. "Feel that breeze! A chill followed by a hot breeze that smells of boiling silk. This is dangerous weather!"

"An earthquake?"

"An earthquake is not the same as weather," said the woman's remarkable voice. She was exasperated. "Blow out that lantern. It will only make us hotter."

The lantern was extinguished. The naked woman's silhouette disappeared from the paper sliding door.

"I heard that a woman died today, one of the cooks. They bound her in a thick fabric and took her out of the palace. They laid her in a cart and covered her with firewood."

"I would think that would be suspicious, carrying firewood out of the palace."

"They joked with the guards as they left the North Gate. The driver said the women wanted a picnic in the woods and they were off to build a shelter."

"So it comes, the plague, always faster than we think." Again, that voice.

"But Lady Utsu! It may really only be a picnic!"

"Goose!" said Lady Utsu.

"They are preparing entertainments for us!"

"Goose!" Lady Utsu said again.

"I heard that when we are taken out, you will not go. Only Aki will remain with you." Matsuhito knew Aki had been Lady Utsu's nurse, and was now the lady's principal attendant. "You and Aki will stay until Lord Norimasa leaves."

"That is cruel!" one said. "Why must Lady Utsu stay behind?"

"He always wants her here."

"There must be a reason."

"I understand farmers have died and fallen into the paddies."

"I've heard that the plague has already begun to worsen. Soldiers are dying. Even the great ones. Not only the *ashigaru*."

"The *ashigaru* are very strong. Foot soldiers always are. Especially ours. They are trained as archers."

"Is anyone going to sleep tonight?"

"Lady Kitsu has fallen asleep."

"Touch her neck."

"It is cool."

"We must try to sleep," said Lady Utsu. "If we lie quietly, pretending to sleep, sometimes it is almost the same thing."

The naked woman, standing in the room. The sound of Lady Utsu's voice. Matsuhito strained toward the dark room. He would like to have seen her.

I never will, he thought.

CHAPTER SIX

MEANWHILE, the plague ran like a tiger through the city. In the beginning, wagonloads of dead bodies were carried away from the capital to be burned in the fields, but later, there were too many. Heaps of corpses began to pile up along the wide avenues of the city. The outcasts, the *eta*, whose job it was to handle corpses and all dead things, could not keep up with the dying. Then they themselves began to die. Men would run senselessly and attempt to scale the walls that surrounded the mansions, thinking they would be safe inside, but if one succeeded in getting in, it would be only a matter of time until one of the rear gates would open and his body would be pitched out into the street.

Dogs roamed there and ate as they would. The terrible, rough sound of the crow was heard day and night. When the few people still left in the palace went up to the third story and looked out from the moon-viewing window, they saw the bodies of people they had spoken with and laughed with a few days before. They lay in grotesque postures beyond their gates.

Noblewomen began to see servants dragging their dead and dying mistresses to the palace walls, hoisting them up, and throwing their bodies over it. Often enough, the servants laughed as they watched the dead bodies fall. Suspicion was uncontrollable. Noblewomen looked at their servants with dread, wondering if the women they believed loved them would throw them from the palace, laughing, or stripping their clothes and beautiful carved combs when they fell ill.

Rough men came in from the country, their faces hidden by hand-cloths. Others wore basket-weave hats that concealed their faces. They stripped the beautiful robes from the dead and made away with them.

One afternoon, a man was heard speaking to one who was still alive. He spoke in a loud voice and what he said was barely intelligible. He spoke as if he had come from another country, so remote was his home place.

"You will not mind if I strip these robes," he said. "Soon the sun will go down and the dogs are not to be borne. If I don't strip the robes now, it will be too late. Please forgive me, but your breath will have stopped within an hour, and, as the sun is still shining, it will not matter."

He left the victim with nothing more than the loincloth that had been beneath his *hakama*.

The dying man gathered all his strength and shouted, "Evil man! You will live in hell on the hill of swords!"

"Then we will meet again," said the robber. "Be reasonable. If you were in my place, would you not do what I did?"

But the man's breath was gone.

The next day his body was a storm of screaming crows.

Soon there were so many bodies there was only a narrow path through the avenues. Carriages were too wide to come through. People began to lash the dead to tree trunks. Finally, more *eta* were brought in from the country. Then the dead were carried out one at a time. The living would laugh at the dead bodies as they carried them.

"Hey, brother! Did you leave me any money? What do you think of me now, being carried by the likes of me? You're food for ravens, you know. Well, so much more rice for the rest of us."

"But at least," one man said to the other, "after he died, he wasn't hungry. Only the living are hungry."

There were reports that the rivers were clogged with the dead. Everyone was afraid of the water that came from the river. People fought over rainwater collected in barrels. It was a common belief that to see one's face in water was a harbinger of death. One of the women spilled a dipper of water trying to avoid seeing her own face in the barrel.

Then came the endless rain and the endless mud. After the rain stopped, the sun shone and the heat beat down. The stench was unbearable. Everyone burned incense inside the baskets meant for that purpose, placing a robe on each basket until the fabric was thoroughly saturated with the smell. The women hid their faces in their sleeves to shut out the odors. The reek grew worse daily.

People left the capital for the mountains.

It was reported that the monks of the mountain temples would not let them in.

Then came tales of men banded together for booty. Women were stolen and taken to brothels. Of the people who left the palace, only two came back. The rest disappeared as if they were smoke that drifted off into the clouds.

Everyone stopped looking out the windows into the avenues.

In a time of such grief, how could one person be properly mourned? How could grief itself survive? The raw love of life—that alone survived.

WHEN THERE WERE INCREASING REPORTS of death in the palace, the shell-matching game was held, and the judging of the newly painted shells took place. The poems, too. The women were encouraged to make a great event of the festival, and they began dressing early in the morning before the sun was up. The day of the festival turned cold. Ordinarily, no matter how hot the weather, most of the women would have worn twelve gowns. Now some of them wore as many as twenty. They were so burdened down that they had to be moved by the servants from place to place, like statues. Some of the robes began to strain at the seams and several seams burst.

"I would think," said Lord Norimasa, "that twelve robes are enough. Tell them, Matsuhito."

"I will tell them," Matsuhito said. "They will be unhappy."

"For what reason?" Lord Norimasa asked.

"They think they will never wear those robes again. If they die."

"Let them wear what they like," Lord Norimasa said, snapping his fingers in exasperation. "Who can tell a woman anything?"

TWO DAYS AFTER THE SHELL-MATCHING FESTIVAL, the heat returned, and with it, great excitement. "An expedition was announced to the great plain to view the full moon. Everyone is going."

"Tonight?" asked the women.

"Tomorrow night," said the minister of the left.

For a moment, the women forgot the plague and twittered like excited birds.

THAT NIGHT, Matsuhito was standing guard as usual.

"So," said Lady Utsu, "it is as I said. The women are to be taken out."

"You're going, too!"

"I will stay with you," one of the women said. "You must have attendants, not just Aki."

"You will all go," said Lady Utsu. "I will choose women from the kitchen to serve me."

"I am staying with you!" Lady Kitsu said.

"You are not. You are skin and bones. You are not strong enough to stay."

Lady Kitsu began to weep.

"Ah," said Lady Utsu, "your face is puffy and your eyes are red. I will be happier knowing that you are safe."

"And will you be safe?" sobbed Lady Kitsu.

"I shall not die of the plague," said Lady Utsu. "I shall stay here and write new poems. I will tell Lord Norimasa stories so he will forget what goes on outside the palace."

"Beg him to let you come with us!"

"I shall not die here," said Lady Utsu. "It is my penance to continue living. You understand my meaning?"

The women fell silent. Even Lady Kitsu did not argue.

AND SO THE WOMEN LEFT. The carriages that took them away were drawn by the most experienced and strongest of oxen. The stout wheels drew the closed lacquered carriages decorated with golden scenes. On the day they left, Lady Utsu stood some distance behind them, watching. When the other women were ensconced, and when they let their shades down so that only their layered sleeves spilled from beneath the bamboo shades, Lady Utsu called out, "Beware the North Gate! You will all break your best hair ornaments when the carriages go over that step!"

She laughed and the women in the carriages laughed with her. To come in through the North Gate was a sign of rank and honor. It was also a terrible jolting and lurching. Every one of the women had broken ornaments and disarranged their hair coming through the North Gate.

"We will meet again," called Lady Utsu.

The carriages began to move. There was the sound of sobbing, low and hopeless.

"Do not cry," Lady Utsu called after them.

The last carriage joined the procession toward the gate. The gate was closed and bolted.

Lady Utsu stood staring at the gate as if she could see through it. Then she walked into her rooms and slid the paper doors shut.

MATSUHITO HAD BEEN WATCHING. He was unable to see her face. She moved so that her great waterfall of hair always hid her face. Now she was gone again, into the dim rooms, attended by three women from the palace kitchens.

That night, as he stood watch, he heard a door sliding open.

"Where are the other men?" Lady Utsu asked him.

"Hidden," he answered.

"I see. If there were too many there, would not someone think a valuable person was inside?" she asked. "I know the state of affairs in the city. I know there are men hidden throughout the palace grounds. I know what is packed in the storehouses. I know how many men there are. I know what Lord Norimasa intends."

Some moments passed. A hot wind blew through the cherry trees.

"You say nothing," said Lady Utsu. "Were you not commanded to obey me in everything?"

"Yes, Lady, I was," Matsuhito said. She was standing behind him. She was speaking to him. He who did not tremble in battle was trembling now.

"Then obey me when I ask you to come into my room," she said.

"Is it permitted?" asked Matsuhito. "I understood men were never allowed in the women's quarters. Only Lord Norimasa."

"You must obey me in everything," she said. "Especially in a time of plague, when there is no reason not to obey."

"Someone must stand watch."

"Aki will stand watch. Aki, stay on the covered porch and make yourself invisible. Take the dog."

He heard a slight rustle.

"Look at the veranda and tell me what you see," she said.

"Nothing, Lady Utsu."

"But the girl is there, and so is her dog. Aki, too, knows how to make herself invisible. Please enter."

CHAPTER SEVEN

INSIDE, the room was dark. There was a strong smell of incense. The young man's eyes were not accustomed to the darkness. Outside, there had been the moonlight.

A lantern sputtered into light. Then Matsuhito could see many screens. Behind them, he thought, were the sleeping mats. There was one tall screen and over it were thrown at least three robes. They glinted in the dim light. Brocade. He had never touched a woman's brocade robe.

"I am here," Lady Utsu said. "I am behind the great screen. Must I come out to get you?"

He made his way forward, his cheeks burning. He stumbled over a headrest, fell forward, and fell against the screen. He and the screen fell together—onto the body of Lady Utsu.

She was laughing softly. "You have not learned your way through women's rooms at night," she said. "It is not easy in the beginning. Do you think you can get up? Your elbow is digging into my hip."

In his hurry to extricate himself, he stood up too quickly, taking the screen with him, and this time the screen toppled backward away from the lady.

"Oh, I am tired of experienced and jaded men," she said, and laughed again. "Try to stand the screen upright. It will be easier if you take the robes from it first."

Finally, the screen was standing.

"Place one robe on each segment of the screen," she said.

He did as he was told.

"In the beginning, before you grow accustomed to dark rooms, it is best to advance shuffling. That way you do not break your neck."

He was sitting on the opposite side of the screen.

"I do not want the screen between us," said Lady Utsu. "Come behind. The night is cold. Are you not cold?"

He did not answer, because he did not know how to reply.

"You will not speak to me?" asked Lady Utsu. "How rude!"

"Yes," he said. "I am cold."

"Take down the robes on the screen and drape them over me," she said.

He did as he was told.

"Now burrow into them. They are warm and they are soft. You hesitate. Do not hesitate when a woman makes such a request."

He slid beneath the robes and lay on his back, rigid.

"Are you not warmer?" she asked him. "I think you are still cold." With both hands, she picked up her hair and draped it over his body.

What would she do next if she thought he was still cold?

"I am quite warm, Lady," he said.

"I will tell you what I want," she said. "I want someone to speak to me. When the women are here, there are always voices. Now that I am alone, all I hear is the sound of the crow. Perhaps I imagine it."

"There are many crows about," Matsuhito said uneasily.

"But you are not a crow," she said. "May I ask you questions? I should like to know the story of the man who guards me."

"Of course you may ask," he said.

"I will begin with simple questions," she said. "How old are you?"

"I do not know the answer to that."

"Your parents did not tell you?"

"I did not know them."

"A *tanuki* dropped you off?"

"I think so," he said.

"I shall not tease you," she said. "You are younger than I am. I can see that. But why do you not know your age?"

"It is a strange story."

She sighed. "It is a night for strange stories," she said.

DURING LORD NORIMASA'S LAST CAMPAIGN in Kai, when the lord was still a member of the Kuronosuke clan, the clan was completely destroyed. Lord Kuronosuke believed that he had reached Kai before his enemies, and took up what he believed was an impregnable position, but the Minagas anticipated his move as they often had before, and were silently waiting in ambush.

During the evening battle, the troops of both clans were dispersed. The darkness was thick. Men fought one another in rivers. Men could not see one another's banners, and so, as was usual, small villages were set alight so that the samurai could see. In battle, no one thought anything of this. Villagers—peasants, farmers—were considered barely human. Lord Kuronosuke had frequently expressed this belief often enough. These lowly beings who toiled in the paddies, what were they but impersonations of humans? "Set fire to the last village," he ordered. "We need more light."

When the battle was over, few remained from either side.

"If we are defeated," said Lord Norimasa, "the others will hunt down every member of your family. We must hide them."

"There is no place so remote or so secret," Lord Kuronosuke said.

Meanwhile, some of the villagers who had not perished in the fire were hunched together, weeping. Parents tried to comfort their children and one another. Two young children caught Lord Norimasa's eye. One was a boy of three or four and the other was a girl. "Look at those children," Lord Norimasa said. "Do you not recognize them?"

"It cannot be," Lord Kuronosuke said. "I sent mine away."

"Yet they are your children," Lord Norimasa said.

"They cannot be," said the lord.

"Who can tell them apart? If your children are to be sacrificed, let these children go to their deaths in their stead."

It was decided.

Lord Kuronosuke took the two children. They were bathed, their hair was cut, and they were dressed in rich brocade robes. Lord Norimasa set off with an escort to find Lord Kuronosuke's own children and bring them to safety. The plan was good. When the children grew to adulthood, the boy could gather their allies and restore the prestige of the clan. Kuronosuke's men were loyal to him and they would rise up to protect his son. In time, his daughter would be married to a powerful lord who would then become an ally of the Kuronosuke clan.

When Lord Norimasa found Lord Kuronosuke's children, he and his horses turned to the north. There they encountered the other party bearing the peasant children.

"Let us switch them now," said Lord Norimasa.

At that moment, what remained of Lord Minaga's men charged down a riverbank, splashed across the shallow water and the Kuronosuke clan turned and fled. They came to a bridge, crossed it and then set fire to it. Here the water was deeper, and the enemy was left on the opposite side.

"Ride north now!" Lord Norimasa commanded. "We will find refuge in Lord Sugimasa's castle."

LORD SUGIMASA WAS AN ALLY and friend to Lord Kuronosuke. He held lands of great strategic value and staunchly supported Lord Norimasa's hope to unify the country under him. He was, therefore, invaluable to Lord Norimasa, and Lord Sugimasa kept the Minaga clan in check and confined them to this province. After the battle with the Minagas, Lord Sugimasa took in Lord Norimasa's men and posted additional guards and sentries, then asked that the children be brought before him.

"Which are the real children?" Lord Sugimasa asked.

"They are all real children," said Lady Sugimasa.

"This is no time for jokes," roared her husband.

There was silence.

"Truly," said Lord Norimasa, "I cannot tell which is which."

"We must question the two boys," said Lord Sugimasa.

"They do not yet speak," said Lord Norimasa.

"This is a fine state of affairs," said Lord Sugimasa. "Did no one think to mark the real children?"

Lord Norimasa did not answer.

"We must hide all four," said Lord Sugimasa. "The Minagas will try to kill Lord Kuronosuke's children. They must remain hidden. Lord Kuronosuke has ordered that they must be concealed. We will say that all four of the children are legitimate heirs of Lord Kuronosuke. He himself does not know which children are his because they were sent away and stayed for so long. We will say that his wife was ashamed because she produced doubles, as a dog produces litters. We will say that the mother was afraid she would be called an *inu*, a dog."

"But," said Lady Sugimasa, "such resemblances are miracles. The gods have done this for a purpose."

"It is Lord Kuronosuke himself who has produced this miracle," said Lord Sugimasa. "I have no doubt that there are other children who resemble him up and down the country."

"Then we must protect all four," said Lady Sugimasa. "For safety, we should hide two in one place, two in another. We can take two as our own. And we must have a burial. We must find two peasant children and bury them with the greatest lamentation and ceremonies as if they were the heirs of Lord Kuronosuke. After that no one will look for them."

"Yes, I think so," said Lord Sugimasa, considering. Why not? If Lord Sugimasa's principal wife had two new children to protect, she would have less time to spend spying on his other wives.

"Let it be done," said Lord Sugimasa. "We will take two. And the other two?"

"They must be well hidden, perhaps in a fishing or farming village," said Lord Norimasa. "They must not be visited by us after we leave them. If we want to see them, they must be smuggled back and forth. Otherwise, it would be obvious to anyone what we have done."

"I know the perfect village," said Lord Sugimasa. "It is a considerable distance from here, a three-day ride. Arrange the details for a journey," he said to his wife. "The other two children can alternate between my castle and the village. We will bring them to us and take them back hidden in wagons with bales of silk. In that way, they can be safe, and when they are with us, they will be educated."

"My lord," she asked, "to what village shall they be taken?"

"Is that your concern?" bellowed Lord Sugimasa. His irascibility was proverbial.

And so it was done, and, from that time forth, the four children did not know who their parents were. The children taken in by the Sugimasa clan believed the lord and lady were their parents. The children taken in by the farmers believed those people were their parents, and accepted the arrangements made for them, growing accustomed to visiting the palace twice a year. At that time, the two other children who normally lived in the castle were sent to Lord Sugimasa's summer villa. And yet all four children were to grow up sensing that something in their birth was hidden. For one thing, there were the servants, endlessly gossiping, and the odd comments they made. Nevertheless, the children were happy.

"AND YOU? Were you one such child?" asked Lady Utsu.

"I was raised as a farmer's child," he said. "Later, long ago, after one of the plagues thinned the ranks dangerously, I ran away and begged an audience with Lord Norimasa. I believe I was ten, although I do not know my own age. My own parents, or the two people I thought were my parents, do not know it. The people who raised me could not tell me who my real parents were."

"Lord Norimasa does not take people in easily," said Lady Utsu.

"Perhaps it was my resemblance to Lord Kuronosuke, who died some years after the battle. They say when he died, Lord Norimasa was inconsolable."

"Not so inconsolable that he was unable to assume Lord Kuronosuke's position," Lady Utsu said.

"That was his duty," Matsuhito said. "An army without a general, a clan without a leader, it is inconceivable. The chaos would have been beyond measure."

"I know all that," Lady Utsu said snappishly. "He has a good reason for everything."

"Quiet!" Matsuhito whispered into her ear.

His rudeness stunned her into silence. Then she heard what he must have heard first, footsteps, but not the kind of footsteps she had heard before. She could see him in the dim light, staring intently at the ceiling.

"They are on the roof," he whispered into her ear.

"The dog is not growling," she whispered back.

"He was taught not to growl if there is danger. Quiet!" he whispered again. She saw that he had belted his robe and that his sword was unsheathed and in his hand.

She remembered Lord Norimasa, when he first showed her the house which was to be hers. "There are nightingale floorboards in the pavilions. No intruder can approach unnoticed. The floorboards squeak. And that is not an ordinary roof. It was quite a feat of engineering. A Chinese man showed us how."

"A Chinese man?"

"He was washed up on the shore near your parents' house. He taught you Chinese. Don't you remember him?"

"The same man?"

"The same one."

"And he built my roof?"

"He showed us how to build it. You will be safe underneath that roof. He was very concerned that it be so."

Suddenly there was a cracking noise, as if timbers were breaking in an earthquake and the roof itself were about to come down. Instead, what appeared were two legs that dangled from the ceiling.

"Get me out of here, you idiot!" shouted the possessor of the legs. But at that moment, there was another cracking sound and another pair of legs made their appearance. "Push up! Push up!" another man was shouting to both of them.

"If we could push up, we would push up! Get us out!" said one of the men. Instead, a third pair of legs appeared, first heralded by the same sound.

"Go back! Go back!" shouted another man. "The roof is a trap!"

It was too late. Blood began to pour through the ceiling and the three pairs of legs pedaled in the air but could neither go up nor fall. Now there were louder footsteps on the roof.

"Should we capture them?" someone asked.

"Torture them! Then kill them!" came the answer.

"That is Sanbashi!" Matsuhito said. "You will be safe!"

He crept to the sliding doors and raised his sword.

Outside, the nightingale floors, as they were made to do, were squeaking and twittering noisily. Someone was coming.

"Not so fast," said a silhouette beyond the paper doors. "It is not over yet, Lady Utsu," the man called into the dark room. "It would be best if you came without a struggle."

"Why do you want me?" she asked.

"You know the answer. You will be a hostage. Get up and come to the door."

"I am coming," Lady Utsu said without moving.

"Faster!" the man said. When he heard nothing, he said, "I am coming in," and as he did, Matsuhito brought down his sword, severing the man's head, and the head rolled almost to Lady Utsu's feet.

Outside, there were three sharp barks. More of Matsuhito's men were coming. They crowded onto the pavilion. "Kill them and torture them all!" Matsuhito commanded. "Two of you light lanterns and search the grounds. Take the dog. Do not leave anyone alive. Send a messenger to double the archers on the roofs."

One of the men suspended from the ceiling shouted, "Kill me! Let me die honorably! I cannot bear this! There is a sharp piece of wood through my thigh. Is this a way for a samurai to die?"

"We are not yet ready to kill you," taunted one of Matsuhito's men. "Six pale worms hanging from a ceiling. It is something to see again and again."

The sound of blood, dripping through the roof.

"Light the lanterns," Lady Utsu said.

"When it is safe," said Matsuhito.

The two sat together against the wall.

"It is amazing," she said, "those legs dangling from the ceiling."

"Caught like rabbits in a trap," he said.

"What is the trap?" she asked. "Lord Norimasa would not tell me."

"Very simple. Thatched sections of that roof are not bound to the beams or the rest of the thatching. Anyone who steps on such a place falls through. Perhaps a child would not, but a grown person, always. Lord Norimasa told me that the Chinese man looked up at the house and said anyone who wants to scale it would come up the south wall. Therefore, build traps on the north. They will be very confident before they come to the traps."

"Very clever," she said, "because very simple."

"As was his other idea, which was to water the roofs in the morning so that they would be that much harder to destroy by fire. Lord Norimasa said, 'I do not mind appearing crack-brained. We will say that we want even our roofs to flower.'"

"Is that what awakens us every day? The footsteps of the gardeners on the roof? We have tried and tried to stop it. We have complained and said we need more sleep, not more flowers."

"Do not try so hard," said Matsuhito.

"Even when we think we are living in peace, we are not."

As if to punctuate her sentiment, a man screamed shrilly.

"One less to worry about," said Matsuhito. "Ah," he said. "They are extracting the six legs."

As they watched, one pair of legs began ascending, complaining as the man to whom the legs belonged went up.

"Three spies," said one of Lord Norimasa's soldiers on the roof. "Not bad for one night's trawling."

"Kill us! Do not make us spies!" one man shouted.

One of the soldiers on the roof laughed. "Pull out the other two," he said.

When it was done, the men were taken away—"To be tortured," said Lady Utsu—and ten men were left outside the house.

"It will be pleasanter to move somewhere else," Matsuhito suggested. "Especially when the sun comes up."

"I want to stay where I am," she said. "I will pull over one of my robes."

"They will be wet," he said.

She sighed and sat still.

"Where is the dog?" she asked at last.

"With Aki. She was told to take him if there was trouble."

"Can he not come in?"

"He is better where he is."

Lady Utsu sighed again.

"It is sometimes said that I am Lord Norimasa's sister. Or his daughter," she said.

"Are you?"

"I cannot say. My parents never hinted at such a thing. It is not impossible."

"Is anything impossible?"

"My character is dreadful. It is like Lord Norimasa's," she said. "I am cruel. Both of us look at people who still live and know they will die, and we mourn for them while they are living, and so it is easier for us to kill. Do you understand?"

When he didn't answer, she said, "How can you understand? Already I am mourning you. Such is my nature."

"I am still alive," he said mildly.

"Yes," she said. "And no." She was silent so long, he thought she had fallen asleep.

"I have never tried to explain it," she said.

"Try. One's mind is sharpened by danger."

"Is mine not sharp enough when there is no danger?" she asked.

"Why must you distract me?" he asked her.

"You are so straightforward," she said. "Men of the court go to China and back to say a simple thing. And we women do the same, with our endless poems."

"If your character is so terrible, and I must guard you, you must explain precisely why you are so dreadful," he said.

He was laughing at her!

"Let me tell you why I am horrid. This poem explains it, although it is not very good. Think of it as a riddle that has an answer.

> What must I prefer?
> The buds so tightly closed,
> Speaking of later rapture,
> Or the open blossoms, white and pink,
> About to fall,
> Speaking of piercing mourning?

"It is not a good poem. I told you."

"But it explains the person you are?"

"It explains why the crack in the cup has come to be there, something not quite whole in me."

"Something to do with piercing mourning?"

"Oh, yes."

"And perhaps loss?"

"Yes."

"And can mourning and loss crack the human vessel?"

"They have done it," she said.

"Mourning and loss are everyone's lot. Not only yours."

They both knew they were speaking with extraordinary openness. They were like soldiers after a battle who have survived together. At such times, it was possible to say anything.

"Perhaps," he said, "such things have made you bitter."

"And cruel."

"If I try to open the riddle," he said, "I will break it. I want to understand the answer exactly as you mean it."

"Ah," she said, falling silent.

"Is it so dreadful?" he asked at last.

Again she did not answer.

"So strange?"

"It is strange," she said.

"I have seen and heard many strange things," he said.

"Have you thrown a torch into a village?"

"I have."

"Yet you knew what the results would be."

"What you yourself have experienced makes it easier. Or harder."

"Easier, I think," she said, "in my experience. I will tell you the riddle. It isn't really a riddle. When I was a child, there was a cherry tree that was planted for me when I was born. After four years, it began to bloom. I waited day and night until the blossoms opened. One night, there was a terrible rainstorm, and in the morning, the petals I had hardly glimpsed had been torn from the branches by the wind. All the petals were veined with brown. Like the skin of the dead. I mourned for that tree. There was nothing in that—if it had stopped there. Most of the poems people write are about the fragility of cherry blossoms.

"But I learned another lesson. After that, I began to look at everything as if it were already dead. I looked at something vivid and new and I saw it as old and dead. From that time forward, I mourned everything, even if it had just been born. And because everything was already dead, there was no need to care for anything while it was still momentarily alive. It seemed quite all right to hasten someone's death—since that person was really already dead. And so I became cruel. Do you understand?"

"I do not really understand," he said.

"Suffering can eventually turn to cruelty," she said. "Have you not seen it? I have."

"I know that to be true."

"From your own experience?"

"No. Not from my own."

"So the riddle means . . . ?" she asked.

"Pain that cannot be endured turns to cruelty. In your life, it has."

"If you knew some of the things I have done."

"I do not want to be told."

"Sooner or later, people will speak of such things and you will hear them."

Morning's thin gray light began to brighten the room.

"Look," she said, and she drew back the curtain of black hair that concealed her face. "Now you can see me in the light."

He found himself looking at the most exquisite woman he had ever seen or imagined.

"You . . ." he said, "you are the one they say is the most beautiful woman alive."

"Lady Utsu," she said. "Short for *utsukushisha*, Lady of Beauty."

"What is wrong in that?"

"So many things!" she said. "Now, because I am beautiful, you will not believe me when I say I am cruel." She snapped her fingers in anger.

The light brightened again, tinting the room rose with the rising sun.

"You see now," he said, "why I thought you would find another room more pleasant."

For the first time, she saw what the room had become. From the ceiling, blood had rained down. Lady Utsu's clothes were soaked in blood. There were bloody footsteps leading from her sleeping mat to the wall against which they leaned. Something like a rag dangled from the ceiling. She surmised that it was a strip of flesh.

"Let us call Aki and tell her to come in with the dog," Lady Utsu said.

Aki and the dog came inside and sat in another corner of the room saying nothing. They, too, were covered in blood.

"A massacre!" she said. She shivered. Still, there was great excitement in her voice. "Yet it did not seem to have been so much."

"You are both in there?" Lord Norimasa shouted. The lord was standing outside before the small rock garden. The sand was raked into patterns like waves, and when the light was bright, the sand reflected the light and appeared to glow.

"The sand must also be drenched in blood," Lady Utsu said.

"It is only sand," Matsuhito said. "We are in here," he shouted to Lord Norimasa.

Lord Norimasa slid open the doors. "A good night's work," he said with satisfaction, looking around, "but not fit for a woman's chambers. Besides, it is polluted by blood and must be purified. If you desire, you can return to the chamber once it is cleaned."

"The blood on the wood will never be cleaned," she said. "I should like the footprints to remain as they are. There is a lesson in them."

"If you wish," said the lord, smiling strangely. "Of course, we will have to bring priests to bless the bloody boards. So, Matsuhito, you have done well. She is alive and you are alive, and we have three spies to torture. We cannot stay in the palace much longer. Our enemies are too bold for us. I am frightened!" And he roared with laughter.

"To leave the ponds and the *koi*, swimming beautifully," Lady Utsu said, "and the dragon boats tied up on the artificial lake shore, and all the beautiful gardens, their paths covered with white sand and combed into patterns, especially the wisteria in the garden in back of the house. There will be much to miss. Once again, leaving."

"And then once again returning. Think of the joy in that," Lord Norimasa said. "Crossing the bridges to the little islands in the lake. Sitting beneath the great willows."

"The joy has already ended," she said.

"I do not like the way you think," Lord Norimasa said. "If we all thought as you did, no one would venture to put on his sandals in the morning."

"When must we leave?" she asked.

"Soon," said Lord Norimasa. "But Matsuhito here, he will continue to guard you. Does that please you?"

"I am not displeased," Lady Utsu said.

"And Aki will pretend to be Lady Kitsu so that people will think the women may still be here. As for the dog, it does what Aki commands it. If Aki wants the dog in the rooms, so be it." He looked around him. "Until the room is purified, I want you to stay somewhere else."

"You have always said," Matsuhito reminded him, "that this roof is the best roof we have in the palace."

"The room can be purified while I wash my hair," Lady Utsu said. "Have someone bring the bamboo rack."

"Is this a time to wash your hair?" Lord Norimasa asked, exasperated.

"It is an auspicious day."

"And when is the next auspicious day?"

"In three months," Lady Utsu said. "Meanwhile, my hair, too, needs purifying. It is drenched in the blood of our enemies."

"Then wash your hair!" Lord Norimasa shouted. "You pay attention to auspicious days only when it suits you!"

"The sun is out," Lady Utsu said meekly.

"Send men to guard her while her hair is washed and while it is drying," Lord Norimasa said. "Have you ever seen a woman like her wash her hair? When the hair is longer than the body itself? Her hair weighs more than she does! Four women to wash it! Four more people to be exposed in the open!"

"We will wash my hair in the walled garden," Lady Utsu said.

"One man at each corner of the wall. Archers!" Lord Norimasa roared. "Can we manage this hair-washing without endangering everyone I go to such expense to hide?"

"It is enough," said Lady Utsu. "Perhaps we do not need the archers on the wall."

"I will decide military matters!" Lord Norimasa shouted at her. "I will send women from the kitchen and someone will bring the rack. You must have your way in everything."

Lady Utsu lowered her head.

"The very embodiment of modesty and obedience," Lord Norimasa said sarcastically. He wheeled and left the room.

"A RACK TO DRY YOUR HAIR?" asked Matsuhito. "When my mother and sisters washed their hair, they went down to the river and swam about trying to catch fish. Then they sat in the sun. Of course, they did not have such long hair as you do."

"Naked? Like peasants?"

"With a robe wrapped around them. Although they did swim naked. They would cry, *'Tasukete! Tasukete!'* as if they were drowning, and we would come running and not find them. They hid in the thick rushes at the edge of the riverbank where there are many hidden places to crawl into." Then he was quiet, remembering.

"And their hair was very clean?"

"As clean as clear water could make it."

"I should like to wash my hair in a river," she said.

"Your hair is so long and the river is so narrow, your hair would stretch from one bank to the other."

"I would like to see that."

"I would not like to see anyone untangle your hair. My sisters screamed when my mother got out the comb. A big rough wooden comb, and yet it would lose its teeth untangling their hair."

"Here the women must gently tease out each knot. It takes an entire day from beginning to end."

There was a small commotion outside. Aki and the dog went to the door and found the gardener dragging a fan-shaped bamboo rack, which he then stood up against the edge of the porch. He went into the walled garden, and on the ground he spread out many overlapping lengths of painted silk, and when he was finished, he placed the rack on top of the fabric.

Meanwhile, four men lugged a big iron cauldron into the garden. First, they built a pyramid of wood, and then went to fetch pails of water until the big iron cauldron was filled. Finally they fired the wooden pyramid beneath the cauldron.

"Within an hour, it should be hot enough," Aki said. "You women! Go eat your meal! Once she has washed her hair, we will be busy until the sun sets. Bring back enough for the guards. And water. And saké for when the hair-washing is done."

The women disappeared. Four men were placed on the garden wall, facing away from the enclosure itself. "Please," Aki said to Matsuhito, "tell them to sit down. They will have enough time to stand watch."

Aki began grumbling to Lady Utsu. "Are you satisfied? Now that half of the palace is busy with your hair?"

"Yes, O-Aki," Lady Utsu said.

"O-Aki nothing!" Aki said. "Take that robe off and put this one on and get into the cauldron."

"You want to scald me," said Lady Utsu. "Matsuhito, is the water boiling?"

"Is this man's work?" Aki asked, enraged. "You should be boiled! Oh, if your mother were alive to see your doings! She was so happy when you were born. She said you were just like a monkey, hair growing down to your eyebrows. How happy she was when she saw you and said, 'This one will not be beautiful! I will keep this one at home! This one will not be sent to the palace!'"

"Did you see me?" Lady Utsu asked. "When I looked like a monkey?"

"No, I had not yet arrived, and you had been sent to a wet nurse's home. Your mother had a fever, and they thought it best to send you away for a time."

"Why was I sent to the palace later?" Lady Utsu asked sulkily.

"You know why! You've heard the story enough! The extra hair on your face fell out and you were the most beautiful of them all. When your mother saw you when you returned, she cried for weeks! And then that driftwood man from China! He taught you Chinese! When everyone thought you slept through lessons! That finished your mother! 'Oh, the Empress must have her because she will teach her Chinese! A man's language!'"

"I cannot help having a good memory," said Lady Utsu. "It was easy to learn."

"Your memory! Only good when it works to help you get into trouble. Into the water! It is not boiling."

The women began buzzing around her. She was wearing a rough undyed robe.

"And you are not coming out until you are clean," Aki said. "You and your whims! Why will Lord Norimasa listen to you?"

"And should I spend three months with caked blood in my hair, covered with lice? Do you think that is a good idea?"

"This way, Lady," one of the women said.

"Make the belt tighter," said another.

"Don't let her hair drag on the ground. It's dusty today," said the first woman.

"Upend the big ornamental pot. Then she can climb in easily," the second woman said.

Lady Utsu climbed up, and now bent forward to test the water. "I will be boiled like plague clothes!" she said.

"Shishi," said Aki, calling Lady Utsu by her pet name, "into the water! It is the right temperature. Unless you've changed your mind."

Matsuhito was standing next to the wall, facing it. He could hear the women and feel the sun beating down, and he tightened his eyes against the glare. Finally, he heard a great splash.

"What have I told you? I have wasted years on you!" Aki said. "You do not dive into a cauldron."

"I drop in like a cherry blossom," said Lady Utsu's voice, coughing and choking.

"Yes, choke and cough yourself silly because you will do things your own way," Aki said.

At that instant, as he stared at the wall, Matsuhito saw another garden, and in it, another version of Lady Utsu as a child, placed on a mat, holding several papers in her hand, her head bending over them, sound asleep. She already had a considerable tail of hair and the round, plump cheeks of a healthy child. "Shishiko, Shishiko," someone kept calling—the child's mother.

"Will you never be where you are sent?" asked a younger Aki. She was tall and strong and big-boned. "I suppose the dog has run off?"

The child raised her head. She gestured to the large cryptomeria tree at her left. "She is tied to a branch," the child said. Her voice was the high voice of every girl child.

"You there, Matsuhito," called the present Aki, breaking into his dream. "Will you not stand guard as well? Do you not have a bow and arrows?"

"Oh, we have enough men for a battle," said Lady Utsu.

But Matsuhito had already climbed onto the wall facing north.

He saw two animals racing toward him, although he could not yet see what they were. Then he saw that the fastest was a fox and the second was a dog.

"There is a fox running toward your rooms," said Matsuhito. "Shall I shoot it?"

"No!" said Lady Utsu and Aki together.

"Shoot anything chasing it!" said Aki.

"It's all right," Matsuhito said. "The little fox has gone under your room. The other animal will soon leave. You must have a den of foxes in there."

"The fox," said Aki, "has come to protest Lady Utsu's defiance of bathing in grounds that are still polluted."

"The fox is here to be sure I do not catch cold," said Lady Utsu. "No one must disturb the fox. Leave food for it outside the wall."

"I have heard of ladies possessed by foxes," Matsuhito said.

"I am one such," said Lady Utsu.

"Take it back!" Aki insisted. "Take it back now!"

"I am not possessed by a fox," Lady Utsu said in a bored voice.

Four tall gold screens were set about the immense cauldron. Six smaller cauldrons surrounded the huge one in which Lady Utsu was submerged. Every so often, she would let her head sink beneath the water, and just as everyone began to feel fear, her head would break the surface. From his place on the wall, of course, Matsuhito could see everything clearly.

The six women divided Lady Utsu's hair into six sections. Each section was washed in its own water.

"It is very bloody."

"It is thick and heavy."

"We must wash it until the water runs clear."

"I think twice more."

"Have the men gone?"

Matsuhito watched as the women combed her hair. This process continued for almost an hour.

"It is clean," someone said at last with a great sigh.

"Well, get her out," Aki said, "and take care not to let the hair touch the ground, or we will be starting all over again."

"You may watch, Matsuhito-san," said Lady Utsu. She had noticed how mesmerized he was by these proceedings.

He saw the small figure in her undyed silk robe stand up in the cauldron. He saw one of the women put an upended pot in place next to the cauldron so that she could step down on it because the cauldron was so high, and to prevent her hair from touching the ground, and she pushed herself up out of the water using the rim of the cauldron. As soon as she stood up straight, the other women held out the long, wet hair they had been at such pains to wash.

Aki clapped her hands and six more women appeared. Each held up the wet strands of hair at midpoint. "Carefully, over to the rack," she said.

"Am I amusing to watch?" asked Lady Utsu.

"Yes, Lady," he said.

She had now reached the fan-shaped bamboo rack. A long, thickly wadded mat was placed on top of it. The women raised Lady Utsu's hair as high into the air as they could.

"Lie down, you annoying person!" said Aki. "Gently! There is no reason to break a bone."

As soon as Lady Utsu lay on her back, the women raised up her head and placed it on a wooden pillow. Then they began spreading out the hair on the rack. Once it was done, the women took combs from the sleeves of their robes and commenced the tedious combing of her hair. Matsuhito watched in a kind of euphoria. As the women combed under the sun, the hair began to fan out like an enormous black nimbus, a black sun.

"I never know: is it easier to comb when it dries, or when it is still completely wet?"

"Every time we decide something else."

And so the women chattered.

At last, the hair was untangled and spread out on the bamboo rack. "Now it has nothing to do but dry," said Aki with satisfaction. "Such beautiful hair." Her own was stringy and thin at the back of her head. "Little monkey," she said, looking at her charge, her voice softening. "And it dries so quickly for all that," she said. She was relieved to see that Lady Utsu's thin, plain robe was also dry, and that every fold of her body was no longer exposed, as it had been while the fabric clung to it.

"Come down and sit here, Matsuhito-san," Lady Utsu said.

"This is scandalous," Aki said, as Matsuhito climbed down from the wall and advanced under Aki's baleful glare.

After some time, without realizing it, Matsuhito began stroking her hair as he once stroked his sisters' hair when they grew hot and feverish and had headaches.

"That is not the behavior for a palace," Aki said.

"It is the right behavior for me," said Lady Utsu. "I have never felt such peace. Do you feel it?"

"Yes," he answered.

No one commented again. After all, the night before they could have died.

"I am happy that Lord Norimasa is such a busy man," Aki said.

"He would not mind," Lady Utsu said dreamily.

"Shishi," Aki said, "even you can go too far." Then she also fell silent, watching them. Tears sprang to her eyes, she did not know why.

A long time passed. "She can get up now," Aki said.

Still holding up her hair, the six women rose as Lady Utsu first sat up and then stood.

"Stand in the middle of the mat and let the hair down," Aki said.

Gently, the women dropped the hair.

Everyone was still, staring at Lady Utsu's hair. It was blue-black, and shone. The soft breeze lifted and dropped the hem of her hair.

"Beautiful," said Aki. "Now we must oil it."

"Can I not leave it like this?" asked Lady Utsu. "It feels so light. Not even for one day?"

"No," said Aki.

"Yet it feels so lovely!" Lady Utsu said.

"And it will be picked up by every breeze and blown into the branches, and loose leaves will tangle in it when they fly," said Aki. "Is our room clean enough so that we can go in and oil the hair?"

"It is, madame."

"The smell of the oil is so wonderful."

"You use it," said Lady Utsu spitefully.

"It is like her incense," Aki said.

And so she was borne off, the women holding her hair aloft, into the rooms, and her hair was oiled, and the sun began to sink, and the blue sky was slowly changed to peach, and then to rose, the color of fire, and her hair was washed.

"Let us hope we escape the plague after this," Aki said.

"The plague is over," said Lady Utsu.

Matsuhito looked down, and right inside, near the wall, the little fox was scampering and investigating the room.

"Are you Lady Utsu?" he asked the fox. The animal seemed to understand. She tilted her head to the left as if she were listening, made a tiny yelping sound and disappeared through the door and beneath the building. I will take care of that fox, thought Matsuhito.

"That fox belongs to me," Lady Utsu said.

CHAPTER EIGHT

UNTIL LORD NORIMASA WAS READY to leave for his country mansion, Matsuhito remained outside the room, but at night, he spent long
nights with Lady Utsu behind her screen, and Aki in a corner of the
room behind her screen. Unseasonably, the long rains began. Both
women were hidden behind their screens. But every night, Lady Utsu
invited Matsuhito in. It goes without saying that they did not continue
to lie like statues, their eyes staring up at the ceiling. Of course, they
became lovers. At night, they talked until the light began to break, and
if Aki made snorting noises, she might as well have been the rabbit in
the moon.

After they slept together for the third night, Lady Utsu said, "This
was the third night. We could be married. All we need is to drink three
cups of saké each and each eat some rice balls."

"Is it possible to marry?" he asked.

"No," she said.

But when they awakened in the morning, the little fox, whom they
had been feeding, was sound asleep between the two of them.

"Like a child," Lady Utsu said. "You know, Aki believes this fox
holds my spirit and I must be careful of her."

Lady Utsu began taming the fox. "No biting, no biting," she said,
again and again, and eventually the little fox did not bite. Instead, she
draped herself around Lady Utsu's shoulders and burrowed into her
long hair. The fox's head emerged through her hair onto Lady Utsu's left
shoulder, her fluffy tail on her right.

"When we leave, I will take her with me," she said.

At night, when the moon was bright and resembled a sand garden on which rain had fallen, Lady Utsu did not hide her face with her hair. Instead, she and Matsuhito would turn to one another and stare at each other's faces.

"You watch my face as if you will never see it again," she said. "But I will see you again."

He said nothing.

"I am never wrong," she said.

"I hope you are not," he said.

The fox pushed herself into the indentation between them, wiggled until she was comfortable, and fell asleep. Through her nose came a tiny snore.

"She is both of ours," said Lady Utsu. "My fox will hold both of our spirits."

"Little fox," Matsuhito said, stroking her. The fox opened her mouth, took his wrist in her mouth. But she did not bite down.

One night, Matsuhito said, "When you were drying your hair, I saw a vision of you as a child. Just as if you were standing there."

"And what was I doing?"

"You fell asleep over some papers."

"And?"

"And Aki came and said you let the dog run loose."

"But I did not. I was always careful with the dog. What was I wearing?"

He could see standing before him the child she had been. "You wore four robes. The top was green and gold. After that, there was a robe the color of a spring sky with coral flowers on it, and after that was a coral-color robe figured in gold. I think the fourth was red."

"And my hair?"

"It was cut short on each side of your face and the rest was trailing down your back, but was bound with a golden cord."

"You did see me," she said at last. "It means something."

"But what?"

"It is enough that it means something," she said. "Time will not separate us forever."

He was silent. She turned on her side and touched his cheek. It was wet.

"Tell me some things you remember so I will have them to keep with me," she said.

"I remember," he said, his voice hoarse, "a procession going over the top of the sand dunes, and old ladies with bells on their hands shaking them so the bells tinkled. I thought it was a beautiful sight. I had no idea it was a funeral. And I remember my father teaching me how to lower bound bamboo twigs and grass into the river so that the fish would catch in them. And I remember a hut, burning, but I don't remember it well."

"I am glad to have those memories," she said.

"Now you are crying," he said.

"I never cry," she said.

They drew together until the tears on their cheeks mingled.

"Never speak of this to Lord Norimasa," she said.

CHAPTER NINE

THE PLAGUE ENDED together with the cooling weather, just as Lady Utsu had predicted, and the population in Lord Norimasa's palace was greatly reduced. Many of the samurai had died burning with fever, begging for water, far from home, lamenting their fate, which was to die a dog's death. The women, those pampered creatures, succumbed in large numbers. One barely wiped the tears from another whose eyes had closed forever, when she, too, fell into a night from which she would never wake.

A great exhaustion gripped the palace. Emotions moved like tides, a high tide of relief that swept in bringing exhilaration at being alive, only to be followed by a great surge of mourning. The women again looked suspiciously at their servants, wondering whether, had they fallen ill, the servants would have thrown them laughing from the wall into the avenue. Crows were everywhere, settling like winged dark beetles on bodies that were not yet cleared away. Servants wept knowing they were suspected, and the more they protested and swore their fidelity, the more suspicious their mistresses appeared to become. There was nothing to be done. Only time's rough tongue could sand away such scars.

"People must mourn," said Lord Norimasa, "but mourning must not go on forever. We cannot explain what has befallen us, but we must give everyone reasons to live. As usual, we will start with the small things."

The fallen leaves rustled like crackling paper and were swept up.

The trees grew black and bony against the sky. The lavender color of the sky changed and turned a deeper hue. Lord Norimasa looked up at the small, pale sun and said, "Snow. On the night of the first snowfall, we will have an excursion." He ordered the women to begin sewing new robes. They were to be well wadded. He had straw raincoats and hats made for all the men and women who were to view the first heavy snowfall from the lake.

The women began to sew, at first slowly, but habit reasserted itself. They began to compete against one another. Little by little, the women who lived their lives in their darkened rooms behind curtains and partitions began to receive visitors late at night. Morning-after poems written by men after assignations were once again written. They were rolled up, tied with paper ribbons and sent to the women the men had visited. A spray of marsh grass, already turned yellow, signifying autumn, that melancholy season, was attached to the poems.

Do you not think that one night passes like seasons?
May our love outlast these yellowing grasses.

And appended to the poem was this note:

See how the grasses rustle like the robes of your gown?
Watashi no kimochi desu.

Conventional poems, conveying little. But sometimes they meant much.

Slowly, gossip, always inevitable in the pavilion, began again. "How did Lord Norimasa have the heart for it?" one woman asked. "In the midst of a plague, in such death, to climb the mountain and kill the *yamabushi*!"

"It was a good strategy," said the woman's lover. "It cheered up the men. They were restless and lonely. And the monks were surprised. No one would have expected it."

"Still," said the woman.

"He was right," said her lover. "If he had waited, more men would have died on both sides."

"That is true," the woman said.

Finally, there was a night sky the color of rose-lavender, a sky with a great deal of light behind it, so that people walking cast long shadows.

"Tonight will be the first snowfall," said Lord Norimasa.

"I have sent the straw coats and hats to everyone," said Matsuhito. Lord Norimasa smiled.

Three dragon boats were already equipped.

At the slightest glimpse of snow, the women were escorted to the artificial lake. For the first time since the women returned, there was the sound of chatter, the peals of laughter, the "Oh, Lady Kitsu, you are so clumsy!" and the lady's indignant response, "I cannot see in this light."

"Do not stand too close to her."

"Are you cold?"

"These straw hats are warm, but they stick you, like needles."

"*Harinezumi*," someone said. Hedgehogs. Needle rats.

"I think there will be little snow."

"But the lord has commanded it!"

"How many robes are you wearing?"

"Six."

"I am wearing eight."

"That is why you are falling down."

They made their way to the lake, protected by their attendants and the palace guards.

"Lady Utsu, into the first boat with Matsuhito," the general ordered. Matsuhito helped her into the boat. Someone was already seated, wearing a straw coat and, beneath his hat, a black hood.

"Ah, so there you are," said Lady Utsu.

Matsuhito said nothing.

Four men boarded and took up their position at the oars.

The night sky deepened to violet.

The boat was rowed away from the shore.

"It is like a great tray of black lacquer," said Lady Utsu. "Oh! Snow is beginning to fall!"

"By the time we reach the center of the lake, the snow will turn to great blossoms," said the man in the hood. Lord Norimasa.

Matsuhito could feel the imprint of Lady Utsu's hand on his own. We survived the plague together, he thought. That is something.

The snow was falling heavily.

"I see again why snow is compared to falling cherry blossoms," Lord Norimasa said. "One knows this is so, but one forgets."

The snow thickened and fell heavily in straight lines. Then the wind changed and the snow was blown directly into their faces. From everywhere on the lake, there was laughter and exclamations.

"It is good to hear that," said Lord Norimasa.

But Lady Utsu said nothing. She was staring into the lake, watching the snow as it reached the black water and then vanished. As if the snow never existed. How nature teaches you the same thing again and again, she thought. Yet it was so beautiful, the silence, the drift of the snow down from the heavens, the disappearance of each flake as it touched the surface of the lake. Surely they live on, she thought.

"And how do you like this?" Lord Norimasa asked.

"It is beautiful," she said.

"Ah, but I know your character," he said.

"Then I need say nothing," she said.

"But Matsuhito, does he know?"

"He knows," she said. "During those long talks in the long rains, we could do little but talk."

"So you were bored," said Lord Norimasa.

"I did not say that," she answered.

Lord Norimasa laughed. They fell silent, watching the snow coat them as it fell.

"We are becoming snow people," he said. "And you are the *yuki onna*, the snow woman. Does he know how cruel you can be?"

"Not even you know that," said Lady Utsu.

"But how could I not know?" he said. "Your character is mine."

"Yes. But we use different weapons."

"Let us watch the snow fall into the lake," Lord Norimasa said. "I believe Matsuhito has not seen snow fall while in the boat."

For a while they sat silently.

"Cold cherry blossoms falling, but without the plague," Lady Utsu said. "It is wonderful."

First, they felt something like peace. Then the beauty of the scene overtook them. In the dark, listening to the black waves lapping at the lake's edge, they smiled senselessly at one another. Yes, thought Lady

Utsu, beauty reconciles. But sometimes even beauty cannot bring about such a result.

"If we could never come back—" she said.

"You would weary of it," said Lord Norimasa.

"Yes, we weary of everything," Lady Utsu said.

"And you?" the lord asked Matsuhito.

"I do not ask myself such questions," he said.

"Perhaps that is best," said Lord Norimasa.

THE OUTING WAS A SUCCESS. When they returned to their quarters, the women chittered like birds. As for Matsuhito, he closed his eyes and saw the falling snow, the white snow-covered mound that Lady Utsu had become, the snow on her hair that covered her face, the occasional sharp whiff of her incense in the pure air, and he knew he would remember the snow on the lake as long as his life lasted. Someday, her hair really would be white. He would like to watch it happen. He knew it was impossible.

EVEN WHILE THE SNOW was deep on the ground and the palace seemed to stand in the middle of a white ocean, there were unmistakable indications that Lord Norimasa was preparing for another campaign. In such deep snow, only a messenger would ordinarily attempt to make his way to the palace, but now there were almost constant disruptions. From the North Gate, wagons arrived empty and left full. Other wagons arrived full and left empty. Men no one had ever seen before were mounted on the palace walls, and couriers on horseback approached over the narrow path outside at breakneck speed, to be heralded by the blast of a conch shell.

Lord Norimasa was said to be shut up with his generals and advisors in a large storage shed, and, because there were rumors of spies, it was said that his headquarters changed daily. From other buildings came the unmistakable sound of armor that needed repairing, swords being sharpened, and a clanking of metal heard everywhere, sometimes like crickets, sometimes like swords clashing.

The samurai hidden in the palace storeroom waited for the beating of the clappers during the Hour of the Monkey. They assembled quietly, left the palace in small groups, wore no armor, wore black cloaks and hoods, and climbed the mountain to the *yamabushi*, the warrior monks, who, expecting nothing to fear from humankind, were instead spending their time chanting in prayer. Two hours later, the *yamabushi*, who had caused him difficulty for so long, ceased to trouble Lord Norimasa. Some of Lord Norimasa's men did not immediately return to the palace, but assembled in the province of Kai, where they were sheltered by Lord Takashima and thought to be safer from the almost extinguished plague, which still very occasionally claimed victims, usually the very old and the very young. But no one was truly safe. Many of the men did not return, and many of the women who did returned to the palace to find their lovers gone.

Now the plague was almost gone, but whatever preparations had gone on while the men conferred about their plans intensified.

"I dislike this," Lady Utsu said. "I dislike being kept in the dark."

"Sometimes it is best you don't know," Aki said.

Aki and the other women were restored to Lady Utsu's quarters, and Matsuhito now attended Lord Norimasa. One afternoon, Aki made note of the route some of the men were making to the warehouse, and hid behind a bush until almost twilight, spying.

"He has never assembled such a multitude," one of the men said.

"It is risky," said the head of the counselors of war, an old man to whom only Lord Norimasa listened when he began to rave without limit. Everyone referred to him only as the "old counselor."

"But if there is a plot to assassinate Lord Sugimasa . . ."

"The entire province will be unsettled," said the old counselor, "and as his allies, we will be endangered."

"The clans are loyal?"

"They do not dare be otherwise," said the one of the counselors of war. "It is Lord Norimasa they believe in. They say he can do anything."

"There is a limit to what any person can do," another of the other counselors of war said.

"We will find out soon enough," said the old counselor.

"But you are satisfied?"

"Yes," said the old counselor. "If the Minagas have killed Lord Sugimasa, there will certainly be war."

"Then we are satisfied, too."

"Even I can be an empty gourd," the old counselor said.

"But you are our empty gourd!" one of the counselors said, and the others roared with laughter.

"So many will die."

"Lord Norimasa does not count the cost."

"If he were not at the head of the troops, there would be rebellion."

"But he is always there."

"They think him invincible."

"He may be," said the old counselor. "The gods choose to weave our destinies for us."

Then they turned and approached their own quarters.

Aki stood up. Her knees creaked these days. It was dangerous to make such sounds, she thought.

She told Lady Utsu what she had heard.

"I surmised as much," she said, and went on with her sewing.

"He will go, of course," Aki said.

"Who?"

"Matsuhito."

"Would he stay here with the ladies?"

"He is one of the counselors of war. If anything happens to Lord Sugimasa, they will all want to avenge him. Even when the others stay behind, Matsuhito goes."

"It is difficult to work with brocade," Lady Utsu said.

"You have come to care about this one."

"I care for everyone," she said with a laugh. She put aside her sewing. Beneath it, the little fox was asleep. "Most especially, I care for this one."

"Complete nonsense," said Aki.

"Humor me. Akahige, stroke my cheek." The little fox lifted its sleepy head and stroked his mistress's face. "Comb my hair," Lady Utsu commanded. The little fox tried to comb her hair, but her hair was too long and the fox's paw tangled in it. Lady Utsu extracted the paw for her. "Good *iiko*," she said. "Good little thing."

"I believe Lady Tsukie is pregnant. Lord Norimasa will be pleased," Aki said.

Lady Utsu's hand, stroking the fox, paused. "Yet another one," she said. "It has nothing to do with me."

"It must go well," said Aki. "Or your jealous spirit will be blamed."

"I am not jealous," she said. "What have I to do with that breeder of babies?"

"They will blame you all the same."

"She was born to have children. She has less trouble than a cow."

"Shishi!" Aki said. "If anyone should hear you!"

Lady Utsu took up her sewing. The little fox struggled up through the brocade folds, stroked the lady's cheek, squirmed, pushed at the fabric until she was comfortable, and fell deeply asleep.

"There are spirits about," Aki said softly, but the lady did not hear her, or if she did, she did not ask what she meant.

THE DISTURBANCE took everyone by surprise. The women were ordered into their palanquins, four in each, and, attended by many men, were lined up in front of the North Gate and began to leave the palace. Many of the women were still putting on their makeup, combing their hair and thrusting combs into it. They left a layer of powder in their quarters, and robes were thrown everywhere. Lady Utsu's carriage was particularly drab. Orders came down that no sleeves were to trail from her carriage's blinds or from any of the other carriages.

Some women were to be returned to their families. Others did not yet know their destination. All of them were to be kept heavily guarded.

"Say goodbye to her," Lord Norimasa told Matsuhito. It was a signal honor.

When he approached her, she raised her blinds. He could see the little fox in her lap. "Please take care," she said.

"I am a peasant for all that," he said. "Peasants last forever."

"But how will anyone know you are?" she asked.

"They will," he answered. He seemed surprised that she had asked.

"Then I shall not fear for you," she said.

"And you, too, will be careful," he said.

"I must care for the fox," she said, smiling.

"Matsuhito!" Lord Norimasa roared. Matsuhito turned his horse's head. "I must go," he said.

"Wait! Say goodbye to Akahige!"

"Goodbye, Akahige!" he called back, and then he was gone, one among the many surrounding Lord Norimasa.

ONCE OUT OF THE PALACE, the men took a circuitous route. They went south. After many hours they stopped, watered their horses and sat on the withered, tan grass. Apparently, the snow had not yet fallen here. Then they remounted, and at a sharp fork in the road leading north, they turned.

"It is a long road," Lord Norimasa said.

"The peasants say all roads are long when you are near the goal."

"What worries me is that we do not know Lord Sugimasa's territories well. We sent out many spies, but will they understand what they see?"

"You must rely on me there," said Matsuhito. "When we are close, but not too close, I will dismount and put on peasants' clothing. I will smear myself with mud and I will say I fell ill on a pilgrimage and say I am so white because I have not been out in the sun."

"Who shall accompany you?"

"It is best if I go the last part alone. All those years alternating between Lord Sugimasa's house and Yasuhiko's hut in the fishing village, I know them both well."

"The horses will do well in their snow shoes," Lord Norimasa said.

"They are all mountain ponies. I thought them best. Your beast is with us, of course, but we should not exhaust him."

"O-Kuro," Lord Norimasa said. "The great black horse. The comfort of animals! If Sugimasa dies . . ."

"I know," Matsuhito said.

"I will level the countryside! I will leave no man alive! The horror will go down in history!"

"Yes."

"And yet you are not repulsed by my savagery?"

"If something must be done, can it be done by half measures?"

"You are cold in that way, like Utsu," he said.

"Lady Utsu, too, speaks of a fishing village and of the whales she saw from the shore, a place like mine, the one where I once lived."

"Does she?" he said, turning briefly to see his face. "The road is beginning to climb."

LORD NORIMASA WAS proverbial for his rages.

"He will end in insanity, like his grandfather," an old man once said, but another man said, "No one knows who his parents were. We know he is of the Norimasa clan, nothing more."

Nevertheless, this man who raged, and once set fire to his wife's palanquin when she would not dismount quickly enough, commanded the utmost loyalty from his men. It was considered unthinkable that anyone might correct a man of his rank and power. Even the Emperor was careful when he had something to suggest. But with his samurai, even with the least of his men, Lord Norimasa was not often cruel.

"I want to know what is in your hearts," he frequently told them. "If you speak what is in your hearts, you cannot make a mistake. If you cannot make a mistake, you cannot tell me a mistaken thing. You must say what you think is best."

In the beginning of Lord Norimasa's reign, the samurai muttered. "The first one who speaks his heart will be the first one beheaded," one said. But after Matsuhito came of age and joined the war councils, he would say, "No, Your Lordship, I think that path is not best."

"And why is it not best?" Lord Norimasa would ask, his face purpling.

"Because it is a path that must go through treacherous marshlands. Horses have sunk in those salt marshes and disappeared."

"They lost their way?"

"No. They sank into the mud and continued sinking until they were gone. I will never forget the sight of a white horse as its ears went under."

"Quicksand," said Lord Norimasa. "I have heard of it. I would like to see it."

The other samurai sat still and silent. On a whim, Lord Norimasa might take an escort and an unsaddled horse and demand that Matsuhito lead him to the marshes. A terrified horse sinking into the earth, how well they knew the lord would like to do it.

"The other way is over mountains," said Lord Norimasa.

"Mountain ponies can manage, my lord," Matsuhito said.

"And all my men will fall from their saddles," said Lord Norimasa, who roared with laughter. "Save your glowering for the battle," Lord Norimasa said, observing his men. "I would not ask this of you were I not sure you could accomplish it."

"Lord Norimasa," said one of the counselors of war, "I have never heard of such marshes."

"And I have never seen a ghost, but do ghosts exist?" Lord Norimasa asked him. "Will you go and will you win?" he asked, challenging them.

They answered with a great roar.

In the end, the campaign was a success.

Still, the men muttered, "Perhaps it is only Matsuhito who may speak to the lord as he does," but as time passed, and Lord Norimasa flew into rages when no one would speak his mind, the men became accustomed to speaking openly.

"Does he ask our opinion because he does not know what is best to do?" asked one of the archers.

"You are a great archer and a great fool," answered the man who rode next to him. "The lord is a great and unusual man." And so they came to feel.

IT WAS A LONG JOURNEY.

The men were released in groups of twenty, at one-hour intervals, each group with a destination that differed from the others, each with its own route. They were to arrive at their destined place, spend the night, and then follow a roundabout track until they reached the borders of Kai. Then they were to return to their assigned place, where they would be hidden from sight and would not easily be discovered by spies. The women, too, were sent by devious routes, to their homes or to convents.

Axles broke, the column stopped, wheels were mended. At night, there was a lacing of frost at the edge of the lake they passed on their right. The light from a crescent moon sparkled on the ebony waters. The mountains were steep and jagged and stood out clearly. There was only the thready morning mists before the sun fully rose. The cries of the birds rang more loudly now that the leaves had fallen and could not muffle them. On the second day, the spies had not yet begun to return, but on the third, a mounted man, his horse lathered, galloped toward them.

He dismounted in front of Lord Norimasa and bowed to the ground. "They are hidden near a mountain, far to the north of Lord Sugimasa's palace. They have massed a great army. Other clans have joined them. They smell victory."

"Is our army less?" Norimasa asked.

"Yes."

"Can we take them?"

"I think not with a frontal attack," said the spy, his head still pressed to the ground.

"Stand up," Norimasa ordered him. "Get some rest. Eat. Take food with you. In the morning, on a fresh horse, you will lead Lord Matsuhito as close to the mountain as you can go without being detected. Then you will leave him. You will arrange to have him meet you at a specified place. Do not lose each other! If anything befalls Lord Matsuhito, you will be crucified. Do you understand?"

"*Wakatta*," said the man in a low voice. "I understand."

Meanwhile, a rustle swept through the men. Lord Matsuhito! Never had he been called that before. Truly, he had become second in command.

"But what are they up to?" one of the counselors asked the head counselor of war, the old counselor.

"Have we not enough on our hands without this girlish gossip?" the old counselor of war bellowed. "Are your weapons in order? Have you fastened your armor behind you securely? These are the questions of soldiers!"

LADY UTSU AND HER TRAIN were heading north. As the road grew steeper, she was pressed back against the seat farthest from the horses.

"This jolting and bumping, how I hate it," she said.

"This is the third time you have complained," Aki said. "Does complaining make the road better?"

"Yes," she said sulkily.

"You will see Lord Norimasa soon enough," Aki said, "although why you must be taken to a battlefield is more than I understand."

"Perhaps I will not go," she said. "Last night, I had an inauspicious dream."

"We all have them. It comes from being pounded about like laundry on river stones. Your hair ornaments are heavy and are giving you a headache."

"I see," said Lady Utsu.

"Well, what was the dream?" Aki asked finally.

"I have forgotten it."

·"What an annoying child!" Aki exclaimed. "Probably you dreamed of catching cold after foolishly washing your hair."

"Probably," said the lady.

She had dreamed that she was lost at night in winter. There was no snow on the ground, although the fallen leaves had faded to a deep tan, and when she walked, the leaves crumbled and crackled. A few snowflakes began to fall, so few she was not yet sure it had begun snowing. But then the snow began to thicken and she stood against a great maple. The snow was falling fast, but it was not covering the ground. As it fell, the snow veered toward her and fell onto her belly, where it disappeared, as if into water. When this happened, a great wave of illness washed over her. Why am I not cold? she asked herself. There was beauty in the dream, and danger. It was not a dream that could be told.

"They say Lady Tsukie is near her time," Aki said.

"Every year, as regularly as the cherry blossoms bloom, but her children are not so beautiful," Lady Utsu said.

"She was not well, and while you were shut up in the palace, everyone thought she had the plague, but it was something else altogether. Lord Norimasa will be pleased."

"Will he?" Lady Utsu said sourly. "If this continues, he will have to build another wing to the palace. How many does she have now?"

"Seven, as you know very well," Aki said.

"A good breeder," Lady Utsu said crankily. "Eight ugly, flat-faced children."

"You have grown fatter," Aki said. "Yet your face is very thin."

"Old age," said Lady Utsu.

"Why did I never notice it before?" Aki asked. "Everyone thought you were an *isshi onna*. A barren woman, a stone woman."

"I don't care what other people think," Lady Utsu said, bursting into tears.

"This changes things," Aki said, pondering. "Do you think Lord Norimasa will send you a maternity belt? Surely the child is his. I know he still comes to you at night, although he swore to Lady Tsukie that he would never again do so."

"This is not his concern, or anyone's," Lady Utsu said.

"You cannot proceed to Kai. It is out of the question. We can stay with your sister in Echizen. You can decide what you will do there."

"Echizen," she said.

"Do you want to keep the child?"

"No!" said Lady Utsu. She began crying uncontrollably.

"Well, we will see," said Aki. "We need not decide everything this instant."

"I have decided!"

"Shishi," she said. "We will see. Calm yourself."

"Children," she said. "I have never seen the point of them."

"Shishi, you have been spoiled. If I were you, I would write more poems. The Emperor is collecting a new royal anthology."

"You mean he will protect me?"

"You need no protection. Lord Norimasa took you as his second wife long ago."

Lady Utsu cried softly. "In name only," she said. "And Lady Tsukie tried to poison me. She was sure I wanted to supplant her and become his first wife. She carried on so that he swore he would give me up. These old stories!"

"If only they were old stories." Aki said. "Open the blinds!" Aki suddenly exclaimed. "A waterfall! Look how high it falls and how it creates a deep green pool! Truly it is like a silver sash! See how it makes the rocks shine! And up at the top, the pines are twisted as if in agony. It is the wind, of course, but those trees are enough to make you believe in spirits. And there is someone beneath the falling water! He must be purifying himself. Now, that is an auspicious sight!"

"Do not worry about me," said Lady Utsu.

"And who else must I worry about?" Aki asked her.

"Soon there will be more snow here," Lady Utsu said.

"If anything happens to Lady Tsukie, you will be blamed," Aki said. "I told you before. They will say your jealous spirit possessed her."

The little fox stirred in Lady Utsu's lap, rearranged himself, and went back to sleep.

"They will say you are a woman who consorts with foxes and they will want to kill the foxes," Aki said.

"No one will touch this fox," Lady Utsu said.

"Mist is covering the mountaintops."

"The weather is changing," Lady Utsu said. She chanted this out loud:

> The pampas grasses wave like banners.
> What makes the grass so strong?
> Does its strength come from the soldiers
> Buried deep beneath the roots?

"It is a good poem," Aki said dubiously.

"You mean it is good that I am writing poems again," Lady Utsu said. "Perhaps you will like this one better.

> Mist covers the mountain peaks.
> Now they do not pierce the clouds.
> Could I climb such peaks?
> Why does the world deceive us?

"Do you like that better?" Lady Utsu asked. Aki said that she did.

"It is good that you do not judge poetry contests," said Lady Utsu.

SHE HAD BEGUN to dream of the palace in Echizen, where it was colder. Night after night, she had the same dream, always repeating the same events. She had been twelve years old. Lord Norimasa had taken her from the Empress's palace to his palace. She was to be a companion to the lord's older daughter and teach her Chinese. The two girls were the same age. Lord Norimasa's young son was only two. He seemed to be a very quick child. Already he was speaking in sentences. But Princess Kiku was slow and cried when she made mistakes, and Utsuhime, as Utsu was then called, was annoyed by her. "It is a disgrace to waste paper on you," she said, irritated beyond endurance. Just then, Lady Tsukie paused near the study and heard what was said. She went to Lord Norimasa. "She must be punished," Lady Tsukie said.

"And what is an appropriate punishment," he asked, "for a bright little teacher who has a slow little pupil?"

His response enraged her. "Lock her on top of the fire towers!" she said angrily.

"And people will gossip and say you are jealous because Utsuhime is so much prettier and more intelligent than our child."

"Our child is prettier! Our child is more intelligent! If you do not like my punishment, devise one of your own!"

"Let your punishment be your own choosing, only let it be clear that you yourself have chosen it," he said.

Her face reddened. "That is not right," she said.

"I command the palace and a good part of the land," he said. "I am not in command of domestic quarrels."

"Then she will go to the fire tower," she said angrily.

"So be it," he said. "You women speak ceaselessly of how little power you have, and how you are shut up in dark rooms and told nothing about our decisions. But you have no responsibilities. Learn what it is like to take on some power."

And he turned back to the scroll he had been reading.

The audience was over.

"But first," he said, turning as if at second thought, "be sure to lock up Aki with her. Aki is to be her companion from now on."

"And is she to be sent to the fire tower? To keep her company?"

"Of course."

"And are any entertainments to be held there? It is a punishment," Lady Tsukie said.

Lord Norimasa waved his hand.

"My lady. My lady. My lady," went the heads bowing, and the chorus of salutations as she departed. Of course, the men and the ladies who attended Lady Tsukie and were near the lord's office heard every word.

"But I am afraid of heights!" cried Lady Utsu.

"Shishi! I will be there with you! Do not disgrace your parents by this wailing!"

"Must we climb the tall ladder?"

"Unless we can fly," Aki said.

And so they climbed up the fire tower.

Lady Utsu sat down on the small platform in the corner, too small to be considered a room.

"You can see the entire city, all the way to the encircling hills," Aki said excitedly. "On the hills, the trees are beginning to redden. Outside the palace, the trailing vines on the houses are half red and half green. Come look, Shishi!"

"I am not looking," said Lady Utsu.

"Oh, it is so beautiful," Aki said. "The sloping tiled roofs, it is wonderful to see. They are gleaming in the setting sun! Hundreds of roofs! Like waves! The red varnished wood is beautiful against the sky. The red *torii* are so beautiful! The avenues are so broad and straight. The oxcarts look like toys! Come look, Shishi!"

"You look," Lady Utsu said. "I am going to lie on the floor. It is hardest to fall off the floor."

"Have you not heard of earthquakes?" Aki asked.

"That Kiku is so stupid," Lady Utsu said murderously. "It is remarkable that she has learned some Japanese."

"The lord knows she is stupid. But you must get on with her."

"She is an imbecile!"

"A sweet imbecile," said Aki. "With a better temperament than yours."

"Then perhaps I should be learning from her!"

"Very true," said Aki, who turned and was now staring into the palace itself. "You can see past the walls into the central palace," she said. "I thought only the birds could see into it."

"Can you see our walled garden?" Lady Utsu asked. A few weeks ago, she had taken off her robes and stepped into the pond. It had been a hot night and the weather was warm, and although the bottom of the pond was muddy, it was deep enough to swim. When she came out of the water, she stood near the wall until she was dry and then put on her robes. But her hair was still wet and it gave her away.

"Could anyone have seen me while I was swimming in the pond?"

"Only the men manning the fire towers," Aki said.

"Can one never be hidden?" Lady Utsu asked.

"Lament your lot. Become a peasant," Aki said. "I am sure they are not spied on if they go into the rice paddies at night."

Even then, Aki had a sharp tongue.

"Ah, the Lady Tsukie! She has gone into the autumn garden!"

"May she perish there!" Lady Utsu said.

"Do not say such things. If a spirit should hear you and decide to obey . . ." She shuddered.

"A ground mist has come up," Aki reported, "and now you can't see anyone's feet, so that everyone resembles ghosts. They glide instead of walk."

This was too much for Lady Utsu, who finally got up and looked out. Aki, she thought, had an unhealthy interest in ghosts.

"It is as if everyone is already dead," Utsu said. "Only we are alive because we are above the mist, and we have feet."

Aki was about to retort sharply, but she stared out, saying, "It is like the Land of the Dead. The Land of the Dead is a comfortable place."

"And they do not know if they are alive or know whether they are no longer alive," Lady Utsu said. She spied something, and now she leaned over the railing as if she had never been afraid of the height. "A fox has run into the autumn garden! Lady Tsukie will kill it! Oh, it has disappeared into the mist! I am sure Lady Tsukie is not liked by that small fox."

They continued to watch the palace until the light faded and a full moon rose. People began to light lanterns inside and out, and the night watchman began his rounds, clapping his wooden sticks together as he went.

"They have chosen a good night to lock us up," Aki said. "We should look again later. The courtiers talk so much of the palace in moonlight."

They heard the creaking of ladder rungs. Finally, a man appeared with warm robes and two stacked baskets of food. They steamed a little in the tiny room. "Lady Tsukie has sent them," the man said. "The ladies are saying how terrible, to shut the two of you up here."

"We will keep ourselves busy," Aki said. "Perhaps I shall begin learning Chinese."

"Bear up!" the man said. "Many of us are watching from below. Nothing will happen to you."

Lady Utsu's eyes filled with tears, and when the man saw that, he left hurriedly.

"Shall we watch for fires?" Aki called after him.

"Why not, mistress?" he called back.

They ate their supper of steamed vegetables, pickled ginger, and steamed fish. When they came to the bottom of the baskets, Aki picked one up. "It feels heavy," she said. She began digging her fingernail into one edge. The basket's floor came loose. Inside were flat *mochi* and sweet bean paste shaped like stars.

"Lady Tsukie did not send this," Aki said. "Right now, every woman in the palace is speaking of her cruelty."

Lady Utsu was pleased to hear it. She ate with relish.

Later, they watched the palace, so diminished by the tower's height. "I like it better this way," said Lady Utsu.

AFTER THAT, Lord Norimasa took care to keep Lady Tsukie and Lady Utsu apart. "I do not like her," Lady Tsukie told her husband. But when there was no answer from Lord Norimasa, she thought, I will be careful. No ill-bred brainless brat will defeat me. And yet she shivered. Lady Tsukie's nurse had once said to her, long ago, "You are overconfident. One day you will pay for it." But the advice of Lady Tsukie's nurse was not borne out by experience. Life had taught her that very few could match her in a contest of wits.

CHAPTER TEN

LORD NORIMASA REACHED KAI, and Matsuhito received his instructions. He and five other samurai were to go on horseback into Kai, where they were to hide themselves in the woods near a little town called Umetani. Under their armor, they would wear robes only a beggar would wear. "If anyone happens upon you, kill them at once," said Lord Norimasa. The men would stay behind while Matsuhito looked for a certain guide who had lived in Umetani for years. Most important, the guide had once worked with Lord Sugimasa, who always trusted this guide and treated him like his own son.

"The meeting place," said the counselor of war, "is at the two waterfalls known as the Sad Lovers. You will hear the falls from a distance. They are said to be very beautiful, and there are legends concerning suicides who died by throwing themselves from their tops, so few people come there, perhaps only criminals."

"Criminals often work as spies," said Lord Norimasa, appearing distracted. "Kill anyone, whether or not they appear suspicious. Remember what I say, Matsuhito."

"And if it is a pale young lady?"

"Women are born spies. Kill her," he said. "But of course you will use your judgment. Still, I am older, and my judgment is better. Remember that."

"If I may be so bold, my lord," said a counselor of war, "the directions given to Matsuhito are not terribly precise. Of course, they point him in the right direction, but—"

"Enough!" roared Lord Norimasa. "We are not asking him to dis-cover one blade of grass in a field of grasses. He will hear the waterfall from the mountain. His legs are strong. Give him more precise direc-tions and someone is sure to intercept him." He turned to Matsuhito.

"I will find the waterfalls," he said.

"Do not make yourself known unless you see a man who looks about as if confused and then falls down in a fit. All that is arranged. "You leave now," he told Matsuhito. Addressing the five others who would accompany him, he said, "Bring him back to me." He was glow-ering at them. "You," he said, addressing Matsuhito, "pick the moun-tain ponies you want."

"I will take the black one," he said. "The other men may decide for themselves."

Once in their saddles, they were given bundles of food which they lashed behind the saddles. They had already donned beggars' clothes beneath their own robes.

"Your armor will be waiting here for you," Lord Norimasa said. "There is no point in sounding an alarm throughout the province. Return alive," Lord Norimasa said to Matsuhito.

"Of course, my lord," Matsuhito answered. "It is your command that we do so."

The ponies galloped off briskly. Lord Norimasa stood looking after them for a long time. "How quickly the dust of the road swallows them up," he said, and still he stayed, staring after them. The others, as cus-tom demanded, imitated their master. He did not turn back for several minutes, and even then, he had unusually shining eyes.

ALMOST IMMEDIATELY after Lord Norimasa left his palace to begin his campaign, Lady Tsukie, who never seemed to eat at all, began eating ravenously. She wanted bean cakes sweetened with beet sugar, and she devoured them almost as quickly as the cooks could prepare them. Within ten days, her stomach grew enormous, and it was clear that the advent of her child was not far off. Her stomach grew greater by the day, so that the lady herself seemed to recede behind it. She was finally stricken with birth pangs. At once, Lady Tsukie's envoys were dis-patched to Lord Norimasa. Lady Tsukie knew her husband would not only remain out in the field, but would probably not answer the dispatches he received. She was alone. Her women, of course, crowded around her. A small house near the wall of the palace was prepared for her so that the birth would not pollute the main palace dwelling. White sheets were spread on the mats and white robes were given to Lady Tsukie. The sacred rope which would enclose her building was made ready. Priests were alerted and began their own purification processes, eating only vegetables cooked in a special pot above a purified fire. The priests prepared to recite the *Norito*, the ritual prayers.

Lady Kago, so named for her passionate desire to travel to distant shrines, asked Lady Tsukie if she wanted anything else. "Have we forgotten anything?" she asked anxiously.

"Oh, by now it is all a matter of routine," Lady Tsukie said impatiently. "Three hours of suffering and number eight will arrive."

"Nevertheless," said Lady Kago, "Lord Norimasa would never forgive me if we did not observe the usual rites."

"More twangings of bows, more pounding on drums, more reciting of sutras, all that intolerable noise, all to keep me safe from evil. It is the worst part. Of course, I want the help of the *kami* and the spirits, but I wish we could summon them quietly."

"Then the usual thing?" asked Lady Kago.

"Less incense this time. Number seven almost suffocated me."

"Yes, my lady," she said. She saw a spasm of pain pass over Lady Tsukie's face.

In the little house prepared for her, Lady Tsukie sat down on the mat. She appeared bored. But as the bow-twanging begun, her pains began strongly. The women helped her upright, but two hours went by, then three, and still nothing happened.

The palace midwife was summoned. "What can you feel?" she asked Lady Tsukie.

"Only pain," she said. "Nothing moves in my belly. Nothing moves down." She was breathing heavily and her body was drenched in sweat.

"I have had so many others," she said, "and never was there anything like this."

"It is different every time," said the midwife.

But when the sun began to set, Lady Tsukie had accomplished nothing. Instead, her pains were clearly stronger.

"I must lie down," she said.

The women looked at the midwife, who agreed.

Lady Tsukie lay on her left side. "I am going to die this time," she said.

"Nonsense," said the midwife briskly. "It is only a large, a healthy baby. It must be a boy."

"I have had boys before," said Lady Tsukie, who seemed to struggle for breath to speak. She did not cry out in pain, as women were not allowed to do so, but she would suddenly seize her abdomen with both hands and roll from left to right and back again. "So many before," she gasped.

Lady Kago immediately ordered the guards to summon additional archers to twang their bowstrings to frighten away evil spirits and sent for a medium who lived in the Ministry of Magic. "Clean the medium as best you can," she said to the women. "She has not been purified."

"Noise, noise, noise," Lady Tsukie gasped. Her voice was growing hoarse.

The din was now infernal. More and more incense was burned to please the priests and a purplish haze hung over the little building.

"We must make her stand up," said the midwife. "It is her only chance."

"No," said Lady Tsukie.

"Stand her up!" commanded Lady Kago. "I will take the responsibility."

"But lady . . ." said one of the women, who knew that if Lady Tsukie died, Lady Kago's own life would be forfeit.

Three of the women dragged Lady Tsukie to her feet. When she was in a squatting position, her head fell forward upon her chest. Suddenly she raised her head, and her eyes opened wide. Her pupils were round and brown. Her mouth opened wide as if she were screaming without sound.

"Lady Kago!" one of the women whispered to her. She was ignored.

"How long can it take to bring a medium? Have we no exorcist?"

"She is outside, my lady," one of the women said.

At that, a small, very old woman was ushered quickly into the room. Her hair was so long it trailed behind her. It was white streaked with black, and her face, dead white, was thickly covered with rice powder. The other women shuddered. She looked like someone who had died and awakened but would soon sink to rest again. Then they looked at Lady Tsukie, who had also gone dead white. The smoke from the incense curled around the floor of the room, and neither Lady Tsukie nor the medium's feet could be seen. They both seemed to float, along with the three women holding Her Ladyship upright.

"So," Lady Kago whispered to herself, "ghosts. An inauspicious sight."

"I know what you want of me," said the medium. "Let me begin at once."

She approached Lady Tsukie and began to chant. The lady's head once more fell to her chest. The medium began to roll her own head violently. Soon her hair was lashing in all directions like the branches of a weeping willow caught in a terrible storm. The hair lashed, too, at Lady Tsukie. The medium's chanting grew to a piercing howl, and the women wanted to clap their hands over their ears, but no one dared move.

Suddenly the old woman was down on her hands and knees and began revolving her entire body. Then she spoke with a young woman's voice. "You have enough," said the young voice. "It is time."

Lady Tsukie raised her head and looked down at the old woman. "I know your voice," she said, her own voice strained and hoarse. "It is Lady Utsu's voice."

"It is she who is bewitching you," said the medium. "Cast her out!"

"I cannot," gasped Lady Tsukie.

"Then I will take her into my body." The medium began lashing her hair again and her arms pointed straight at Lady Tsukie's belly.

"Something is moving," Lady Tsukie said, and her head again fell forward.

"It is the bad spirit, coming out," said the medium.

Now an exorcist arrived, and began her spells to help evict the evil spirit from Lady Tsukie's body.

"It is a little better," Lady Tsukie said, her voice muffled by her drooping head.

"Blood!" said the midwife. "Lay her down!"

The three women helped Lady Tsukie lie down on the white mat. The red stain was spreading.

"I will die here," said the suffering woman.

"You will not die," said Lady Kago. "I have seen dying women, and never do they look as healthy as you."

"He is out!" exclaimed the midwife. "A boy! Enormous! Do you hear that, Tsukiko?"

But Lady Tsukie had fallen asleep.

"Try to wake her!" commanded Lady Kago. They called to her; one shook her wrist and finally Lady Kago pulled her hair, but she did not move.

"Is she dead?" asked one of the women.

"She is not dead!" said Lady Kago. "Do not use that word to describe her again!"

The midwife was packing clean rags between the lady's legs. They were quickly soaked with blood and then replaced. It was night, and clouds had hidden the moon when the bleeding stopped. Lady Kago placed her hand on the woman's chest. "She breathes," Lady Kago said. "Now we must wait and see. Where is the child?"

"With the wet nurse. He bellows like an ox."

"Send servants to the child," Lady Kago said. She was kneeling beside Lady Tsukie's body. "Is there nothing you can give her?" she asked the midwife, who shook her head.

"But there is something!" the medium said. "It is dangerous, but I have seen it work. Someone must send to the monastery. Someone must go to Yamababa. No one knows her real name. She is up on the mountain just before the monastery. She makes up potions from herbs and roots, and Lady Tsukie's mother, Lady Kinchi, always told me the old woman of the mountain had saved her life."

"Now we rely on an ignorant old woman whose power rests on roots and berries?" asked Lady Kago.

"Look at her," the medium said, staring at Lady Tsukie. Her breathing was so shallow that her soul seemed to have fled her body. Her face, which was white before, was now almost translucent, and every blue vein was clearly visible. "You take a chance if you do not summon her."

There was a silence.

"Send for her," said Lady Kago.

"Have someone take me to Yamababa," said the old woman. "I will know what to tell her."

"And what good will come of this?" Lady Kago whispered to herself.

"We must take desperate measures," said the midwife.

"I would not do it for anyone else," said Lady Kago. She turned to the medium and said, "A samurai will bear you on his back. Take four men," she said, addressing the others. "When one is tired, the second will carry her. Bring her back quickly. Do not persuade yourself you are seeing evil spirits on the mountain. If you see such things, it is the work of the spirit who inhabits the lady."

THE MEN WERE summoned and rode out through the East Gate and galloped on horseback to the eastern mountain. One of the men had the medium securely tied to his back. When they reached the steep slope of the mountain, they dismounted and began climbing.

"You hop like a rabbit," said the old woman. "I am old."

"Don't complain," said the samurai, panting.

The night was dark, and several times the men thought they had lost the trail, but each time the old woman would say, "It is there," or, "It is a little to the left," and so they made good progress.

"How many times have I climbed this mountain?" the medium said, speaking to herself. No one answered. There was the sudden, startling sound of a belling deer. An owl hooted.

"An owl is an unlucky thing," said one of the samurai.

"What ignorance!" said the old woman. "An owl means knowledge, which we are about to receive."

"Old woman," asked the man who carried her, "what is your name? Once you had a name, did you not?"

"I should not like others to know it," she said. "I should not like others to know what I have become."

"But someone knows," said the samurai.

"Certainly," the old woman said. "Lord Norimasa. He calls me *uguisu*, nightingale, because he has heard my chanting. That is name enough for you."

Now the other men began to insist, "Tell me your name! Tell me your name!"

"All right," she said. "Then I will say it's *onibaba*, evil devil woman of the mountain."

At that, the men fell silent. An animal snapped a twig as it made its way toward its den.

"It is not far now," said the old woman. "There it is!"

The little hut on the mountain was half propped against an ancient beech tree and was so covered with vines as to be almost invisible. The hut belonged to Yamababa, a woman so old and so reclusive that everyone but the medium had forgotten her name.

"Put me down," said the old woman.

"A pleasure to oblige," said the samurai, "although you weigh nothing more than a leaf."

The old woman went up to the hut and called out to the old woman in the hut, "Shirofune! It is me! We need your help!"

The door creaked open. An ancient creature holding a lantern stood in the doorway.

"So, it is you," Shirofune, the ancient woman, said. "I thought you had forgotten me."

"I am too old to walk up the mountain," the old woman said. "You of all people understand."

"Then what do you need from me?" Shirofune asked.

"Lady Tsukie, wife to Lord Norimasa, whom I serve, will surely die unless you can help her. She has lost a great deal of blood in childbirth."

"Come in," Shirofune said.

The two old women disappeared inside the hut.

"Were either of them once human?" one of the samurai asked.

"They are only old," one answered.

"Then," said the first, "it is true what they say. Better to die in battle than to live on and then die on the mats."

"It is true," said one of the men. After that, they fell silent, thinking their own thoughts.

INSIDE THE HUT, Shirofune busied herself fumbling through stacked boxes. She set aside two small piles, and then picked up two bottles. Next to that, she placed two earthenware cylinders. "Now," she said, "the medicine in this tall bottle is dangerous. Give her very little. The medicine in this small bottle is powerful, but not dangerous. She can drink all of it. Will you remember that, Umeko?" she asked the medium who had refused to tell the men her name.

"I am younger than you are!" the medium protested.

"And you are still attached to the court?"

"I never stopped living for it," the medium said.

"We were never the same," said Shirofune, "although we loved each other."

"Days too far to remember."

"Too painful, you mean," said Shirofune, busy with her medicines.

"Where is your sleeping mat?" the medium asked, looking around.

"Those pine boughs," said Shirofune. "I sleep on them. You know I always slept well."

"And do you still?"

"Why not?"

"But you never had trouble staying up all night during unlucky times when terrible spirits were about. It was I who fell asleep."

"And I who shook you," said Shirofune. "Well, it is done. Go quickly. If the lady lives, ask her to come up the mountain when she is better."

"I will do it," said Umeko. "She has lost so much blood. Her skin is whiter than snow."

"Then take these to her quickly. There is not much time."

And then the old woman was carried down the mountain, this time at a trot.

"Why are you twisting about?" asked the samurai who carried her.

"I was trying to see the hut until it was out of sight," she said.

"It is out of sight now," said the samurai. "Please sit still."

IN THE LITTLE ROOM, Lady Tsukie lay as before. The women had plainly tried to change the bloodied cloth of her mat, but were afraid to move her lest the bleeding, which had stopped shortly after the old woman left, begin again.

"I have the medicine," said the medium. "She is to drink all of the small bottle, and if that does not revive her, she is to drink only a small amount from the tall bottle. That one is dangerous."

Lady Kago, who was exhausted and deadly pale herself, gave Lady Tsukie the first medication drop by drop. "Green liquid," she said softly. "What can it be?"

Then they sat and waited.

After a short time, Lady Tsukie began to moan softly. She turned her head and lay still.

"It is not enough," said the old woman. "You must give her some of the second medicine."

"How much?" asked Lady Kago.

"Five drops," said the medium. This liquid was the deep color of blood. When Lady Tsukie drank the fifth drop, a shudder ran through her entire body. A rasping sound came from her throat.

"Is it a death rattle?" asked one of the women, but no one answered.

Another rasping sound followed, this one stronger. Then Lady Tsukie's fingers began to twitch. After that, she sighed deeply, turned her head to the right and seemed to fall asleep.

The women looked at one another in horror.

"But see!" said the medium. "There is color in her cheeks!"

"Give her more drops!" said Lady Kago.

"No more," said the medium. "Let her sleep."

"So," said one of the women. "It was Lady Utsu's fault."

"Oh, come!" said the medium. "Lady Tsukie hates Lady Utsu. That is why she thought she heard Lady Utsu's voice. Did her voice sound like Lady Utsu to you?"

The woman agreed that it had not.

"We summon spirits, but they are mischievous," said the medium. "It makes coming worth their while, playing tricks on us."

"That is true," one of the women said.

"Once," said the medium, "the lady of the mountain told me never to forget the tangled ways of spirits. It is not good to be too credulous."

The women nodded their heads in agreement.

Just then, Lady Tsukie moaned gently in her sleep and picked up her right arm and placed it over her chest.

The women smiled.

"Let the fire burn strongly. Keep it warm in here," said the medium. "Do not rejoice yet."

DAYS PASSED, and time returned Lady Tsukie to what she had been. But she did not ask to see her newborn child, who was given over to a wet nurse, and there was something sad about her, as if at last she realized that she would not forever remain in this world. Her women, seeing this, did their best to amuse her, and puppeteers put on shows for the children of the palace, and, as usual, it seemed as if the mothers laughed most of all.

One morning, when the sun was just beginning to rise over the horizon and the dew still on the grass lit up like gems, Lady Tsukie awoke in an ecstatic mood. She gave no explanation for her extreme happiness, and the women did not question it. Every morning, for days, she would awaken in the same state, because every night she had the same dream. To her, it appeared too precious to tell to anyone.

In her dream, she was young again, and she and Lord Norimasa had just married. The dream always began that way—just after the two of them had exchanged their cups of rice wine. Then they stood in the middle of a large valley, and Lady Tsukie would draw something like clay from her pocket and hand it to her new husband, who would take the magic material and begin to build their palace from it. "Just here we will put the walled gardens," he would say, "and here the sleeping quarters for the women." She would hand him more clay, and he would say, "Just here we shall have the open pavilion." When it was finished, Lord Norimasa would say, "How bare it looks. We must have fruit trees and one twisted pine. And a small river must run through the grounds right here and end in a pool and the pool must be filled with *koi*." Then she would hand him more clay, and the trees would appear and blossom as she watched, and beautiful red and gold *koi* would leap from the pool and splash as they fell back into the water.

Night after night, Lady Tsukie had that dream, and night after night, the palace was built again and again. The two of them were particularly proud of the *shinden*, or the main hall, and of the four-footed gate and its sloping roof of green tiles. And each night, the dream grew longer, continuing as it added new events.

Lady Tsukie became more and more curious about the meaning of this continuing dream. Although she did not want to share it with anyone, she wanted to know its meaning. Surely no one had ever had a more auspicious dream. At last, she decided to call for the medium, the old woman whom Lady Tsukie believed had saved her life.

The old woman came and knelt, her forehead touching the reed mat.

"Please rise," said Lady Tsukie.

The old woman assumed a kneeling position.

"I have had a dream. It continues. Every night, another chapter is added," she said, and she proceeded to describe the dream. "I know it is a good dream and I would like to know what it portends."

But the old woman did not look up. Lady Tsukie could feel waves of uneasiness radiating from the old woman.

"What is it?" she asked.

"I had not believed jealousy could be so strong," the old woman said. "You wish that you yourself had created this palace, as you have created a child. Such jealousy does not bode well."

"It is not a dream of jealousy! Leave me!" commanded the lady.

The old woman got slowly to her feet.

"If it were a dream of jealousy, it would not make me happy!" Lady Tsukie burst out.

"You would destroy the entire world, except for Lord Norimasa and your palace," said the old woman. "Even your children are not exempt. Listen to me, Lady," said the old woman. "Your delivery was difficult. You are still angry at the child who almost killed you. Your anger has been like a spade. It has dug down and brought this jealousy to the surface. Perhaps the dream is warning you to keep such jealousy under control. I have told you what I know, but I cannot make you believe what I say."

"Yet why should I be jealous?" asked the lady. "Look about me. Is there something I lack that would cause jealousy?"

"There is always something someone believes is lacking," said the old woman. "Find that thing and the jealousy will lose its power over you."

"You are a foolish old woman!" said the lady. Then she began to weep.

"Those tears tell me I have spoken the truth," the old woman said. "I wish you well."

"You may go," said the lady.

But it is an auspicious dream, she told herself. And then she heard the voice of the medium saying that spirits were mischievous and could not be trusted. She had heard those words even as she slept.

"But there is nothing I lack!" she said out loud.

"My lady?" called one of the women.

"Nothing is wrong," she said. "I am getting old and talking to myself."

LADY UTSU SETTLED IN with Aki and Lady Utsu's sister, Harume. When her birth pangs began, there were no twangings of bows, no chantings of sutras, no burning of incense. In twenty minutes it was over, and she was the mother of a daughter.

"Oh, she is certainly your child," said Aki. "Look how her hair grows down to her eyebrows."

"I will give her away," said Lady Utsu. "No one is to know about this."

"Think carefully, Shishi," Aki said. "What is done cannot always be undone. You cut a branch from the cherry and you cannot put it back."

"There are barren women among the nobility. We must ask discreetly."

After some time, Aki said, "It would be easier if the child were a boy. There is always some head of a family who has not produced a child and who would adopt a boy of good birth to continue his name."

"And there are always mothers who have nothing but sons and want to play with a girl as with a toy," said Lady Utsu.

"It is true," said Lady Utsu's sister, Harume.

"Make inquires," Lady Utsu told her sister. "Be circumspect. Say that the mother has not yet decided to give up the child. Say that the mother of the child is afraid that her husband's principal wife will try to kill it. Do not tell them everything at once. Make them extort the information from you. Then they will be sure the child is of noble birth."

"I do not see how you can give up this child," Aki told Lady Utsu. "Now that you have seen her."

"I am not destined for a peaceful life," said Lady Utsu.

"And how do you know that?"

"I have always known."

"Who will hand the child over?" asked Aki.

"Harume must do it," said Lady Utsu.

Five days passed, and the hair fell from the child's forehead. It was evident that she, like her mother, was to be a beauty. "Will you not keep her as your own?" asked Aki. "Even so small a child as she is resembles you so closely."

"Has Harume any news?" asked Lady Utsu.

Eventually, Harume heard of a noblewoman who wanted to adopt a female baby. "She is a distant relative of the Norimasa family," Harume said.

"It is destiny," said Lady Utsu.

"But there is a condition. You must never attempt to see the child again."

"Of course I agree," said Lady Utsu.

And so it was arranged.

Aki and Harume both swore themselves to secrecy.

"This is a blood oath," Lady Utsu said. They cut their palms and each mingled their blood with one another's. When this was accomplished, Lady Utsu said, "The child has drifted from our sky as a cloud drifts by. I hope she will be happy."

"We shall never know," said Aki. "That is the worst of it."

"Make me a figure of a doll," Lady Utsu said. "I will burn it. After that, she will truly be gone from our lives."

Aki and Harume looked at each other. Harume found some scraps of cloth and some twigs. She made a face out of paper and took some of the child's hair which had fallen out when she was five days old and used clay to fasten the hair to the top of the head.

"Must we burn it?" asked Harume.

"Yes," said Lady Utsu. "I myself will light the pyre."

They took the figure outside, poured fragrant oil on it and set fire to it. A small fire burned and a small puff of smoke drifted upward like a tiny cloud.

Aki and Harume cried inconsolably, but Lady Utsu remained dry-eyed. "It is done," she said.

CHAPTER ELEVEN

LORD MATSUHITO PROCEEDED with his five men farther into Kai. Soon after, a courier came bearing news of Lord Sugimasa's death at the hands of the Minagas. When Matsuhito and his men came to a thick wood where even the sunlight did not penetrate, Matsuhito said, "We will go on foot here. Dismount and lead the horses." When they reached a particularly dense and dark place, they took off their fine clothes and instead wore only the rags of peasants. Each wore a loin-cloth, a rough coat and baggy, stained pants held up by a length of rope.

"You go no farther than this," Matsuhito said. "I am going to find the village of Umetani. Watch my horse. Above all, remain quiet. If anyone approaches you and suspects you own the horses, let them suggest that you are bandits and you stole the horses. If they suspect anything, kill them quietly."

He tied up some food in the cloth that served for that purpose. He took his short sword, and cut down a thick bough.

"Well, I am ready," he said.

"But how far is Umetani? You do not know."

"I will find it," he said.

"Take the sword," said a samurai named Takamasa. "You must have something."

"I have my short sword and dagger. How would a beggar come by a sword?"

"Send a messenger if there is trouble," Takamasa said.

They watched Matsuhito as he walked through the wood.

"He does not turn to look at us," said one of the men. "How he trusts us."

"Rest assured," said Takamasa, "he is listening for the sound of snapping twigs or rustling leaves. It is second nature. But it is true that he trusts us or he would have hidden his horse somewhere else. And his sword."

"Where is his sword?" one of the men asked.

They looked for it. It was not fastened to the saddle of the horse. It was nowhere in sight.

Takamasa roared with laughter. "He has hidden it!" he bellowed.

The five men laughed until they collapsed on the ground.

"And yet he seems simple," said Takamasa, once more bursting into laughter.

"He is like a conch shell. It looks as if it could make no noise, but it splits heaven and earth with its blast," one of them said.

ONCE FREE OF THE DARK WOODS, Matsuhito found himself treading a dusty red clay road in bright sunlight. He shielded his eyes against the light. To his right were flat rice paddies. The crop was harvested, and only spikes remained of the rice plants. To his left was the forest, where the land was also flat. He surmised that paddies would appear on the other side of the woods. There was the rich smell of mud and the unmistakable smell of night soil. In the far paddies, a man was squatting, fertilizing his own land. It was a sign of courtesy to squat in a paddy and relieve oneself. Fertilizer was hard to come by.

He could feel the road beginning to climb. Ahead was a mountain. At its base would be one town, and farther along another. One of them, he was certain, was Umetani. He was using the thick branch as a cane, but it stirred up dust, and he thought better of it and hoisted it to his shoulder. Down the road, a large cloud of red dust was rapidly approaching. Bandits. He stepped off the road and waited for them to reach him.

"Who are you?" called out one of the men. Yes, they were bandits. They were dressed in unmatched pieces of armor, and the leader wore a fearsome helmet adorned with antlers.

"A poor man on his way to the shrine in Umetani," he said, speaking with the dialect he had learned as a child in his fishing village.

"There is no shrine in Umetani," said the bandit.

"Ah, how people play jokes," Matsuhito said. "My knee is failing. They said I was sure to be cured there."

"One of us will take you to Umetani," the leader said. "It is bad to walk on a weak leg."

"Knee," said Matsuhito.

"Take him," the leader told one of the men. "Can you stay on a horse if you hold on?" he asked Matsuhito.

"I will try," Matsuhito said.

"The worst you can do is break your back," the leader said, and the men laughed loudly.

"Good luck," the leader said. "We are in a hurry. There is an army massing near here. We want to be far from it. That is our motto: 'Be far from a battle, but be close when it is over so we can pick the bones.' Is it not a good motto?"

"The best," Matsuhito said. He pretended to have difficulty mounting the horse.

"Get down and help him," the leader said. "Someday we may need help.

"What is your name?" the leader asked.

"Taki," he said.

"A good name," said the leader. "I am Hideo, the greatest bandit there is. Do not go beyond Umetani or go over the mountain. The army is assembling there."

"I thank you," Matsuhito said.

"I am Shinda, the man who makes other men dead," said the man to whose back he clung.

"A frightening name," said Matsuhito.

"I chose it myself," Shinda said.

"Then you are not troubled by spirits?" said Matsuhito. "Even saying the word for death makes most people tremble."

"Spirits fear *me*," he said, and he dug his knees into the sides of his horse, and the two of them sped away toward the base of the mountain.

"Umetani," Shinda said when they arrived. "Mud and straw huts. As you can see, there is no shrine. But the mountain is red and yellow. Maybe the shrine is the mountain. I think the people here may worship it. Someone has put something over on you."

"I will get down," Matsuhito said.

"I felt the dagger beneath your robe," said Shinda. "Best to be prepared. I must get back to the others. Remember. Straight ahead."

Matsuhito began to walk away up the road. Shinda's horse snorted, and Matsuhito turned in time to see horse and rider wheel and ride away. In the distance, there was a blackness to the left. That must be the trees, he thought. Now to find the two waterfalls.

When he reached the wood, and found a path beaten down by deer, he could already hear the sound of the waterfalls. As he proceeded, the sound grew weaker. He turned so that the sun was at his back. Immediately the sound of the waterfalls grew louder. The trail was narrow and overgrown and the soil was sandy. Here and there, tangled masses of roots had been washed away by the rain. Rocks large and small lined the trail.

Suddenly he came upon an archway in the trees at the end of the trail, and beyond it, a yellow brilliance tinged with green. Now the roaring of the waterfalls was quite loud. He walked on, went through the arching trees, and found himself in a meadow. The beauty of the sight stopped him. The grass was lush and deep green. At the far end, a deer was grazing with its fawn. A stag was approaching them, then changed its mind and went back into the woods.

It is an enchanted place, Matsuhito thought.

He turned in the direction of the rushing water. There were the two waterfalls, two beautiful ribbons of silver light falling into pools. The water splashed up white as it fell, and the pools themselves were the color of dark jade. I have found the most beautiful place in the world, he thought, and at that moment, he thought of Lady Utsu, whose black hair often seemed a strange, dark waterfall.

There was a special light in the valley, a sacred light. He had heard of such things. The gold light appeared to fall into the valley alone. Even the grazing deer were tinged with gold. When he turned to look at the waterfalls again, they were a lighter green than the pools into which they fell, but they, too, sparkled with gold. This, thought Matsuhito, would be a good place to die.

Someone was treading on fallen twigs. He felt for his dagger beneath his coat. An old man hobbled from the fringe of the woods carrying a bunch of ferns, fell on the ground, and was taken by a violent seizure. White foam spilled from his mouth. Matsuhito watched, horrified. The man grew still.

Matsuhito approached the man cautiously. He was dressed like a pilgrim and had little bells attached to his sash. Pinned to his back was a piece of dirty white paper on which someone had written, "Umetani." So this was the man for whom he was waiting.

He crouched in front of the old man. "I am Matsuhito," he said softly.

The old man opened one eye. "I am Sato," he said, without moving.

"Have you news?" asked Matsuhito.

"I know everything," said Sato. "Do not be deceived by this disguise. I have powdered my hair and my white beard is false. I am as strong as you are." He sat up, looked around and opened his kerchief and began eating a rice ball. "Have you nothing to eat?"

Matsuhito took the pack from his back and opened his own bundle of food.

"We cannot drink better water," Sato said, indicating the waterfalls. "They say they are blessed because so many people have prayed here for the souls of the sad lovers. If they appear to you, they say you will live forever."

"Have you seen them?"

"No," said Sato. "Now, this is where we are. Everyone believed the Minaga army would encamp on this side of the mountain. But they settled on the other side. The spot is shut in by this mountain on one side, deep woods on the left and the right, and only a narrow pass between two small mountains at the far end of the valley. There are two, although from a distance, they seem to be only one. This means that your men will have to enter one or at most two at a time. They will be ambushed and massacred. The archers are already stringing their bows, and daily new bundles of arrows keep arriving. They outnumber you by three to one. Perhaps this is a battle to avoid. And there is more trouble brewing. The Minagas are planning to fight on two fronts. They believe their palace cannot be breached, surrounded by water as it is. There are already troops billeted there. When this battle is over, the rest of the men intend to reinforce them there."

"There is always another way to get into a palace," said Matsuhito, who seemed not to have heard him. "Every burrowing animal knows enough to dig out two doors."

"You would be better off as a bird than as a burrowing animal," Sato said.

"This mountain," Matsuhito said. "Can we climb it?"

"Of course. We should start at night. We must borrow the dogs of a peasant I know. The dogs know the way. I can speak for that man. I know him well."

"Tonight, then," he said.

"But all you will see is the instrument of your coming defeat."

"Tonight. The two of us, the peasant and his dogs."

"We must rest," Sato said. "We will be up all night. Let's sleep in the shadow of the trees. No one will harm us. The peasants worship this place. It is sacred to them."

Matsuhito followed Sato to the broad, thick strips of shadow cast by the trees, shadows that would only lengthen as the sun went down. "Here?" asked Sato, and Matsuhito nodded. The two of them made themselves comfortable in the shade, and within minutes they were ready to fall asleep, but not before, as Sato noticed, Matsuhito had placed his hand on the handle of his short sword.

"Long habit," said Matsuhito, noticing Sato's eyes.

Sato grunted, and fell asleep.

Matsuhito was not sure how long they had slept, but he became aware that someone was watching him, and he knew without opening his eyes that it was already dark. He slowly opened his left eye. Sitting cross-legged, watching him through slitted eyes, was Shinda.

"Do not move," Matsuhito said. "I would not like to kill you."

"Why kill me? I was only curious. I told our leader that I knew you had a dagger and you might be up to something, and he said to go find you and see if anything worth mentioning was going to happen."

"Like what?"

"Killing. Plunder. Food. It's lean times here. Our band can help you."

"How can you help us?" Matsuhito was aware that Sato was awake and listening, his hand also on his short sword.

"Who knows the land better than a bandit born on it? I know every bridge I can hide under when people pursue me, and I listen, smiling, knowing that they will not find me."

"Do you know your way over the mountain?" Matsuhito asked.

"No," said Shinda. "One person cannot know everything. But the woods on the other side, that is another matter. The one on the south of this valley is almost solid—brambles, thick bushes between the trees, thorny vines, barely passable trails that twist back on one another. The natives call that wood *Jigokumori*, Hell Wood. Yet we know our way through it. There are thick pine needles there, so thick you can sleep on them. We know where all the Minagas are. The wood to the north is another story, also hard, but not for us. There is a difficulty. It is the Minagas' land and they also know the wood."

"And why should we trust you?" Sato asked.

"We know there is a large army not far from here. You must be their scouts. We would not take on an army of Lord Norimasa's."

"You know too much," Sato said. "Perhaps you are Minaga's spy."

"Everyone who creeps on this earth of Kai tells us what he knows if he does not want his throat cut," said Shinda. "That's how it is here. It was no different when you were born."

"And Lord Norimasa," Sato asked, "what do you know of him?"

"Cruel and ruthless, like us. We are no lover of the Minagas. They hunt us like rabbits."

"We could take a chance," Sato said. "If we don't like him, we can cut off his head."

"Do not cut off my head. I need it," Shinda said.

In spite of themselves, the two men laughed.

"We will try you out," Sato said. "In a few hours, we are going over the mountain."

"Impossible," said Shinda.

"Do not be so certain," Matsuhito said. "Nothing is impossible, especially to someone who is willing to try it."

"If there are men on the other side, they will hear us coming," Shinda said uneasily.

"Are there?" asked Matsuhito.

"Yes. I don't know if there are few or many."

"We will find out," Matsuhito said.

Just then, another man emerged from the wood. In his hands, he carried ropes tied at one end around the collars of two white dogs.

"That is Kenji," Matsuhito said. "We were told to expect him."

"These dogs know the way," said the new man. "Who is this third person? he asked, seeing Shinda. "He does not look like one of yours."

"His name is Shinda," said Matsuhito. "He is ours. Now."

"Shinda the Butcher? What is he doing here?"

"He thinks he can help us."

"Help us to heaven, he means," the new man said. "See the dogs bare their teeth? They do not like him. My name is Kenji. Sato told me to come. Ask him. See? He is happy to see me. The big dog is named Okii Inu, Big Dog, and the small one is Inu. A crescent moon. That is good. Enough light, but not too much. But we must take care. There will be thunder and lightning and perhaps rain. Up until now, there has been only one rainy week. It has been dry for a long time."

"And why will there be thunder and lightning?" asked Shinda.

"Because the dogs are shaking," Kenji said.

"They are shaking because they fear me," said Shinda.

"They would tear you apart if I gave the command," said Kenji. "They have no fear."

"Are we to sit here forever?" asked Shinda.

"We can go now," Kenji said. "Keep this Shinda in the middle of us."

The four men crossed the valley. Kenji loosed the dogs, who ran ahead and waited for them at the foot of the mountain.

"Can horses climb that mountain?" asked Sato.

"Mountain ponies," Kenji said. "If the dogs lead them."

"Horses would be heard," said Sato.

"Decide these things when we reach the other side," Kenji said.

They began climbing. The dogs rushed off, then stopped and waited for them.

"They are like lanterns, those white dogs," Shinda said.

"The woods are full of these white dogs," said Kenji. "To the left. Follow the dogs."

The slope was steep. They slid downward easily, and each time this happened, there was a noisy shower of stones. The earth was sandy. Finally, they caught Kenji's rhythm, and pulled themselves from one bough to another.

"How far?" Shinda asked.

"We have only begun," Kenji said. "Conserve your strength."

The higher they climbed, the less they seemed to accomplish. Now they could not see the top of the mountain. The mountain was so thickly forested they could barely see the light of the crescent moon, sailing quickly through the inky clouds.

"We will stop here," Kenji finally said. "The dogs are going to the stream to drink. I will go, too. The water is good."

The other three men followed them wearily. At the stream, they discovered their thirst. "Put your heads in the water," Kenji said. "You will come alive once more. Shinda first. Good, no?" Kenji asked. The dogs were back, shaking water from their fur.

"It feels good," Sato said when it was his turn.

The dogs were whimpering softly, running up the slope and coming back down to them as the men quenched their thirst.

"The dogs say it is time to go," Kenji said.

Their exhausting progress began again. With every step, there were small rock slides. Eventually they began to see the dim ridge of the mountain, even blacker against the sky.

"Not far now," said Kenji, panting slightly.

"And then?" asked Shinda.

"And then we come to a sheer rock face. Farther north are the paths down. But from that rock face, we can see everything in the valley below. The sun is already coming up. We will see well. Let's go," he said.

"Why do the dogs not bark or whine?" Shinda asked.

"They were taught. They know they may be told to attack, and they are taught to make no noise and give no warning. They are deadly. But loyal to their owners. There!" he said suddenly. "Go slowly! You don't want to fall over the edge! The dogs will stand at the edge. Stay a little behind them."

"You are not going down?" Shinda asked Matsuhito nervously.

"Only observing," Matsuhito said. He studied the scene below him. "It is like a box," he said.

"It is a trap," Shinda said.

The valley was shut in on all four sides. To the east, the mountain on which they stood created one boundary. To the west, another, smaller mountain formed another perimeter. The Minagas were massed near it. Gradually they saw the natural arch that led from the small mountain and into the valley. To the south was Jigokumori, Hell Wood, and to the north was the Minagas' own land, and on it their fortress in their dense wood.

"They think," said Shinda, "you will be drawn in through that narrow pass. Because no more than two can come through at a time, they will slaughter you. You will be caught in there."

"Would Norimasa's men be stupid enough to continue coming

through the pass only to be murdered?" Sato asked. "The Minagas may be massing there because they think it is safe."

"A trap is a trap," said Matsuhito. "A different prey can be caught in it."

"What are you thinking?" asked Sato.

"We will go back and I will talk this over with the Council of War," Matsuhito said. "I have a plan, but there is a great hole in it."

"Now what? We climb down again?" asked Shinda. "There will be no battle?"

"We may have need for you after all," Matsuhito said.

"We must be rewarded," Shinda said.

"You may pick the bones of the dead, whichever side wins, and if we win, you will have a share of the bounty. That is, if our plan comes to include you."

"Shinda," said Sato, "Lord Norimasa enjoys nothing more than the sight of a severed head, especially one he has beheaded himself. He is fond of crucified men, too. When they are taken down, he cuts off their heads himself."

"The roads are now full of our spies," Shinda said. "If a bandit tries to alert the Minagas, if they learn a man has climbed this mountain, such a man will be flayed alive. It may be that Norimasa is fonder of flaying than cutting off a head. What do you think, Matsuhito?"

"First he would do one, then the other," Matsuhito said.

"Did you notice the waterfall?" Kenji asked. "And the sound it made? And the stream running through the valley? It is dry weather now, but some time ago, it rained for over a week. Everything else is dry, but the stream is swollen and noisy. All that is good."

Matsuhito nodded. "Let us report," he said.

"You will not tell me what you are thinking?" Sato asked him.

"You will find out soon enough."

"And will you give me a hint?" Shinda asked.

"Certainly not!" said the other three men at once, at which point the two dogs growled and put their ears back.

"Those dogs are like ghosts," Shinda said.

"Their teeth are not the teeth of ghosts," Kenji said. "Should we kill Shinda?"

"No," said Matsuhito. He laughed. "I like him. He is funny."

Shinda scuffed his sandals against the dirt. He did not look up.

"You have made him blush," Kenji said.

"Do not laugh at me!" Shinda bristled.

The three men laughed heartily.

"You will not be happy until you wake the Minagas," Shinda said sullenly.

"So," Matsuhito said, "how can I find you? We will need all of you."

"I will find you," Shinda said. "You think you know everything, but you don't."

"Enough," Matsuhito said. "We will trust you to find us."

CHAPTER TWELVE

IN THEIR CAMP, after Matsuhito arrived with Kenji and Sato, Lord Norimasa's Council of War assembled in front of a fire. The flames were reflected on the men's faces. They looked as if they had already been bloodied.

"So, have we forgotten anything?" Lord Norimasa asked.

"I am not sure about these bandits," said the old counselor of war.

"I am sure of Shinda," said Matsuhito.

"On such cobwebs hang destinies," said Lord Norimasa.

"The plan is good," said the old counselor. "But there is danger in it."

"The idea," said Lord Norimasa, thinking aloud, "is to catch the Minagas in their own trap. But once we begin down the mountain, they must not escape through their own woods."

"I have heard of something," said the old counselor, "that happened a long time ago, before the time of the Taira. Some men holed up in a box canyon. They had the Minagas' idea. They would kill the men as they came in through the single entrance. But the enemy was clever. They knew the dimensions of the opening and built a wall of wood. They kept it in place nobody knows how, but the men inside could not escape. The canyon was full of trees. The enemy sent in burning arrows. The trees were like tinder. Everyone in there died. It was the smoke more than the fire that got them, although many were burned to death."

"A wall," one man said.

"It could be done," said Lord Norimasa. "But not, I think, a completely solid wall. There should be slit-openings for swords, and square slits, higher up, for flaming arrows. What would hold the wall in place? Heavy timbers?"

"Heavy timbers, wagons, stones and men," said the old counselor.

"They will escape through the north woods, which they know well," said Lord Norimasa.

"This is why we need the bandits," said Matsuhito. "They know the woods as well as the Minagas. They can fire the woods."

There was a great muttering about the bandits.

"We have never made use of bandits before," said the old counselor. "Nevertheless, they are fearless to the point of stupidity."

"We want such men," said Lord Norimasa, "and when have we shied from using whatever useful thing or person that presented itself?"

"Let us think," said the old counselor.

"And you, Sato," Lord Norimasa said. "Tell me your thoughts."

"I understand the plan. It may work."

"They are clever, those Minagas," said Lord Norimasa. "But we are clever, too. Well done," he said to the old counselor. "You have shored up the hole in the plan. I think it will work."

"It must work," said the old counselor. "We must avenge Lord Sugimasa. He protected us in this territory. Unless we defeat and contain the Minagas, we will never be supreme in this territory, and we will never be able to take control of this country. They stand between us and our hope of restoring peace to the country."

"Not one Minaga must be left alive," Lord Norimasa said. His voice went cold and sharp, as if a sword had spoken, not a man. "Not one woman, not one child. *Wakatta?*"

"*Wakatta,*" answered the council.

"And if the bandits do not keep their word?" asked the old counselor.

"They will," said Matsuhito.

"Yes, they will come," said Sato. "Hideo, who heads the gang, has never been part of such a great event before. Curiosity and greed will bring him. The rest of the band will follow."

"I think he is right," Kenji said. "Shinda was afraid of my white dogs, but he was fascinated by them."

"Then we have a few more hours to sleep before dark, and we should take advantage of them," said Lord Norimasa. "Be sure the sentries are alerted. You, Kenji, can you sleep yet watch over the dogs? We must not lose the dogs."

"The dogs will watch over me," Kenji said.

"Who will bring the coals we need for the arrows?" asked the old counselor.

"See to it," Lord Norimasa said. "It must be one of the samurai. It is too important to be left to the *ashigaru*."

"The *ashigaru* have good experience in such things," said Matsuhito.

"Set some of them to work," said Lord Norimasa. "In the morning, before first light, we will go over our plan again."

IN THE MORNING, when it was still dark, most of the men opened their eyes, found their clothes damp and thought it was already raining, but they soon found there was no rain, only a dense moistness in the air. When the sun did come out, and the morning mists scrolled and drifted from one end of the valley to the other, they could see themselves only from the waist up. The sky resembled a sunset rather than a sunrise. It was a bright red sun that dyed the sky red. Almost everyone turned to look at it. As the sun continued to rise, it turned paler, but it remained red, and the few thready clouds drifting across it were a lighter red that soon turned a deep rose.

As the men busied themselves checking their equipment, bundling their armor and fastening it to the saddles, they cast frequent eyes up at the sun. The Norimasa clan used red banners, and its *mon*, the insignia of the clan, was a stylized dark red maple leaf. The men worked soundlessly. Many of them thought such a sunrise augured well, but others thought differently, and a sudden clatter of crows crossing the valley and settling noisily on the pines behind them made many shiver. But it was the moisture that most troubled them because the men had heard that fire was to be used as a weapon in the battle, and if it rained, fire could easily be put out.

By the time the men began eating, there were discussions in low voices about the weather.

"It's going to rain," someone said.

"No," one of the *ashigaru* said. "The mists will clear off. It will threaten, but it will not rain."

"Why not?"

"Fishermen always know," said the ashigaru.

"Were you? A fisherman?"

"Of course."

"Fishermen are always right," someone said.

"Not always."

"Who can be right all the time?"

"Believe what you like," said the fisherman. "It will not rain today."

"Tonight?"

"Not tonight, either."

"A large party of samurai will be climbing a mountain dressed in armor. On horseback," someone said.

The men chewed and ate. News invariably leaked out from the War Council, and such leaks were the bane of Lord Norimasa and leaders of all groups, large or small. "I think," Lord Norimasa often said, "there is always someone in an army who has the ability to turn into a very small mouse, and when the council is over, the mouse turns back into a man and tells everyone what it has seen, and lucky for us, a mouse does not have an excellent memory." It was as good an explanation as any other. In the Norimasa clan, spies came to be called *nezumi*, mice, and Lord Norimasa showed a great delight when someone brought him a dead mouse before a battle.

"Does it not augur well?" the soldier would ask, and Lord Norimasa would always say that when the battle was over, the mouse killer would certainly receive a promotion. When the man was out of sight and sound, Lord Norimasa would say, "They are all like children," at which point the old counselor would reply, "We are all like children," and there the matter would rest.

The Council of War reconvened. Shinda arrived and was introduced to the others. "I trust him," Lord Norimasa said. "Matsuhito trusts him. That is enough for me."

"If there is no rain, I think we will succeed," said the old counselor.

"This large wooden wall," Lord Norimasa said. "It will not do to have banging and sawing filling this valley. Someone will see it or hear it."

"Lord Norimasa, it is already being taken care of," said Shinda.

"And how have you taken care of it?" asked the Lord. "I hear nothing."

"But there is a great deal of noise in Sanomi," Shinda replied. "It is such a small village that it is named for the village elder. Until last summer, it had no name."

"And are they making the wall there?" Lord Norimasa asked. "How do they know what to do? When did you speak to the bandits? Why should Sanomi agree to it? Will others not be suspicious of the noise there?"

"It is a clan of carpenters. They are like a guild. It's always noisy in Sanomi. They are always cutting wood there. It would be suspicious if the town were quiet."

"Why should they help us?" asked the old counselor.

"Because," said Shinda, "they have family members in our band. Also, we threatened to burn their town to the ground and then behead them if they did not help."

"A sizable motive," said Lord Norimasa. "But still, I must ask. How did you give word to the rest of your gang?"

"One came to meet me yesterday. I knew someone would find me and he did. He remembers every word anyone ever says, a real nuisance."

"Still, Sanomi . . ." said the old counselor. "We are relying on strangers."

"They hate the Minagas," Shinda said. "Sanomi was set on fire once before, when Lord Kuronosuke fought the Minagas. They were loyal to Kuronosuke. Lord Kuronosuke's palace was the Minagas' handiwork. That, too, was burned to the ground by fire."

"The sleep of revenge is better than the sleep of the dead," said Lord Norimasa, "because it can awaken."

"It will always awaken," said the old Counselor. "And when it wakes, it is like fire. Uncontrollable."

"We have made good plans for using fire," the lord said. "We do not intend to be burned alive by our own flames."

"Good," said the old counselor.

"How long will it take to build this wall?" Lord Norimasa asked.

"That is the bad part," Shinda said. "It will take all day and all night. But it will be ready tomorrow. Maybe even tonight."

"And how will they transport such a thing?" Lord Norimasa asked.

"They will put it on wheels and oxen will pull it. If anyone asks, they will say they are building a shrine near the Two Lovers and this is to be one of its walls. They are always doing such things."

"All right," said Lord Norimasa.

The plans for the night were rehearsed again and again.

"Some of you will leave as soon as possible, in small groups, wearing gray clothes without the clan *mon*. The men on foot will leave when night falls. When it is very dark, the samurai on horseback will leave in groups of five, and Kenji and his dogs will accompany them," the lord said.

"The dogs can ride horses, my lord," Sato said.

"Indeed?" asked Lord Norimasa.

"They are very well trained."

"Put a cloth over them. They are so white," Lord Norimasa said. "Otherwise, they will be like lanterns, especially if there is any moon. Now we must ask the gods for dry weather."

Soon the first parties of five were setting out toward the valley, while others were setting out for Sanomi.

A large force of samurai remained behind, inspecting their weapons, and when they were done, they lay down intending to sleep. Not long after noon, they were addressed by Lord Norimasa. "When it comes to climbing the mountain, Sato will be your guide in everything. He knows the ground. He has Kenji, and Kenji has the dogs. Until you reach the top of the mountain, Sato is your superior. Do not curl your lips. Without him, it cannot be done. You will go halfway down the mountain and await two signals. Matsuhito's falcon will be let loose and you will see him swooping. At the same time, a gong will ring out three times. When these two things happen, the two of you with conches will loudly sound the alarm. Then you must make as much noise as possible. Shouting, gongs, war drums, whatever you can think of. Terrifying screams are good. Rocks rolled down from the mountain are useful. You will use your own imaginations. If the dogs howl, let them howl. If all goes as planned, we may not need to fight. But if it rains, we will be outnumbered and we will fight as usual, man-to-man combat."

"Can the entire plan be made plain to us?" asked one of the samurai.

"It is always best if the council alone knows all the details of the plan."

"Lord Norimasa," said one of the older samurai, "you worry about spies among us, but the bandits know everything."

"You are resentful," said Lord Norimasa, "for no reason. The bandits must know certain details of the plan. Do you not believe me?"

"How can I question your judgment?" asked the samurai, bowing low, touching his forehead to the ground.

"Get up!" said Lord Norimasa angrily. "Such prostrations are not for a man of valor! Do not mock me! If you do not know what to think, and believe I have lost my senses, you must go on faith!" he roared.

The samurai got up and walked backward into the waiting troops.

"Would it be best to slaughter you all?" Lord Norimasa roared. "Must everything always be done as it was the time before? The bandits are a tool, like the conch shells. We make use of them! Fools!"

"Please excuse me," said the samurai who had spoken out.

"Yorihige-sama, there is nothing to excuse. You had your opinion and you spoke." Now Lord Norimasa was smiling. His face returned to normal. "Waiting is hard," he said finally. "We have all day to get through. Everyone go to sleep. Face east as you sleep. Schedule the sentries."

Like soldiers everywhere, the men settled in and fell asleep immediately.

"Now I am going to sleep," said Lord Norimasa. "Sato, you and your dogs will sleep on one side of me."

And so the valley fell silent, except for the cawing of the large crows which seemed to be waiting for something in the trees, but the men slept soundly and did not hear them.

Lord Norimasa was another matter.

He lay awake, thinking and rethinking their plan, anticipating what could go wrong. Occasionally, he would fall into a light sleep, and then he would awaken and begin reviewing matters again. Finally, he sent for Matsuhito.

"Of course, everything can go wrong in a battle," Lord Norimasa said, "but I think the one thing we must fear most is rain."

Just as Matsuhito was about to agree, there was an enormous clap of thunder, and then a loud rumbling, as if huge stones were falling from a great height.

"It will rain," Lord Norimasa said. "I have not thought of a good plan to follow in case of rain."

"Please excuse me," said Matsuhito. "But it will not rain."

"And you guarantee that?"

"Of course," Matsuhito said, and both men laughed.

The thunder and lightning roused the other samurai, who were beginning to stand up.

"Yet it's very dark," Lord Norimasa said.

"Then we can start out early," Matsuhito said.

"Give the command," said Lord Norimasa.

THE LIGHTNING and thunder continued as the men set out through the thick gloom.

"A doomed enterprise," one of the samurai whispered to another, and the other man nodded. The comment spread through the troops.

They rode two by two along the narrow road. Two farmers stood up from a paddy, looked at them in surprise, and Norimasa gave the command to cut them down. Their headless bodies were thrown back into the paddies.

The horses did not gallop because the old counselor advised against it. Galloping horses would make the ground tremble and alert the countryside. And so they advanced slowly.

When they reached the base of the mountain, Sato got down and released his dogs. Then he mounted his horse again.

"You will follow Sato in everything," said Lord Norimasa. "You remember the signals?"

"The falcon, followed by three gongs, and then by conch blasts," Matsuhito said. "Now I will go around to the other side of the mountain. I am responsible for the bandits. It was I who brought them."

"Go," said Lord Norimasa.

SLOWLY, Lord Norimasa's men began climbing the mountain. There was a great crash of thunder as they entered the thickly wooded foliage.

"But it is not raining," said Lord Norimasa.

The two dogs were as visible as moons and stars would have been.

Lord Norimasa followed Sato, Kenji and the dogs, and the other samurai followed him.

"Why must you always be up front?" asked the old counselor. "Most generals stand on their war stool and watch the battle."

"Do not ride abreast," said Lord Norimasa. "The path is too narrow. And, to answer," he said, "my feet fall asleep if I sit on a war stool."

"*Kichigai*," said the old counselor. "Crazy."

"There are two trails coming down the mountain," Lord Norimasa said. "Will you command one?"

"So, you do not think I am a useless old man," the old counselor said with a wide smile.

"That is because I am *kichigai*," said Lord Norimasa, laughing softly.

"And Sato knows of this?"

"Of course. I know you will do well. I do not feed you for nothing."

"If I were standing on the ground, I would prostrate myself before you."

"And make me listen to those creaking knees as you get up?"

"Ah, you never change," said the old man.

And so they kept climbing.

ON THE OTHER SIDE of the mountain, the men who had hidden themselves during the day began to mass not far from the opening to the valley. Everyone was quiet. The thunder and lightning continued. Horses whinnied, but their sounds were drowned by the thunder.

"No one will expect us on such a night," Matsuhito said. "Shinda! Has anyone seen him?"

Suddenly a brilliant bolt of lightning flickered in the sky and they could see Shinda on his horse, and behind him, men dragging something enormous. In front of those men were the rest of the bandits on horseback.

"They've brought it," said Matsuhito. "And they've brought it early."

Hideo, the leader of the bandits, was in full armor, antlers on his helmet and his face mask horrifying.

"Come on, come on, it's not so heavy," Hideo was saying. "Do you want to shame me in front of the samurai?"

The men pulled harder and the object approached. It was indeed a wooden wall.

"Made of pine, as you asked," Hideo said. "Although pine is softer and burns more easily."

"I want it to burn easily," Matsuhito said. "Minaga's men expect us to come in here. As soon as they are alerted, it will be time to begin the distraction. At the next lightning flash, stand the wall upright. The thunder will drown out the grunting of the men."

"The wall is upright," Hideo said presently.

Matsuhito let his falcon loose.

"If they do not see it in such darkness?" Shinda asked doubtfully.

"The falcon will land on Lord Norimasa's arm. He will feel it."

"And then what will happen?"

But before Matsuhito could answer, there was an enormous conch blast from one side of the mountain, and then another answering blast from the other. Inside the valley, the enemy turned and looked up at the mountain in alarm. The lightning flashed again and they saw the samurai silhouetted on top of the mountain. They saw, also, that they were beginning to descend, and as they did, gongs rang out and war drums began pounding and the men coming down yelled bloodily.

"To the rear, to the rear!" someone was shouting inside the valley.

"Put in the wall," Matsuhito commanded. "They are all looking away!"

The wall was pushed into place. The bandits took up their posts at the wall and waited for the men inside to try to come through where a narrow space had been left open. When a few men tried to come through, the bandits slew them with their swords.

Now some of the enemy saw the danger at the entrance to the pass.

"Break it down!" someone shouted.

The wall, however, had been carefully constructed. There were slits wide enough for swords to thrust through, and there were the openings for arrows.

"When the enemy presses against the wall trying to topple it, kill them through the slits. They can see nothing in the dark."

As if the enemy were obeying the Norimasa clan, many of them began to attack the wall when they saw that they were boxed in. The samurai thrust their swords through the wall again and again and more and more men fell.

"Fall back!" they heard someone shout.

"Lord Norimasa and the others are near the bottom of the mountain, waiting," Matsuhito said. "Loose the flaming arrows!"

The ashigaru went up to the archers and set the arrows on fire.

"Let them go now!" Matsuhito commanded.

The flaming arrows sped through the wall. Inside the canyon, where the grass was tall and dry, the fire caught immediately. There was shouting from the men, and the unmistakable sounds of confusion.

Now Lord Norimasa's men began to loose their arrows from the mountainside.

"The trees are beginning to burn!" one of the bandits said joyfully. "It is as you said it would be."

"It may still rain," said Matsuhito grimly.

Suddenly a temple bell began to toll.

"What's that?" asked Matsuhito. "Is there another force hidden?"

"That is our signal," said the bandits. "My men will wait a short time. Then they know what to do."

"Retreat! Retreat!" came a loud shout inside the valley. "Into the north woods. Into the palace!"

From his perch, Hideo could see the trapped men turn and run toward the north woods. They were falling over one another in their hurry. He saw them begin to disappear into the darkness of the trees.

"Fire the woods," whispered Hideo. Suddenly fire broke out in the north woods. "My bandits are doing their job. The men of Sanomi are in there, too."

Now the screams in the woods began.

"The trees are going up!" said another man who watched from a small window in the wall.

"Fire the wall!" shouted Matsuhito.

The bandits turned to him, disbelieving.

"Some will try to escape the fire and try to break this down. They will try to die fighting. Fire the wall!"

The archers let loose their flaming arrows. The wall began to blacken, then smoke, and then crackle as the sap caught fire. Lightning flashed again.

"They are climbing the other side of the wall like ants!" called Hideo. "But they are falling off."

"If anyone goes through, kill him," ordered Matsuhito. "Be prepared!"

Now Lord Norimasa's men entered the valley. They stayed on one side of the river, which protected them from the fire.

The wall was beginning to fall.

"They have to fight or be burned alive," Matsuhito roared at them. "Don't leave one alive!"

The wall fell backward, toward Matsuhito's men. "Back!" ordered Matsuhito. "Stay away from the fire!"

The enemy began to emerge from the opening, their faces covered by soot, coughing from the thick smoke inside.

"Let them come to us," Matsuhito ordered. "The smoke and the heat have weakened them."

Nevertheless, the enemy, expecting to die, fought strongly. When lightning flashed, the archers let their arrows fly and many men went down. The others were met by Matsuhito's men and man-to-man combat began. There were screams from the north woods and the enemy often turned toward those sounds, and in that moment, a sword flashed, and a Minaga head rolled on the ground like a stone.

Finally, there were almost none of the enemy left.

"I am Minaga Yatsuhiro," one man called out. "Let someone of equal rank fight me."

"Lord Norimasa is not here," said Matsuhito. "He has just climbed down the mountain. I am second in command."

"I demand to fight Lord Norimasa," Lord Minaga insisted.

"I am here," said Lord Norimasa, driving his black horse through the opening. "Give Lord Minaga a horse! A good one!"

"Give him mine," said Hideo.

Lord Minaga mounted the horse.

Both men rode away from one another.

"I do not like this," said the old counselor, who had just appeared on the other side of the wall. "Now he will fight amid corpses and smoldering grasses. He will do foolish things."

The two men turned and began to ride toward one another. Lord Minaga had a naginata, halberd, and also a sword. Lord Norimasa rode more slowly, his sword extended.

"He is wearing those infernal stirrups," the old counselor said. "If he wants to stand up high, he can stand up. He is going to try something." The men fell silent, watching.

Minaga's horse was at full gallop. Lord Norimasa's was trotting slowly. As the men neared one another and began to close, Lord Norimasa wheeled his horse about and stood up in the stirrups. Using the higher of the two slots in each stirrup, he appeared as if he were standing on the horse's saddle. The startled Minaga shot past him. When he turned back to face Lord Norimasa, it was too late. Lord Norimasa, still standing in his stirrups, said something to his horse, which reared up. When the horse came down, so did Lord Norimasa's sword. He struck

Lord Minaga from above. His head fell into two halves, like a melon cut through with a sharp knife.

An enormous roar ran through the Norimasa clan and did not stop. It died down, then began again, like the thunder.

Lord Norimasa's horse pranced toward them.

"It did not rain!" he shouted to the men, and burst into loud laughter. The men echoed the sound.

"Now," said Lord Norimasa, "look to the horses. See if their hooves were burned in the valley. The rest of you, hunt down and kill everyone in the valley and in the woods. Tomorrow, we will level Minaga Palace." He raised his sword and rode back into the valley. The men followed him, shouting.

Lord Norimasa turned back. "Where is Hideo?" he asked. "Where is Shinda?"

"We are here," they answered.

"I know what you have accomplished," Lord Norimasa said. "I shall raise you all to landed samurai."

"But," said Hideo, "we are happy as we are."

"Speak for yourself!" said Shinda. "I have an old mother and two sisters no one will marry!"

"Someone will marry them now," Lord Norimasa said. "Hideo, you men decide among yourselves." He turned to Matsuhito. "It is almost over," he said. "But there is bound to be a contingent of samurai in the castle. They will expect us tomorrow night, but we will come in the morning. No one must be left alive! I want to make their deaths as terrible as possible! If even one is left breathing, we will have failed. Sugimasa will not rest. It is bad enough that I was not there in time to close his eyes."

Shinda rode up to Matsuhito. "I beg the favor of speaking alone," he told him. Lord Norimasa heard Shinda and nodded his permission, and the two men galloped farther down the valley.

"Lord Norimasa," he said. "He is preparing for a frontal attack on Minaga's castle?"

Matsuhito said that he was.

"The gates of that castle are thicker than iron," said Shinda. "While they are breaking down the gates, Minaga's men will hurl rocks from the roof and pour rivers of boiling water. The water will pour through the holes in your samurai's helmets, scalding them."

"Yes, they will do all of those things," Matsuhito agreed.

"If there were another way . . ." Shinda said.

"Is there another way?"

"There was always a legend of another way into the castle. Today an old man from Sanomi told me what it was."

"Bring the old man to me," Matsuhito said.

"We must go to him," Shinda said. "He is that old."

"If there is another way, Lord Norimasa will want to wait until he hears it," Matsuhito answered. "I will tell him."

"FIND THE OLD MAN," said Lord Norimasa. "Don't waste time."

Matsuhito and Shinda galloped off together. The night was dark. It was not difficult to believe that a man was hidden behind every pine tree they passed. As he rode, Matsuhito rehearsed the battle to come. How many times since coming to this place had Lady Utsu's face appeared before him? Where was she? And if he never saw her again? But she had told him that could not happen. Never before had anything distracted him once the fighting began. I must train harder, he told himself. I must become more disciplined.

They came to a small village with steep thatched roofs. There was the smell of raw pine in the air. At the edge of the village, a tiny house was set slightly apart from the others.

"The old man lives here," Shinda said. "I got him drunk last night. His life hangs by a thread. I thought, No one else will give him saké. He should die with his throat oiled."

"He knows another way, and you almost killed him?" Matsuhito asked angrily.

"Without the saké, I would not know about another way," Shinda said.

The men dismounted. Shinda knocked loudly at the wooden door. "He is a little deaf," Shinda said. "But his mind is good."

The door creaked open. The oldest creature Matsuhito had ever seen was facing them. He had no teeth. His cheeks had sunken in. His eyes receded into their sockets and his skin was the dead white color seen on recently killed men. Some spiderwebby hair drifted across his skull.

"Tell him," Shinda said.

"I am Kyuzo," he said. "Sit." He indicated his rush mat. "I was the first to take up carpentering. I was one of the men who built Minaga Castle. None of the others now live. You want to know about another way, the secret way in. I know it," he said. "I am the last who knows. Lord Sugimasa took my daughter into his family. She bore a son by him. Twice the Minagas have set fire to our village to light up their battles. If you have killed many of them, I am glad."

"There are more men in the castle," Matsuhito said. "Is it true that there is a sheet of metal between the two wooden panels of the gates?"

"It is true," Kyuzo said. "I would offer you tea, but my hand trembles."

"Make tea, Shinda," Matsuhito said.

"The way in is useless unless there are men who swim," Kyuzo said.

"We all swim. We were trained to swim in armor in Lord Norimasa's lake."

"Lord Norimasa can swim?"

"Very well. And the horses can swim."

"The horses will not help," Kyuzo said. "Is there no saké left?" he asked Shinda.

"As soon as you explain the way in," Shinda answered.

"This is the way," Kyuzo said, wheezing. "I helped to build it. There are three moats before you reach the castle wall. Behind the castle is a river that feeds the moats. Where the back wall meets the side wall on the west, there is a way in. You must swim through the water in the last moat and dive down. There you will see a cave under the water. If you swim into it, you will find that the cave slopes up and the water suddenly grows more shallow. You will soon be able to breathe and crawl on your knees. When there is no more water, you will come to a tunnel above you. If you climb up on the stones and go through the tunnel and reach the end, you come to what seems like a blank wall. But it is a door, and it swings open when you force it. If you go through that door, you will find yourself in the deepest level of the castle. You will be in a vaulted place where the servants and women bring beheaded men to clean them up after a battle. After that, it is up to you. You will see steps leading upward. You will find yourself in one of the corridors. If I were you, I would put on the clothes of some slain Minagas. It should not be hard to kill them."

"So?" Shinda asked Matsuhito.

"Stealthy men, good with swords, men with sharp wits," Matsuhito said.

"Take some of the bandits," Shinda said. "Why do you think we became bandits? We were burned out by the Minagas."

"And you were cruel and greedy," Kyuzo said to Shinda. "But you had your reasons. "One more thing," Kyuzo said. "There are tunnels all through the thickest of the castle walls. If the Minagas knew what was happening, they would hide inside those the walls. They would think they were safe there."

"That is important," said Matsuhito. "You would not set a trap for us, or tell us fairy tales?"

"I have thought about Minaga Castle for almost eighty years," said the old man. "Every night, before I went to bed, I remembered it. I was the only one left. I taught the secrets to my son, but he was burned alive in one of the battles. So long ago, I no longer remember his face. If I saw him now, I would not know him."

"Here is the saké," said Shinda. "We will drink together."

"Lord Norimasa must be told at once," Matsuhito said. "We must go back."

"Find someone to share the saké with you," Shinda told Kyuzo.

Kyuzo cackled, wheezing. "That will not be hard," he said. "If the plan works, please come tell me. My son's spirit will be soothed."

"I promise," said Matsuhito.

CHAPTER THIRTEEN

"So," said Lord Norimasa, "we swim in like fish and burrow in like moles."

"That is the long and short of it," said Matsuhito.

"It may be a trap," Lord Norimasa said.

"I think it is not," said Matsuhito.

"Collect the strongest swimmers and the strongest men. How fast can they be ready?"

"Before your men pretend to attack the front gates."

"And you are sure they cannot be broken down easily?"

"I am sure. And the Minagas would be defending their own ground. They might fire the castle to avoid our taking it. This way they will assume they are safe inside. Imagine how they will feel when they find we have somehow made our way in. They have always counted on the castle being completely impregnable."

"They will be terrified!" said Lord Norimasa with satisfaction. "When the men have killed as many as they can and when they see no more of the enemy, they are to leave the castle and swim back through the river. Then we will fire the castle. We will do that in case there are men hiding in the walls. They will be burned like beetles. Let them die in utmost terror! When you are back on the other side of the river, send a burning arrow into the castle and sound the conch. Leave the bows and arrows and the conch on the shore before you enter the water to approach the castle. Do not make them obvious. This Kyuzo has nothing to lose. He is going to die anyway. He may be deceiving us."

"If you saw him, you would not think so. When he thought of the Minagas dying in the walls, his smile was terrible. In this," Matsuhito said, "I go first. Is it agreed?"

Lord Norimasa nodded.

"Assemble the men," he said. "We will watch from the woods. Some of our men will feign an attack. Before you enter the water, take clothes from the dead Minagas and put them on even if they are stiff and caked. They will soften in the water. Go!"

Twenty-five handpicked men were to swim the river, all of them in Minaga clothing. Among them was Shinda, who had been a fisherman, and the *ashigaru* who had also been one. He was the man who had sworn it would not rain.

"One at a time, no splashing," said Shinda.

One by one, Lord Norimasa and the others saw them disappear.

"Three moats!" he said aloud. "Look! They have reached the second!"

The dark shapes progressed and then disappeared. "We cannot see them now," Lord Norimasa said uneasily.

"If the cave has collapsed, or if it has filled with silt, they will not make it," said the old counselor.

No one answered. In the castle, all was silent. An occasional lantern moved from place to place.

"The rest of the Minagas are in there," said the old counselor. "If it is so quiet, our men have not made it in."

The men stood still, staring up at the castle.

"I think they have not made it," said Lord Norimasa.

And then a huge gong struck, and the air seemed to tremble with the noise. Now the lanterns in the castle moved about crazily, like fireflies, and loud shouts were heard easily over the sound of the river.

"They are in," said the old counselor.

"The enemy was taken by surprise," said Lord Norimasa.

"Which means," said the old counselor, "that Minaga's men have been drinking."

"Let us hope they were that stupid," said Lord Norimasa.

The shouts and the sound of the gongs continued, and then everything grew still. "The Minagas may have taken refuge in the walls," Lord Norimasa said.

"Or they may all be dead, both ours and the others," said the old counselor.

"Old men grow foolishly pessimistic," Lord Norimasa said. "We can only wait."

Time passed. They listened to the sounds of the river and the wind, coming up strongly.

"Will it rain?" someone asked, but no one answered.

"All this waiting," said Lord Norimasa. "If I had a *ryu* for every hour spent waiting."

Lightning flashed, and then thunder. "Again," the old counselor murmured.

"I think," said Hideo, "I heard the conch when the thunder sounded."

Now every eye was riveted to the spot where the men would emerge.

"The arrow!" said Lord Norimasa. "There it goes!"

The flaming arrow was streaking toward the castle.

"They made it back!" said the old counselor.

The men in front of the castle began to send in more flaming arrows. They aimed for the artificial gardens where the rustic thatched huts added such charm in the daylight. There was shouting from the castle and the sound of men running.

"When they try to leave through the gate, our men will be waiting for them," Lord Norimasa said with satisfaction.

At last they heard the sound of swords clashing. "It will be over soon," said the old counselor. "There cannot be many left and we have many men." It was not long before the noise ceased.

"There may still be trouble," said Lord Norimasa.

But the men, disguised with the Minaga *mon*, were beginning to return.

"Not one has been left alive," said Matsuhito, collapsing on the ground. "The castle is in ruins."

"The old man told the truth," Shinda said, falling to the ground near Matsuhito.

Suddenly they heard a scream. Everyone was on his feet at once.

"Someone just killed the *ashigaru* fisherman!" a man shouted.

"Find someone wearing the Minaga *mon*," Lord Norimasa roared. "He came back with us!"

"Loose the dogs!" Sato shouted to Kenji. "Everyone lie down! Then the dogs will not attack our men!"

The white dogs streaked through the darkness. The silence of the forest was broken by growling and a man shrieking.

"The dogs have him," Sato said with satisfaction. "There will not be much left of him."

Then there was another outbreak of barking, followed by more shrieking.

"Two came back!" said Lord Norimasa. "I did not think of this!"

"If there are two, there may be more," said Matsuhito.

"Not for long," said Sato.

Another outburst of barking began and another man shrieked and was still. The men looked at one another and then watched the forest. A short time later, the two dogs, their muzzles bloody, returned.

"What are the bandits doing?" asked Lord Norimasa.

"Some have gone in, looking for plunder," one of the men said. "The rest are going through the fallen bodies trying to find anyone who might be playing dead. They are beheading each man as they go. Also, they are taking weapons."

"Let them take what they want," said the old counselor wearily.

"I should like to see them at work," said Lord Norimasa. "The lightning will be better than the moon. Is Minaga Yatsuhiro's head stitched up? I have special plans for that head. I will go alone to watch the work in the valley," the lord said, but Shinda immediately said it was not safe.

"I will go with you," Shinda said. "I am not afraid of dead bodies."

The two men set off. It was a sight to see, the head of a clan and a bandit of no particular distinction.

"More foolishness," said the old counselor. "But this is a battle to remember. If it was a battle, in the old sense."

"Ah," said Matsuhito. "Remember what you taught us. This was war. 'The only reason for war is to kill the enemy.' This we have done."

"So many tricks," said the old counselor sadly.

"We fought fire with fire," said Matsuhito, laughing. "'Always fit the weapon to the nature of the attack.' How many times have you said that?"

"Lord Sugimasa has been avenged," said the old counselor. "We have secured a great part of this province. This war was good."

"By your standards, too," said Matsuhito. "You remembered the wall and how to use it. It must have happened long ago."

"When members of my family still lived, very long ago," he said.

"Time takes some of us and leaves the rest of us behind. The ones left behind are not the lucky ones."

Matsuhito looked at him, but said nothing. He did not speak when there was nothing to say.

Hideo rode up. He looked like a happy man.

"People will remember us and speak of us," Hideo said. "We outcasts have become part of history."

"I wonder," said the old counselor. "Already a myth is hardening around us. Who knows what they will say of us? Or of you? People may tell the story so that it is our clan who won the battle. Or they will forget you. Or they will forget all of us."

"None of us will be forgotten!" Hideo said confidently.

"Of course not," said the old counselor.

"We will be sorry to leave you," the bandit said.

The old counselor smiled. "I would slap you on the back, but I would fall off my horse," he said.

CHAPTER FOURTEEN

LORD NORIMASA WAS not a superstitious man, which made him almost unique in his country. When people spoke of portents and inauspicious days and directions and occasions, he would avert his face. There was only one thing about which he was superstitious, and that was the charm from the Grand Shrine that was meant to protect him from all misfortunes. He wore this charm in a small purple pouch at all times. In times of danger, he had a habit of touching the toggle from which the small pouch hung, to make sure it was there. He could no longer remember who had first taken him to the Grand Shrine southeast of the capital, but he was taken sometime after *O-Bon*, or the Festival of the Dead, and every year since then, he returned to Ise so that the charm could be burned. He would make a contribution to the shrine, and a new charm would be given to him to keep him safe for the next year. It was considered of great importance to return the charm at the end of the year so that the spirit that inhabited the charm could be released and take up its good works in another, perhaps a charm against drowning or dying in battle.

One of his men was approaching him at a full gallop, and seeing this, Lord Norimasa automatically touched the toggle of his little pouch.

"Honorable lord!" said the samurai without dismounting. "A man was seen fleeing from the Minaga castle not moments ago. He was carrying a reed basket of some kind, and it appeared to be full of papers!"

"Find that man and kill him!" Lord Norimasa commanded. "Take twenty men!"

"He may only have been a scavenger," Shinda said.

"I have always heard rumors," said Lord Norimasa, "that Minaga Yatsuhiro held something in reserve against us, something to do with the four children. If he had such documents, they cannot survive this battle."

"Send our men," said Shinda. Lord Norimasa ignored him and watched more of his men setting off.

When this was done, Lord Norimasa turned to Shinda and said, "It is almost dawn. We will see quite clearly." Shinda knew what he meant. Lord Norimasa was eager to inspect the carnage at the site of the battle.

"The green grass will be red and slippery with blood," Lord Norimasa said, almost dreamily.

The old counselor rode up and reined in his horse next to Lord Norimasa's.

Already the outlines of the ruined castle were visible. The Minagas had built their castle of stone, and the shell of the castle remained, but it was open to the sky where the fire had broken through and destroyed the roof, and the rooms of the castle, always so gloomy and murky even at high noon, now were illumined by the thin light that poured through the roofless structure. Here and there, portions of ramparts had given way, and the morning mists curled through the first levels of the castle in a most ghostly scene.

Lord Norimasa smiled. "Shall we rebuild it and keep it for our own?" he asked.

"It could be done. But we have always preferred our fortifications built on a height," the old counselor said.

"I wonder if any of the polished wood floors have survived," said Lord Norimasa. "They were so dark and shone so. Only old age can give cypress such a patina."

"It should not be a principal place of defense," said the old counselor. "Perhaps a residence."

The sun now came unstuck from the rim of the mountain, tottered there for a moment as if it were going to fall forward, and then rose higher and brighter.

"The valley!" said Lord Norimasa, and he and the old counselor galloped away from the castle to the scene of the first battle.

The bandits were still at it, systematically beheading dead Minaga after dead Minaga.

"Is it not a wonderful sight?" Lord Norimasa asked. "Look how fast the scavenging begins!"

Not far from them, they could see a wild boar devouring the stomach of a fallen soldier. Two of the boar's offspring waited their turn. As the men watched, an enormous flight of crows descended, cawing loudly, and another cloud of crows flew upward into the pine boughs. The crows descended on the heads of the bodies and began ripping flesh from their faces. The fallen Minagas were soon covered by crows savagely thrusting their beaks into the feet of the dead men. When they were finished gorging, some of the crows, bearing shreds of the red sandals the men had worn, disappeared into the distance. "They are building nests," Lord Norimasa said approvingly.

The packs of wild white dogs had already begun arriving and were feasting on hands, feet and faces. Those who were no longer hungry had begun to tear through the armor and the clothing and sank their fangs into the flesh wherever it seemed fullest simply for the joy of the activity. One dog, having finished devouring an entire leg, wrested loose the long bone of the man's arm and went to the edge of the valley, where it chewed on it.

"Why are they taking so long with Yatsuhiro's head?" Lord Norimasa asked impatiently.

Throughout this, the old counselor kept silent. He looked at the white bone of a knee, from which the flesh had been eaten. He observed again the improbable, almost comic, postures into which the dead had fallen. One man was so covered with arrows that he had the appearance of a feathered creature. He must have taken a long time to die.

"Would Lady Utsu like this castle?" Lord Norimasa asked.

"She is accustomed to her own palace," the old counselor said.

Other men were lying on their stomachs, but their heads, severed from their bodies, gazed up into the sunlight. He could not see them without believing that they could still see and wanted to run, but were unable to move.

Deer were moving cautiously near the edges of the field, fearing the white dogs and the other animals that began to come out of the woods. A dog's growl would send them leaping into the safety of the darkness.

"It is incredible, still, after all this time," said the old counselor.

"Beautiful!" said Lord Norimasa, who sighted a mounted man approaching him. "He has the head!" Lord Norimasa said excitedly. "I hope he has stitched it up well."

The two halves of Lord Minaga's head were sewn together with thick black thread.

"He looks like a monster," Lord Norimasa said, gratified. "Nevertheless, there is no question that it is Lord Minaga. Good work!" he told the samurai. "Send someone for a stake!"

"Must you do it?" said the old counselor.

"I have been imagining this for a long, long time," Lord Norimasa said.

The stake was brought to him. Lord Norimasa dismounted and watched as the stake was driven into the earth.

"Now," he said, "give me the head!"

The head, with its seam running down its face, was given to Lord Norimasa, who handled it as if it were a jewel. The head had been washed and the hair oiled and combed. Someone powdered and rouged the face. "So we meet at last," Lord Norimasa said. "Now there is one final thing to do for you." He raised the head high above the stake and then brought it down with an enormous force so that the stake protruded from the top of the head like a horn. The breaking bones of the skull were loud and easily audible for a distance. "It is that sound I wanted to hear," said Lord Norimasa. "Is there a more lovely sound on earth? You are an *oni* now," he said, addressing the head. "You look like the demon you are. But you will not cause us trouble again."

Some of the samurai feared that the spirit of Minaga Yatsuhiro would exact revenge. Others, more intelligent, again saw the extremes to which Lord Norimasa could go and knew that such cruelty could be equally inflicted upon them. But, they inevitably thought, as long as we remain loyal, we are safe. Lord Norimasa is a man who will protect his troops. One man, who watched closely, thought, The man is mad. Sooner or later, that madness will break forth like a volcano and none will be safe.

"Collect the heads!" Lord Norimasa ordered. "Bring the women of

Sanomi here to clean them and we will begin to take them back to the city."

"The women of Sanomi are not used to such things," said one of the samurai.

"They will get used to it," said Lord Norimasa. "So, it is over," he said. "The man who escaped from the castle! Has anyone found him?"

"Kenji has gone to look. He has taken his dogs," said one of the men.

"And the battlefield? What are we to do here?" asked the old counselor.

"Collect any worthwhile weapons and armor, wash them and let them dry in the sun. Leave everything else as it is. The scavenging beasts will see to the rest."

"And Lord Minaga's head?"

"Make special preparations. And his son. Have someone find his son. I want those two heads taken especially."

"And the dead? Are they to be buried?"

"Leave men hidden on the mountain or in the woods. Prevent any attempt at burial," Lord Norimasa ordered.

"That is hard," said the old counselor. "And next you will have to answer to Lady Tsukie. I have seen you throwing away her letters." There was a note of vindictiveness in his voice.

CHAPTER FIFTEEN

THE OLD COUNSELOR had long observed that husbands and wives came to resemble one another, or to act for one another. Lord Norimasa always had a cruel streak, but after he married, it intensified. At first, the old counselor believed that Lady Tsukie, who daily demonstrated little cruelties, was influencing her husband as her spirit was absorbed by his. But with time, the old counselor came to think that the reverse was true. Lady Tsukie had a capacity for small cruelties, but large ones were, as yet, beyond her power. As time passed, the old counselor began to see that Lady Tsukie was most cruel after a battle, as if the lord's cruel spirit had somehow possessed her. So it came about this time.

The death of others one loved, but especially one's own near death, as all the samurai knew, changed a person, and the old counselor sensed that such a change had taken place in Lord Norimasa's wife. He intended to observe her closely.

He began by making a ceremonial visit to the new child and congratulated Lady Tsukie on having such a beautiful infant who so resembled her mother. He realized at once that he had said the wrong thing, because the lady looked at the child with narrowed eyes. He decided that she was still angry at the pain and danger the child had caused her and decided to look into it further.

"Lord Norimasa created a brilliant strategy, but very dangerous," the old counselor told her. "Already it is referred to as the Battle of

Sanomi. So many times my lord's life hung in the balance," he said. "He had not one moment to think his own thoughts."

"He did not have one moment to think of his family at home," said Lady Tsukie. "Couriers were dispatched on our fastest horses, but what was the possible death of one woman among the slaughter of war?"

"Were couriers sent?" asked the old counselor. "Surely I would have seen them."

"Loyalty can be carried too far," Lady Tsukie said as she toyed with the edge of her robe. "Perhaps your devotion to the lord blinded you to the presence of the couriers as the sun sometimes blinds us when we walk." There was an odor of menace about her.

"Have you changed your incense?" the old counselor asked. "It pleases me to think that everyone in the palace was safe while we ventured into a world that spiraled around, dizzying us."

"Ah," said Lady Tsukie, "so you did have time to think of us at home, burning our incense and hanging our red and gold robes over our incense baskets."

"The smells of war are unpleasant, and so we like to think of other, more pleasurable things. That way we continue to believe in the world for which we are fighting."

"And the sounds of war are unpleasant," said Lady Tsukie, whose eyes were cast down. "Did you often recall our singing and playing?"

"The sounds of war are drowned out by our heartbeats," said the old counselor.

Lady Tsukie smiled, her lips thin and white. He had won this round.

"It is odd," she said, "but all the trouble began when Lady Utsu left the palace. I wonder if she, too, missed the palace and thought of it with melancholy. Beneath her calm exterior, I have always considered her quite excitable."

"That is why her poems are so extraordinary," the war counselor said. "She has great passion. She finds beauty in everything and so she has no time for the darker passions."

"Darker passions?"

"Like anger and revenge," the old counselor said. "I have known many poets in my time. I myself have two poems in the next royal anthology. You cannot imagine how it pleases me to know that my name will be recorded there forever! If she feels anger or wants revenge, she knows she will be able to fill her poems with those emotions. Once she has expelled them, they will no longer exist for her. Her mother was the same. The daughter reproduces what the mother once was. Once I loved her mother, but I came upon her too late."

"It was an inauspicious time for a battle!" Lady Tsukie burst out.

"My lady," said the old counselor, "since Yoshitsune, all warriors have agreed. If the weather and position favor a battle, and even the winds are for you, there is no time to cower on the shore awaiting an otherwise auspicious time. In battle, the conditions determine the auspicious time."

"You know very well he has no use for auspicious times and auspicious directions. He is not ruled by such superstitions. He will do as he pleases!"

Never had she criticized Lord Norimasa so openly.

"Right now, he is shut up in his rooms, seeing no one, because it is a taboo day," the old counselor said.

"He wants peace! He is angry because I did not produce another daughter to marry into the Emperor's family!"

"Honorable lady," he said, falling silent.

"So even you tire of defending him!" she said. "And what was that childish prank? Standing up on the saddle! Is he still a young man who can do anything? Think what was at stake there! He is reckless! Some people would call him mad."

"He stood up in the stirrups, not on the saddle. I have never seen a man with such balance," the old counselor said mildly. "It succeeded. Success is never criticized."

"The risk was mine as well as his! And while I was in seclusion, and my blood was flowing out, a red fox ran under my shelter. Utsu and her love of foxes! They are ill-omened animals!"

"Sometimes yes, sometimes the opposite. Perhaps it was sent to protect you," the old counselor said.

"This family is rocked by her when she is here, and it is even worse when she is gone!"

"Honorable lady," said the old counselor again.

"The other clans of Kai have submitted to Lord Norimasa," she said bitterly.

"Your family is secure," he said. "Your family is very powerful. Who will challenge you?"

"My husband," she said.

"Will it not be the other way around?" the old counselor suggested.

"I have known you since my eyes first opened," said Lady Tsukie. "Now I ask you to leave me."

"Please send for me when you are happier," he said. He stood up, knees cracking, and walked backward out of her presence.

"Was there need for that?" she asked her women when he had gone.

"My lady, he thought there was," said one of the women.

"Yes, yes," said Lady Tsukie, "he can advise, but it is my lord who makes the decisions. I wish to speak to my brother. Send word."

"Yes, my lady," the woman said.

Later, the women who attended Lady Tsukie whispered among themselves in an adjoining room. They said that Lady Tsukie was calling for her brother and would give him the task of spying upon Lady Utsu. Perhaps, they said, Lady Tsukie suspected that Lord Norimasa had taken Lady Utsu to the place of battle with him. "She has never gotten over the passion Lord Norimasa showed for her. Indeed, I believe he loved her."

"And she, him."

"Why did he not keep her as his second wife?" asked one of the servants.

"She herself was too willful. How often she said, 'I shall never marry.'"

"No. She said, 'I shall never marry and grow into a Lady Tsukie, who spends her time jealously spying on the rest of the people in the palace. I will not let myself be distorted in that way.' And, as bad luck would have it, Lady Tsukie heard every word."

"Lady Tsukie attacked her, didn't she?"

"She intended to do her harm. She flew behind Lady Utsu's screen and meant to tear out her eyes, but Lady Utsu simply stood still and looked at her without even blinking. For once, Lady Tsukie was afraid, who knows of what? She retreated to her own quarters, and would not speak to Lord Norimasa. Then she ordered her carriages and returned to her father's palace."

"But it was more complicated than that," said another servant. "When Lady Utsu came here, she was only twelve. Lady Tsukie thought of her as her own child. How could she forgive either of them when Lady Utsu and Lord Norimasa began their assignations? And when he spoke of making her his second wife, Lady Tsukie was outraged. She said her child had betrayed her with her husband, and her husband had betrayed his own child. After that, she was uncontrollable, and when she became quiet, her stillness was that of a sword in its sheath. She would take out that sword and use it now—if she could. But, of course, she cannot say more against Lord Norimasa, and to move against Lady Utsu is the same as setting herself against him."

"Then does she hate him?"

"Many would like to know the answer to that."

"Truly, she will grow horns," said one attendant. "She is mad with jealousy. Of Lady Utsu, of course."

"The potion may have changed her," suggested another servant.

"We do not know what was in it, or what it did to save her," said another attendant. "These ancient women, they say they can command spirits."

"They have been employed by many emperors."

"Perhaps it is the end of love. The old counselor used to say that habit was worse than love."

"His sayings are often impenetrable."

"It is a good saying."

"Even the simplest things he says twist and turn."

"He speaks brutally to Lord Norimasa."

"They are soldiers together," someone said, and the women fell silent.

Outside, there was a great commotion. Something was happening in the avenue near the palace.

"It is only the heads on stakes. They are putting them up on poles now."

"The crowd is noisy."

"Ill-omened day or not, Lord Norimasa will have to appear."

"And why is that?" Lady Tsukie asked, noiselessly sliding into the room. "It is hazardous, his love of admiration and display."

Lord Norimasa had also entered without making a sound. Now he asked angrily, "And would you have me hide in the palace as if I felt shame in winning?"

The two of them, thought the female attendants behind their screens, moved as if they had no bodies, as if they did not touch the floor. The women were silent.

"What is this endless arguing?" asked Lord Norimasa. "In the old days, when we were young and I returned from battle, you said you were angry at me because I had made you afraid for me and the fear had made you angry. But now it is something else. Tell me, if you know."

"I do not know," said Lady Tsukie, speaking, as was not her habit, the plain truth.

CHAPTER SIXTEEN

THIS, THEN, is the beginning of the story I wanted to tell about the four children. Lady Utsu, my mother, and Lord Matsuhito, whom I now believe to have been my father, no longer live. The third one, the monk, has now died, and the fourth one, a child said to have resembled my mother, has never been found.

I have paused here to consider their lives. Lady Utsu, Matsuhito and Lord Norimasa have reached the height of their power. They will never again be as beautiful or as powerful. Already, Lord Norimasa and Lady Tsukie are beginning to lose the force and beauty with which they were ready to meet their destiny. What is this but the ending of youth? The passions, the jealousies, the extreme loves and hatreds, the impulsiveness, ambitions never scrutinized, infatuations taken for grand passions: what is that but youth? Already my own youth is going.

Shinda, I understand, still lives, and sends messengers telling me he will return with the rest of the monk's many newly discovered scrolls; they continue the story of the four children. I have eight more scrolls I have yet to read, but cannot get to them. My own children suffered many illnesses this winter. My son's terrible fever kept us all occupied and I was unfit for reading anything. Now I cannot reach the scrolls because of the snow. When I saw how busy I was going to be, I had the scrolls put into our storehouse, and now the snow is so deep there is no approaching the storehouse until spring causes it to emerge from the drifts again.

So I have transcribed the rest of the scrolls I still have in the house.

I think it is best if I let the monk speak for himself until the hot sun melts the snow and lets us reach the rest of the scrolls. If anything should happen to me, I have instructed everyone to take the scrolls and copy them so that the truest story of the four children can become known. I myself would like to finish reading the rest of the story, but nature and obligations do not permit it, at least not for several months.

Here, then, is the monk, relating his tale. He is contemplating the lives of two of the four children, those two being my mother and my father.

I CANNOT SAY how long I have lived like a monk in this hut on the mountain. Certainly, I have seen the seasons repeat and repeat. I have written of Lord Norimasa, Lady Tsukie, Lady Utsu and Matsuhito. When I remember the old counselor, I feel great sorrow. But I have reached that point where I begin to lose sight of them, although they will come into view again. For now, it is time to leave them where they are.

Can anyone imagine that either Lady Utsu or Lady Tsukie, or that lovely kitten, Lady Kitsu, would end her days as a nun in a convent, her hair cut off as a symbol of her withdrawal from the world? Can anyone imagine any one of these women sitting on a low stool, six feet of her hair clipped and falling to the floor, and the lady saying, "Oh, it is cold without my hair"? And can that woman succeed in renouncing the world, so that when she sees those she once loved, they mean nothing to her, as if she had never known them, loved them, cared for them? These things can happen. The old counselor lived out his life happily. When Lord Norimasa forbade him to engage in a campaign several years after the Battle of Sanomi, he dyed his white hair black and went into battle. He killed many men before he received his death wound, and when Lord Norimasa stood over him, the old counselor smiled and said, "I was fortunate. I did not want a death on the mats." He was, indeed, fortunate. Few men accomplish what they most desire. So it is time to leave them there, young, caught up in that storm we call youth, and see how they proceed into autumn and then winter. There is nothing else they can do.

But there are a few shreds I can still write down.

Lady Utsu's daughter, for example. Lady Utsu, who gave her daughter away, grew to love that daughter's memory although she never saw her after the day she gave birth to the child. I often think she, rather than Lady Tsukie, who hated one of her sons, should have been the one to have eight children, but she was so certain she wanted none that she gave away the only one she did have. At the time, she believed she had no regrets. And she was a woman who saw into herself with exceptional clarity.

Her child remained undiscovered. Only Aki and Lady Utsu's sister knew the parents to whom it had been given. But that information died with their deaths, and when that happened, it was too late for Utsu to find her daughter.

Yet she was found, but not by Lady Utsu.

She was found after Lady Utsu left the palace.

Lord Norimasa had organized a hunting party and the men found themselves near a prosperous village in Chubu. At that time, Lord Norimasa decided to find someone new to help care for Lady Tsukie, whose strange whims needed attention. He inquired of many noble families, but had found no one to suit him.

Late one afternoon, his falcon still on his wrist, he saw a low wall, and inside were many persimmon trees. He was riding his black horse, son of the mare had he always ridden, and like his mother, the horse was famous for his ability to jump higher than any other horse. He often demonstrated his ability by jumping over another horse on whom a samurai was mounted. It amused Lord Norimasa to do this because the sight of a horse flying overhead never failed to turn the other samurai pale with fear. And so, without thinking, and accustomed as he was to doing whatever came into his mind, he and his horse jumped the fence, and there Lord Norimasa pulled down persimmons, eating them to his heart's content. Without warning, he caught sight of a woman's robe flowing out from behind a tree.

"Please come out," Lord Norimasa asked her. "I am Lord Norimasa. You may have heard of me."

Still, the woman did not move.

"Please do come out," said the lord. "It is I who am intruding. You must feel free in your own walled garden."

The woman slowly moved into view. She was a young girl, perhaps thirteen.

"It is not possible!" Lord Norimasa exclaimed. He, who never turned pale, felt the blood drain from his face. "Are you a ghost?"

"A ghost, my lord?"

He believed he was staring at Lady Utsu, Lady Utsu as he had once known her, her face unlined, her hair disarranged by the wind, her perfect face restored to what it had always been, the face he always saw before him in the instant before he slept.

"Who are you?" he asked.

"My father's daughter," she said.

"His name?" asked Lord Norimasa, his voice choked with emotion.

"Lord Nakamura," she said.

"And you have lived with him since birth?" he asked her.

"Of course, my lord," said the young girl.

"And you have been well educated?" asked Lord Norimasa. "You speak Chinese?"

Now the young woman appeared frightened. "Yes," she said. "Yes, my lord."

"And there was an old Chinese man who taught you Chinese, a man once washed up on this island after a shipwreck?"

"How can you know such things?" asked the young girl.

Clearly, Lord Norimasa thought, the same man who taught the mother had somehow stumbled across the daughter.

"I am frightening you," he said. "You bear an astonishing resemblance to a woman I once knew." How the past comes back, he thought. But never as you expect it.

"And is she dead, my lord?" asked the young girl.

"I no longer know where she is."

"You miss her," the young lady said.

"Yes."

"I see."

"If I spoke to your parents, and they consented, would you come to my palace near the capital and wait on my wife, the Lady Tsukie?"

"I am happy where I am," the girl said, "But I have always wanted to live near the capital. They say the women there are so clever and life there is so interesting."

"And the women complain of sitting in dark rooms and spending their lives waiting," he said.

"I am sure it is not so!" the girl blurted out.

"I will arrange to meet your parents," Lord Norimasa said. "What are you called?"

"I am called Sadako, my lord."

"And your mother, does she resemble you?"

"Not in the least, my lord."

"Then how can it be?" he said aloud.

"My lord?"

"I spoke without thinking," he said.

And so it was arranged that she was brought to his palace.

Lord Norimasa felt as if his youth had been restored to him by the persimmons in the garden.

Lady Tsukie was another matter entirely. She grew mad with jealousy. "This is your child, whom you have hidden all these years!" she burst out resentfully. "It is worse than having Lady Utsu back! After all those years of swearing that she meant little to you and was tied to you only by friendship! Now she walks the palace as if she owned it! I will not stand for it!"

"Then you may return to your family's home," he said.

"And my children?"

"Your children are grown, except for the boy."

"I will go to my family's home. And perhaps I will not return!"

"If you are happy there, stay as long as you please. When you disabuse yourself of your fantastic illusions, please return. The girl is not my daughter. And if she were, what would you have to fear? A love affair with my own child?"

"Then she is your child!"

"Once," Lord Norimasa said wearily, "it was possible to open my heart to you."

He summoned Lady Kitsu and asked her to make preparations for the journey to Lady Tsukie's home. "And will you go?" he asked her.

"Of course, my lord."

The women left in splendid palanquins, followed by the many oxcarts holding Lady Tsukie's possessions, and they were accompanied by an escort of many men and many soldiers.

I do not know if she ever came back.

I have heard it said that as he grew older, Lord Norimasa had a tendency to sit for long hours in the open pavilion looking into the garden, staring at nothing and frowning. They say, as a result, his mouth began to turn down, and anyone looking at him would think he had led a very unhappy life. I cannot imagine him in that way. Whenever I saw him, he was laughing—unless, of course, he was red-faced and roaring at one of his entourage.

And there the mist refuses to part again over that time in their lives, and for a long time, I know nothing about them. Life is like that, a book left in the rain, ink erased by water, entire chapters disappearing. And then the story continues, and you must imagine the missing chapters that went before. Rest assured, it has continued, their story, although no one was there to let me read it. But since I began to write, I have come to know the rest of it, and so I will write it down.

I MUST PICK UP again here. I have read the rest of the scrolls and it is my duty to order them sensibly. As he grew older, the monk began to jump from one time to another, so that deciding what passages belonged to a particular time has been difficult. It has also been difficult to read the story of my mother's life, even though, in the end, I believe she found happiness. But you must decide for yourself. I believe she was happy because I must. Otherwise, her story is intolerable to me.

BOOK TWO

CHAPTER SEVENTEEN

THE HORSE WAS rearing against the sky. It was a brilliant gray sky, almost silver, with much light behind the clouds. The entire sky was the color of the moon, silvery gray. The animal's woven shoes had worn off, and the horse was frightened, and therefore dangerous.

Mud was everywhere. It was slippery and difficult to avoid mistakes in one's footing.

The horse was mad with fear. It whinnied loudly. When it stopped rearing, it could strike one of the farmers lying injured in the mud. Worse, it might grow wilder and try to break out of the enclosure made up by the huts of the village. Inside the huts, the women and children were hidden.

Shizuku, the head of the samurai who had come to protect the village, saw the horse rear. Like many men who once had glorious reputations and whose names were still known throughout the country, he now had no master and had chosen a name that was not his own. This avoided pity and the inevitable satisfaction that showed in other people's faces when they realized how the mighty had been brought low. Better to begin again, as if he had no history, as if he had been born when the sun came up. The bloody sun, the red sun.

He had a gift with animals. He had a gift for warfare and strategy. He had once been known as one of the best archers in the country and admired as a brilliant military strategist. He had immense patience. He lost his temper only when people insinuated that he himself ought to be head of a clan. He was one of the most loyal men alive. Really, everyone said, there was nothing he could not do. He was once second in command to an impossible, unreasonable lord. When the lord caught a fever in battle and died soon after, it was Shizuku who led the troops to avenge their lord's death.

The horse, rearing. The thick mud, slippery.

He acted without thought. He approached the horse head on. He stood still. Seeing him in his armor, the light glinting on it, the horse grew even more wild. His hooves came down. He reared up again, his front hooves making a sucking sound as they came free of the mud. There was nothing in the samurai's mind but one thing. The horse must be stopped.

Although he was unaware of it, he began to speak to the horse. The horse must have listened. His ears tilted forward. And then, in one fluid motion, the samurai himself jumped at the rearing horse, grabbed its bridle and was somehow in its saddle before the horse came down. The other samurai were shouting at him. He should come down. He should stop. "*Abunai yo! Yamete! Yamete!*" He didn't hear them. He heard the panting and gasping of the horse. He leaned forward and wrapped his arms around the horse's neck. He kept on speaking to him. "*Abunai yo! Yamete! Yamete!*" The shouts rang out. "You must calm down or they will hurt you," Shizuku said into the mane of the horse. "I will not hurt you. Why should you throw me off?"

The horse turned his head, as if to see him better. "So, I am only a man on a horse," he said. "Come with me and be my horse," he said. "I have not had a horse of my own for a long time. My horse was black, just like you. The same. I feel I know you. Come with me and I will tell you stories and you will tell me yours." Later he could not have said exactly what he told the horse; he only knew that he had to keep speaking. The horse reared up again, but this time when he came down, he stayed still. Again, it twisted his head to see if the man was still on his back. The horse was trembling badly. Its mouth was frothing. "You will come with me and I will tell you stories?" the samurai asked the horse.

"Get down and we will kill it!" one of the other samurai called.

"Don't touch this horse!" Shizuku called. "It is my horse."

"It's mad. It's a mad horse," called Bokoshi, one of the samurai.

"Don't touch this horse!" Shizuku ordered.

The horse whinnied, this time softly. It was a sad sound.

"The horse will be all right now," Shizuku said. He sat in the saddle as if he had no trouble with the animal. "How many bandits?" he asked. "How many left?"

"They are all dead!" shouted one of the women within the hut. "Dead, all of them!" There was a chorus of village women answering. They were weeping with fear and relief.

Shizuku surveyed the town from the horse's back. There were bodies everywhere. Covered by mud as they were, they appeared inhuman, as if they were born of the wet, slippery earth. The mud men who lived in swamps, that old legend.

"What next?" Bokoshi called.

"It is time to bury the dead or there will be pestilence."

The villagers began to come out and the men dragged the dead from the river and piled them up along the bamboo fence nearby. The river was raging, its color sometimes brown and sometimes greenish, white foam spewing up into the air. "And what will we do about the enemy dead?" Bokoshi asked.

"Separate them from the others," Shizuku said. Without hesitation, they began their task. It was unpleasant work. The faces had to be washed because the dead were encrusted with a mask of thick mud. The women brought pails of water and began the work. When a dead villager was discovered, there was a pause and a silence, and then a terrible wailing from the family of the dead man.

"You trained the village men well," said Bokoshi.

"I was trained well," Shizuku said. "I did what my lord would have done." They must obey instantly, the lord had said. If possible, give a reason, but later. If you do not give a reason, they must still obey without question. If anyone demands a reason, behead him. Later, he said, after you have beheaded two men, you will not need to behead another. He was always right, in those days.

The first time the lord ordered a man beheaded, he spoke to the man in front of the troops. "You know why you are losing your head?" the lord asked him. "You remember the *kappa*, the water sprite who can do so much damage? The one who gets his power from a liquid in a depression on the top of his head? Even a *kappa* will obey customs. If you bow before a *kappa*, the *kappa* will bow in return. Finally, he will bow so low that the water on top of his head will pour out and then he can be killed. That is how important it is to obey customs. Everyone must obey my orders. That is my custom." And so saying, he withdrew his sword and immediately beheaded the man.

"Order a ration of saké for everyone once the sun sets," Shizuku told Bokoshi. "When it grows dark, they will see ghosts everywhere. When it is dark, they will begin to know what they have lost."

Bokoshi went over to the men and women helping with the dead, and announced the coming distribution of saké. "And if there is any rice to cook, we will make *mochi*," Bokoshi went on. "We will give thanks to the *kami* of the village."

The men turned and smiled. The women shook their heads, smiling sadly. Before this, they would have cheered, but there were the dead, their eyes looking up into the moonlit sky.

Bokoshi returned to Shizuku. "Now they begin to count the cost," he said.

"The bandits should not be buried with reverence," Shizuku said.

"They cannot stay as they are."

"I would like to throw them in the river!" he burst out. The horse whimpered. "But the water feeds these fields."

Bokoshi scuffed at a plank and did not look at Shizuku.

"We should try to burn them in a pile and use dried manure to light the pyre," Bokoshi said. "The villagers will like that. Even better, strip the bodies first and burn them naked and unwashed. That will make them happy."

"Give the command," Shizuku said.

Bokoshi went back to the women cleaning the dead and gave the orders. When they heard the commands, there was a fearsome shout. "*Yokatta, yokatta*," said Bokoshi, returning again to Shizuku. "They would like to behead the bandits before they burn them."

"*So desu.* Has anyone seen Takai?" he asked.

"No," said Bokoshi.

"Go look through the dead," Shizuku told him. Bokoshi trudged through the mud back to the dead bodies. Takai was not there. There were still ten or twelve bodies left, but all the dead had been short, and Takai, who was very tall, was not among them.

Bokoshi sighed and walked back to Shizuku. "Takai is not there," he said.

"The hut that was on fire, look there," Shizuku said.

Bokoshi was about to set off again when three women carrying something approached them.

"A body on a wooden plank," said Shizuku. "Dead, I think."

Then the man on the wooden plank coughed.

"It is Takai," one of the women said. "He helped put out the fire, but he stayed too long in the smoke."

The coughing grew stronger.

"He must take deep breaths," said another of the women.

An old woman, her face deeply pleated with wrinkles, said that breath must be pushed into him. "I will do it," she said. "Once I saved my son after a fire."

The women carried the man on his plank onto the high porch of the elder's hut. The old woman was helped to her knees. She knelt in front of the motionless man and began to breathe into his mouth.

"Pinch his nose shut," one of the woman said. "*Obaasan,* have you forgotten?"

"What do I forget?" asked the old woman. But she pinched the man's nostrils together and resumed breathing into his mouth.

"See! He is pinking!" said the old woman's granddaughter.

The old woman ignored the world around her. She breathed into the silent man. Time stopped. Then the man began to cough and move.

"Help him up," the old woman said.

The man's eyes opened. "I am not dead," he said, astonished.

Everyone began to laugh.

"When we set the fire for the dead, he must not breathe in the smoke," the old woman said.

Shizuku would have liked to ask why, but the old woman would not have been able to tell him. The old customs came down and were observed, but the reasons behind them were lost.

"Make soup and give it to him," the old woman said. The other women helped her up. She looked around. "How quiet it is," she said. "Now things are put right." She looked up at the sky and beyond the village into the fields. "In a week, we must plant the rice," she said. "Now we can all squat in the paddies!" The women laughed noisily.

A softer, warmer air blew through the village.

"Spring has come," said the old woman. "You two," she said, looking at Bokoshi and Shizuku, "you two need more than soup. Prepare food for them and then for the others," she ordered the other women. "We can eat horse meat after a battle," she said. "It is the custom."

"Clean all the dead horses and butcher them," Shizuku said. "They are still fresh. Leave alone the ones that live."

"Horses are worth money," the old woman said. "We are not stupid."

"We will each want a horse of our own," Shizuku said. "And a saddle."

"I see you already have one," said the old woman. "He is already your horse. The others can choose for themselves. That is best."

"We will bury our own dead," Shizuku said.

"They were once ours," said the old woman. "We will help, if you will accept our assistance."

"We shall be honored," said the samurai, bowing.

EVERYTHING WAS DONE. The beheaded were burned in a great pyre fueled by dung. The fire would smolder for weeks as bodies near the fire turned to ash, and the fire would be built up again for the ones not yet burned. Meanwhile, the women were carrying the rice seedlings to the edge of the paddies and the planting was already going on. The men and women sang as they planted, old songs from the beginning of time.

The villagers were as grateful as ever, but the samurai could see that they were no longer needed, and it would not be long before the villagers' gratitude would begin to wear thin, and they would be unhappy to defer to them and cook for them. It was time for them to go. The three samurai were agreed.

"Tomorrow, we will be leaving," Shizuku said to the village elder. "We wish you a good harvest."

"You will come back if we need you?" asked the elder. He was half teasing, half not.

"If you can find us, we will come back," Shizuku said.

"But honorable one," said the elder, "you cannot leave tomorrow. We have to prepare your provisions for the trip. It will be accomplished the day after tomorrow, not sooner."

"Then we will wait," Shizuku said.

"It is not good to be hungry in the countryside," the elder said. "Until you learn to scavenge. But if you are lucky, the food will last you until you reach a large town."

Shizuku bowed deeply.

The elder bowed even more deeply.

"Now you are like two *kappa*," Takai said, laughing.

The elder laughed heartily. "A good joke!" he said. "Wait until I tell the others."

When the elder left, Shizuku said, "They are still trying to decide if we are human."

"It is indeed time to go," Takai said.

When the villagers made the provisions ready, and sacks were stuffed with uncooked rice, and bags were stuffed with rice cakes and vegetables and smoked horse meat, the samurai mounted and stood staring up at the burial grounds of their four dead. A sword was placed upright in each mound. The three men stared at the dusty mounds. It had been dry and hot for five days, and the wind blew dust from the mounds toward them.

"Well," said Shizuku.

"Well," said Bokoshi.

A crowd gathered around them.

"We must leave," said the samurai.

Suddenly one of the villagers knelt and bowed to the ground.

"Please," said Shizuku. "Get up. Do not kneel in front of us."

"We will remember you," Bokoshi said.

"Please remember them," Takai said, looking up at the four burial mounds of the dead samurai.

"Every year at the *O-Bon* observances, they will be remembered," said the old woman.

Then the men turned their horses and slowly rode down the road and out of the village. When they turned to look again, the villagers went back to their planting in the paddies. As they went, the samurai heard the sound of singing begin, and they knew the villagers were planting in time to the rhythm of the ancient song.

THE ROAD OUT OF THE VILLAGE was steep. Because they expected a long trip, the samurai dismounted and led the horses. The season had changed since they arrived. The mountains around the village were greener and puffier. One at a time, the three men realized that they had not had time to look around while they were defending the village.

Shizuku thought, Roads take you somewhere you have not yet been or they bring you back to where you were. Some roads lead to the future, some to the past. Then he thought, That is not right. All roads do both. They were now nearing the highest point of the road and the summit of the hill. Here the three of them paused and looked down at the village. From here, the old-fashioned wood huts looked like mushrooms. Their thatched roofs were steeply pitched and came down almost to the ground. Light glistened on the paddies and the people were moving about, but were featureless from this distance. Occasionally, the sound of singing drifted by like a light wind.

Without saying anything, the samurai began descending the other side of hill. When the sun started to sink in the sky, they stopped and ate their meal. Takai wanted to go farther and find a good place to sleep. The others agreed. They could hear a river in the woods to the left and they led the horses into the woods. When they came to a meadow, they decided to stop and sleep. "I will stand guard," Takai said automatically. He had always taken the first watch while they were in the village.

"What are we guarding?" Bokoshi asked.

"Takai is right," said Shizuku. "It is a lonely place. We have horses and food."

"It will be a dry summer," Bokoshi said. "I feel it."

"It will be hot, we know that much," Shizuku said.

"Will you need to sell your armor?" Bokoshi asked. "I don't think I'll need mine again. I have no house in which to display it."

"I would sell all of it, but not my sword," Shizuku said. "And I will take my bow. It is part of my hand."

"Of course not your sword," Bokoshi said. "Or your bow."

"And not my helmet or my faceplate," Shizuku said.

"Why? Because the faceplate is so terrifying?" Takai asked.

"Because it was given to me," he said in a manner that closed discussion.

"The helmet is heavy," Takai said.

"I am still strong," Shizuku said.

"We are all still strong right now. I think I would like to run an inn," Bokoshi said. "I would like to sit and listen to the stories of the people who come."

"And you?" Shizuku asked Takai.

"I will go to my family home. My father may need help. He cannot keep accounts."

"Ah, you are lucky," said Bokoshi. "All my family is gone."

Shizuku nodded and said nothing. He rubbed his shaven head.

"People," Shizuku said, as if he did not know the meaning of the word. He got up, sat down and propped himself against a tree, and was sound asleep.

"A real samurai," Takai said.

"The best," Bokoshi said.

"Three days more, and we're there," Takai said.

Bokoshi turned away, lay on his side, and fell asleep.

The mosquitoes were already swarming. They were early and buzzed about Takai's head. He looked at the two sleeping men and saw that the mosquitoes were after them, too. Still, they slept on. The horses lashed their tails and tossed their heads. Someone in the village—who?—had given them a pot of ointment for the beasts, saying it would keep off the flies. But it was cool, and he, too, was tired, and soon he was asleep.

IN THE MORNING, Shizuku, who had the last watch of the night, heard the small rain begin. He gathered more twigs and put them on the fire. It would be much harder to keep the fire going if he waited. Then he sat against the tree and watched the shimmering drops fall on the new, bright green leaves. One at a time, the drops depressed each leaf, which then sprang back. The gray sky was brightening, a new kind of silvery fire, and lacquered each leaf as if it were dusted with gold powder. How many dreams does a man have? he thought. As many as there are leaves on any one tree?

What was there to watch for here? Not enemy spies, estimating the forces of their opponents. Yet there was always something to require vigilance. Bandits, animals, wild boars who ran straight at you without the least fear, mad, foaming dogs, making right for you, a snake slithering toward you. But these were anyone's dangers, not only the opponents of soldiers in armies.

Takai was stirring, and Bokoshi would soon be awake.

They ate their rice cakes, looked up at the sky, and at one another. The little rain intermittently continued.

"It feels good," Bokoshi said, looking up, letting the rain wash his face. Some raindrops fell into his eyes and he rubbed his hands.

"My *obaasan* always said, 'Do not let rain fall into your open eyes.'"

Then they fell silent. Was there anything that wasn't forbidden by someone? There were people at court, Shizuku remembered, who believed that if rain fell on the eyes of a dead person facing the sky, every memory of the people he had loved would be washed away. Did the world not frighten everyone enough without these endless superstitions? Shizuku suddenly turned his face up and opened his eyes wide. There were times, and this was one, when he would do anything to forget the image of that woman, her hair, her face. Her voice, too, but the raindrops would not help there.

Soon they were on their way. The little rain darkened the road to reddish brown, and as they rode, no clouds of dust arose to annoy them. The mosquitoes, too, had been driven off by the rain.

"An early start," Bokoshi said cheerfully. Shizuku asked himself, An early start to what?

The road, which had been going up, began to go down suddenly.

"I think I will leave you here," Shizuku said.

"*Nani?* What?" said the other two together.

"It is as good a place as any other," Shizuku said. "I am going north."

"North!" one of the men exclaimed.

"I have heard about it for many years," Shizuku said, as if that were an explanation. "I hope to reach Echigo before the snow."

"What madness is this?" Bokoshi asked angrily.

"Whatever it is, it is my madness," Shizuku said.

"There are many clans who want you," Bokoshi said. "You are a prize. Is there no other lord you can work for? Your usefulness is not over."

"It is over."

"Why say such things!"

"I cannot pledge myself to another lord. I was happy enough while it lasted. Now my life is my own."

Bokoshi and Takai regarded him in horror. "Truly, you are mad," said Bokoshi.

"Let us part as friends," said Shizuku.

"*Baka!* Of course we are friends!" Bokoshi said.

"There will not be enough work for both of you in the town," Shizuku said.

"Do not speak of the town to which you are not going!" Bokoshi said, enraged.

"Here there is a good entrance into the woods. It looks like a good mountain."

"It is a mountain! A steep mountain!" Bokoshi shouted. "At least find a pass!"

"Look at that willow down the road, on the left. I wonder how it got there. There must be a buried spring near it. Already it has turned green. Stop under a tree like that when it is time to eat. I am going now." And he turned his horse into the gap in the woods.

"What are you doing?" Bokoshi bellowed.

"We will meet again in another existence," Shizuku called back. "I am sure of it." Then the horse began to climb, and Shizuku disappeared into the woods. They heard a rain of pebbles. He was gone.

THE INCLINE WAS STEEP, and it was difficult for the horse to avoid slipping back. As he climbed after the horse, the samurai, too, had difficulty until he began to grasp tree boughs and hold them until he advanced a few steps. Then he would catch on to another, and so he would progress. The horse seemed to be finding his own way, digging into the earth with its black hooves and then moving forward. Finally, the horse grabbed a branch with its mouth, and, like the samurai, made its way upward. It occurred to the samurai that the horse was imitating him. He was an intelligent animal.

The horse tired before he did, and whinnied, and when they stopped, he heard the sound of running water. The ground leveled out and the horse repeatedly tried to move to the left, to the sound of water.

"We will go to the river," The samurai told the animal.

The water sparkled clear over the shining black stones and both of them drank their fill.

The samurai was fatalistic. Whether he lived or died on this mountain or on some other was a matter of indifference to him. If he hoped to sum up his own life in the silence created by the absence of others, he had not yet framed such a hope. He had heard of people who went mad in such solitude, while others thrived on it. Whatever happened did not matter. For the first time, no one was his master. It occurred to him that he had so far spent his life believing that floating without roots was not a good thing. Now he was not sure.

"People see things in the woods," he said aloud, and then laughed in delight because there was no one to hear him. Still, the horse turned when he spoke. "*Shimpai shinasai*," he said. "Don't worry." He would begin to worry about what he would do when he had to pass checkpoints and barriers, but he had a Lotus Sutra scroll from the village elder. He had a note Bokoshi had written, saying that he was a monk traveling to Echigo, where he was to take up residence in a monastery. Long ago, he had shaved his head. "What do you want with a note like this?" Bokoshi had asked, and the samurai said, "It is a joke. Your handwriting is better."

He heard the tinkling bells of a man on a pilgrimage, and the sound of his stout stick. The guards at the barrier would let him through. If not, he could avoid the passes and find a mountain he could climb. He hoped to take the horse with him. He had several sets of wicker horseshoes in his saddlebags. He knew how to make more.

The horse settled himself on the ground and watched him.

"You behave like a dog," the samurai said. "I have never seen such a horse."

The horse lowered his head and then rolled onto his side.

"Get up," the samurai told the horse, which obliged. "You cannot be comfortable lying on saddlebags," he told the horse, and proceeded to remove them. He strapped on his long sword and lay down against a tree. The sound of running water, the soft wind, the sweet smell of wet earth and decaying leaves made his eyelids droop. The horse again settled himself on the ground. "Sound the alert if you hear anything," he told the horse.

She was weeping without sound. He watched her quietly. Finally, he turned to her, but her hair hid her eyes.

I was dreaming, he thought, opening his eyes. Her hair, he realized, was black streaked with gray, but it had not been cut. Whoever she was, she had not become a nun. His eyes closed again. He dreamed that she was waiting for him and that he would find her, yet he was not sure who she was.

Now the great lord was ill. At first it seemed nothing, but when the lord began to grow hot, he grew hotter and hotter. His wife and servants left the chamber. They claimed that when they bathed the lord's forehead, the water rose up as steam. It was as if he were being consumed with fire.

"We will survive and we will fight again," the lord said. So hot! The waves of heat, he remembered, reached him where he knelt at the edge of the lord's mat. Lady Tsukie spent little time there. She used her time discussing what the priests should do, how many sutras must be copied in gold ink, how many archers must twang their bows.

"It is too bad the old woman died," said Lady Tsukie. "She saved me." She smiled the smile of a snake.

I cannot forgive Lady Tsukie even now, he thought, as he knelt by the lord. She drove Lady Utsu out with her jealousy. And the girl who so resembled Lady Utsu, had it not been for the lord, she would have gone about in rags, and her fingers would have been pricked raw from sewing for the royal children and grandchildren. Regardless of what the lord said and did, Lady Tsukie saw to it that the girl knew she was hated. She did not flourish. "We should marry her off," Lady Tsukie said again and again.

But the girl did not like courtiers. She preferred the samurai and their roughness, their directness. Nevertheless, Lady Tsukie arranged a meeting with a courtier's family. The man was of high enough rank so that the lord would not object, but the girl despised him. He was tall and fat, and filled out his ceremonial robes as if he were an ever-expanding cloud. He was addicted to gold on gold, and his head, resting on top of his elaborate and expensive brocaded robes, was far too small for his round body. He had a white face and a small red mouth, the kind of man who not so long ago would have been considered the most handsome of men and who would have been pictured as the handsome man in the scrolls of the *monogatari*.

"But he alights so gracefully from a carriage," Lady Tsukie said. "Unlike your samurai, who trip and fall and drench themselves in mud puddles."

"It happened once," the lord said.

"I hate the sight of him," the lord said to Matsuhito. "Can you imagine him wearing armor? Or mounting a horse? The crows would hover overhead at the very sight of him."

Lady Tsukie had taken to dressing in red and orange and black. Her robes managed to be both garish and fit for mourning at the same time.

Her clothing eschewed all the auspicious designs—cranes, turtles, plum blossoms, pine trees—and eventually she only made use of unique patterns that meant nothing, but were invariably geometric and harsh in their angles. Privately, her women said that she had come to hate the world. Every year, her lips were pressed tighter together, whiter and thinner. Once the lord fell ill, she was everywhere, watching everyone, summoning everyone to her as she sat behind her screen. She was said to move through hidden tunnels in the palace and listen to what was being said in the corridors and the rooms. It was believed that she listened with great attention to the servants. "They know everything," Lady Tsukie once said to one of her women.

Now, as the lord lay there, predicting recovery, he grew even more hot and began raving. Matsuhito was startled and horrified when the lord turned toward him and loudly said, "You! I thought I had you on a stake! Why did no one obey? I will do it myself!" he shouted, and he tried to stand up.

"I will cool you, my lord," he said, "as you warmed me in that terrible winter while we lay siege to the palace in Omi."

He poured cold water on his clothes and lay down on the lord's body. Truly, the lord's body was so hot that Matsuhito's clothing began to steam, and soon it was dry. Once again, he wet his clothing with cold water and lay across the lord's body.

"How touching," said Lady Tsukie, who slid back the paper door. "But it will not help."

"Of course it will help," the lord said, quite lucidly. "I am not so hot as I was."

"I must ask the doctor if this coldness is acceptable. I pray you do not catch still another cold. Whatever you suffer from is bad enough."

"Do not call the doctor," said the lord. "My spirit will come after you if you call him and I die here. Leave me!"

Matsuhito continued soaking his own clothes in cold water and covering the lord with his body.

"Ah, that is better," the lord said. "Help me into my armor. If I die, I do not want to die in this shroudlike garment."

"I will do it, my lord," said Matsuhito, "but not until the fever breaks. You are so hot your skin will heat the metal and it will burn your body."

"But I am growing cooler," the lord said petulantly.

"As soon as you are cooled enough," Matsuhito said.

"Give orders to my men," the lord said. "That woman is not to enter my room alone. Post men in front of my door."

"How many, my lord?"

"Six. Have them stand watch. Two at a time. She will try to slither in like a snake under the door."

"There will be no slithering, my lord," Matsuhito said.

A hint of a smile lit up the lord's face. So there is hope, Matsuhito thought.

Finally, the fever seemed to have broken. Matsuhito did as he was told and brought his armor. "My lord," he said, "it is heavy. Are you sure you want it on?"

"Yes," said the lord.

"It will exhaust you," Matsuhito said. "Even the bear-fur boots? They are so hot."

"Put on the boots."

Matsuhito sighed and put them on.

"Your helmet, my lord?"

"You mock me," he said. "I cannot lie on my back wearing my helmet. Call the members of the Council of War to me. Help me into my chair."

When the counselors of war arrived, they prostrated themselves in front of the lord. They wept with happiness.

"Let us touch you, my lord," asked the old Counselor. "For so long, we thought you were almost a ghost."

The lord nodded his head in assent.

The old counselor felt the lord's head. "It is cool," he said, returning to his place. The others approached, one at a time.

"How long I will last, I cannot say," the lord said. "You know who I want to take my place in military matters. He has been my second in command for a long time. Matsuhito makes few mistakes. What I want from you is to swear to protect my oldest son against rivals. It is my will that he rule in my place if I do not survive. He will rule once he has been fully trained and once Matsuhito agrees that he is ready to take my place. And more, I want you to swear to protect the Lady Utsu, should she be found, and the Lady Sadako, whom I have taken in as my ward. Your enemy will be Lady Tsukie. She is a redoubtable foe, but she is mortal. I leave her to your own devices. Do you agree? Lady

Tsukie is not to arrange a marriage for Lady Sadako without her permission. If there is danger of such an outcome, you must get Lady Sadako out of the palace and to young Prince Sugimasa's castle. Do you promise me?"

They promised.

"As you fear my restless spirit?" asked Lord Norimasa.

"As we revere you," said the old counselor.

"Swear," said Lord Norimasa.

"You have our pledge," said the old counselor. "Say it." He turned, addressing the others.

"I swear," said one after the other.

"I shall be a relentless and fearsome ghost," said Lord Norimasa.

"We would expect no less," said the old counselor. "We will leave you now. You must rest."

"Lord Matsuhito will remain. When the time comes," said Lord Norimasa, addressing the old counselor, "tell Matsuhito everything you know."

Matsuhito looked at the lord as if to ask questions.

"Not now," said the lord. "See you in hell," he said, addressing the others. He was smiling.

THAT NIGHT, Matsuhito, who had fallen asleep, his head on the edge of Lord Norimasa's mat, was awakened by the lord's shouting. "Why is that man's head still on his body? Twist off his head! Twist it off!" Then the lord began tossing and turning. "Matsuhito!" he said. "Take off the armor! It burns me! My shoulder plates burn me, and the plates of my chest! Take them off!"

Now Matsuhito became aware of how hot he himself was. Perspiration dripped from his face and from his chin. He began removing the lord's armor as fast as he could. "Someone come in and help!" he called through the paper door. One of the men came in and both of them worked to remove the armor. "He is hotter than ever," said the other man. "It is not good."

"We will try cold water again," Matsuhito said. They began to apply cold clothes to the lord's body, but there was the sound of steam. Nothing helped.

The lord began calling for water. "How it burns!" he said. "More!

More water! There is acid in it! Someone is poisoning me! Is it you, Matsuhito? Never would I have expected it of you! More water, even if it is poisoned!"

"Does the old counselor know any remedies?" Matsuhito asked desperately.

"There are none. He said so before," came the answer.

"Ah! The town is on fire! It is so bright! We can see everything! Loose the arrows! This will be over quickly!" A great smile spread over Lord Norimasa's face. The two men watching stared intently. Suddenly Lord Norimasa began shaking violently. Matsuhito threw himself on the lord's body to calm him and prevent him from hurting himself. "Oh, so you attack me in front of my troops!" Norimasa raved. "So that is what you are!"

"You had better get off," said the other samurai softly.

Matsuhito hesitated, and then rolled from the lord's body and to the edge of the sick man's mat. He sat and watched.

Lord Norimasa suddenly sat up, his eyes wide, and said in a terrible voice, "I see it all now!" Then he fell back and they no longer heard the rasping sound of his breathing.

The samurai placed his head on the lord's chest.

"His spirit is gone," he said. "*Shindayo*. He is dead."

Lady Tsukie, who must have been listening, came in. "Matsuhito!" she said. "You have killed him! You poisoned him and smothered him!"

The old counselor, who had been sleeping in the corridor, came into the chamber. "Take care, Lady Tsukie," he said. "If the lord was poisoned, would not such a person want to poison his lady?"

She went white.

"Make preparations for the funeral and the burial, and do not waste time making dangerous accusations," the old counselor said.

"How you speak to me!" Lady Tsukie gasped.

"Do you deserve better?" asked the old counselor. "Lord Matsuhito was given the lord's commands should he die. We were there and heard him. Now he is dead and matters are in our hands. He spoke of sending you from the palace."

"Sending me? Me?" she asked, her voice rising.

"To a convent, my lady," said the old counselor. "It is written down. The convent's name and what should be given as presents when you arrive there."

"Where are the papers?" she asked, her voice deadly.

"They are safe, my lady, and far from the palace," said the old counselor. "Is it not so, Yamamizu?" he asked one of the counselors.

"He tells the truth," Yamamizu said. "Your eldest son is to continue as the head of the clan and he is to assume power when he is of age, but the lord said he wanted peace in the palace at any cost. To achieve that, he made provisions to take you to a convent."

"I do not believe it!" said Lady Tsukie, sinking to her knees.

"Enough!" Matsuhito boomed. His voice echoed through the palace corridors. Everyone fell silent. Never before had Matsuhito raised his voice indoors.

"I was given charge of keeping peace here," he went on loudly, addressing Lady Tsukie. "You are only one of his three wives. Go to your chambers and remain there."

"You have all been waiting for him to die so that you can ruin me!" she shrieked. "But I will not cut my hair and go to a convent!"

"Chambers! Now!" Lord Matsuhito commanded.

The lady bowed low, and slowly left the dead man's chamber.

"Now," said the old counselor, "you are truly Lord Matsuhito. What are your commands?"

So LONG AGO, thought the samurai, shaking his head as if to clear it. The rain had stopped. The moisture was oppressive and mosquitoes were again beginning to swarm.

"I have ointment for you, Kurokuro," the samurai told the horse. "And then we will go on and find a place with green grass and I will eat as you graze."

He took out the grayish ointment and smeared the horse's nose with it. "What a smell," the samurai said. "But now you look happy. I will put some around your eyes. Are you ready?" he asked the horse. "I will lead you until we see what the terrain is like."

A good place for an ambush, he thought. Then he thought, All that is over. I must not forever think of strategy and victory. I must notice only things that do not have to do with war.

"It is stony ground," he told the horse. "It will wear out your wicker shoes."

They climbed steadily, weaving between trees, and eventually they came to a clearing. "Here is your meal," the samurai said. I feel tired, he thought. "Before, I never noticed how fighting sapped my strength, but now, Kuro," he said, addressing the horse, "I can rest when I please."

He let the horse loose. The animal looked back as if to see if it was all right. "Go," said the samurai. "Although," he said, as if speaking to himself, "it is only the first day and already I am afraid to fall asleep and dream."

The horse, halfway across the meadow, again turned his head, as if to ask if he should return.

"Go, go!" the samurai said.

Something will happen here, he thought. I sense it.

He found a good tree, its trunk moss-covered. Soft, he thought. From where he sat, he could see mountain upon mountain, some lavender, some blue, and clouds like banners obscuring some of the summits. Here and there were shining silver streaks, as if light had struck an unsheathed sword. Waterfalls and rivers, he thought. How far away can they be? Impossible to estimate distances when faced with such a landscape. He could be seeing things fifty miles away. More.

I will sleep and I will dream, he thought uneasily. But he was tired and he fell asleep at once. He was awakened by the wild whinnying of his animal, who was pawing the ground in front of him.

"What is it?" he asked the horse. "What is happening? Why are you nervous?" the samurai asked. He got up and took the horse by the reins. "Show me what it is," he said, and as if the animal understood, he began pulling on the reins and moving toward the meadow's farthest edge, the samurai following. Once there, the horse stopped suddenly and turned to look at his master. The samurai could see nothing, but just as he was about to turn back, he heard a hideous whimpering, the very sound of desolation.

"A baby," he said. "Left out here. We will look into that," he told the horse, and, dropping the reins, he walked into the darkness amid the pines. The whimpering continued. "Remember, you cannot tell where a sound is coming from if you remain in one place. Turn to the left and to the right," he recollected the lord saying.

Left, the sound was definitely coming from the left.

He pushed back the undergrowth. The sound grew louder, but it was a weak sound, as if it came from someone or something that was not grown or strong. He pushed his way through a thorn bush and found himself staring down into the eyes of a baby fox. The little fox tried to rise, but its feet would not support him.

It is hungry, the samurai thought. Had the horse pitied the sound? The samurai went forward slowly, asking the little fox, "Are you hungry? Do you want to come with me? Once I had a fox bigger than you are, and at night he slept on my chest."

Now he was almost upon the fox, and with one quick swoop, he had the fox in his arms. The little animal began to gnaw on his wrist as if it intended to escape. "And where will you go?" he asked the animal. "No biting," he said, clamping the muzzle shut gently with his large hand. "You are cold," he told the fox. "If I put you into my robe, you must not bite me."

He slid the little fox inside his robe, and the fox scrabbled and fought against the cloth. Then it was quiet. It began moving again until his muzzle emerged from the robe. It looked up at the samurai and drew back into the robe as if into a cave.

"What to feed you?" the samurai said aloud.

He could hear the fox breathing rhythmically. He was asleep. I had better boil some rice, the samurai thought. But if it wakes up before it cools, I do have some rice balls. He stopped, tethered the horse and set about building a fire, and used the small pot the villagers had given him. It makes no difference whether we go on now or later, the samurai thought. I have no destination.

"That is a kind of destination, to have no destination," he heard the old counselor say. He would have to take care. Solitude did strange things.

The horse, who was well fed, lay down on the grass, his neck stretched out, watching the samurai.

"When a fox is ill," he heard Lady Utsu saying, "first feed him rice water. If he tolerates it, you can try a few small grains."

Soon, thought the samurai, he would see ghost people moving through the woods.

I will call the fox Utsu, he thought.

"Even if it is a male?" Lady Utsu asked with a laugh.

You are tired, the samurai told himself.

As the smell of the boiling rice grew stronger, the little fox began to stir.

When the rice was cooked, he filled a small cup with rice water and waited for it to cool. The fox's little head emerged from the samurai's robe. It was wrinkling its nose. From his place on the grass, the horse watched attentively. The samurai held the cup to the fox's mouth. The fox began to lap up the rice water. It looked up questioningly at the samurai, but when nothing happened, it began to drink again. Several times, the samurai took the cup from it so that it would not drink too quickly, but soon it had drained the liquid. A short time later, it began to emerge from his robe, and the samurai held it as it climbed onto his shoulder and surveyed the scene. It was startled by each thing it saw: the horse, the man's hands, and each time, the samurai said, "*Shimpai shinasai*, don't worry." The fox appeared reassured and sat down on the samurai's shoulder. It fit between neck and shoulder quite nicely.

After some time passed, he offered the fox a few grains of rice. Not knowing how to eat them, the fox nipped at the samurai's finger. From then on, the samurai rolled the rice into a ropelike shape and offered the fox the tip of the rice. The fox ate greedily. When it finished two such strips, the samurai told the fox it had had enough, and replaced the rice wrapped in leaves in his leather saddlebags. He brought the fox over to the horse's head and said, "This is what you heard. It is also your fox." The horse snorted and put his head down. "And you?" he asked the fox. The fox gave a little cry and disappeared into the samurai's robe. "You will get to like him," said the samurai, "in time."

And so there are three of us, the samurai thought, walking back to the tree and sitting down with his back against the moss. How much more green the world was than yesterday. Soon it would be summer. He would, he thought, take the fox wherever he went. It was light enough to carry.

"Why, when we spent so much time together," Lady Utsu asked, "did we not speak more of our lives?"

"I hardly knew what mine was," Matsuhito said.

"Why did you not tell me you loved me and that you pined for me? That was expected. That would have been courteous."

"You knew," Matsuhito said. "And I did not know. Did your heart belong to Lord Norimasa or did it not?"

"Once it did," she said. "But when I met you, it did not. And now time has gone on and I have not been . . ." She hesitated. "Good."

"Bad, then?" he asked.

"Very bad."

"What has that to do with me?" he asked. "You can never be bad in my eyes."

"You are still innocent," she said. "Wise in the ways of war, and guileless in everything else."

"Guileless, my lady?" he asked. "I have forever had your image before me. I wanted no one else."

"Not even the women of the palace? Not even the night before a battle?"

"Warm creatures in the dark, featureless and speechless."

"Speechless?" asked Lady Utsu.

"I had nothing to say."

"And did any of them have a fox?" she asked, smiling.

"No foxes, my lady. They were unsurprising in every way."

"Boring, then?" she asked.

"Yes, boring."

"And so you still do not know women," she said.

"I knew you."

"That is your greatest delusion," she said. "Lord Norimasa, is he dead?"

Matsuhito told her of the lord's death.

"Your fox is waking up," she said. "Keep her close to you. Let her lie on your chest. She will like the way it rises and falls."

"Her?"

"It is a female fox," Lady Utsu said. "You see how little you know?"

Then he opened his eyes. The little fox climbed back onto his shoulder. The horse was standing. The light was still bright. "We will go a little farther," he said to the horse, and they began making their way into the woods.

CHAPTER EIGHTEEN

SOONER OR LATER, the samurai knew, he would come across someone else, even in this wilderness. Bokoshi had told him as much.
"There is never complete absence," he said. "There are endless pilgrims
tinkling their bells to scare off demons. There are hermits who have
lived in the mountains for years, most of them barely sane. And thieves
and bandits hiding in the woods until it is safe to come out, or because
they are hiding and burying their treasure. It is not the absence you
think it will be."

"But it will not be a town or a busy thoroughfare," the samurai said.
"And if you fall ill, who will help out?"
"It does not matter," the samurai said.
"Then you are going into the forest to die," Bokoshi said.
"Just the opposite. I am tired of the dust of this world."
"And so you seek another kind of dust?"
"There must be another."
"I do not think so," Bokoshi said. "All dust is the same."
"There must be better worlds," the samurai said.
"Has anyone yet spoken of them?" Bokoshi said.

THEY TRAVELED for two hours, up and up the mountain. "You can go
too far," Lord Norimasa said. "And then you are on the other side, and
you are free of the mountain's spell."

When he was in sight of the timberline, the samurai, thinking the ground would hurt the horse's hooves, and aware that he would find little for the horse and fox to eat, stopped and made a camp.

Whenever he stopped, he put the fox on a little nooselike rope and, if he intended to sleep, attached one end either to his own leg or to the pommel of the horse's saddle. He was beginning to notice that the fox had little inclination to stray very far, but he was not yet ready to let her loose and run. He did not want to lose her.

While he cooked his rice, he stared up at the timberline through the steam. How gray and like clay the rock looked. He could see few handholds on it, but to the left, he began to see trees. The mountain must be less high there. He would go that way, to the west, and then he would again go north. He had heard of snow country, of the great blizzards that buried the houses roof and all, so that the people had to dig out one window in order to let light and air come in, and the tunnels that were dug through snowdrifts over twenty feet high, because when the snow fell, there was no other way to cross from one side of a road to the other. He had heard many sad stories of people in the north who set out in clear weather, but when it began to snow, they could go no farther, and were often undiscovered until the snow melted late in the spring. Snow country, white blossoms and the white face of a woman who sometimes appeared in front of him when he closed his eyes before sleeping—any one of these things reminded him of the other two.

There was a sudden disturbance in front of him. The horse was whinnying in a complaining way, and the samurai saw that the horse followed the tugging fox, who went to the edge of the woods and disappeared inside the darkness, still tethered to the rope. Unexpectedly, the fox reappeared excitedly, ran over to the horse and lay down next to him. She had something in her mouth. The samurai went to investigate. The little fox had caught a very large rat, and the rat was twisting its head toward the fox, hoping to bite her and then escape. He took out his sword and beheaded the rat. At first, the fox seemed disappointed, as if the rat might still be alive so that she could enjoy torturing it. She then began to tear off its fur and to devour it with her sharp little teeth. She might be growing tame, but her nature would not change, he thought. The fox had taken the rat's head in her mouth and was offering it to the horse for inspection. The horse tossed his head in annoyance. This made the samurai laugh.

"When you finish eating," he said, addressing the animals, "I will tie you, little fox, to my leg. You are taking command of that horse."

He scooped the rice from its pot and poured a scoop through a square of material that served as a sieve. When he had eaten, he offered the little fox a scoop of warm rice water and rice. "You do not need as much as usual after eating such a large rat," he told the little fox. The fox promptly devoured her meal.

After that, the samurai tied the fox's rope to his leg and went to sleep sitting against a tree. When he again opened his eyes, the sun was going down and a brilliant red glow streaked with apricot streamers illumined the mountaintops. Soon the shadows would be gone until the sun came up. He became aware of a weight on his chest, and looked down to find the fox, curled there like a snake, sound asleep. She fights small wars, he thought. Her stomach was plump, as it always was after she ate. He touched the fox's belly gently, and she sighed in her sleep. Lady Utsu Fox. He had heard men swear that they had seen foxes transform themselves into women. Transform yourself, he thought, silently addressing her. Not surprisingly, nothing happened. Somewhere, he could hear the sound of a waterfall. Tomorrow, he would look for it. If he was unfortunate enough to stumble into a town, he would try to find paper and a writing set. He could keep a journal. It was something to do. Lady Utsu had once said, "I cannot keep a journal in the palace. People would take it and read it," she said bitterly. "Here everything must be shared. But I will have time and more time. Then it would relieve the boredom."

"Are you often bored?" he had asked her.

"Unless I am lost in my own strange world," she replied. He knew she would not admit openly that his presence brought her happiness. He thought she was superstitious. If she were to openly say that she was happy when he was with her, something was sure to go wrong. It had, in any case. Better to have said what she had to say.

The fox stirred, looked up at him as if to say, "Are you still awake?" and put her head down and went to sleep again.

It occurred to the samurai that he was happy. He rarely asked himself, Am I happy? Am I not? Always he had asked himself, What must be done next?

In the morning, he and the fox ate the rest of the rice, and the horse grazed in the meadow. Then, while the light was still dim and an orange and purple sunrise streaked the sky, they set out, heading west. The sunrise resembled the one that had dawned over the Battle of Nigawa. He remembered Lord Norimasa saying, "If you could wrap a woman in a robe like this, I think she would stay with you forever." He was so astonished to learn that Lord Norimasa thought of women while preparing for battle that he asked him to whom he would give it.

"Not to my wife," he said, laughing.

"Who, then?"

"First, I must meet a woman worthy of such a robe," Lord Norimasa said.

Ever since Lord Norimasa's death, the samurai seemed to hear his voice more clearly and loudly, as if, in dying, he had gained in strength. I wonder where you are and how you have fared, he thought.

He and the fox and the horse traveled in this way for two days and still they had not reached the mountain edged with pine trees. The samurai felt an overpowering desire to sleep early in the afternoon, and so he tethered his horse, and he leashed the fox to his leg. He was awakened from a deep sleep by the sound of the fox whining and making little yelps. As soon as he was awake, he heard the tinkling of bells.

Someone is nearby, he thought. When he rescued the little fox, he had not realized he was acquiring the best of sentries.

"You are looking too far afield," a man said.

The samurai turned suddenly to his right, and there was a man, sitting cross-legged on the grass.

The samurai watched him and said nothing.

"I know, I know," the man said. "You can easily cut me down with your sword, although," he said, "the fox might get in your way."

"But my dagger would not," the samurai said.

"*Honto*," agreed the man. "What are you doing in my mountains?"

"Your mountains?"

"I have lived in them for years."

"Then you can tell me how far I am from that mountain topped by trees."

"Another day's journey," the man said. "What are you doing with that fox?"

"I like her," he said. "Don't touch her."

"The last time I saw a fox, I picked it up and it cut through my tendon. One of my thumbs is almost useless."

"Which thumb?"

"Ah, you are still a samurai," said the man, laughing. "You want to know my strengths and weaknesses."

"If we go down the mountain, if we come to a hamlet, what will happen there?" he asked.

"A good question," said the man. "If they know you are a samurai, they will try to kill you. To be safe, they must think you are someone other than what you are. And, of course, they will try to steal your horse. I can invite you to my hut and we can think further."

"And will you try to kill me?" the samurai asked. "I know the ways of bandits. They send out men looking for prey."

"I have never had the privilege of being a bandit," the man said. "But you must decide for yourself." The fox went to the man. Without hesitation, she climbed into the man's lap.

"I will leave it up to the fox," the samurai said.

"You are a wise man," he said. "Small animals, small children, they are never wrong."

"It would be pleasant to believe that," the samurai said.

"Just a little way down," said the man. "It is my summer hut. I also have a winter hut. You see how wealthy I am."

To reach the hut, they proceeded down the mountain, this time following a path barely wide enough for one man. The pine branches brushed against the horse, and sometimes caught in his bridle and then snapped back. The fox, snuggled in the samurai's robe, poked out her head, sniffing at everything.

CHAPTER NINETEEN

HUTS ARE NOT PALACES, but this one was poor by any standard. The man had built his roof at a steep angle, and then covered it with thick bundles of thatch. The roof was supported by thick tree trunks. There was only one wall, the back wall. The floor of the hut was packed dirt, and there were some rough mats clearly woven by someone who did not know what he was doing. In one corner was a straw mat stitched clumsily together with long vines from which the leaves had been stripped. In the middle of the hut was a fire pit, really no more than a large hole dug out of the ground. In another corner, a pile of pine branches were drying out, to be used for the cold that could come even in summer to someone living high up in the mountains. A few utensils hung from the ceiling by hempen loops.

"A fine hut," said the man with satisfaction. You see how I have placed stones in front? And farther down the mountain is a sandy place, and I carried the white sand up and poured it between the gray stones. There is more sand in back of the hut. The only trouble is, when the rains fall, most of the sand is washed away. I spend too much time going down the mountain to bring up my sand. Would you prefer pine nuts and rice or rice and pine nuts?"

"It is hard to choose," said the samurai.

"I am almost fifty," said the man. "Who could have foreseen my destiny in the beginning?"

"Or mine," said the samurai. "Or anyone's."

"What did you expect to happen?" the man asked. His back was to him.

"Please do not laugh," said the samurai, "but I expected to remain faithful to the lord I served, and when he died, I expected to succeed him."

"And when he died, the intrigues began and you were supplanted," the man said.

"No," said the samurai. "When he died, the lord had already lost a decisive battle. Still, we ruled for some time after that, and I believed we could struggle on and succeed, but during a great battle the weather was against us. A sudden flood drowned many boats full of our soldiers. Men well hidden, anticipating an ambush, were undone by the lightning storm that left them in full view. And then there was an earthquake and eight hundred men died at once. The clan had to disband and flee. People said I brought these disasters upon us."

"When things go badly, that is what people always say," said the man. "And for equally stupid reasons, they will give you the credit if there is victory. Is it not so?"

The samurai did not answer, but lowered his head. The man looked at him and busied himself stirring his pot.

"Now, I was meant to bring a defeated clan back to life," the man suddenly said. "Everyone was wiped out but the two children who remained of the clan. I was said to be one of them. I was hidden so that when the other clans rallied to me, I would take over as the legitimate heir when I was grown. But there was an absurd accident. Apparently, the lord who remained loyal to my father—or the man thought to be my father—noticed two children, the sons of farmers whose village had been set on fire by the soldiers. There was a red sky, I remember the lord told me that, like a blazing sunset, although it was the red of burning huts. The two children were said to be identical to my sister and to me. In their hurry to create doubles who could impersonate the real heirs and face whatever dangers were in store for them, they dressed the two from the village in rich robes. Then they couldn't tell them apart from the noble's children. The lord was furious. He threatened to kill the men involved, but they were still under attack, so nothing was done.

"At the time, I was an infant and my sister was not much older, and so was the daughter of the nobleman. I was too young to speak, even though I was almost three. Men on horseback were milling about, arrows were shooting at us from the woods, and in the lord's hurry, we four children were completely confused. To this day, I don't know if I was the heir of the defeated lord, or if I was the peasant child. The same fate befell my sister. In the end, the lord who still lived decided arbitrarily. I was said to be the real heir, and the other child was sent to a blacksmith, where he was safe in the village. My sister, if that was who she was, was to be sent to the lord's palace, or to another family. I heard that years later. They say that when all that took place, my sister and I bore a strong resemblance to one another, but the lord insisted that one girl baby had nothing in particular to set her apart from any other baby. He always said, "Babies are babies. What they look like as an infant is not what they will resemble in six months." So I do not know if my sister resembled me. And she, wherever she is, does not know if she was the dead lord's child or the child of a peasant whose parents were killed when the village was set on fire. I tried to find her, but it was like looking for one grain of sand amid all the sand outside the hut here. What luck could I have? Even if I had found one of the two girls, how would I know which was my sister?"

Could the same events have happened twice? The samurai thought. He did not think so. This man must have come across documents which had been hidden. He remembered the man who escaped from the Minaga Palace with a batch of papers; Lord Norimasa said the papers might be about the four children and what had happened to them. This man seemed to know everything.

The samurai studied his face but saw no trace of any resemblance. His own face was clean-shaven except for a small moustache, but the other man's face was obscured by a full beard. In any case, if this man's sister was Lady Utsu, he clearly did not know where she was, or if he had ever seen her.

"Does it matter so much?" the samurai asked. "In the end, you will share the same destiny."

"How can I know even that? She may have been brought up in a fisherman's village, while I was tutored by scholars and finally taken in by a nobleman's family."

The samurai realized that he was jealous of the man. If the man was

Lady Utsu's brother, he was even more closely tied to her than Matsuhito was.

He is not Lady Utsu's brother, he decided. He realized that he no longer cared who his real parents were, or where his sister was. All that was over. He felt sorrow for the man in the hut who kept these questions alive, who let them lodge in his heart like arrows. Probably, he thought, if the man met his sister, he would not like her. His own desire to find Lady Utsu was probably as doomed and as pitiful.

"I never knew my parents," the samurai said. "They were killed when they were caught up by an advancing army. Then I was put in the care of farmers. They were nice enough, but I was not meant for farming. And they wanted me to be good, like the other children, so I was beaten like every other child in the village. I found it impossible to be good. I kept running away from home. And to make matters worse, I had dreams of glory. I knew every bridge for many miles and which were safe to sleep beneath. One night, I heard some bandits discussing breaking into a nobleman's storeroom. I spoke up and said, 'What about me?' First the bandits thought the bridge itself had spoken. Then they slid down the bank itself and found me. I asked them to take me with them. They wanted to know what I could do. I said I was small and could wriggle into narrow places and that I was a very good liar.

"They asked about my parents. I said they were dead and no one would come looking for me. I told them I could cook and I had very good eyes and ears. They laughed at me and said I was certainly confident. Then I learned archery from one of the band, and swordsmanship from another, and how to fight man-to-man from still another. Much later, I found out that they were all renegade samurai who had lost their clans. It was good while it lasted. A good life. They were good to me."

A shadow fell and dimmed the hut. A young man was standing facing into the room.

"My son," explained the man. He looked up at him. "He is also a bandit, as you were. A scholar and a hermit like me, producing such an industrious son."

The son stirred, bristling. "People have a way of killing bandits," he said to the samurai, "and you have a samurai sword."

"Please do not worry about me," said the samurai. "I have no interest in killing people."

"What is that wriggling in your robe?" the son asked.

"A fox," said the samurai, glowering. "She is mine. It would be unfortunate if anything happened to her."

"Please do not worry about me," said the son, imitating him. "Your name?" he asked the samurai.

"The samurai," he said.

"I am Yoshida," the son said.

The two men bowed to one another.

"So you travel with a fox," Yoshida said. "I have heard of a woman who took her fox wherever she went. She was very famous. A real poet, in the royal anthologies. I suppose the fox became famous, too. No one knows where she is or if she is still alive. Or her fox."

"I should like to find that woman," the samurai said.

"It could be done," said Yoshida. "I tell you what. Tonight, we are breaking into a storeroom. Come with us and we will inquire after that woman."

I am tired of being good, the samurai thought. Any cause, after all, is a good cause. I have led a good life and still I am not happy. Perhaps I should try the other side.

"All right," the samurai said. "Who will watch my fox and my horse?"

"I will," said the man.

"You will lose your head if you break your promise," the samurai said.

"Oh, he has been a priest for some time now," Yoshida said. "He only sits and thinks or sits and reads. He is not happy I am here. He doesn't like humans any longer, or so it seems to me. He will do what he says."

"And you?" the samurai asked Yoshida. "Will you keep your promise?"

"Why would I harm you? A good man is invaluable. You may want to continue with us," Yoshida said.

The samurai shook his head.

"Why predict the future?" Yoshida said. "Why look further than tonight?"

CHAPTER TWENTY

THE STOREHOUSE was in a fortified mansion, but it was not heavily guarded. The noblewomen, their attendants and many of the samurai had gone to see the maple leaves in Atsugawa, and the mansion was quiet.

"We've been planning this for a long time," Yoshida told the samurai. "The storehouse is built into the back wall. The Kashiwa family is as interested in protecting the storehouse from fire as from robbery, so it is built of stone. The door is solid metal, impossible to open without a key. The Kashiwas often take pilgrimages and see the sights. It has been quiet for them since the Minaga clan was defeated. While they were gone, my men have loosened the stones at the edge of the storehouse. Now we can pull them out more easily than teeth and we will be in."

"What is it you want in there?" The samurai asked. "Money?"

"Money, rice, anything we can sell well. There are other noblemen who want treasures for their houses. Screens, Chinese paintings, Chinese robes, anything Chinese. Rolls of silk—the Kashiwas are famous for their dyeing—and scrolls. People will pay a fortune rather than copy another scroll. They say that one or two of the Lotus Sutra scrolls are well illustrated, which makes them very rare. We already have our customers."

They reached the slope far above the palace, tethered their horses and began to climb down. More and more men joined them.

"Don't light any candles or lanterns until we're in the storehouse and have closed it back up," Yoshida ordered them. "There are archers left to guard the house. Most of them are drunk on saké, but even drunk, they can hit a hawk's eye in the darkness. Don't get careless."

The men were soon in the storehouse, replacing the loosened stones. Then they lit two lanterns. There were remarkable things everywhere they looked. The scrolls were there, in gold cases. The gold screens glowed in the lamplight, and some of the men began to them to inspect them. The samurai saw a painting of a woman and went to look at it. The woman was pictured half sitting, half lying, her hair hiding her face, a magnificent red and orange robe swirling about her body. She is the one I am looking for, he thought.

Yoshida came up behind him. "They all look like that," he said. "Look, Shinda, how many times have you seen the same painting? From time to time, the style of the robe changes."

"Shinda?" the samurai said, turning suddenly. There in back of him was the short, stocky man who had helped them at the Battle of Sanomi. "Shinda!" he said. "Is that you?"

"Who else is there named Shinda?"

"To meet again, how strange," the samurai said. "What path brought you here?"

"Bandits are hunted down," Shinda said. "Most of the men you knew have sunk beneath the ground. I escaped. I had to find somewhere else. I remembered hearing of Yoshida, so I came here."

"Did you not think we would protect you?" the samurai said. "Lord Norimasa would never have forgotten your help."

"Noblemen take us up like rags and throw us down when they are finished," Shinda said.

"It would not have happened that way," the samurai said.

"Where is Lord Norimasa now?"

"Dead. The clan was defeated. I left. Now I haunt the mountains."

"Then why are you here?"

"It is hard to let go of the excitement."

"It is impossible," Shinda said.

YOSHIDA, who had been supervising the removal of the storehouse treasures, came back in. "The clouds are drifting away from the moon," he said. "It's time to go."

The men began to leave one at a time. Just as the last man left, they heard the unmistakable sound of an arrow humming through the air, and one of the men who had just left the storehouse dropped to the ground.

The samurai looked around him and saw an archer on the wall. The samurai withdrew an arrow from his quiver and shot. A man fell from the wall, and then a second. After that, there was silence. The samurai hid in the shadow of the wall and waited as he watched the corner. He could see no one. He began to walk toward the woods.

"Do you see anyone?" a man called from the wall.

"No one," the samurai answered. "But they are about somewhere."

"Keep looking," said the other man. "We're searching the grounds.

"I think they're in the woods," the samurai said.

"Go there," the man said.

The samurai walked slowly, looking this way and that, as if he were searching. When he reached the woods, he heard the whinny of a horse, and followed it. The bandits were assembled.

"Don't waste time," The samurai said. "I told the mansion guards I thought you were in the woods."

"This way," Yoshida said, pointing. They rode off as quickly as they could, and soon were on the narrow path that led to the priest's hut. "There are caves in the rock above the hut," Yoshida said. "We will go there. You," he said to the samurai, "you go to the hut. Take Shinda."

"I need no protection," the samurai said.

"My father does," said Yoshida. "He does not know the world as well as he thinks he does. He has lived alone in the mountains too long. I will come with you."

YOSHIDA'S FATHER WAS waiting inside the hut.

"How many killed?" he asked.

"One of ours," Yoshida said. "By an archer."

"How many killed on their side?"

"I think three. All by the samurai. He could shoot a speck of dust."

"So," said his father. "You were right to take him. And you, Shinda? Usually you are suspicious of new men."

"I know this man," Shinda said. "We were in battle together. He made our band famous."

"You must tell me that story," said Yoshida's father. "But right now, you must have things to discuss. It is always good to consider the past."

"The past is gone," the samurai said to Shinda. "Tonight, I broke all my rules. It feels good. But there is one part of the past I would like to find. One sliver remains. I would like to find it."

"So," said Shinda. "A woman."

"She left Lord Norimasa's palace. No one has heard of her since."

"Probably she is now a woman with no feet," Shinda said.

"She traveled with a red fox. Always."

"Yoshida said you have a fox."

"Don't harm that fox," the samurai said.

"Two of you with foxes. It's unusual," Shinda said.

"It is," said the samurai.

"But," said the father, interrupting them, "a woman who travels with a fox, she might be tracked down. Through the great web of bandits."

"It's possible," Shinda said.

"Try," said the father.

"You have a fox and you look for a woman who carries a fox," said Shinda. "Is that not a mystery?"

"Certainly," the samurai said. "I should like to get to the bottom of it."

"Like throwing yourself into a well," Shinda said.

"Sometimes," said the father, "I think we are all flies caught in a web. The web gives a little and we move from one thread to another, but still, we are caught. Shinda! Make inquiries about the woman with the fox!"

"You will not find her," the samurai said. As he said it, he knew it was true. If Lady Utsu had disappeared, if she wanted to disappear, she would be harder to find than smoke dispersed into the air.

"Perhaps you will," said the father. "The web gives a little. Not often, but now and then."

"And what will it be like," the samurai said, "if these two trapped flies meet in the web that holds them?"

"My son was right," the man said. "Don't look too far into the future. As for you, aren't you heading north?"

"I'll leave tomorrow," the samurai said.

"You do not belong here," the man said. "You are looking for a dif-

ferent life. You miss the company of a clan, even if it is a clan of bandits. You miss hitting your target. You miss matching yourself against
others. But you are tired of it. What you want you cannot find here. If
Yoshida and his men learn anything, they will find you."

"How?"

"They will look for a man carrying a fox," said the man, laughing
shortly. "Be careful at the barriers and checkpoints. Shinda! Find
Yoshida and give this man false papers."

"Can I go with you?" Shinda asked the samurai.

"Yoshida's father was right," the samurai said. "I started out alone,
and I will obey my first intention. Otherwise, you would be the man I
would want to bring."

Shinda shuffled his feet and looked down at the floor.

"Go find Yoshida!" the father commanded.

"You have always been good to me," said Shinda. He fled the hut.

"You inspire loyalty," said the father. "I also appear to inspire loyalty. I think both of us are the same age."

"I think so," the samurai said. "I would like to have had a son. Or
a wife."

"I have a son and a daughter, and I tell you," the man said, "it is
better to raise radishes."

The samurai laughed.

"Here is your fox," said the man, handing the fox, whom he had
picked up, back to the samurai. "At least an animal is grateful."

"Men are capable of such sentiments, too," the samurai said.

"Men, sometimes," the man said. "But not women."

THE NEXT MORNING, the samurai was ready to leave. He watered his
horse and let him graze in an open pasture. The night before, the sky had
turned light purple. Lord Norimasa, the samurai remembered, used to
say that a purple sky at night meant the gods and the Emperor were
arranging things. "These are auspicious nights," he would say. When it
suited him, he believed in auspicious and inauspicious dates and signs.

The samurai put the horse's woven weed mat on his back and he
was starting to saddle the horse when Yoshida's father came out. The
samurai realized that the man still had not told him his name.

"You've got plenty of food in these sacks," the man said. "You won't go hungry. Eat the boiled chicken today or it will spoil. Let the fox gnaw on the bones. Where will you go now?"

"North," the samurai said.

"Yoshida and Shinda have been talking," the man said. "Sooner or later, you will have to go into a village. Villagers don't like samurai. You know that. Around here, every village was built from the ground up after samurai set them afire when they fought night battles. So you should not go in as a samurai. Better go as a bandit, or even better, take your sword and wear nothing but a loincloth. If it's cold, put on a fisherman's straw coat. You can steal one or buy one from someone in the town. All the women make them. Act strangely. Hide your horse. A horse means you're a samurai, especially a horse like yours. You don't want to run into another samurai and have him think you killed another samurai and stole his horse and helmet. Or go as a beggar or a monk. Either make a spectacle of yourself so that people will think you mad, or be as inconspicuous as possible. You'll be able to go anywhere with Yoshida's papers. They're the real thing, taken from a dead man. And," he said, "forget you ever saw any of us. If we hear anything of a woman who travels with a fox, my son will keep our promise and send him to you. You two seem destined to meet up in this world."

Then the two of them walked to the edge of the meadow and stared out over the mountains.

"Mist in the mornings," said the man. "How beautiful it looks when there are no people to spoil it."

The mist was still obscuring the trees and bushes, but their outlines were now visible. The sight from the meadow was breathtaking. On the mountain above them, bushes appeared as purplish clouds at the foot of the cryptomeria trees, and the trees were graying in the light and stood up straight in line after line. Above each set of bushes and trees came another set, all lit differently by the rising sun, all tinted differently. Nothing was sharp or boldly colored. The sun changed as it continued to rise and the scene was bathed in a soft greenish gold. It looks, thought the samurai, like a beautiful scene painted on silk after it has faded. In the center of the meadow, the greens were washed out, misty, although now there was no mist, and the bushes and pines were a brilliant green touched with gold.

"I love to look at this," said the man. "You can see the same sight everywhere in the country, and everywhere it is beautiful. When you go farther, you will come to a waterfall. If you can, go to see it. You can get there on foot, not with the horse. How," he said, turning to the samurai, "is Little Lady Fox?"

"Comfortable in my robe," said the samurai.

"Don't take her into a village. Peasants are very superstitious. Be careful. Carry your bow and arrows, at least when you're on the mountain. The peaceful places always have the most sudden dangers."

The fox's head had emerged and was straining toward the man. "May I pick her up?" he asked.

"Please."

"She has lice and fleas, but so do we," the man said. "A person could get used to a fox. Do you want to sell her?"

"No," said the samurai with a slight laugh. "We are married."

"Of course," said the man. "She has bewitched you. When you look at her, you see the woman she has made."

"I see another woman, not a fox transformed into a woman," the samurai said.

"A very powerful fox," the man said.

I wonder if we will meet again, the samurai was thinking. Even if this man was one of the four children who had been switched, the samurai had no desire to get to the truth of the matter. He had led his life, whoever his real parents had been. And last night's escapade, in which he had killed three samurai, now cut him off from his past altogether. Except for the woman.

The man took a knotted rope strung with coins and handed it to him. "Yoshida and the men decided. You deserve a share of last night's earnings. Take it. They have enough. When they have too much, they go into a town, get drunk and barely escape with their lives. I cannot wait for them to leave. Take it, take it."

The samurai bowed and accepted the money.

"It will buy food for your fox," the man said. "I hope we meet again in this world of ours."

The samurai nodded.

"It is as if we have always known each other," the man said.

"I, too, feel the same. How curious it is."

"YOSHIDA!" the man called out. "The samurai is ready to go."

Yoshida and Shinda came out of the woods and walked over.

"Take care," Yoshida said.

"Shinda, take care. And you, Yoshida," the samurai said.

"I will not watch you go," the man said. "It is bad luck. But Shinda and Yoshida have no such worries."

"We will ride partway down with you," Yoshida said. "When we come to the lane going east, we will go back."

"If you want to become a bandit, come back," Shinda said. "Yoshida said so."

"My fox," the samurai said. The man handed her over.

"Watch him, little fox," the man said.

"All right," said Yoshida, tapping his horse's side with his heels, "let's go!"

They set off. When they reached the narrow trail, the men dismounted. The three tried not to look at one another. "We will meet again," Yoshida said.

"Somewhere," said the samurai.

"Somewhere," Shinda agreed.

"Take care in dry weather," Shinda said.

Then they mounted, and the samurai headed east, and the other two began their climb back to the hut and the band hidden in the woods.

The samurai rode in silence. Then the fox began to stir in his robe. With her left leg, she began scratching violently.

Fleas, the samurai thought, and began scratching his own chest. "Now we go back to the way we were," he said aloud. The horse, Kuro, sped up as if happy to hear it.

CHAPTER TWENTY-ONE

AFTER FOUR WEEKS, the samurai found himself in rocky country. Little grew there. He was beginning to worry about food. He had no desire to descend into a village. But the fox had to be fed, and so did the horse. By scavenging for grass several hours a day, the horse was satisfied, but the samurai was beginning to feel hunger, and he believed the fox was, too.

When they reached clumps of brush or stands of trees, he would let the fox loose, and often she would return with a rat or a mouse. Late one day, when the sun was dying and the sky was dark except for a bright gold and peach ribbon outlining the mountains, he saw a hawk. He took an arrow from his quiver, pulled back his bow, sighted along the arrow, and shot the hawk down. He watched where it fell. To reach it and retrieve it, he had to tether the horse and climb up a steep rocky slope. When he reached the hawk, it was not yet dead. One sharp twist of its neck ended its life. Then he slung the hawk over his back and began the climb back, but just as he was on level ground, his ankle twisted, and he knew he had sprained it. He limped back to the horse and the fox. The horse, as usual, had lain down, and the fox was ensconced on one side of the horse. She looked very comfortable.

"I have this for you," he said to them. "We will have to stay here for a few days and there is not much to hunt for. So we will eat a little at a time."

He defeathered the hawk, built a fire, and began roasting it, holding it to the fire with skewers made of branches. While it was still bloody, he cut a leg loose and gave it to the fox, who began devouring it greedily. As each branch burned down, he replaced it with another one, and in that way the hawk was finally cooked. The samurai cut off a good piece for himself, and then continued to cook the hawk. It would last longer without spoiling if it was well cooked. He decided to save the bones to make soup if they could find nothing else to eat.

"And would you share a rat with me?" he asked the fox, who looked up questioningly. "I think you would," the samurai answered himself. "Probably you believe I am your mother." The fox looked up again. "How displeased you look, you imperious creature. No doubt you think I am your servant."

The fox dragged her hawk leg up to the samurai. Then she climbed into his lap.

"This is why I am always washing my clothes in streams while the horse drinks," the samurai said, sighing.

The fox raised her head straight up and pressed the back of her head against the samurai's chest. "You are a good fox," the samurai said, and the fox growled contentedly and then went back to gnawing and biting. The horse was now sitting, front legs tucked under, watching him. Such strange animals, the samurai thought. It is going to get harder to feed all of us.

So it proved. They had reached a barren country. The little fox caught fewer and fewer rats. The hawk had been eaten days ago. All that remained were a few rice balls that the samurai parceled out to himself and the fox. The horse managed to find enough grass, but even grass was becoming more scarce.

"Hunger," said Lord Norimasa, "does terrible things. It's interesting to think of what the people in that castle are doing."

The lord had laid siege to a castle, and his men were encamped around it. There were deep woods nearby and it was early autumn, and the scavenging parties returned with wild vegetables, berries, nuts and deer. Often, they came back with a wild boar. There were figs and other fruits and they ate well. "I have seen what men will do when they are hungry," the lord said. "I saw a man kill his horse and eat it. The man loved the horse. It had saved him many times. In the end, it saved him one last time."

I will not kill my horse, the samurai thought.

They continued traveling and he gave the last grain of rice to the fox. "Now we are in for it," the samurai said. "We won't find people here."

The next morning, they got up and started again. The fox was beginning to nip at his robe and his wrist. The samurai would stroke her and eventually she would calm down, but this, he knew, would not appease her indefinitely. They headed for a small clump of bushes and pines clinging to the rocky slope below, and there, to his astonishment, he saw a hut. The full force of his hunger hit him. He got down, ordered the horse to lie on the ground and put the fox on the horse's flank, tethering her to the horse's tail. Then he went down slowly. He walked silently. His sword did not clank, his robe was tightly belted so it would not blow and rustle in the wind, and he put his arm up to his bow so that it would not easily hit anything or fall.

Finally, he reached the hut. No smoke came through the chimney hole. Empty, he thought. Then, inside the hut, he heard the sound of scraping and clawing. He thought, An animal has gotten in and found something. He went up slowly to the opening of the hut and poked his head in. He did not want to cast a large, warning shadow. What he saw shocked him. An old woman was lying on her back, her eyes open and staring at the ceiling. She was so old that her scalp was exposed and only a few wispy hairs remained. She had assumed the skeletal face of someone who had recently died. Her mouth was open, and both her arms were raised as if to take something someone was offering her. In the dimness, he could see another human. He was digging frantically in the earthen floor with a wooden plank.

The samurai's hand automatically went for his sword.

"What are you doing?" he asked the man.

The startled man turned to him, eyes staring.

"Digging," he said. "I know she buried food here."

"Did you kill her?" he asked.

"No, master."

"But she is dead," said the samurai. "Explain." He unsheathed his sword. He had learned that the simpler the peasant, the craftier. The man was filthy. Dirt was rubbed into the creases of his forehead and those on the sides of his mouth. When he spoke and his mouth opened, the samurai saw a few blackened teeth, but what he saw most clearly was a mouth like a black hole that went right through this world to a world beyond his own.

"I found the hut. I came in. I saw her there, dying. She would die soon without water or food. I didn't try to give her anything. She didn't need help from me. It was a waste of time, understand? She told me there was food under the floor. She was hungry, but she couldn't get up. She could only lift her head or turn it. I started digging. I found three radishes and ate them and she watched me the whole time. Then I dug again and when I turned around, she was still watching me.

"'Close your eyes, Mother!' I told her, but she kept staring at me. It gave me the shakes. Finally, I turned back to her and she was staring up at the roof, just as she is now. I thought I heard a chicken. Have you heard a chicken?"

How can such people live? the samurai thought. The creature does not look human. Then he felt his own hunger. "I have not heard a chicken," he said.

"They hide them sometimes up on the roof. Doves, too. Parts of the thatch lift up and there are little animals underneath. They are clever, the old people who live up here."

The samurai saw that the man was trying to make him an accomplice. Let him think so, he thought.

"Where is the food buried?" the samurai asked.

"She said near this wall," the man said.

"I will help you dig," he said. He took out his dagger and began slowly pressing it into the ground. Finally, he felt something. "Dig here," he told the man.

The man saw both the sword and the dagger, and began digging. "A box," said the man. He dug, loosening it, and brought it up.

"Give it to me," the samurai said. He took the wooden box and opened it. It was stuffed with dried chestnuts and dried persimmons.

The samurai left the box near the dead woman's feet and began to use the dagger again. Once more he felt something. "Dig," he said.

This time the man brought up a sack of rice wrapped many times in rough fabric. "Give me that," said the samurai, then he put the sack near the wooden box. He was careful not to turn his back on the man.

He went back and began probing with his dagger. "Dig again," he said. Another box emerged, filled with dried yams. The next box was filled to the brim with strips of smoked deer meat.

"Give me something!" the man insisted. "I am dying of hunger."

"As you gave the woman food when she asked for it?" the samurai said. "Help me slide her mat over to the other side. Her best things will be under there."

He probed where the mat had been, and found several boxes and several more sacks of rice. There were clay bottles sealed up with pickled radishes and other vegetables.

"Give me something!" the man demanded. He began to scrape at a loose mound of dirt. When he stood up, he held a dagger. "Give me something!" he said again.

"Take it from me," the samurai said. "What good will it do you? The angry spirit of that woman will turn that food to poison. You slept with that old woman before she died, didn't you?"

The man turned scarlet. "Take it back!" he said.

"You did, didn't you?" asked the samurai.

"Don't give me that nonsense!" the man said. "She hasn't been dead long. She's still warm. You can still use her."

"Animal!" said the samurai.

The man knew he was no match for the samurai, but anger and hunger were in him and he lunged. In an instant, he lay stretched out on the floor, his head attached to his neck only by a flap of skin. He lay at a right angle to the woman's feet.

"Abui yo," said the samurai, the word for "goodbye" that a bandit would use.

Outside, the horse was lying down, but the fox was alert and watching. The samurai brought out the boxes and the sacks and fastened them to the horse's saddle. "Get up," he told the horse. They would have to find another hiding place, and then they would eat. Before he mounted his horse, he took a dried yam he had put in his robe and gave it to the fox, who growled and began gnawing. At least someone is not hungry, the samurai thought. The dead woman in the hut is not hungry, nor was the man he had deprived of his head.

They traveled for the entire day, only stopping to eat. On the highest slopes, the trees, still bare of leaves, were ashen and looked dead. Slightly below them, the young leaves had come out and were a brilliant yellowish green. Where the samurai now rode, the trees were fully leafed out and were a deep green. Occasionally, there was a rustle in the leaves, a new leaf would drift down and eventually a bird would fly out, swoop over them and return to the trees. Birds repairing their nests, the samurai thought. The song of the birds caused the fox to wake up and her muzzle emerged from his robe. She looked around, saw nothing she could catch or eat and went back to sleep.

He was passing through magnificent scenery, places few people had ever before seen. To the left of the road, there was a steep falling off, and below it, a gravelly plain filled with enormous rocks that resembled a grand structure now in ruins. From another point of view, the rocks looked like a crop sown by giants. The rocks were light gray streaked with black, and huge as they were, each one longer and taller than a mansion, they were sheared off at the top as if a monster had harvested them and cut through them with a sword. The samurai stopped a moment, made note of the place and where it was should he need to find it again. It was an excellent hiding place. Then he went on. He absorbed very little of what he saw. Instead, he was riding through a scene made up of a dead old woman lying on her mat and the dark shape of a man scraping at the earth.

Yes, the world is like that, he thought. There are people who live and die like that. They are born into that world and they never escape it.

"If someone dies a horrible death, and that death haunts you," said Lord Norimasa once, "I know a remedy. You must take an image of that person and burn it. While it burns, you must say a prayer for the dead, and apologize to the dead person. You say these things while the image is burning. It need not be a work of art. Two twigs, crossed at right angles to each other, and a scrap of cloth, and on it you write the name of the dead person. If you do not know the name, you write something like, 'Dead person on the plain.' After that, you will no longer be haunted."

The sun was dropping in the sky. The samurai stopped and let the fox into the woods. He followed the fox and snapped some twigs. When he came back to the road, he made a little cross to represent the dead woman and tore a little piece of cloth from his robe. He would not be able to write the words 'Dead woman in the hut' on the small piece of cloth, but surely, he thought, he would be heard if he intoned the words while the fire burned. When he finished the image, he dug a little pit and started the image on fire. The pine sap spit and crackled as if it were the old woman's body. "I am sorry," said the samurai. "Now your spirit will be at peace, dead woman in the hut," he chanted, as if reciting a poem. "Let us both be at peace. I would not have killed you," he said.

The little fox returned, once again with something in her mouth.

"How did you get a bat?" the samurai asked her. "You are a most redoubtable fox. Will you eat it?" he asked her, but she was already eating it. Bats have such sharp teeth, the samurai thought sadly. The fox takes too many chances. "But that is what it is to be a fox," Lady Utsu had said, about what he could no longer remember. Perhaps the bat was already dead when the fox found it, the samurai thought. He did not like to think of harm coming to the fox.

He looked around him. Below, there was a river winding through a deep gorge. The sun turned coppery, and the river was liquid copper, and in it, a brighter path of the same color seemed to lead through the river as if it were a road that would bear people and carriages. It is beautiful here, he thought. He looked around suddenly. Everything had turned sharp. The old woman was gone, or at least not so vivid. To live to such an age and die that way, the samurai thought. I do not want to live that long.

The wind was rising and the sun declined. It was colder than he had expected in these mountains. He thought of widening and deepening the pit he had just built and warming himself at a fire, but the smoke would be visible to anyone who might be nearby. He decided instead to cut some tall grasses and bind them. When they dried, they would keep him warm. He would do that tomorrow. Tonight, he and the fox would sleep next to the horse.

He had, perhaps, an hour of daylight. He remounted, and they left the road and entered the woods. He tethered the horse to a tree and went on foot. When he came to a flat rocky face where there were no trees, he went back for the horse. "We are staying here," said the samurai. Then he started a small fire and cooked a little rice. The fox seemed anxious to go into the woods and explore, but the samurai told her that she had had enough of the woods for one day, and so kept her tethered to his leg once they began to eat. The horse was loose and began grazing at the grasses between the trees. The fox observed this, and regarded the horse balefully. "Really, you do not know what is good for you," the samurai said. He fed the fox some rice. It seemed to the samurai that the fox ate with a poor grace. "When he comes back," the samurai said, "I will give you a strip of deer meat." The fox considered him as if she did not know whether that promise was sufficient. Then she whimpered and curled up on his chest. The fox, the samurai thought, was a person of some character. She seemed to have been born believing she owned the world. He envied her. He had never felt at home in the world, and certainly not as if he were entitled to privileges.

"Take what you are offered," Lord Norimasa had said. "These things are not offered twice."

"But if I do not deserve them?" the samurai had asked.

"How many men deserve what they are given, either good or bad?" Lord Norimasa replied. "Take them. You would take Lady Utsu if you dared. And I think she would go."

He looked at the ground.

"I have embarrassed you," Lord Norimasa had said, laughing.

"I am only her bodyguard," Matsuhito had said.

"Only," repeated Lord Norimasa. "Think again."

WHEN THE SUN came up in the morning, the river below was bathed in gold. When the water looked like that, the *kappa* and the *oni*, said to be lured by the gold, leaped into the water and drowned there. The trees were still dark, almost black. The samurai munched on a rice ball and watched the trees as the brightening light tinted them pale green. "There are remarkable places in this world," he told the fox. "Later, you can go into the woods. If there is no danger." The fox had come to understand the words "woods" and "danger." She kept quiet. Probably she was still half asleep. The horse got to his feet and the side he had slept on was dusty. The samurai pulled up some grass, clenched it in his fist and used it as a brush to groom the horse's head. Then they set out to find water. It was not difficult. Little ponds were everywhere. We could stay there, he thought. But the idea of snow country drove him on.

He realized he missed the sight of the sea and the sound of waves pounding on the high rocks. On rough days, the foam was high above the rocks, almost like cliffs. Then everyone began to fear a typhoon. He remembered the salt smell of the sea, and low tide, when the sand below the cliffs was patterned like a sand garden in a castle. I cannot go everywhere, he told himself.

The sky was darkening, as if predicting rain. The air was moist and the temperature suddenly dropped. The samurai got off the road and looked down. Below were vertical rows of gray rock, almost obscured by mist. At the bottom, the water was bright blue, very odd in a vista like this one. The mist, so resembling a spider's web, rose up from the river and now threaded its way around the rocks. The vertical rocks resembled a cemetery, and the mists, spirits of the dead. Let us get out of here, the samurai thought. Inside his robe, the little fox was restless, as if expecting something. "This is no place to hunt," he told the fox. "This is a place where something will hunt you."

It turned still colder, and when the samurai again looked out over the mountains, he saw the trees covered in frost. There was a cracking sound. A tree must have broken under the weight of the leaves weighted down by the ice. Above him, he heard the sound of cracking ice. The mist on the pines near him hardened, and when the wind blew, the ice cracked and sparkling icicles fell.

The samurai asked himself, Should we stay here or should we go down? He looked at the piles of straw he had bound up and tied to the horse. We will take our chances here, he thought. When the light was almost gone, he ordered the horse to sit down, and the horse obediently sat on his side. The fox climbed out of his robe and onto the horse. "I will sleep next to you, Kuro," the samurai said. "Try not to move." He took the three bundles of straw and covered himself with them. They were surprisingly warm. "Come here, lady," he told the fox, but she was content where she was. However, in the morning, when the dawning light awakened them, the little fox was curled up against his side, having burrowed beneath the bundled straw.

We have found a good place, the samurai thought. It has been a while since we've seen so much as the roof of a hut. We will go on as we were. North, always north.

It was a peach and orange sunrise and the ice reflected the colors. Truly, this is paradise, thought the samurai. He and the fox ate as they rode. The path was going down. He expected to find a small meadow where the grass was not frozen, but they did not find one. Finally, the horse decided for himself, and left the path of his own accord. He happily ate the grass, now more snowy than icy, and the samurai realized that the horse was drinking as well as eating.

After that, they went on.

They were still on territory the samurai believed was free of people, but at a bend in the road, the scenery abruptly changed, and they found themselves in a bamboo grove. Bamboo lined both sides of the road and met overhead. Now the samurai was cautious. These trees had obviously been planted deliberately. The presence of the bamboo implied the presence of people, people who might have died and gone, but also people who might still be alive. Already, the fox's head had emerged from his robe and her nose was twitching the air. "People," the samurai said aloud.

He slowed their walk and let his right hand rest on the sword hilt. The light was now going. In half an hour, it would be dark. And then he heard voices. The fox's ears were up and inclining toward the woods on the left. "This time we go together," the samurai said, speaking gently. "I trust myself, but I cannot be sure you two will be safe alone." So saying, they entered the woods.

Gradually, the voices became louder. These were the voices of men, rough voices, raucous, some angry, some laughing. What is this place? he asked himself. Abruptly, the trees cleared away and he saw a meadow and many white stones. A cemetery in the middle of nowhere. "Who goes there?" he shouted.

From behind the stones, men began to emerge. In the half-light, they resembled spirits risen up from graves. "Speak your names and your reason for being here," the samurai demanded.

"We live here, sir," one man said softly.

"You live in the cemetery?" the samurai asked.

"We are outcasts," the man said. "We have handled the dead and butchered animals and made things from leather. There is no place else we can live."

"And when you are not here, you raid villages," the samurai said. "You are bandits. Tell the truth. I do not dislike bandits."

"We are not bandits," said another. "We are *eta*, the unclean. We remove night soil in the darkness. We could not be bandits. Even a bandit despises us."

"*Eta*," said the samurai. "Is this true?"

"You are uneasy with us now that you know we are *eta*. You will not want to touch anything of ours, much less touch us. We know how it is. No one speaks to us. If people need something to be done, they leave notes for us and we take them up and read them and do what we are asked. They leave money for us wrapped in vine leaves. They do not like to see us. They hate the sight of us, and if you were honest, you would say you do, too."

"Where are your women and children?" the samurai asked.

"Come out," said the soft-voiced man.

Women and children, half starved, resembling the men, began to appear from behind gravestones. "So you are not bandits," the samurai said. "You would not bring your families with you if you intended to pillage and burn."

"Bandits are a great deal wealthier than we are," the soft-voiced man said. "We are worse than bandits."

"And what made you worse?" said the samurai.

"We were born worse," said one of the men.

"I should like to stay here," said the samurai. "No one is happy to see a samurai enter a village. And my fox," he said, tapping his chest, "she would not be a pleasant sight for the villagers who think foxes are evil."

"I beg your pardon, my lord," said the *eta*. "It would be best if you did not stay here. Too many of us have had friends and relatives killed by samurai at crossroads when they saw an *eta* and decided to test their sword on him. We know that it is permissible, and that it is not permitted to complain to the authorities. They are completely uninterested in the doings of *eta*. You yourself may have used an *eta* for such a purpose."

"No," said the samurai. "If I needed a body to test, I went to the jail and used a body already in the morgue."

"I have often wondered," said the soft-voiced man, "why samurai are not also *eta*. You kill others, sometimes in great numbers, you cut off heads and put them on stakes. You are always soaked in blood. Why are you not an *eta*?"

"Some people think we are and look down on us," the samurai said. "The courtiers at the palace, for example."

"How can you stay here?" asked one of the men. "We will pollute you."

"Who will know?" asked the samurai.

"If you are found in our midst, it will not be you they will beat or kill," said one of the women.

"Quiet!" said the man with the soft voice. Apparently he was the leader, or one of them. "One of our daughters escaped to a village far from here. She married a man and had two daughters. Somehow it was discovered that she was an *eta* who was passing as a human being. She was dragged from her house and burned at the stake. The villagers stabbed the children before burning them. That was the villagers' mercy. Since then, we are closely watched. Every three or four months, someone comes and counts the adults. If anyone has died, we must show the corpses. This is not a good place for you."

"I think you will be safe while I am here," the samurai said. "In return, I will ask you to watch over my horse and my fox. Do not let the fox venture too far into the woods. She has a peculiar passion for rodents. Do not let me disturb you. I will go behind the highest stone."

"Please do not come too close to us," said the leader. "You will be polluted."

"If I am not already polluted, I will not be polluted now. As you said, I have killed many men and shed human blood."

"Don't listen to him," said one of the women. "He has a sword. He may be tempted to use it on us. He may be a spy tempting you to say something you can be punished for."

"Are you a spy?" asked the leader.

"No," said the samurai.

"Can you not treat me as one of you?" asked the samurai. "I have heard of *eta* and seen *eta*, but I know nothing of their lives. I should like to know."

"We are *hinin*, nonpeople," he said. "We are dangerous to others."

Without warning, the fox let out a sharp wail.

"Someone's coming," the samurai said.

Silently, as if they had never existed, the *eta* disappeared. Now there was the faint sound of voices, and as he listened, the voices grew louder.

Thieves, criminals, thought the samurai. He went in the direction of the stone behind which the leader had disappeared.

"What do they want?" he asked.

"They have killed a man and now they want to bury him here where the body will not be discovered. We must allow it or they will kill all of us. When it is done, they will kill one of us and threaten to come back to kill the rest of us if any of us speaks of what happens."

"A dead body could be useful to you," the samurai said. "One of you could escape. When the authorities come to count, you could show them the body and say it was one of your own who died. But this time they will not kill any of you. Someone tether the horse, and don't speak," he said. "Go behind the stones. Leave this to me."

The samurai put on his helmet. In the moonlight, he looked monstrous. He strapped on his quiver and slung his bow over his shoulder. He sheathed his sword and moved silently into the woods. Once behind a tree, he looked into the cemetery. The place looked entirely deserted. The voices were becoming distinct.

"No one's there?" a rough voice asked. "Where can they go? Are they all dead?"

"If they've tried to escape, we will hunt them down," another answered. "If they talk, we'll be crucified."

They rode up to the cemetery and the man called roughly, "*Hinin!* Come out or we will kill ten of you!"

There was no response.

"Come out! I will not call you again!"

An unearthly yell split the silence. The men looked at one another.

"A spirit?" someone asked.

Another, more horrible shriek rent the air.

The horses were moving about restlessly and the men turned to look at one another.

"*Hinin*, are they shape-changers?" asked one of the men. No one answered him.

The samurai stepped out into the open. He wore his helmet, his faceplate and a loincloth. He had heard enough mediums so that he could easily imitate them. He knew how horrifying he looked, especially in the dim light of the thieves' lanterns. The faceplate was a dark red, and particular attention had been paid to its mouth. Instead of the usual black hole surmounted by a white moustache, the mouth was filled with the teeth and fangs of an *oni*.

The samurai let loose his war shriek again. "Answer!" he thundered in his terrible voice. "Who are you? Explain why you pollute sacred ground."

One of the men laughed nervously.

"This ground is already polluted," said the leader. "The *hinin* have polluted it." His voice trembled in spite of himself.

"I decide what pollutes," said the samurai. "Are you the ones I am waiting for?" He took an arrow from his quiver and prepared to shoot it. "Leave the corpse here and go," he ordered. "I, the *obakemono* of the cemetery, command it."

"He may only be human," one of the men said. There was a rumble of assent.

The samurai let an arrow fly and the leader fell.

"You have heard of the scream that kills?" the samurai asked. "You will all die in agony. But you," he said, looking at the man standing next to the fallen leader, "I will waste an arrow on you. I need corpses! I look at you and see you are already corpses! I will have corpses! Ones in good condition!"

He loosed another arrow and the second man fell to the ground.

"If there is a deaf man, and he is alive after the death scream, I will shoot him," said the samurai. "Now I begin. I am opening my mouth." He began his war scream, but the men turned and fled. "Come back! Come back!" called the samurai. "I need more corpses! You are stealing my corpses! Come back at once!"

But the men were fleeing precipitously down the mountain. The samurai heard a loud thud and a shriek of pain. A horse whinnied in panic.

"They will not come back," said the samurai, sitting down on the ground cross-legged.

After some time passed, the samurai ordered, "Come out! It is safe now. Take the two corpses and dress them in clothes so they will look like you. Three of you can escape."

"Three?" said the leader of the *eta*.

"The dead man they brought, and the two I killed. Now I am tired and my throat is sore. If you will bring me water, and water for my horse and my fox, we will sleep behind the tall stone. Do not try to ambush us."

"We are indebted to you," said the head of the *eta*. "But we cannot repay you. We have nothing."

"When morning breaks, I will ask you a question. Its answer is important to me. And I will be curious and satisfy my curiosity by seeing how you live. There is nothing I want that I don't already have."

"What can we know, living here?" the leader asked.

"Go to sleep!" the samurai said.

"At night," said the leader timorously, "we keep watch."

"Why not? It is a good idea," said the samurai.

He led his horse to the tall, thin gravestone and tethered the horse to it. The little fox, who was disturbed by the samurai's spectral screams, began to stop moving about. "A good night's work," the samurai told the fox. "Time to sleep. I like to kill as much as you do. I tell myself all that is over, but when there is an opportunity, I am happy. Sit down," he told the horse, who lay down in front of the stone. He lay next to the horse's back and piled his straw bundles over him. In an instant, the three of them were sound asleep. He did not hear the *eta* woman who stole up to look at him and see that he was warm enough. The little fox peeped up at her, decided there was no danger and went back to sleep herself.

"An escapade worthy of you," said Lord Norimasa. "Military tactics are one thing, but tricks are best."

"Thank you, my lord," said the samurai.

"You are on the right track," Lord Norimasa said. "Information. That is what you need."

"But does she still live?"

"Information," Lord Norimasa said again.

The samurai stirred in his sleep. The fox moved out of his robe and settled herself on the horse's side.

The morning dawned gray and lifeless. Mist was everywhere, hiding most of the gravestones, exposing parts of them as it began to lift.

"It will rain today," said the head of the *eta*.

This was a signal to begin building cooking fires, and when the fires caught well, the *eta* began cooking what they had. To the samurai watching, it seemed as if everything the *eta* owned went into a pot of water and became a soup, all the ingredients indistinguishable. The samurai took down a little rice and some dried strips of deer for the fox. The horse was already grazing, moving from tree to tree.

The samurai placed his pot near the fire of another *eta*. Immediately an uneasy silence fell.

"What is the matter now?" asked the samurai.

"My lord," said the *eta*, "it is not safe for you to eat so close to us. For your own sake, move off."

"You believe other people's superstitions? About you? As if they were true?" asked the samurai. He continued building his fire. "Suppose the villagers begin to say that you eat bodies? Will you believe it?"

"There is always truth in superstition," said the elder. "If not, why would it exist?"

The samurai felt his anger rise up. Was it possible that they were as credulous as they appeared? Had they not just witnessed a display in which he imitated a ghost who was part *oni*? Then it occurred to him that perhaps they believed he was the *obakemono* he claimed he was when the thieves appeared carrying their corpse.

"Such superstition is invented to serve the inventor. When we knew a battle was to begin, we invented many superstitious rumors.

None were true. What was true was our determination to win. That appetite fed our ingenuity, but the superstitions we invented existed only in our minds, and then, by contagion, in the enemies'. We did not fall victim to our own traps."

"The nobility is different, my lord," said the *eta*. "Our tradition tells us what is true."

"It is useless, talking to you," said the samurai.

A short little wail pierced the scene of mists and smoke. "Now what?" asked the samurai, looking down and seeing the little fox looking up at him. "Someone is coming." The *eta* again disappeared as if they themselves had become part of the mist.

A frightful-looking being was emerging from the mist. It wore a helmet and faceplate. "Where is Matsuhito?" boomed the apparition.

"Shinda! Is that you?" the samurai asked.

The apparition removed its faceplate and Shinda's face appeared.

"You have news?" the samurai asked.

"Only that she is alive. And her fox is probably alive. But no one knows where she went. Is that news enough for you?"

"Yes," said Matsuhito. "It is enough and more than enough."

"So now you will try to find her. Take me."

"We have been through this before," said Matsuhito.

"I hate graveyards," said Shinda, looking around uneasily. "They say men who are not quite men live here."

"Come out!" called Matsuhito.

The *eta* began to appear. Their fear made them approach slowly and circuitously. In the mists, they were like creatures of smoke and cloud.

"They are real?" Shinda asked. "If they are real, I can defeat them."

"Remember this place," said Matsuhito. "It is one you can come back to if you need to hide. They will help you."

"*Eta* will help us?"

"I will ask them to."

"We do not need help from the *eta*," Shinda said angrily. "You are a strange samurai. First bandits, now *eta*. They say samurai are fearless, but you are beyond that."

"If I thought only as a samurai," he said, "I would have been dead long ago. I was lucky to be raised in the country."

Shinda snorted. "Yoshida said I had to find you and tell you what he knew. A slave woman told him."

"Her name?"

"She would not tell it," Shinda said. "We will meet again," he said, turning his horse and riding off. The mists swallowed him.

The samurai sat down and began eating. While he had been speaking to Shinda, an enormous cauldron big enough for three men to bathe in appeared and was placed in front of a fire. Protruding from the cauldron were a horse's four hooves. The water was bubbling violently, and grayish bubbles emerged from the gray, scummy water and then collapsed into it again.

"What is that?" the samurai asked.

"A horse, my lord," said the *eta*.

"You are going to eat him?"

"We will eat him, my lord, but first we will remove his hide to make leather. Then we will eat the rest of him."

"Is the head in there, too?"

"The head came with the horse, my lord."

"When you get a dead horse, you simply put him into a pot?"

"Oh, no," said the *eta*. "First we take out his insides. They are not always good. If they are, we cook them separately. We think horse meat is very good."

The samurai got up and went to the cauldron. The horse was placed in upside down and the water sometimes made it rise up and then let it fall back again. He stood for some time staring at the horse's four feet. It does not pay to die, thought the samurai, and sometimes it does not pay to live. I will see this sight in my dreams, he thought. He went back to his place. The leader of the *eta* approached him. "Wicker shoes for your horse. Sandals for you. A wadded blanket, a little dirty, but if you tie it with ropes and put it in a river on a warm day, it will come clean and dry quickly on the rocks. Several sets of polished chopsticks. Some dried *tanuki* meat. We see the fox likes it. Dried persimmons. A wicker basket hat to keep off the rain and hide your face. These things are not heavy. We have thought things over. Three of us will try to escape. One could come with you."

"No companions," said the samurai, eating his rice.

"I understand," the leader said.

"You heard me send off Shinda, and he is my friend. It is not because you are *eta*. But I have a favor to ask. I used to hear that all *eta* families were in communication. Is it true?"

"We try."

"Then someone, somewhere, may have heard of a woman who travels with a fox. Has anyone heard of such a person?"

"Yasue, you have come the farthest. Have you heard of such a woman?"

"I have heard," Yasue said.

"I want to find her," the samurai said.

"It may not be possible," Yasue said. "She was heading north and there was a rumor about an island. I heard she was looking for a boat and a man to take her, but the sea was very stormy. After that, the story ends. If she persuaded someone to take her, she may have drowned. If she did not drown, who knows what island she was taken to? A woman traveling alone, anything can happen."

"Who told you this?" the samurai asked.

"An *eta* who cleans dead fish from the beach."

"He would tell the truth?"

"He is a stupid man. He does not imagine what he doesn't see or hear."

"I would ask you to continue to gather information about this woman," the samurai said. "I will also be going north. Can you find me if you learn anything?"

"We can find a man who travels with a fox," Yasue answered.

The samurai nodded. Then he said that he must leave, and he was grateful to have been treated with such hospitality.

"You embarrass us," said the head *eta*. "We do not know where to look." It was true. They did not.

"The three of you who are leaving," he said, as he mounted his horse. "Plan your escape carefully. Clean yourselves and find good clothes. Fix your hair like other people. Walk the roads as if you belong on this earth. If you do all that, you will succeed. Until we meet again!" he said, and turned and left the path that led through the woods back to the larger road.

CHAPTER TWENTY-TWO

SHE WAS DREAMING, or she was a spirit dreaming, or she was a cloud of energy that refused to disperse, or she was about to cross over into the land of the dead where everyone who comes to that point begins to dream of what has gone before, and in her dream, she could see the green mists of spring. She was asked for by the Empress, and so she went to the palace to teach her Chinese, and she and the Empress grew very close.

But it was not spring. It was the second week of the eighth month, and the heat had been unbearable for weeks. Even when the rain fell it did not cool. Instead, a hot wetness bore down upon everyone. There was no one who did not complain of the weather. People moved languidly, and the blinds were shut against the heat.

At that time, most of the court ladies repaired to the slightly cooler northern wing of the palace, where they put up their screens and were sleeping in a room together. For a time, she slept next to Lady Kitsu, both of them behind a screen. Because they could not sleep, they began to compose poems. From time to time, Lady Kitsu would whisper her name, and if she answered, Lady Kitsu would read out a poem. At times, she read out a line only. Then she would revise the line and read it again. She would say better or worse or try again. Every so often, she would read out a line of her own to Lady Kitsu. Eventually, one of them would call softly, but there would be no answer, and so she knew that the other had fallen asleep.

But as the heat increased, Lady Utsu became convinced that it would be cooler in the old room in the east wing because the stream beyond her veranda, swollen with recent rains, rushed onward making its happy, cool sounds. Because the Empress often called upon her late at night when she awakened, the lady was given permission to move as she wished from one part of the palace to another.

She got up, telling no one, and, wearing a light summer robe, made her way back to her old room. The nightingale floors, especially made to squeak and alert the inhabitants to intruders, sounded as she walked, and as she passed, one or two guards raised their heads, but when they saw her, they again lowered their heads and fell back into sleep. She lay down on the mat next to the blinds and was about to raise them a little when she heard a man's voice say, "See how the clouds roil, and how disturbed nature itself seems."

Life can be decided in an instant.

She was certain she recognized that voice. Moreover, she felt that she had been waiting years to hear it.

Another man answered, "I think a storm is coming soon."

"How often," said the first man, "lightning flashes down like a silver arrow."

There was a rumor that one of the princes had fired an arrow at a man to discourage his pursuit of a certain woman. The two men were talking of this incident, but they were circumspect. Instead they spoke of roiling clouds, disturbed nature, bolts of lightning.

It would not do for her to hear them, she thought.

She lay as close to the blinds as she could. Her robe was soft, but she was nervous. The slightest rustle would alert them. And of course she was terrified that she might sneeze.

The night before, there had been a festival, a poetry contest, and the man who had spoken first now began to recite one of the poems that had made an impression on him.

"Did you take particular notice of her poems on waiting?" he asked. Then he said, "'While inside her breast, her heart chars.' I thought that was a most remarkable line."

"Lady Utsu is a most exceptional woman," the other man said. "But she is too passionate. I speak for myself, of course."

The first man laughed. "You with your principal wife and many consorts! How could you live with a woman of strong passions?"

Just lately, the women had heard that the Empress herself was so enraged with the Emperor's acquiring yet another consort that she picked up a vase covered with phoenixes, a vase which everyone admired, and, when she heard her husband's voice in the hall outside her partition, flung it over the partition at him. It shattered, and the Emperor was greatly shocked. The Empress retreated into her own room and allowed none of her attendants inside. Instead, she lay on her mat, heaped with robes as if she were freezing and it was the dead of winter.

"Women with strong passions are for the young," the second man said.

The first man did not reply.

Meanwhile, the moon freed itself from the thready clouds, and where she lay, the room was flooded with moonlight.

Without thinking, she turned to her right, found her inkstone, applied some water and slid a thin sheet of white *michinoku* paper toward her. She wrote this with her brush:

> *The moon that has obscured the clouds*
> *Now shines out brightly.*
> *I find myself carpeted in silver.*

She dried the ink with white sand, folded the poem into three, twisted both ends, and then placed the sheet of paper on a small tray of silver. She thrust the tray through the blinds onto the veranda, making as much noise as she could.

Then she lay absolutely still and waited.

Both men fell silent. She could see them through a crack in the blinds. Their posture bespoke danger. Then the second man saw the sheet of paper.

He inclined his head. The man whose voice had so arrested her was closest to the paper. He bent down and picked it up. Now her heart pounded until her body shook, and she thought, Surely the wrong man will take this paper and read it. But it was the man the poem was meant for who took it up and read it.

"So," he said. He slid the paper into his robe. "The palace still stands. A foolish poem by a woman," he said.

Her body burned. She thought of the months she had spent training impulsiveness out of herself. Useless.

"Aren't they all in the north wing?" asked the second man.

"Someone has wandered in the heat," said the first man.

"She came for the river," said the second man. "It has a cooling sound."

They both nodded.

The second man laughed softly. "Remember your proverb," he said. "'A cool man and a hot lady make poor companions.'"

They began moving away as if nothing had happened. But just before they reached the arch of the bridge that spanned the little river, the man whose voice she seemed to have listened for forever turned and stared intently at the blind through which she had thrust the poem.

In that instant, she was convinced her face was visible to him. In the dark, she reddened.

He will not find me out, she thought, and, as a flush spread through her body, she felt intolerable regret. She thought, I will make him pay for this.

Then he turned away, and he and the other man quickly passed over the bridge and disappeared into the deep shadow cast by an enormous oak.

Again, she lay down on the floor next to the veranda and tried to sleep, but her eyes would not close.

Again and again, she thought of what she had written. Repeatedly, she burned at the inadequacy of what she had committed to paper.

Now she heard the small sounds of people stirring in the palace.

It would be best, she thought, not to be found here when dawn broke. She went back to the north wing and lay down next to Lady Kitsu. She heard Lady Kitsu stir in her sleep as if she had heard her.

She thought, It means nothing. Who is he to me? He will not find me out. Still, she burned with humiliation. And confusion: what had possessed her?

Then she must have fallen asleep.

TIME PASSED, and she did not see him or hear him again. Because she had not signed her name to the poem, she thought he would not know it was she who had sent it. Yet every day she hoped for a sign from him.

One night, the women were awakened by the fire drum. At first they did not believe that there was a fire in the palace, but they soon noticed that the room in which they slept was too hot even for summer, and guards were pounding on the lattices shouting, "Wake up! Wake up!" The ladies in the north room threw thin robes over their heads, whereas others, who had experienced fires before, simply rushed out of the rooms with their heads uncovered. They shielded their faces with their long sleeves.

She was still hesitating when she saw an odd flickering on the polished wood planks of the floor, and realized she was seeing the shadows of the flames themselves. At that point, she grabbed Lady Kitsu by the wrist and dragged her out of the room. The entire north wing was in flames. The fire had a voice of its own, and roared like the orange beast it was. Several guards were mounted on the fire towers, in which huge kegs of water were kept for such emergencies, and the guards began pouring the water down onto the flaming quarters of the north wing. At first, the corridors lit up with an orange glow, and then the fire burst forth, and the corridors were consumed and collapsed immediately. As the women watched, one room after another was filled with an orange light and then seemed to dissolve into smoke and ash as if the partitions were nothing more than a sheet of paper thrown into a brazier. Great clouds of smoke rose above the red and gold flames, and when water was thrown down, a terrible hissing filled the air and clouds of steam rose up. The two women stood as if paralyzed, staring at the north wing, which had so suddenly been erased. At times, the smoke covered everything, but suddenly the flames would break free of the thick smoke, and then they saw the flames' wild dance. It was impossible to believe that the flames were not themselves alive.

Many of the soldiers arrived, and the women who had been in the north wing were roughly pushed away from the scene of the fire. Lady Utsu was still holding on to Lady Kitsu when a strong hand grabbed her own wrist and began pulling her in the direction of the gate that led out of the castle into Ichijo.

"Please get into the palanquin," said the voice of the man leading her. She recognized his voice immediately, and without hesitation went to his palanquin, dragging Lady Kitsu with her. Lady Kitsu appeared incapable of speech, and if left alone would have continued staring at the burning wing of the palace.

When the two ladies were seated in the palanquin, the man opened his fan and placed a letter on it. "A letter from your brother," he said. "I was about to bring it when the fire broke out."

She had no brother.

She took the letter and put it into the sleeve of her robe.

She had not thought to cover her face when the fire was discovered. The flames were so bright that the scene was lit up as if by daylight. Her face was plain for anyone to see.

"How disgraceful to be seen like this," she murmured. She put up her sleeve as if to shield her face, but soon realized it was not possible to remain hidden. The excitement of the fire, the agitation caused by the letter, the sound of the man's voice, her mortification at the smudges streaking her clearly visible face—all these together made her teeth chatter as if frozen with cold.

"I shall try to look the other way," the man said. "Although Mount Fuji itself is not disgraced when clouds make their way across the summit, just as soot on your brow cannot disgrace you."

She was mortified.

"Your hair trails from your cart," the man said, and indeed, it was sweeping the dust. Her hair was almost two feet longer than her body. She was as well known by her hair as by her poems and by her insolent treatment of men who approached her. She drew her hair up as if it were a rope and twisted her hair so that she could place it on her lap. She knew that her face was scarlet, and she knew, too, that her face was unadorned by makeup. She was beside herself with worry, because she had not heard the fate of the other women in the north wing, and did not know if all of them had gotten out. Although she thought of Their Imperial Majesties, who might still be in danger, she was dismayed to find herself worrying about the spectacle she now presented. Her face was smudged! Perhaps the smoke had drawn two sets of eyebrows onto her face. For reasons of vanity alone, she was in agonies.

Four of the other women were thrust into her carriage, and the man gave directions to the driver, and the ox yoked to the vehicle was soon jostling along. When the carriage reached the palace gate, an enormous jolt sent them all flying into the air, and she remembered the many times each of them had been thrown about in this way.

The fire was contained, and after several days they were again settled in the castle's east wing. The heat of the fire and the heat of the summer combined to torture them. The heat of the unopened letter burned even hotter.

When they had moved into their rooms again, when she was once more behind her screen which had miraculously survived the fire, she unrolled the sheet of paper twisted at both ends. Paper cherry blossoms were attached to the sheet. In the moonlight, she could read what had been written there:

> *The perfume of summer:*
> *And yet the aroma of cherry blossoms wafts toward me*
> *As if a door opened in the moon*
> *To remind us that spring, although gone,*
> *Remains waiting behind the silver door.*

So it was written by the man whose voice she had heard that night! The letter he had given to her was written by him, not by her imaginary brother. He had not wanted others to know of his interest in her. He would have exposed her to others who might have tried to persuade her to spy on him.

Beneath the poem, he wrote, "Even those who live to the left of the north rooms minister to those who write such superb poems."

Then he was the minister of the left, a man known for avoiding entanglements by women. Her heart grew heavier as she thought of this man whom others called "the minister who avoids women." And yet he knew she had written the poem passed to him that night, and now he had written back.

She rolled the letter into a small scroll, again twisted its ends, buried the paper cherry blossoms in one of her robes and lay down to sleep. But she did not want to sleep. Again and again, she conjured up his voice and everything he had said.

In the morning, the Empress called all of them to her, saying that she wanted to see for herself that all were uninjured. She was wearing an apple-green robe of the thinnest silk, the hem thickly embroidered with deep red chrysanthemums, and beneath it, she wore three light silk purple robes, the first quite light in color, the other two deeper colors of the same purple shade. Before she dismissed the women, she said, "A moment, Lady Utsu. You have been having adventures." It would be futile to conceal anything about the letter she had been given.

"Might you have the letter?" the Empress asked, and when the lady produced it from her sleeve, the Empress laughed and said, "As precious as that? Carrying it about in your sleeve, afraid of the cold, like an egg about to hatch?" And then she read the letter.

"So," said the Empress. "Even the minister of the left is susceptible. His calligraphy is unmistakable. He is a most remarkable man. Perhaps it was your calligraphy that drew him to you?"

Then she knew that the Empress had seen the letters she had written that hot night when she thrust it through the blinds and sent it forward so rashly.

"How much more interesting than a fire this is," said the Empress, and the lady again thought how lucky she was to be in this court, and not in the somber court of the retired Empress, and once more thought how adorable was the Empress, and how beautiful she always was, and how lovely were her emotions.

"You may see him again someday," the Empress said, "and next time, it may not be necessary to burn down a wing of the palace to accomplish it."

"Your Majesty," she said, but the Empress interrupted her and said that she found both of their poems quite interesting and quite unusual, not the kind of poems recited again and again during the poetry contests.

"But they are full of mistakes," the lady said.

"These are poems of the heart," said the Empress. "I find them beautiful and accomplished. You will attain more than any of us who scribble correctly." From her sleeve, she withdrew a thick sheaf of paper.

"I am giving these to you so that you will cover these sheets with writing. I await the notes you shall write on this paper."

The lady was stunned, and did not dare look up at the Empress. The Empress smiled and said, "I only wish I could see the minister of the left so I could give him a gift of the same paper and ask him to write down his notes about his life for me."

At that point, the Empress took pity on Lady Utsu, and because the women were all steaming their robes over incense baskets that day, she sent the lady back to the others.

What began by sending the letter, thrust from the blinds with such heat, was as yet not clear, but would become so.

She stirred in her sleep. In her sleep, she asked herself, Why am I remembering this? It was not the minister on the left who wrote the poem. It had been a young samurai. What was his name? If I cannot remember his name, does it mean he has died? She began to sob, and when her eyes opened, her cheeks were wet. But as her eyes opened, the name came to her.

But, she thought, if I looked for him and found him, how disappointed he would be. Not disappointed: horrified. "How time does such things to us!" she said aloud, and began weeping again. Her hair was streaked with gray, her face had wrinkled and when she last caught sight of herself in her rain barrel, she thought she saw that her teeth were yellow. Near her pillow, the animal stirred. He was a red fox, and as she looked at him, she saw how gray the fur of the animal's muzzle had become. Time touching us all like frost, she thought. Was she remembering the young samurai because her life was coming to an end? She had not dreamed like this before.

Everything was garbled. Events of which she dreamed were out of order or distorted. The minister of the left was an old man when she received the samurai's poem. The man she heard speaking outside did not have his voice, nor had he the voice of the young samurai. She remembered that young man's voice.

It was some time since she had dreamed of the Imperial Palace and the Empress. If only she could dream of Lord Norimasa, now gone up in smoke. If she could dream of the samurai who stayed with her during the plague. It was, she thought, part of her punishment that these men would not appear to her, not even in dreams. But the frozen man appeared to her often. She had dreamed of the frozen man, and it was her punishment to have him appear in her most precious memories when she did dream.

Then she remembered, as she always did, that he had been killed because of her whims, and that many still remembered what had happened, and continued to hate her. The frozen man—his voice was the voice she had heard in the dream.

She rarely dreamed of the man to whom she had fed ground glass so long ago. People cannot suffer forever. In time, she persuaded herself that when she ground the glass to the powder that killed him, she had not acted on her own will. Lord Norimasa had commanded her. She had no choice. If that were true, she now believed, the evil was not her own, any more than a messenger delivering a scroll was responsible for the words written on it. But it was also true that she had taught herself never to think of Lord Tsurunosuke. If she thought of him long enough, the old, corrosive acid returned and ate at her heart.

She was a woman who killed her men. She often asked herself, Would I do it again? The answer she gave was always this: "I would not." But how, with a past such as hers, could she ever be sure?

CHAPTER TWENTY-THREE

THE SAMURAI TRAVELED NORTH and north and again north. He became accustomed to seeing people and scenes from his past appear as if they stood there in front of him. He understood that this happened after he traveled many days without enough food and without speaking to another human being. He was happiest when he stumbled upon a place that looked as if it had never been visited before. Not long after noon, he came to a birch forest and a light rain began to fall, almost a mist. The scene had a vividness of its own, as if the samurai were seeing it in ghost light. He stayed on his horse and looked at the view for some time. It was strange, he thought, that often, as he first saw something, he knew he would remember that thing forever. He would remember these white trees, these fluttering green leaves, the small rain almost like a mist, forever. He asked himself, Do I really want to find the woman with the fox, or was it human nature to need a goal, something to pursue? As if asking the question summoned her up, he saw her lying beside him on the mat of her room, the two of them covered by her robes. He knew at the time that he would not forget that night. What he could not know was how much he would continue to long for her. He believed Lord Norimasa when he said, "Love is like brocade. It fades, not in the light, but in time as it passes." Yet often his memories were more brilliant than what he saw when he looked about him.

And what had that time meant? They were both exhausted by the plague. They both wanted comfort and some happiness. He told her things he never told anyone before, and she did the same. It was an interlude, and it would fade. Yet as time passed, their nights together grew brighter. He wished she were here to see these birches, or that he could describe them to her. It was so still with the rain falling soundlessly, so unearthly, as if the scene before him were bleached.

After all, he thought, I must have loved her.

Of course she had not loved him. Why should she have?

THE FOX WAS now becoming restless. She was growing larger and it was less comfortable having her in his robe. She no longer had the look of a nursling. Soon she would be the size of a dog, but she had no sense of her own size, and she was puzzled and angry when she could not rest inside his robe. Instead, he took to holding the fox in his lap and keeping one arm around her. They rode slowly because of the rocky, steep paths, and the horse responded easily so that he could control her with one hand. The fox would reach up to lick his cheek, intending to nestle beneath his chin, and would then discover how uncomfortable she was. She would look up angrily at the samurai, as if he had done something to disturb their pleasant arrangement.

"If you grow any larger, you will need your own horse," he told her. He decided to get down and to let the fox down. He would follow her into the birch grove. All of them were hungry. The horse could graze while they went in.

The fox bounded happily into the grove. The samurai stood staring at the trees, one after another, lined up like soldiers. Even though there seemed to be little light, what light there was illuminated each tree trunk so that the trees resembled lightning in a dull sky. A lightning forest, he thought. The idea made him smile, these trees rising up in a storm and fracturing the night sky.

Three sharp yelps brought him to attention. The fox had found something. He went farther into the grove, his hand on the hilt of his sword. There is nothing here, he thought. He still did not see the fox, so he continued on. Suddenly the trees gave out and he found himself in a clearing, and at its far point was a hut tilting crazily. "Utsu!" he called to the fox, who ran to him. "Must you find houses everywhere?" he asked her. "Now we must worry."

The door to the hut was gone, and even from the outside, he could smell damp and mold and decay. There was a small pile of rat droppings in the corner, but even the rats were gone. Someone has died in there, he thought, but when he went inside, there was no one. No footprints disturbed the dust that had blown inside. The ashes in the fire pit had been dead for a very long time. On the floor were more rat droppings. At least that meant there would be no mice. The farmers had taught him that rats and mice would not occupy the same space.

"So," he said to the fox, "someone always leaves something behind. But there is nothing in this place." The fox ran outside and looked up at the roof, whimpering. "Rats?" he asked the fox, who began running back and forth frenetically. "I will help you up," he said, and picked up the animal and set her down on the deeply sloping roof. Almost immediately, there was a small shriek. The fox must have found a rat.

Something must be left, he thought again, and began to walk around the tilting house. A violent rainstorm could bring it down, he thought. Its wood was so old it had silvered and so soft that he could press his fingernail into it. He could see the ground here was good and rich. Someone must have planted something at one time.

He came to a place where the grasses were thinner than the rest and he began to look, parting the grass. There was the unmistakable sight of radish leaves. That would keep them going. He used his dagger to dig up many of them, putting them in his robe until he could carry no more. Then he saw the kind of vines that meant melons and followed them until he found the fruits. They were not completely ripe, and if left alone they would grow bigger, but he cut them loose and made a small pile of them. There are yams here, he thought, looking for the leaves that would betray them. He found them and dug up as many as he could find. His sacks had been almost empty. He would fill them up.

The samurai went back and forth to the horse, picking up sacks, filling them and returning. The fox was still up on the roof. Every now and then, the samurai heard another little shriek, and he knew what the fox had found. Then came an abrupt flutter and cheeping of birds, and two suddenly flew up into the greenish sky. The fox had found a nest. He came closer to look. The grown birds had flown, but he was sure the fox was eating the eggs in their nest. He finished filling his sacks and sat down on the grass. There were wildflowers everywhere, yellow and purple, and huge red poppies. Someone once planted them and they spread. There had been a great bed of poppies near his quarters in the castle. He cut some and decided to take them with him. They would wilt quickly without water. He found some large plantain leaves soaked with rain and wrapped them around the stems. Now they would last longer. He was not, he saw, resigning himself to the transience of things.

The light was going. If there were a rainstorm, the house, bad as it was, would afford shelter. He sat down again on the grass. It was unpleasant to go into a house like this whose inhabitant had vanished from the face of the earth with barely a trace. "It is like entering a tomb," he said aloud.

He intended to call the fox, but he could hear her up on the roof. He sat down beneath the overhang. It came almost to the ground. Someone had wanted shelter from the hot summer sun. Long, long ago, *nagai aida,* but the sun was as bright and hot as ever.

He rode up to Lord Norimasa, who was overlooking the charred remains of the valley after the Battle of Sanomi had almost ended.

"I wonder," Lord Norimasa said, "how long people will remember this. And what they will think of it. If they remember it at all."

"They will remember it as a great battle won by a great commander," said Matsuhito.

"As the old counselor said, already it is hardening into myth," Lord Norimasa said. "There is talk of my cruelty and your cunning. That is what will remain. Such is my thought."

"Myths can last forever," said Matsuhito.

"They can," said Lord Norimasa. "But the men in those myths do not resemble the men who lived. And the events do not duplicate the things that did happen. You may be the hero of the myth and I will vanish, or it may go the other way. It will all be a fairy tale," he said, sighing. "Who will remember Lord Sugimasa? Who will remember how he inspired such loyalty? Who will remember why we fought this battle? How many hundreds of battles have been fought and forgotten? Chance, all of it. Yet we must live our own lives, without regard to what people as yet unborn will think. We are so careful not to stain our honor, yet who will remember we even existed? Will even a whiff of incense be left? A faint smell of charred wood?"

"They will remember," Matsuhito said confidently.

"Does it matter?" Lord Norimasa said, turning cheerful. "We have won the battle and when everything is over, we will get good and drunk! That is what matters! No more of this drifting into the mist as if I had already become smoke! It is a good life!"

"It is our life," said Matsuhito.

"Whether we have chosen it or not," Lord Norimasa said, turning to look at him.

What people remembered of Sanomi was Lord Norimasa and his cruelty. People recited in detail Lord Norimasa's order to stitch together the head of Lord Minaga, and everyone went into the greatest detail when they described how the lord insisted that he himself impale Lord Minaga's head on a stake. Matsuhito was known as "the man who came from nowhere" and worked with bandits to trap the Minagas so that they were burned when they tried to climb the wall he had put in place, and, like ants caught in sap, they burned and crackled as if they were already in hell. "Such cleverness amounts to evil," someone said, and so the myth had hardened further, and Matsuhito was thought to be an evil man. Nevertheless, he was greatly admired.

Matsuhito remembered Lady Utsu's polished metal mirror, and how, when you looked into it, only one small part of the oval remained in focus. Everything else distorted or vanished. Mirrors gave warnings. The women of the castle would do anything to acquire a good mirror. Lady Utsu feared her mirror. "Suppose it truly reflects the world as it is?" she asked him. "Then it is a terrible world."

"It is only a mirror," said Matsuhito.

"You know better!" she said angrily. "Why try to comfort me about what cannot be changed! At least we can recognize the truth!"

He had never met a woman like her before or since.

"Utsu!" he called out, summoning the fox, who jumped down from the roof and loped up to him. "It is nice up there, *ne?*" he asked her. "We will cook some yams and tomorrow we will set out again."

The horse, well stuffed, was returning from the grove.

"We will sleep in the house tonight," the samurai told them. "It is a house beyond defilement."

The yams were stringy, but the samurai found them delicious, and the fox could not eat enough. "Do you want me to starve?" the samurai asked her. Her ears went down and she lowered her eyelids and looked away. How human she is, he thought. "It's all right," he said to the fox, who crept toward him and climbed into his lap. "You are getting very large, Lady Utsu," he said. "In the winter, when it comes, it will be pleasant to have you lie on top of me like a thickly wadded robe."

He stroked the fox, who grew so happy that she let her head droop over his lap, so relaxed that her tongue hung out. The samurai thought that she might be getting too tame. How would she survive if something happened to him? Yet he was sure Utsu would be a redoubtable foe to someone who might attack her.

"How cold it is," the samurai said aloud. "Let us go inside."

He took up a thick bunch of pine twigs he used as a broom and swept the floor clean.

"It is very cold," he said, shivering.

The fox came close to him and stood up, her front paws on his thighs.

Is something wrong? the samurai asked himself. She rarely does this. The fox yelped sharply, and, puzzled, watched him closely.

Probably a rat in the walls, the samurai thought, and he ordered the horse to lie down, lay down himself next to the horse's back as was their custom and the fox clambered up onto the samurai's side, moving up his body until she could see his face. She seemed to be watching it.

"This red face you see is a sunburn," he told her, and then they were all asleep.

SOMEONE STABBED HIM. He grabbed his dagger, and when he tried to rise, he could not get up. Someone has stabbed me and set the hut on fire, he thought. How hot it is here! We must get out at once!

But there was a moon, and he clearly saw that he was alone in the hut, the horse was asleep, and the fox was watching him worriedly. As he began to reason more clearly, he felt the repeated stabbing in his side continue. He felt his wrists. They were hot. His blood pounded through his veins. His eyes were sore. The fox whimpered and began to wash his face with her tongue, and when he reached up to touch his forehead, it was very hot. I have Lord Norimasa's sickness, he thought. He comes to me so often I have caught it from him.

He wanted to relieve himself, but that meant he would have to get up and go out of the hut. After several attempts, he was upright, and he staggered through the doorway and barely got some distance from the hut. Ridding himself of his full bladder burned horribly. He remembered that Lord Norimasa had complained of the same symptom. After that, he thought that he felt a little better, but the stabbing continued, and now he was extremely thirsty. The clay water jug was back in the hut, and after steadying himself, he slowly made his way to it. He managed to open the jug, drank a great deal and, exhausted, collapsed near the horse. The fox was patting his face and licking him wherever she could reach his skin.

The samurai liked being licked by the fox. Usually such washings left him sticky from the fox's saliva, but now the saliva cooled him as it dried. He felt for the place where the daggers were driving into him, but found nothing there. By now he was shaking, shuddering, as if he were having a fit. He could not control the shaking. He knew his body was hot, but he felt as if he were freezing in the snow.

The yams must have been poisonous, he thought, but then the fox was as healthy as ever. If I did not know better, he thought, I would believe a spirit was inhabiting this house and meant us no good. He had brought a horse into the house. Such a thing would anger any spirit.

He lay still. The daggers became less sharp, but he was growing hotter and hotter, and the fox was beginning to yelp softly. She began to dig at his clothes as if she wanted him to go with her.

If I am going to die, the samurai thought, she may know a good place. Again, he managed to get himself upright, and, with the fox tugging his robe, he went into the meadow, half stumbling.

"I cannot go any farther," he told the fox, intending to lie down in the grass, but the fox was insistent and kept dragging at him. "I will collapse," said the samurai. "Let go of my robe."

But she continued to lead him. He followed, stumbling, his eyes closed. It was too much effort to keep them open, and even the light of the moon hurt his eyes.

He heard the sound of rushing water. He opened his eyes. There was a clear stream. "You want me to drink?" the samurai asked the fox.

The fox yelped in annoyance, let go of the samurai's robe and walked into the river. She looked back at the samurai on the bank and began yelping again and again. She wants me to come into the water, he thought, but the water is cold and I am already shivering. She yelped again and the sound hurt his head badly. Before she could yelp once more, he waded into the river and immediately slipped on a rock and toppled into the water. The fox made her way to him and climbed onto his back as if to keep him where he was.

After the first shock of the cold water, the samurai began to feel better. His head stopped pounding and sounds did not torture him. It was comfortable lying in the water, and so he remained there. After some time went by, the fox again began her yelping, but now, when she tugged at his side, she seemed to want him to come out of the water. Now he did not want to go. The fox began yelping. She sounded like a very strange baby, crying.

"All right, all right," said the samurai. "*Takusan.* Enough."

He had less trouble walking and he followed the fox back to the hut. The stabbing in his side turned to a dull pain and his blood still thundered through his veins, but he was better than he was.

He thought of removing his wet clothes, but the clothes were cold and comforting. He lay down near the horse, but the fox interposed herself between them and tried to roll the samurai away. It was easier to move away from the horse than to argue with the fox, and he moved away from the horse. He must have fallen asleep.

A thin, milky light filled the room. When the samurai opened his eyes, the fox was standing beside him, watching him. His clothes had dried in the night, probably because his body was so hot. It was still hot. He staggered to his feet and went to the jug of water and drank deeply. There was not much left. He would have to carry it down to the stream, but he felt too weak to make the attempt. As the sun brightened, he saw that his wrist had a yellowish cast, and when he pulled open his robe, he saw that the same was true of his entire body.

Moxa. An herb to cure illness. The bandits had given him some, and so had the *eta.* "A man on a horse will not outrun an illness, even on a road," the *eta* leader had said, and he stuffed both into one of the sacks. I am too tired. I will look for it later, said the samurai, lying down, and in an instant he was asleep again.

He was dreaming. He was asking, "Will I die here?"

A woman stood wearing a long white robe, with her face to him, and said, "No, you will not. But you must sleep. Obey the fox."

"I am so hot," he said.

"Obey the fox," she said again.

"My body aches and I am yellow," he said.

The woman laughed. "Men make such mountains of these things. Yet they will put up with a wound and not whimper." The leaves began to rustle and her hair began to whip in the wind.

"Go to sleep," she said, and then she was gone.

"Are you dead or alive?" he called after her.

"I am not dead," she called out. But it was only her voice, borne on the wind.

After that, he stopped tossing and fell into a deep sleep.

When he next awakened, his body and his clothes were drenched.

Exhausted, he went to the water jug and found it empty. After he walked back, he immediately fell asleep. The fox lay down next to him, but did not touch him. The horse wandered out of the hut and was grazing in the meadow. Then he disappeared into the grove. The fox yelped sharply, as if to remind the horse to return, and the horse whinnied in the birch woods. The samurai forced himself to get up and go down to the river to fill the water jug.

Days passed. The fox spent her time on the roof catching rats and occasionally going into the woods and eating other things. The samurai knew this because she came back with a scratched nose and blood on her muzzle. He looked carefully at her and went back to sleep. When his eyes again opened, she was lying along his side, her long nose just beneath his ear.

One morning, the light was very bright, and although it hurt his eyes, he was very hungry. He drank the rest of the water in his clay jug. He found it much easier to move. He went down to the river and filled up the jug and returned tired, but not exhausted. One more day, he thought, and he could again ride his horse.

This time he made some *moxa* tea and drank it. He ground up the *moxa* leaves, lay down and put little cones of ground powder on his chest and set them on fire. This would draw out the illness. The fox, however, would not put up with this, and tossed them off his body with her tail, and then rubbed her bottom and tail against the damp dirt floor. After that, he gave up.

The samurai made a fire pit and boiled some rice and then waited for it to cool. The fox stood up near him. She believed that the rice water belonged to her. When the rice cooled, he ate voraciously. When he had eaten all of the rice, he gave the fox the rice water. She was always playful after being given rice water.

After two days, he felt strong, and decided to go on. It seemed to him that the days were growing chilly and the nights were cold. If he was to reach snow country, he would have to keep going. Now, while traveling, the fox, who was less and less comfortable in his lap, began running along with the horse and darting into the woods, often coming back with a bird or a small animal. He always greeted the fox happily, even when she returned covered with mud. He believed the fox had saved him by dragging him to the river. She was a female, after all, he thought. She must already have known what she needed to do.

North, and again north. Day followed day. He came upon gorges that seemed bottomless but must have had rivers that ran through the beds because he could hear the sound of running water. At such times, the fox watched him suspiciously, as if he were thinking of trying to climb down. They came to a large river bordered by a wide sandy beach, the sand brown and carved by the waves. He tried to remember all the different colors that combined to create a sunrise and a sunset. His face became weathered by the sun, which no longer bothered him. When the fox grew tired, she would yelp, he would stop the horse and she would jump up in front of him and sit across the saddle, rammed against the red wood pommel. She was becoming heavier. Now, when she jumped on, the horse turned to look at her and tossed his head.

Finally, they came to another gorge. When he looked down, he saw red leaves, and red vines climbing the light-filled trees. Autumn was coming. He had a wadded silk jacket, but little else. It was time to begin looking for shelter.

The samurai thought it would not snow for some time. Instead, there was a heavy downpour, and after several hours, the rain appeared to have no intention of stopping. They were in stony mountains, and he began to look for a cave. In the last few days, they had passed many, but now he could see none. The bedraggled fox, her fur beaten down, looked half the size she had seemed before the rain began. They went on because there was little else they could do. The lightning split the sky, and thunder began to roll. The fox heard that and jumped back up onto the horse, who appeared to stumble, but then soon got his footing. "Get down," said Lord Norimasa. "Before the lightning strikes you."

The samurai got down, and the fox came with him. They continued to walk. It was difficult to see. The rain poured down so heavily that his eyes continually filled with water. He blinked ceaselessly. Once he blinked and saw something dark in the mountain face on the right. He blinked again. It might be a cave.

It was not difficult to climb up to the dark place, and the dark place was, to his great relief, a cave. It was large and deep and tall. He went back for the horse and led him up. The three of them were soon inside. The samurai looked out through the opening of the cave and could see nothing but a dense wall of silvery water.

"We were lucky to find this," the samurai said. He took off his wet clothes and lay them on the horse's back. They were thin, and the heat of the horse would dry them quickly. He unpacked his straw raincoat and put it on. It scratched, but it was warming. "When the rain stops," he said, "we will find wood and start a fire." The roof of the cave and the walls were damp and cold. The fox whimpered and lay down near the horse, and the samurai lay down near the fox. It was dark in the cave and the samurai could not see anything in the depths. He could see only the heavy water, like a waterfall, curtaining the cave opening. He fell asleep.

He sensed that the fox was going out and coming in, but he did not wake. He had heard of fierce bears who lived in caves, but there was no sound but the heavy rain falling.

He opened his eyes in the morning to find the horse standing and sunlight streaming in through the opening. Now he could see the outlines of the cave and how deep it was. He went outside, hoping to find something dry enough to use as a torch, but everything was soaked through. Then he thought to look in the cave. Surely someone else must have taken refuge in it before.

Near the south wall, he found a small cache of firewood. He took one branch, used his flint, finally lit it and began to explore the cave. The walls were smooth, but looked as if steps had been cut in them. The firewood was burning slowly because of the dampness. He continued deeper into the cave. That was when he saw him—a samurai sitting upright, propped against the wall.

"Did you, too, take refuge from the storm?" Matsuhito asked. "We have some food."

The other samurai neither stirred nor answered.

Matsuhito had thrust another stick of firewood into his sash, and he lit that one, too, and went closer. What he had mistaken for a living man was a skeleton still dressed in elaborate armor. The cords that bound the metal plates of his armor were purple, a color afforded only to people of great importance. The samurai must have held a very high rank. He must have removed his *mempo*, or faceplate, before he died. The skull was fearsome. The samurai went back for two more sticks of wood. He sat down in front of the dead samurai and contemplated him. No odor of death or decay emanated from him. He had been dead a long time.

But what had killed him? Matsuhito's first thought was that the samurai had been killed through violence, either by bandits or thieves. The skull, however, showed no evidence of having been cracked. No hole attested to a lance thrust through the man's skull. He moved closer. The parts of the bones that were exposed by the armor showed no signs of breaks. He had simply found his way in and died here. Starvation or illness must have killed him. If the plague was raging, and he had been on a campaign, he might have been left behind by the others, and he might have looked for a place to shelter himself.

The sticks flared up and he saw a piece of paper next to the man. He bent forward gingerly and picked it up. It was the man's death poem.

> *It is dark*
> *And it has always been dark.*
> *I go now into a greater darkness*
> *With a heavy heart.*

He put back the paper and moved away from the dead samurai. He thought of the slanting hut in which he had sought shelter and where he himself had almost died. He knew nothing of this man. He might have been a great warrior, even a *daimyo,* but there was nothing to say who he once was. Matsuhito might have heard stories of great courage performed by this man, but all that remained was a skeleton and armor. If only he had worn a banner with a *mon* on his back, then there would be hope of finding out who he had been. Now there was nothing.

The fox approached and began gruffling. Perhaps she could still smell the stench of death. She was uneasy faced by this phantom. The samurai, nevertheless, felt reluctant to leave him. Once he left, no one might set eyes on this man again. He lit another stick, and carefully placed it against the breastplate of the armor. "At least you will see for a small time," he said. He watched the light flicker over the dead man. He thought he saw him move. He took a second stick, broke it in half, and broke one in half again. Then he stripped the bark from one piece and used it to bind two pieces of the branch into a cross. That would serve as an image of the dead samurai. He took the little image and placed it against the burning branch propped up on the dead man's breastplate. The image caught fire. A white smoke spiraled up from it. "Now you are going up, at least a little higher," said Matsuhito. He got up, and he and the fox walked back to the entrance of the cave.

Yes, his spirit was going up, he thought. But did not really believe it. The dead samurai was still alone in a greater darkness, and his heart was still heavy.

CHAPTER TWENTY-FOUR

THAT NIGHT, and for many nights, he dreamed of the dead samurai. At times, he thought he saw his face and a pink flush that showed he was still alive. But usually he saw the skull and the black hole beyond the teeth, and then it seemed to him as if he heard a great rushing of air and felt himself drawn through those teeth that looked so like tombstones into the wide darkness beyond. He would awaken in the morning and think, All roads never end. Even if you are not walking in a circle, the road never ends. Every step you take toward snow country takes you farther away from it. By now, snow country had become a mythical land, something as unreachable as heaven. He tried to remember the stories he had heard about the snow country, the women who wove silk all winter in their dim rooms, and then spread the silk out on the snow to bleach it, doing this again and again. Someone told him that when the narrow street filled up with snow between the houses, the people walked on top of the packed snow. Every so often, someone slipped, and once a peddler fell down the slope of snow and burst through a family's window, bringing a small avalanche with him. He would like to see such things. More and more, he believed he would not.

Summer was turning to winter while he journeyed north. The ravines, gorges and mountains blazed red with maples. He often stopped to take up the most beautiful red leaf he had yet seen, and threw out the one he had been keeping in his sack. He never had that leaf for long, because he immediately discovered one even more beautiful. Autumn, that season of melancholy things. Instead, the brave display of color gave him happiness. The leaves knew how to die as well as samurai did. Look how they made a celebration of their death! He was fascinated by the spectacle, as if he had never seen it before, and he neglected his preparations for winter. Only when he stroked the fox's fur did he realize how much thicker her fur had become. In the mornings, when the horse snorted, white mist rose from his nostrils. Time, he thought, to gather more firewood. The horse could only carry so much. He would have to strap a large amount to his back and begin to walk on foot. He would have to find grass and begin drying it and tying it together into mats beneath which he and the fox could sleep. The horse, too, would need a straw blanket. Now that the samurai knew what had to be done, he set out down the road in a cheerful mood.

Both sides of the road were deeply wooded. It had been some time since he had found a good meadow. When the sun rose in the sky, it was small and pale, resembling the moon when it appeared before the sun set. There was a chill in the air that touched the cheeks gently and reminded him of chilled jellies kept in the palace storehouses. The leaves that had not yet turned color looked as if they were spun out of gold and jade. Truly, he thought again, this is a beautiful world.

The fox returned with something in her mouth and disgorged a large cicada, and the samurai took the insect in his hand and watched it move about. The cicada let out its strident song. Soon the sound of the cicadas would be gone.

"Good fox," said the samurai. The fox must have carried it very carefully in her mouth, and he reached down and gave the insect back. The fox hesitated and dropped it. She was thinking about jumping up onto the horse and trying to fit herself between the samurai and the pommel of the saddle but decided against it.

"Don't worry," he told the fox. "When we find a meadow, we can lie down together." They set out down the road. Sometime after noon, the temperature dropped suddenly, the sun went behind a cloud and the wind came up. A thunderstorm, thought the samurai, but the fox was not betraying her usual nervousness. The boughs of the pines were rising and falling in the wind and red leaves began to float down toward them. The sky turned a deep silver, as if the great dome above had tarnished. To the samurai's disbelief, snow began to fall. The snow fell lightly at first, small, feathery flakes, but before they reached a bend in the road, the snow was falling thickly in large flakes that blew toward them in slanting lines. Then the wind changed, and the snow began blowing straight at them. There were sounds of branches cracking and a large bough fell in front of them. The weight of the leaves and the snow on the leaves was bringing the weak boughs down. If this had happened when I lived in the palace, he thought, soothsayers would have been summoned, and diviners, and the Ministry of Magic would instantly have been consulted. Would the snow augur well for the Norimasa clan or for the Minaga clan? It was hard to believe that only he knew of this spectacle and there was no one to tell of it. It came upon him as suddenly as the snow had appeared in front of him: the world had nothing to do with humans or even with animals. The world and the weather turned on their own wheels and what happened, happened. Nature was as irrational and precipitous and impossible to predict as any one man. He would have to get down. The road was too slippery for the horse.

He was reminded of an early battle when Lord Norimasa intended to set fire to a castle using spinning, flaming arrows. Metal boxes full of live coals were brought for that purpose. And then it began to rain and finally to snow, and all the fiery arrows were extinguished and the Norimasa army was forced to retreat. In another campaign, a castle held out against Norimasa's siege until torrential rains began and overran the river that protected the castle. He and Lord Norimasa watched while the river rose and continued rising until the waves began to pour through the castle walls. Inside, the men were in danger of drowning. "So their defenses turn against themselves," Lord Norimasa said with satisfaction. "The storerooms will flood and the mud holding the stones of the castle walls will crumble and they will be at our mercy. It will be like shooting nightingales in a cage." How strange our lives were, how much stranger if we tried to anticipate what would happen in them.

"Many are the times when I've thought we rely too much on human ties," Lord Norimasa said. "How much better it would be if we could ally ourselves with the weather. Then we would always be victorious."

The snow continued to thicken. The colored leaves changed to white. The travelers themselves were white, a white ghost, a white horse, a white world. The samurai stood still, deciding. They could not stay on the road. In the woods, the trees and the leaves would shield them from the snow, but there was danger of falling branches and trees.

Yet the samurai decided that they would be safer in the woods. He got down and walked in front of his horse into the woods. The ground was treacherous and full of holes and dips in the ground disguised by the blanket of snow. He walked carefully, and if the ground felt unsafe, he left the horse and found a safer path. The fox was leaping happily through the snow and throwing up sprays with her muzzle. She leaped up to catch snow in her mouth.

There is always someone who is happy, the samurai thought.

The wind died down and then it was silent. The snow continued its quiet falling. He remembered his mother saying, "You must not say, 'Yuki ga furu.' That only means that snow falls just as rain falls because it is in the nature of snow to fall. Instead, you must say, 'Yuki ga futte imasu.' Snow is falling. Do you see the difference?"

As a child, the samurai was impatient. Why would someone say that snow falls if it were not snowing? "No, I don't understand," he said, and his mother sighed. She was such a gentle woman, this woman who became his mother after the battle that killed his true parents in the village. "Please think about it," she said. "Always try to know where you are so you can get back," his father had told him. "Really it is not so hard. The sun comes up in the east and goes down in the west. If you are facing the rising sun and want to go north, you make a left turn. How hard is that? You must remember it." But the young boy said, "I always know how to get back."

"And if you got turned around in the snow? Or if you are in a deep wood and begin walking in circles? The sun is there to rescue you."

"Also to make the rice grow," said the boy, and his father struck him. "If you do not listen," he said, "one day you will perish for no reason."

Now, as they searched for a clearing in the woods, he realized for the first time how far they had come and how isolated they were. It was possible that they might find a naturally made clearing, but unlikely that they would find an abandoned hut. It was also likely that tomorrow the sun would come out and the snow would begin to melt and the world would be as it had been a few hours before. Yet in the meantime, they could freeze to death.

None of them were hungry, so they kept walking. There were no cleared spaces. They were going in deeper and deeper. How had he failed to realize that they were so far up? Who would choose to live here, especially when winter set in and the snow closed the doors to the rest of the world?

The samurai was tiring. Even the fox was beginning to pant. The horse stopped and willfully refused to continue. "Shall we lie down in the snow and die?" the samurai asked them angrily. But animals did not obey him as his own men had. "A little farther," he said, tugging on the horse's reins. They went forward slowly.

The snow suddenly stopped, as it will, before starting up again, and the samurai saw what he thought was smoke and not swirling snow ahead of him. He thought he smelled burning wood. He looked at the fox, who bounded in front of him. Something was there. If there was a fire burning in this snow, there must be a person who had built it.

The samurai's legs turned to stone. He found it difficult to lift one leg, then another. The horse, too, was struggling, and snorted with every step. But the fox was already in front of the place from which the smoke was coming and she yelped sharply.

"Let's go," said the samurai. "Bear up!"

He went forward, the horse following. Finally, he could see the outlines of a dwelling, but at that moment, the snow began falling again, and the hut vanished. The samurai thought he had imagined it. The fox yelped again, and then again.

He could walk no farther. When the horse lay down in the snow, he would lie down on top of him.

A dark body walked out of the curtained snow. "Will you stand there forever?" she asked the samurai. "Come inside. These things happen in the mountains. Didn't you know?"

With his last strength, he lurched forward. The woman grabbed his arm. She was surprisingly strong and she pulled him inside the hut. He saw the fox come in after him, and then he sank down, insensible.

BOOK THREE

CHAPTER TWENTY-FIVE

WHEN THE SAMURAI began to stir, he did not know where he was. At first he thought he had gone blind in the snow because he could see nothing, only a whiteness. There were frightful, jabbing pains in his feet and knees, and the same stabbing in his nose. Someone is torturing me, he thought. Then he became aware of something covering his face and raised his hand to remove it, but his hands felt like blocks of ice. Still, he did not disturb the cloth over his face. Finally he moved it so that he could see into the dim interior of the hut. The cloth was cool but not cold, and as he tried to remove it altogether, a hand replaced the cloth and put it back where it had been.

"So," said a woman's voice, "you are alive."

"These pains, like needles . . ." he said.

"You were too long in the snow. You were beginning to freeze. These cool cloths will help."

"Warm ones," he said. His throat was hoarse.

"I will warm the cloths slowly," she said. "The needles will come out." She removed the face cloth. "Look at the room," she said. "Does it hurt to move your eyes?"

"No."

He looked carefully about the dwelling. He was not in a shelter that resembled the tilting hut they had last used. Here the floors were polished, and as the woman moved about, he thought he heard the squeaks of a nightingale floor. The insides of the walls were fitted with planks of wood, probably teak, and were done with great skill so that there were no drafts even when a stiff wind blew. Above, there was a ceiling also made of wood. The fittings reminded him of the palace, where everything was done by master carpenters. There was an oiled paper window on one side of the room. In the middle, there was the usual fire pit, and in one corner, a huge cauldron made of brass. A woman could not have carried anything so heavy.

He turned his attention to the woman. He had never seen anyone who resembled such a figure. She was dressed in a quilted and wadded black robe that wrapped around her, and the black robe's hood covered her head and came down to her eyebrows so that he could not see her face. At first he thought she was enormously fat, but then, as she moved, he could sense the extreme heaviness of the robe she wore. I am not really awake, he thought, because from here, it looks as if a black tail is trailing out from beneath her robe.

The fox! Had the fox frozen?

"Utsu!" he called, his voice hoarse. The woman turned sharply, then turned back again to whatever she was doing. The fox, who had been asleep in another corner, got up and sat down next to him.

"The horse?" he asked the woman.

"In a room behind this one," she said.

"A stable?"

"Yes," she said.

She seemed disinclined to offer information.

"How did you get here?"

"A long story," she said. "A tale told around a brushwood fire."

"But this is where you live?"

"Yes."

It hurt to speak and so the samurai fell silent. The fox rumbled and moved closer.

"Not too close," she said. "A fox's body is very warm."

The fox placed one paw on the samurai's chest.

"Utsu," he said softly.

The fox placed her head on the man's chest and began to rub the underside of his chin. So we are all fine, thought the samurai. So this woman is not my fox transformed into a human. He would not like to think such a thing had happened.

The woman brought him a ladle of barely warm tea and helped support his head while he drank. Then she carefully lowered his head to the mat, went back to the low table and began to chop things he could not see. The cold seemed to have made his sense of smell far more acute, and he thought he smelled raw radishes and yams, but he was equally willing to believe that he was dreaming and that there was no woman, no one chopping anything, no hut fitted out like a room in the castle and no beautifully lacquered low table where the woman was doing her chopping.

"Is it still snowing?" he asked her.

"Yes."

"Will it go on?"

"Yes," she said again, and took something from a wicker basket near her table.

"Will we all die here?" he asked.

"No," she said.

The prickling pain was becoming less acute. Now it was more like mere stinging. He was tired and wanted to turn on his side, but he sensed that the woman would get up and prevent him from doing so.

"It is best if you sleep," the woman said. He closed his eyes and the scene disappeared.

He dreamed he was back in the castle and the plague was raging. The heavy odor of dying and dead bodies was everywhere. There was a woman he was supposed to watch—who was she?—and she made up two balls of fabric soaked in incense. She kept one to her nose, and so did he. In his dream, he grew certain that he had died and so had she, and the odor came from their own dead bodies. He woke with a start.

"A bad dream," she said. "The snow brings them on when you are out in it too long. I have to go out," she said. With her back to him, she removed the black robe. Beneath it was a thick, shorter robe, and as he watched, she pushed her feet into boots made of bear fur. Then she put on a woven straw coat, blue leather gloves painted with flowers, wrapped a cloth around her hair and fastened a large wicker hat over it, tying it under her chin. "I will be back soon," she said. "We need water and some things from the storeroom."

The fox, seeing her stir, got up and looked at her.

"She wants to go with you," the samurai said. "You need not be afraid of her. She is tame."

She nodded. She pushed the door to shove away the snow outside, and then she and the fox disappeared through it. For a moment, the room lit up, but the woman must have closed the door and it grew dim inside.

He again examined the room. The floor kept attracting his attention. It was, he was sure, made of cypress, a nightingale floor, entirely inappropriate for such a hut. The planks were patterned oddly, some far shorter than the others. He had seen that done somewhere, too. Usually it meant that parts of such a floor could be lifted out and beneath it were storage areas. But what would a woman alone in the snow have to store? Unless, of course, she had a husband. She must. That would explain why she was still alive in such an isolated spot, and why she had food to chop on her table.

As for the woman, he realized that he had no idea what she looked like or how old she was. When she wore the long black robe, she was a chilling spectacle, almost spectral, and her face and hair were hidden. He remembered the tail of her hair that protruded from the long robe, and the bits of white hair, or fur, visible in it. Conceivably, he had dreamed of that tail. She walked and talked like a human being.

After a short time, the door opened and the samurai could hear the door squeak against the snow. The woman was wearing snowshoes. She took them off outside the house. He was afraid that they would be buried under the snow, but said nothing. The woman seemed to know what she was doing. The fox hesitated at the door, looking at the woman as if asking for instructions. "Shake the snow off," the woman told the fox. The fox shook herself all over. "Good fox," said the woman, and the two of them entered the hut. She was carrying a large clay jug and it sloshed as she moved through the room. She went back to the wall, removed her straw jacket and hat and put her long robe back on. Once again, she was as well hidden as if behind a high screen.

"Where is your husband?" asked the samurai.

"Husband?"

"The man who built this hut."

"I have no husband. I have never had a husband."

The samurai thought this over. If she had no husband, surely she had a protector who had fitted this hut out for her. If that were true, she was probably happier than she would have been with a husband.

"Someone built this hut," he said.

"Of course someone built it. Huts do not build themselves."

It was possible she had gone on a pilgrimage and stumbled upon this hut and decided to live in it. But if that were the case, why did she not have the problems everyone had in such country? Everyone he met was desperately fending off starvation. Yet she seemed well supplied with food. It was not impossible that a samurai once came here to live out the rest of his days, stocked the hut and died there, and she took up residence in a then-vacant hut. Birds did that.

"You should sleep again," she said. "Afterward, I may be able to remove the cloths." She was replacing the now-cold ones with warmer ones. The needling pains were gone, and the stinging was lessening. This time, when she replaced the cloth that covered his face, she did not cover his eyes.

"You are a samurai?" she asked.

"I was."

"Then you do not need to stay awake protecting yourself from me," she said. "You have a bodyguard," she said. "That fox. What is her name?"

"She has many."

"I thought you called her Utsu," she said.

"One name among many."

"A strange name," she said.

"She was called Utsu when I found her," the samurai said.

"And she has many names? You are afraid that if I know her name, I will gain power over her. That will not happen. She belongs to you Utsu," she said, addressing the fox, who trotted over. "Stay with him," she said. The fox obediently lay down next to the samurai.

"Good fox," said the woman.

"Good fox," heard the samurai, drifting into sleep. Good fox. There was something in her voice, reminding him, but of what? Good fox, he heard the voice again, and then he was asleep.

The next time he opened his eyes, he realized that the woman had removed his wet clothes and was covering him with a black robe identical to the one she wore. The hut was warm now. He could see that she had placed more wood in the fire pit. Then she went to another corner of the room, sat down on a mat, picked up a scroll and began to read. She read quickly. Every so often, she got up, went to her low table, where a writing desk and paper had replaced the radishes, and wrote, also quickly. Then she returned to her corner and again began reading from the scroll.

"These are the occupations of a noblewoman," he said.

"I suppose so," she said. "I was in service to a noblewoman who taught me."

The samurai kept his eyes almost closed so that, from her position, he would seem to have fallen back asleep. In this way, he could watch her. Regardless of how he watched, he could not get a glimpse of her face. When she read and when she wrote, she bent her head, and if that were not enough, her hood fell forward as she did this.

Finally, she stood up and walked over to him. She nodded, and went back to her corner. Evidently, she was satisfied with his progress. The fox crawled closer and part of her body pressed against his chest. He saw the fox steal a glimpse of the woman, and seeing that she was occupied, the fox crept a little farther onto his body.

It was peaceful in the hut, and warm. I am not destined to reach snow country, he thought. That is why snow country has come to me.

Some time later, the woman saw him stirring, came over, helped him up, and asked him if he could eat the food she had cooked. "It is warm," she added. "Now you can eat and drink warm things."

He became aware of how hungry he was, and said he would be happy for the food, whatever it was.

"It is bear meat stew," she said.

Bear meat. Who had killed a bear for her? Or had she found a dead bear? But few people would attempt eating the flesh of a dead animal, especially a bear. Dead things usually died for a reason.

"The meat is good," she said, as if divining his thought. "I myself smoked it. I have been eating it for weeks and I am still above the ground, as you see."

He was embarrassed and did not respond. He saw the fox, ears up, sitting attentively near the fire pit. I wonder if she will feed the fox, he thought. Otherwise, I will have to do something.

There was a castle once and they laid siege to it. Lord Norimasa said, "Find bear. These mountains are full of them. Be sure to shoot them before they kill you." Inside the castle, the men were starving. It was the castle of Kumanojima. "When we have bear, we will cook them when the winds blow toward the castle, and they will smell the meat. Then they will give up and we will press them into our army."

The men in the castle did not give up. Instead, those who died were cooked and eaten by the others. When Lord Norimasa's men finally entered the castle, they found living skeletons devouring the roasted carcasses of those who had died. Matsuhito watched Lord Norimasa. He expected to see the excitement that such spectacles created in him. But there was no light in his eyes, only darkness. "I did not want to reduce them to this," he said. "You are looking at very brave men."

The old counselor said, "They would have been braver to die without such a meal," but the lord did not think so.

"They wanted to fight on," he said. "They did not do this to preserve their own lives."

"We do not agree," said the old counselor, who turned his horse and rode out of the castle grounds.

The woman returned with a metal plate and a small amount of food. "You can have more later. Small amounts are best. But you, Utsu," she said to the fox, "you can have a large meal." She set a plate near the fox, which began to eat ravenously.

"A healthy animal who recovers quickly," he said.

He heard the whinny of his horse. "He has been fed and watered," she said, "and a straw blanket placed over him. He lies down on his side like a dog."

"He is a strange horse. He learned to imitate the fox."

The woman nodded again and went back to her corner and began reading. Apparently, she had already eaten.

The next morning, blinding light spilled into the hut. The sun had evidently come out and was glaring on the white dunes of snow. He knew people could go blind in such light if they were outside too long. Now he could see every grain of each plank of wood. The surfaces of the planks were dark from long use and they gleamed with a light of their own.

After a time she was again cooking, and set out three plates.

"I should like to see your face," the samurai said.

"Why?"

"You can see mine," he answered.

She laughed softly. "A child would answer in that way," she said.

"Nevertheless," said the samurai.

"When I have finished eating," she said.

"When I lived in the castle," he said, "the women always had to be hidden behind screens. Or they shielded their faces with their fans or their screens or their sleeves. Or they wore gauzy veils. Only once did I see a woman's face clearly."

The woman sighed. "It is best for women to keep their faces hidden," she said.

"I know the custom," the samurai said. "But what is the reason?"

"The prevention of foolish jealousies and wild inflammations of the heart," the woman answered.

"And does it work?"

"No," she said.

She moved closer. This time, she sat near him as they ate.

"May I see your face?" he asked again when the plates were empty.

"And if I say no, will you continue to ask?"

"Yes," he said.

She lowered her robe and raised her hood. Then she raised her head.

That face! Surely he had seen it somewhere! But where? Did she resemble his mother, who had died in the fire, whose face he could never summon up? He returned again and again to her eyes. They were rounder than most women's and so made her appear as if she had just seen something so astonishing it had widened her eyes in surprise. As a result, she had an air of wonderment. Her hair, which was parted in the middle, as the ladies of the castle had worn it, seemed twice the thickness of other people's hair. Her mouth was very small and very red, but the flesh above her mouth was scored with vertical lines, and when she spoke or smiled, little wrinkles appeared at the edges of her eyes. She was no longer young.

"That is my face," she said.

The woman's hair was streaked with gray, and that made her appear older. She began to put up her hood.

"Please don't do that," the samurai said. "May I see your hair?"

The woman sighed and stood up and let her robe fall to the floor. She moved a little to the right so that he could see her better, then turned her back to him. Her hair fell to the ground and trailed on the floor. No wonder he'd thought she had a tail.

"Living like this," he said, "I should think you would cut your hair."

"I am not a nun," the woman answered.

Smoke from the fire pit rose in the room and obscured the woman as if she were behind a veil, and in that instant, he saw how beautiful she still was, and he could imagine how beautiful she must have been.

She moved to the fire pit, added more wood and stirred the coals. The fire burned brighter and the smoke began to clear.

"How it stings your eyes," the woman said. "Why do you stare at me?"

"Because you are beautiful," he said.

"If you knew how tired I was of being told that," she said. "I have looked forward to old age which would crumble my beauty. I thought it had happened."

"Why wish for such a thing?"

"Beauty has not brought me joy. Quite the reverse. I did not want to be born beautiful. My mother did not want it. But because I was, things happened that ought not to have happened. We all have our regrets," she said, putting her robe on and taking up the plates. He could see that the discussion was over.

"I should like to see my horse," he said.

"To look at his face?" the woman asked, mocking him.

"So that he will know he has not been left alone."

"The fox visits him."

"That is not the same thing," said the samurai.

"Tomorrow," said the woman. "I give you my word. We have not been eating him." Again, that note of mockery.

"Where do you find water for him?" he asked. "He drinks a great deal."

"Snowmelt," she said. "Every time I go out, I fill the jug with snow and it melts in the stable. There is also a pile of snow in one corner of the room where the roof is not tight. He licks at that as well."

"I will fix that roof," said the samurai.

"You would not know how."

"I was not always a samurai," he said. "Once I was a child and then a young man. In those days, I mended the house and did chores."

"Later, I will think about it," she said, and he heard clearly what she did not say: If you stay.

The next day, he was well enough to get up and begin pounding nails into planks on the north wall that had loosened in the storm. Now the samurai often experienced a sensation that was halfway between happiness and peace. At night, when he lay down in the room on the other side of the pit and felt the warmth of the burning coals, he was content.

The samurai was also fatalistic. If the woman decided he must leave, he would leave. He did not think, however, that she would ask him to go until the snow was gone. He found the twig brush and began to sweep the floor. He did whatever he could. Finally, he decided that it was only right to help bring in the firewood. That meant going out into the snow. He asked permission to use the woman's snowshoes and, when she did not argue, went out and followed a well-beaten path that the woman always appeared to follow. After going a short distance from the hut, the path led into the woods, and there he found a small clearing, and on the edge, a large, rickety roof held up by four slender tree trunks. Beneath the roof was the firewood. It was packed to the ceiling with branches and even logs, and not for the first time it occurred to the samurai to wonder whether or not there was someone helping the woman. How, for example, could she have stood up so high in order to pile up the topmost layers of wood? And then there was the degree of craftsmanship in the hut, almost a display of ostentation, but so poor-looking on the outside that few people would think to look in. He had now seen food and clothing emerge from the storage spaces beneath the floor, and he knew that those places were well stocked. The daily life of the woman pointed to one who lived alone, and simply, but there was a mystery. Who looked after her and made certain that she had everything she needed?

The samurai began pulling wood from the lean-to, and, judging the amount to be sufficient, trudged back through the woods. The snow was very deep. The sky looked more like twilight than sunrise, and the trees were covered with puffy snow. There were still dead leaves clinging to the branches, and large puffs of snow built up on them like blossoms. Every limb of every tree was outlined by snow which lay along the tops of the branches. Since he had been in the hut, the temperature must have risen and the snow on the trees must have melted so that when it grew colder the branches had become coated with a clear, crystalline ice. Even in the gray morning light, the trees glistened and shone. The woods looked as if it had been created by a giant jeweler. It was like a magnificent scene etched on a woman's comb. He felt his feet growing slightly numb, and continued along the path with his burden. He opened the door slowly and silently, as had long been second nature.

The samurai found himself looking at the woman, who was sitting on the reed mat next to the fire pit, where she was stroking the fox and plucking lice from its fur and throwing the lice into the fire. Then she picked up some rice from a bowl, placed it on her upturned palm and extended her hand to the fox, which quickly ate the rice. The two of them looked as if they had always lived together. When she finally saw him there, she looked startled. "She was hungry," the woman said.

The samurai nodded and put the wood against its usual wall. "The sky looks like snow, but it does not feel as if it will snow," the samurai said. Then he selected a thick branch and began to whittle. The woman watched curiously but did not ask what he was making. "It is calming to carve, and a satisfaction," he told the woman. "I am making a figure of my fox. I carved figures during sieges. At one time, I had many such carvings even though many people asked for them. At night, the carvings seemed to come alive. I would open my eyes and see them where I did not think I had put them when I went to sleep. It was my theory," he went on, comfortable in his whittling and in the warmth from the fire pit, "that some of them did not like each other, and while I slept, they quarreled and moved about to be close to other figures they preferred. They were very lifelike. Probably I have lost the skill."

The woman considered the samurai quietly and continued stroking the fox. The samurai returned to his whittling.

Her voice, when she spoke, startled him. Often he fell into a kind of reverie, almost a trance, as he carved. "I should like to know more about your life," the woman said. "I know it is not polite to ask in this way, but your life has been very different from mine."

"My life is ordinary," the samurai said. "I am not special."

"Yet you have participated in battles. You have killed men, and no doubt you beheaded the ones you killed. When you left the battlefield, the ground slippery with blood, you went back to your own home and family as if you had gone for a stroll. That does not appear ordinary to me."

"Nevertheless, it is the lot of all samurai, and so my life was ordinary," he said.

"And your wife? What did she do when you went off? Did she worry?"

"I have no wife," he said, looking up quickly and then looking away. "Or children. I was a lone crow, a *hagure karasu*. I had a lord I loved and followed. In that regard, too, I was like everyone else."

"The other samurai were unmarried?" she asked innocently.

"No. They were married."

"Why did you not marry?"

"You ask many questions for a woman," the samurai said.

"I have grown rude and hungry for stories, living in these mountains," the woman said. "Tell me why you did not marry. You were not a monk? You did not take a vow of celibacy?"

"Perhaps I did, but not in the way you think," the samurai said.

"I should like to know," the woman replied.

"A long time ago, when I was young, I met a woman I loved. At the time, I knew I loved her, but until we were separated, I had no idea how much. Even in the madness of battle, her face would appear in front of me and often I believed I fought to keep that face safe, wherever it was. My lord said there were men like that. They fall in love once, and no other woman can take the place of that first one. So it was with me, he said."

"But you did not go back for her and find her?" the woman asked.

"I could not. She disappeared as if she never existed. My lord made inquiries. Men were sent out to search, but no information came their way. Some suggested she died. But I never really believed that she ceased to live. More and more, as I go through the mountains, her face becomes more vivid."

"She was young?" the woman asked.

"We both were," the samurai answered. "Then."

"I have rarely heard of such devotion," the woman said. "In stories, but not in life."

"There is no great value in such devotion," the samurai said. "I was made as I was when I was born. The devotion was always in me."

"Nonetheless, I have not come across many such men," the woman said. "I do not think you were ordinary."

The samurai looked up, but she busied herself with the fox's paw. "She has a splinter?" he asked the woman.

"She is fine," the woman said. "Very well cared for. With her, too, you have been devoted."

"And you? Have you married."

"I was cruel and afraid of marrying. I had my own money, inherited from my father. It was not necessary for me to marry. I was suspicious and jealous by nature. I set trials for men who thought they wanted to marry me. People thought I was afraid someone would marry me for my fortune, but the men around me were far more wealthy than I was. I was afraid that a man would marry me for my beauty and then tire of me almost at once. Even the most beautiful screen in the castle soon becomes invisible, its wonders dimmed."

"Trials? What kind of trials?"

"Trials to prove a man's sincerity," the woman said. "But one went wrong, and after that, I was not wanted in society."

"I have been traveling alone for some time," the samurai said. "I, too, would like to hear stories. Particularly this one."

"This is a terrible story," the woman said. "To tell it is to reveal my nature."

"I loved my lord, whose nature was badly flawed. He had a cruel streak that frightened others. But when he was not cruel, his nature was altogether different. Then everyone loved him, and people said of him that his cruel actions were caused by a spirit that inhabited him. People have many natures."

The woman considered the samurai from beneath her hood. "Why not tell you?" she said. "Then you will understand why I am being punished as I deserve."

The samurai put down his work and sat cross-legged. The fox, seeing he was unoccupied, got up and lay down next to him, her paws on his thighs.

"What would you think of yourself if you killed the fox?" the woman asked suddenly.

"I would not be happy whenever I remembered what I had done, and I would remember all the time, or so I think."

"Then you may understand what happened to me," the woman said. "This is my story.

"*Mukashi, mukashi,*" she said, as if she were telling a fairy tale. A long time ago.

"A long time ago, there was a little girl whose mother loved her so much she wanted to keep the child with her. The mother and the child had scholarly inclinations, and a long time ago, a ship coming from China was wrecked on the cliffs not far from their mansion. The servants and some attendants were sent down to see if there was anyone who could be helped, but they were more anxious to see if there was any treasure they could bear away. When the attendants got there, the wind was so strong and the waves so high and wild that they could see only the white spume of the waves. Finally, they saw a man on a very high rock which ordinarily stuck out of the water like a miniature mountain. Because the water was so high, the rock was almost submerged, but it was enough above water for the man to cling on there.

"The men had brought up stout ropes in the hope of hauling cargo from the water onto the dry land, but when they saw the man on the rock, they decided to rescue him. If they succeeded, they thought, he could be tortured and he would tell them what of value was in the hold of the ship.

"After many attempts to throw him a rope, an archer who had come down to look had an idea. He fitted the rope onto an arrow and said he was going to send it straight to the man in the sea. 'How can you do it without killing him?' everyone asked, and spoke against the idea. But the archer, whose name was Hatsuie, said it could be done.

"Hatsuie was already known as one of the best archers in the land. He used an enormous bow and although he himself could easily pull it back in order to launch an arrow, no one else could do it, so strong he was. It took two men to draw back his arrow and bend his bow. Hatsuie was also known for his temper, so that everyone was unwilling to oppose him. Meanwhile, the waves in the sea were rising even higher. Something had to be done.

"Hatsuie readied his bow and his arrow, to which the heavy rope was attached, and the arrow flew. It flew over the rock, but when it dropped down into the water, the rope lay across the lap of the man in the sea. The man took hold of the rope and many men began to drag him toward the cliffs.

"Finally, they got him to the cliffs. The men pulling on the rope were tiring, but soon he was on land. The noise of the sea and the noise of the rain made it impossible to talk to him. They took him back to the castle.

"My mother gave him dry clothes and made tea for him. The next day, when the sea was calmer, our men went out to look. The man from China was upset because an oilskin pack full of scrolls was lost. The men found pieces of highly decorated furniture, one very good mirror, far better than anything we had, but the oilskin package was not there. Every day, my mother made them go back to look. On a day when the sea was calm, someone saw what looked like a dead fish floating on the water. Hatsuie was summoned, impaled the object and brought it onto dry land. It was the oilskin package.

"The Chinese man did not want to go back to his country, although he would not say why, and we knew that we should have reported his presence in our castle, but my mother pleaded that he be left with us so he could teach us. She found out he was a scholar.

"It would not be too much to say that the mother and the daughter fell in love with the Chinese man. For his part, he fell in love with the daughter, whose intellect was so quick, and who, as he said, grew more beautiful by the day. 'She is the castle's treasure,' said the man from the sea. And then one day, after some years, he simply disappeared. My mother thought that he returned to the sea, and boats were sent to search, but there was no sign of him.

"Meanwhile, I was taught to read Chinese and I had spent a good deal of my time writing Chinese poems. When the Emperor and Empress visited the castle, the Empress was very pleased with me, and decided to bring me to the palace with her. My father said he himself would accompany me.

"What I wanted back was the man from the sea who had been so kind, and taught me so much, and could have taught me much more. I was twelve when he left. I thought him cruel to leave without a word, and inside I repeated again and again, How could you go and leave me alone? In time, that sorrow turned to anger and a great suspicion that all men were disloyal. I knew my parents would never have allowed us to marry, but I also knew I was clever, and I believed I could somehow bring this event about. When the man from China disappeared, all my plans were ruined. We never knew why he left.

"My father knew what I was thinking. He told me, 'You cannot dwell on this forever.'"

"I grew more angry and bitter. After that, I decided I would not accept any suitor who proposed to me, and announced that I should never marry. I meant what I said, although no one believed it. The man from China once expressed the opinion that mine was a terrible will. He said I must tame that will, and not exercise it on small things. When he was gone, I was at the mercy of my own dreadful character.

"When I was summoned to the palace, the Emperor and Empress and I grew to be close, and the Empress and I studied Chinese together. This was, of course, not considered a fit subject for a woman, but who would contradict an Empress? I got on well with the other ladies, but I was soon to develop a reputation for cruelty to men. I was given the name *Kumo*, or Spider, and people spoke of my writing as the *kumonosu*, or spider web, made up of the threads of my poems. And so life went on in that way. It was well known that men died fighting over me, and when I heard such news, I was indifferent. People concluded that I was cold. But I was not cold. I was still burning with anger.

"And then one day I was secluded with a man who was ordered to watch me. All but one of my female attendants had been sent away, and there was a contingent of soldiers in front of my pavilion, but the man was ordered to stay with me. I have never known what love is, but I think it is a strange thing. It is like the weather, unpredictable and inevitable. There is always weather. You cannot escape it.

"I thought I was toying with him, as I had with so many others before, but when he was sent into battle, I was stricken with a sorrow that threatened to break me. The lord of the clan, who doted on me, called for diviners and exorcists. Of course, nothing helped. Then the lord himself was called away for battle. I decided to disappear. I was taken by palanquin to a place far in the north, and there I realized that the man who had once been set to watch me was the cause of my trouble. Again, I began my silent chant. Why did you leave me and leave me here alone? It was then I realized that I loved the man who had guarded me more strongly than I had once loved the man from the sea. But it was too late. He had gone into battle, and when I had left the palace, I left without leaving a trace, as if I never lived there.

"The bitterness increased, as one would expect in a person of my character. Eventually, I was tempted to take refuge in Lady Miko's castle because she, too, was interested in scholarly pursuits and writing. She was a dreadful poet, absolutely hopeless, but a very kind woman. In her castle, things went along well enough.

"Then one day, a nobleman caught sight of me, and after that, I was plagued by a perfect whirlwind of love letters and love poems. He was an excellent poet—his poems are in the royal anthology along with mine—and he interested me. But really, I wanted no one else. And I swore that I would not again experience love for a man. Well, that was stupidity, but I thought I had made a resolve I could keep. Why go through the storm that brought your world down as typhoons bring down trees?

"Aren't you bored by this?" the woman suddenly asked the samurai. "For me, it is such an old story."

"I am not bored," said the samurai.

"Should I go on?"

"Please," he said. And she continued her story.

"The man who wrote poems persisted. Eventually, I began to be tempted by him. It was a severe winter, and I thought to test him. I said I would consider marriage if he would come to the castle every night without fail for one hundred days, and each night use his dagger to make a small notch on the shaft of my palanquin. You see what a monster I was?

"The first week went smoothly. Then the weather changed and the snow fell interminably, yet he came every night through the snow, made his notch, and then left. Around the ninetieth day, his mother began her dying. He would stay up with her all day and almost all night, but when it was very late, he would make his way to the castle and notch the shaft of the palanquin. Everyone knew what was happening, and people were full of praise for my suitor, who was so persistent and who was even willing to risk his life. By now there was almost no one who would go abroad in such weather. Everyone thought I should release him from his vow. But I refused to consider it. He continued to come, and the full moon that would mark the end of the one hundred days was fast approaching. He came all through the last week, but on the very last day, he did not appear, and no notch was left in the palanquin's shaft.

"I said that the test was over. He had failed, and I wanted to hear no more about it. My ladies and I were building a snow mountain in the winter garden when a courier came, and, as was proper, we hid our faces with our winter fans. 'My lady,' he said, speaking to me, 'I have news. Please stand aside from the others.'

"The news was catastrophic. My suitor, who had appeared every night for ninety-nine days under the most difficult of circumstances, missed the last night because he had fallen in the snow and was unable to get up. The snow covered him where he fell. They found him two days later, stiff as a board, his beard and his eyebrows covered with ice. He was blue with cold. In his hand, they found a red sheet of paper, and on it was written, 'Lady, forgive me.'

"I can see you disapprove," the woman told the samurai.

"Disapprove?" the samurai said. "I am trying to understand."

"What is there to understand?" the woman asked. "I was evil. I am still evil."

"I do not think you are evil," said the samurai. "I think it was something else. That is what I'm trying to understand. Tell me what happened next."

"Next," she said, sighing. "After that, everyone spoke of my cruelty and hard-heartedness, especially since I showed no inclination to mourn. He had, after all, taken his chances, and if he had survived the task, I would have kept my word and married him.

"The lady of the castle was so horrified that she had me brought by sled to see the frozen corpse. His skin was white tinged with blue. From the tracks in the snow, it was plain to see that he had dragged himself forward, trying to reach me, when really, it would have been more sensible to try going back to his own mansion. And that night, as he died, his mother died as well. It was said that my spirit had killed her, too.

"Lady Miko considered asking me to leave, but she herself was happy in my presence. The lord, who had loved the dead suitor, said to her, 'It is like harboring a snake.'

"Nevertheless, I stayed for a while. I became an emblem of cruelty and people everywhere spoke of me. 'How much better to marry the person your parents choose for you,' everyone said. That was the lesson to be learned from my story. I now had a reputation for beauty, for poetry and for cruelty. People regarded me with fascination, the fascination of a snake. Men were tempted to see if they could break me as if I were a horse that was running wild. I grew colder and colder. Still, there were women who admired me, one of whom came in the middle of the night and said she wished she could do what I had done. There were so many angry women. I found that out.

"I began to fear that the lord in whose palace I had once lived would hear of me when the winter's snows melted. I knew I could not remain hidden in Lady Miko's castle for long. One day, I decided to vanish forever, and I put on pilgrim's clothes and went out the back gate, completely alone. When I saw a place I liked, a tree or a gate, I left a little poem stuck to it and went on. I never signed anything, and much later, the legend of the traveling ghost who wrote poems became well known. Eventually, I found myself here. Now I regret my mad will and what it brought me. Why should the man have died for me in the snow? But dead is dead, and the dead cannot be revived.

"So that is my story. It is very long to tell it, but when it happened, it went by in a flash. After the man died, time slowed and each day was endless. I was happy to rescue you from the snow. I thought the spirits were taking pity on me and had brought me another test, and I was determined not to fail in this. So you are alive and now I do not know what to do with you. I cannot keep you here. Sooner or later, I will turn on you as I have turned on everyone throughout my life."

The samurai said nothing. Finally he said, "You will not turn on me, and if you do, it will make no difference. I have come to the end of my life."

"There is a great deal of life left in you," she said. "What would your fox do if you died?"

"It is true that she ties me to this life, but it is not a strong tie," said the samurai.

The woman said, "It is stronger than you think." She got up, took some firewood, broke the twigs into pieces and stirred them among the dying coals of the fire pit. She was thinking, Our lives are inexplicable, even to us, but she did not say anything.

The two of them sat silently, not looking at each other. Both of them were lost in their own memories. "Memories are a dark wood," Lord Norimasa had once said. "Do not enter them."

CHAPTER TWENTY-SIX

THE PLAGUE WAS RAGING. He was entrusted with the safety of the woman, Lady Utsu, who, one night, bored and frightened, had invited him in. He had never been that close to a noblewoman before. He had only spoken with one through her screen, and then only briefly.

When he entered her room in the castle, he could barely see, so dim was the light shed by one torch mounted on a wall. There were shimmers of gold everywhere, gold screens which glinted richly in the dim light. Everything in the room was muted. There was a strong odor of incense that the samurai had come to associate with that room and now with the person who occupied it. She said, "Come lie here with me."

After he had stumbled and thrown down the screen, he righted it and they lay on their backs, staring up at the ceiling, like brother and sister. Then she turned toward him, and his eyes, accustomed to the dim light, saw her face for the first time. He had never seen anyone so beautiful. I will be killed for coming in behind the screen, he thought. He looked at the screen, her rich robes thrown over it. They were brocaded silk and gleamed in the darkness. He tried to make out the patterns. Surely one was a crane, and on another robe, fiery phoenixes.

The lady reached out and touched his cheek, softly, as if she meant to comfort him. The touch was so soft and spoke so of compassion that he felt tears well up in his eyes. "We will be all right," the lady said. "Don't fear the plague. I was not meant to die in a plague, and neither were you."

"Turn toward me," she said, "so that I can see your face. I have seen you many times, through screens, and every time, I have wondered what you would look like if you had not been covered by those spider webs."

He turned toward her. And she did another strange thing. She took his head in her hands.

"A strong face," she said. "The courtiers have doughy faces, as if they had no bones. I saw one a few days past, and he wore so many robes he looked as if three people were hidden in his costume, and his round head was so small it looked like a ripe cherry. How did it happen that women came to admire such formless men?"

He listened to her without speaking. At that moment, if her voice had gone on and on forever, day after day, season after season, until he grew old and white and the bones of his body began to creak and snap, he would have been happy to die on the mat with her.

"During times like this," she said, "anything is permissible." She was encouraging him. When he was younger, he would run away, sometimes for long periods, and return when he was hungry. When he came back, he slept with young girls in his village, but he thought nothing of it. He would have said he was curious about the village girls, and he was curious about how his own body suddenly developed ideas of its own, but he felt little for them. "You have no feelings!" his mother would say again and again. "You run away from home and worry us senseless! And if that were not bad enough, you know the lord would behead us if he found we were not capable of taking care of you!"

He could not bring himself to say he was sorry. Although this woman treated him as a mother, he knew his real mother had died in a fire. Yet this one had been very good to him. She died before she could see him safely ensconced in the lord's castle, where he often carefully disagreed with the generals in the war council, was often listened to by the lord, who told the other members of the council that the samurai was to sit in on their meetings as part of his training, and as the samurai grew older, the lord was inclined to trust his opinion over any other's.

He was staring at the lady's face. Her eyebrows were shaved, as was the proper way for a woman of her station, but she had neglected to put two smudges, one above each eye, in place of eyebrows. When he saw that, something cracked in him, ice breaking on the surface of a deep pond. He felt something like pity for her, pity that he was all she had as the hot days continued and the men of the castle began to throw dead bodies over the walls. His own hand moved to her face, and after that, there was no stopping.

"Ah," said Lady Utsu afterward, "there is always happiness some-where."

He thought, If this were happiness only, it would be better. This is what people call love.

"I love you," Lady Utsu said.

"Don't say such things," said the samurai. "That is an important thing. You must mean it."

"I do mean it," Lady Utsu said.

"It is because you are alone and in need of comfort," he said.

"Do you think I am so weak? Do you think I am like men, who will say 'I love you' when they feel no such thing? I would not say it until I meant it."

"You mean," said the samurai, "you thought for a moment you loved me, but tomorrow you may not."

"I mean no such thing," said the lady.

"But Lord Norimasa loves you," the samurai said. "You are his."

"Even if he thought of me as his, I would still love you. The lord loves me, but not in the way you think. I am his foster daughter. He has sworn to protect me. He took me from my parents after I left the palace and brought me to his castle and said he would keep me safe. People gossip so in a castle. People even believe I am the daughter of a lord who was slain in battle, and that I am one of the two remaining heirs of the family. There are some who believe I am Lord Norimasa's illegit-imate daughter. Lord Norimasa loves to look at me, and when he is unhappy, I read my poems to him. I love him as a daughter loves her father. Not like you!" she said, suddenly poking him in the belly. "Not like you!" she said, poking him again.

Was she telling the truth?

"Stop that or I will poke you back," said the samurai.

She poked him again.

He began to tickle her. She shrieked and moved away from him, and then turned and attacked him. They were both laughing like children.

"Oh! I am exhausted!" she said when it was over.

"Completely exhausted?" he asked her. "'The rain, when it falls, does not hear the trees saying, 'Stop!'" he said, quoting from an ancient poem.

"It doesn't?" asked the lady. "And must I be such a tree? A tree in a poem is not a normal tree." He opened her robe and lay down on her body. "Such small breasts, such large nipples," he said. "You were meant to bear children."

"I do not want children," she said.

He was already entering her. Her body arched to meet him. Their love cries must have been plainly audible, but who was there who could disapprove of Lady Utsu? Her two attendants were asleep behind their screens, or pretended to be so.

This went on throughout the night. The room was lightening, and he raised his head when he thought he heard a cock crow. Then he heard it again. The night was over.

"And will you write me a morning-after poem?" Lady Utsu asked him.

"No," said the samurai.

"Why not?"

"Because such poems mean nothing. They must be written. They are written out of obligation. Someday I will write you a poem when there is a good reason to write one."

"A scandalous, rude person," said the lady. "But you are right. I have written enough morning-after poems in my life. When the night comes to an end, the men dress hurriedly, say they are sorry to leave and rush home to write their morning-after poem. They send them to us by an attendant. Meanwhile, the women in question cannot go to sleep until they write one of their own in return, and then they send the poem to their lovers by their own attendant. On those mornings, you would think the whole world felt nothing but love. What a farce it is! But it must be done."

"And must I say I love you?" he asked. "Is that also required?"

"No."

He knew he had hurt her. "Yet I do love you," he said.

"Ah," she said with a long sigh. "I thought so. And did you believe me when I said the same?"

"No," said the samurai.

"But I did mean it, and I do now," she said.

"To feel love," the samurai said. "I never thought I would feel it. I believed I was incapable."

"I once loved one man, but I was young then. It was the bud before the blossom."

"Why should we feel love for one another?" the samurai asked. Really, he thought, he did not know. He was a child in these matters.

"Now you are asking questions that have no answers. 'Why does the sun come up in the morning? Why does it go down?'"

"Must it go down?" the samurai asked.

"In my case, the sun always goes down," she said.

"Perhaps the same will be true of me," he said.

"I think you are different. I think your heart is not deformed as mine is."

"How can you say such things of yourself? Your heart is not twisted. You insist that it is and you come to believe that what you say and think is true. You may turn from me, but your heart will still be good."

To his surprise, the lady began to weep and wiped her eyes on her sleeve.

"Now you are like a poem," said the samurai. "'She wept until her sleeves were drenched.'"

He held her tightly, but she continued to weep.

"I am sorry to have caused this," he said.

"Women sometimes cry when they are happy," she said.

"I understand," he said.

"Do you?" she asked. "I am crying because you believe my heart is good."

"That is nothing to cry about," the samurai said.

"It is!" Lady Utsu said, and began weeping once more.

"I, too, cannot complain about the rain and ask it to stop," he said. "How can it happen that you weep and yet your weeping makes me happy?"

Her face was buried in her robe, but now she lifted her head. Her face was shiny with tears, but what he saw was happiness.

"I cannot breathe through my nose," she said.

He laughed. "These are the kinds of tragedies we must expect," he said.

"Sometimes," she said, "you seem so young, and sometimes you appear to have lived forever."

"I think we are all like that," the samurai said.

"Yes," said Lady Utsu, sighing again, and burrowing into him.

And that was only the first night.

CHAPTER TWENTY-SEVEN

"ARE YOU HUNGRY?" the woman asked.

"No," said the samurai.

"I will soak some dried yams and fry them," she said. "Probably you will feel hunger soon. You were so quiet. What were you thinking?"

"I was thinking . . ." he said, and then he broke off. "I was wondering," he said, "if you have heard of a woman who traveled with a fox."

"As you do?" she asked.

"As I do," he said.

"I think once," she said. "But that was a long time ago."

"Do you know what became of her?"

"No one does," said the woman. The samurai was getting up to tend his horse. As he was about to leave, the woman said, "There are two things I should like to ask of you. First, you must have noticed that there is a second story above the stable and that sometimes you may have heard footsteps above you. Please do not go up there. Second, there are times when I walk alone outside. I will tell you when those times are. You must promise not to follow me or even to open the window and look out when I ask you not to. Can you promise?"

"Are these tests?"

"I am not testing you. When you come back, you must tell me your story," she said. "It will pass the time."

"My story?" said the samurai. "I am a simple person. I loved a woman. She was above me in rank and talent. I was called to war, and by the time I returned, she had vanished. Everyone has such simple stories."

"And did you look for her? This woman?"

"No one knew where she was. I thought, if she wanted to see me, she would have stayed until I returned. After that, I busied myself with the lord's occupations and had no time for anything else. The lord was always at war with one or another of the clans, so it was an exciting life. I can't complain."

"Ah," she said. "Complaining is what I do. What is writing poetry but complaining? You take something, refuse to let it go and remind everyone it has gone. Is that not complaining?"

"I know little about poetry," the samurai said. "I read it, but I rarely write it. But I know when my horse is hungry."

"It is not right to let a faithful animal feel hunger," she said. "You must go."

When the samurai returned, the woman was restless. "I am about to go for the walk I mentioned. You will not watch me or look out the window until I return?"

"Very mysterious," said the samurai.

"You must promise," she said.

"I will be as a blind reciter of ballads until you return."

"*Yokatta*," she said. "Good."

THE WOMAN PUT on her cloak and pushed her feet into her bearskin boots. Outside the door were her snowshoes. When she left, her shadow crossed the window, but he did not rise to try to see where she went. Her snowshoes made an odd swishing sound, like the hem of a silk robe sweeping against a polished castle floor. A little later, he heard her again, and once more her shadow passed the window. This time his fox began yelping and whimpering and jumped against the wall and began to use her claws as if she intended to break out of the hut.

"What is wrong with you, Utsu?" the samurai demanded. "Sit down! There is nothing so terrible out there! Only a woman!" The fox came and sat down with him, curled herself into a ball and glowered at him. "Do I not take you for enough walks?" he asked the fox. "I will take you out later. You cannot go everywhere with the woman. Do you think there is something I should look into?" he asked the animal.

"Normally, I would do it, but I promised that I would not look into this." The fox answered with a little snort and turned her head away.

"I DO NOT UNDERSTAND HER," Lord Norimasa said irritably. "She delights in mystification. She will give everyone almost anything, and then she will refuse to say what ingredients she uses for one of the incense cakes she no longer makes. She mixes her own dyes and colors the silk in her own way, but she could not be more careful if the entire castle were full of spies who wanted to know how to dye silk. But if one of the women needs a robe because she has worn all of hers before, she will throw that woman three robes as if she were throwing off poor versions of a poem written on crumpled paper. Why this passion for secrets?"

"We live in such close quarters," the samurai said. "Perhaps these hidden things give her privacy. Surely there are times you yourself long for it."

"If I could find that place called privacy without dying first, I would be happier than anyone in the land. I go to my innermost chambers, and although I seem to be there alone, I know that behind the wooden walls, many samurai are watching and attending. Nothing must happen to me. At night I dream of eyes. They float by like fish. Why should she need privacy when the other women surround themselves with chattering creatures telling one another everything they ought to keep to themselves?"

"Because she is not the same," the samurai said.

"She is not the same," Lord Norimasa said, nodding gravely. "There can be no better answer."

THE SAMURAI WAS beginning to drift off.

"You cannot go in there without your ceremonial hat!" the old counselor was shouting.

"If I knew where the hat was," Lord Norimasa shouted back, "I would put it on my head! It makes no difference. I am ruler here. They will remember my face even if I am not wearing the hat."

"How rough and ridiculous you are," the old counselor said. "But you will have your own way!"

"And should I have someone else's?" the lord asked, his voice angry.

"Go in there uncovered and make a fool of yourself," said the old counselor.

"Do not presume so much," said Lord Norimasa.

At that, the old counselor purpled, the veins in his forehead pulsed and he went through into the great hall.

Later, the samurai stopped the old counselor. "We should play a joke on him," the samurai said.

"No one can play a joke on that willful beast," said the old counselor.

"This is what we will do," he told the old counselor. "If the plan does not appeal to you, I will say I did it myself."

"Have I no courage?" asked the old counselor, puffing up. "But really, how can the lord lose so many hats? It has been years since I consulted with a hatmaker. I have bought him ten hats. Now they are gone. These lacquered black hats are not made in a day. I cannot even think where I can find a maker of hats."

"Let me do it," said the samurai.

Several days later, he came back with a large box wrapped in an embroidered cloth. On the cloth was a gold phoenix, and the embroidery was so thick and elaborate it seemed to rise up from the fabric itself.

"Come into my chamber," said the old counselor. "Everyone behind the walls is now blind," he announced to the seemingly empty room. "See to it!"

The samurai took off the cloth and opened the black lacquered box. The box stood on four feet.

"It is big enough for a suit of armor," the old counselor said. Already he was smiling. "Open it! Open it!"

The samurai opened the box. "You lift it out," said the samurai. "You had the worst of the argument."

The old counselor began to lift the object from the box, and when he held it up before him, he roared with laughter.

"Let me put it on," he said. He put on the new black hat and his head promptly disappeared into the hat, which had settled on his shoulders.

"It will be difficult to lose that hat," said the samurai.

Behind the polished wooden walls, there was stifled laughter.

"Remember! In there, you are blind men!" the old counselor said, and then his laughter broke out again.

"Is there any way to wear such a large hat?" asked the old counselor.

"Oh, yes," the samurai said. "If you tilt it backward, it will stay on."

"Find a mirror!" the old counselor commanded.

One of the guards hidden behind the wall emerged from a panel and carried a mirror. He had obviously been laughing until tears wet his cheeks.

"Show me how to put it on," the old counselor said.

"Tilt it like this," said the samurai.

As soon as the enormous hat was on his head, the old counselor demanded the mirror. "Oh, what a thing!" the old counselor said. "How ridiculous it looks!"

"Less ridiculous than no hat at all?" asked the samurai.

"No!" said the old counselor angrily. "A lord must wear a hat."

"He will not wear this one," said the samurai.

"Don't be so certain," the old counselor said. "He is a most peculiar man. He will not easily be tricked."

At the next council, the lord again had no hat.

The old counselor said, "I knew you had not replaced that hat. I have bought you another, better hat." And he handed the lord the big box.

"Here, let me take it out for you," the samurai said.

"No, no, I will do it," said the old counselor.

The hat emerged. Lord Norimasa's face turned red, and then he suddenly began to laugh. He laughed until he cried. "I will wear that hat forever," he said when he could speak. "Who could ask for a better hat?"

"You will wear that into the Council of War?" asked the old counselor, scandalized.

"It is a hat," said Lord Norimasa. "I will put it on."

At once, his head was swallowed up by the hat. Lord Norimasa removed it and said to the samurai, "I am sure you know how to don this hat. Please put it on for me."

Lord Norimasa went into the Council of War looking as if an enormous black gourd had grown on his head. Thereafter, that was the only hat he would wear for formal meetings. That hat, of course, was spoken of far and wide.

"You see?" the old counselor told the samurai. "You cannot win even a game of *go* with Lord Norimasa."

ANOTHER SUDDEN TANTRUM on the part of the fox awakened the samurai. His fox was flinging herself against the door and scratching the wood.

"Stop!" said the samurai, and the fox dolefully agreed and returned to her place by his side. A moment or two later, the door opened and the woman came into the hut. "Very cold," she said, shaking some snow from her heavy robe.

Utsu went up to her and was sniffing the robe's hem. The fox looked at the samurai as if to ask for permission to jump up on the woman.

"No jumping," the samurai said.

"She smells a dog I kept once," the woman said. She put the robe on a peg, and to the samurai's astonishment, the fox grabbed the robe's hem and began lashing it back and forth as if the fox thought it were an animal and she intended to break its neck.

"Utsu!" shouted the samurai. "Stop!"

The fox was yelping as she attacked the robe. "Stop!" the samurai said again. This time, the fox obeyed and returned to him.

"Animals have lives and wills of their own," the woman said. She seemed entirely unperturbed.

"*Gomen nasai, gomen nasai*," he kept repeating. "I'm sorry. I'm sorry."

"There is no need to be regretful," she said. "I am surprised that the fox obeys you so well."

"She does not normally act this way," the samurai said. "I apologize. She seems to think she can go anywhere with you."

"Do not apologize for her," said the woman. "The fox is loyal to you. She thought there was danger and so she set off an alarm. If she scratches my door, I am not worried. It was well scored by my dog."

The samurai thanked her, bowing.

"Tonight," she said, "I will make a meal of smoked river fish, clear broth and pickled radish. Everything I have is either smoked or pickled. In the mountains, one must have food that will outlast the winter."

She went to her table and placed a large wooden board in the center and then went back to the robe and took a large radish from its sleeve. She began chopping it. The fox crawled slowly on her belly back to the robe. "Ignore her," the woman said. The fox crept back to the samurai. "I still have a few vegetables buried under the straw in the stable," she said. "They will keep there for a while. Tomorrow, I will bring some pomegranates and I will stew them with sweet beans. In winter, they keep illness from taking hold. Also, they are delicious."

The samurai acknowledged this with a low bow.

"I have thought of a story to tell you," the samurai said. "About a lord and a large hat. Have you heard such a story?"

"No," said the woman.

"Shall I tell it to you?"

"Please," said the woman. "An entertaining story makes the chores fly."

The samurai told the woman the story of Lord Norimisa's hat, but he did not tell her the lord's name.

"A difficult man," said the woman, smiling. "How all of you must have laughed!"

"He had that hat on just before he died, although at the end we had to take it from him. He was so hot, the old counselor was afraid he would set the hat on fire."

"The old counselor," the woman repeated in a soft voice.

WHEN DINNER WAS READY, she placed a bowl before the samurai, then set her own on the table and they both sat down.

"When I lived in a castle," she said, "it was my task to tell stories, especially on the unlucky nights when we were not allowed to fall asleep."

"Tell me a story, then," said the samurai.

"It is hard, have you not found it hard, to refrain from telling those you meet, 'I was such and such a person in such and such a life'? When you are cut off from what you were, you want to believe you were the person you were before, and so you are forever telling people, 'This and this is what I did, this and this is what I was.' Do you not have this impulse?"

"I think, never," said the samurai.

"Your character is strong," the woman said. "Women are not so strong. They are forever telling those who will listen, 'Now I am old, but once I was young. Today, my face frightens people, but once I was beautiful.' It is the death of beauty that stabs them the most deeply."

The samurai looked at her and smiled. "Are you telling me how beautiful you once were?"

She flushed. "If I wanted to tell you that, I would tell you clearly," she said. "I was not thinking of myself. I was thinking about people and how they age, even in their minds."

"When does a woman begin to know she is old?" the samurai asked. The smoked river fish was tough, and he chewed slowly at it.

"There is one sign, and every woman I have known believes it to be horrible—when a woman sees herself in a very good mirror or reflected in a very still, clear pool, and her face has changed in this way. There are perpendicular lines that score the thin band of flesh above the top lip. A woman from the castle saw this and went entirely mad. After that, she was sure her husband intended to poison her and that her children thought she was a burden and were attempting to assassinate her. It was necessary to guard her day and night. But she was not watched carefully enough. In the end, she procured some poison and they found her dead around the Hour of the Ox. Then rumors flew! You know how people are in the castle, hundreds of moths in a small box. Many thought the husband somehow gave her the poison. Others suspected the children. In fact, I thought everyone was relieved, or would have been, if they had not thought they would meet the same end. Those lines above the lip sound like a gong in a woman's mind, and what they say is, 'Old! Old! Old!' Once some women hear it, they can hear nothing else."

The samurai seemed surprised that beauty was so important.

"What else does a woman have?" she said with a touch of scorn. "She sees herself growing older, and it is as if someone were stealing every bit of her money as she watched, knowing that in the end, she would have nothing. You cannot reason with someone like that. Perhaps no one should try. A woman valued only for her beauty is right to believe that she is now bankrupt."

"And when you grew older?"

"I never believed that I would be the one exception, the woman who would never age."

"I wish," the samurai said with a sigh, "that there were many stories about women. They are so difficult to understand."

"Only because no one thinks them worth understanding," the woman said.

"No," the samurai said. "Especially if a man wants to understand a woman, he has the greatest difficulty of all."

"Why do you say that?" she asked.

"Because when you truly want to understand someone, when you are not content with surfaces and poses, when you want to know the truth of another human being, the truth of anything is almost impossible to find. And women are not like men. They are not as direct. Even in their minds. They think and then speak through many screens. Even when they wish to speak directly, they cannot do it."

"Yet some men and women achieve it—understanding," the woman said.

The samurai regarded her and said nothing.

"You think it is impossible," she said. "Perhaps it is."

"Someone should write a story about this problem," the samurai finally said.

"I may know one," she said. "Although it is not exactly the same thing."

"Please tell it," he said.

"Probably it is a foolish story," she said. "And perhaps you have heard it. 'The Man Who Wanted to Paint on Skin.'"

"I have not heard it."

The fox walked to the door and began to whimper softly.

"When you come back from a walk with the fox, we shall have some saké, and I will tell you my foolish story," she said.

CHAPTER TWENTY-EIGHT

THE SAMURAI and his fox returned. The woman asked him what he expected of the weather. "More snow," he said, and she nodded in agreement. She went to the door and opened it. Snowflakes were beginning to flutter, very few, the small flakes easily mistaken for ash coming up from the fire pit. She asked the samurai how much snow he expected, because, after all, he had already seen the snow beginning when she asked him to predict the weather. He laughed and said, "Look at that sky. What can come but a storm?"

"Up here," she said, "the snow can grow so deep it blocks the window and then it is always dark inside."

"I will dig out a path so we can open the door and go back and forth to the stable," he said. "Do you know enough stories to get us through a snowstorm?"

"I am made up of stories," she said.

"Well? Will you tell me one now?"

"It will not be exactly what you meant," she said. "I told you."

"Whatever it is, I will like hearing it," he said. "I once knew a woman who liked to tell me stories."

The woman nodded, settled herself comfortably on the mat, propped her elbow up on an armrest and began.

"This story is called 'The Man Who Wanted to Paint on Skin.'"

He waited expectantly. She poured each of them a cup of saké, and now she sipped at hers. Finally, she began.

"*Mukashi, mukashi*, there was a man who wanted to paint on skin.

He thought skin was more beautiful than any paper and that anything painted on it would be illuminated and change day to day as paper never could. So he persuaded several people to let him try skin painting. His pictures were very beautiful, and in those days, he excelled in painting images of longevity—turtles, cranes and pines. His sunsets and sunrises were miraculous. At that time, too, he painted only on people's backs, but the paintings were so beautiful that the people on whom he painted wanted to see his paintings easily, and so he began to paint on stomachs, thighs, legs and arms. But there was one flaw to his idea. The paintings would not last. When the people he painted bathed, the paintings would slowly begin to fade.

" 'This is not what I wanted,' said the man. 'I do not want my paintings to vanish. I want them to change as the person's body changes. I will have to think of something else. Fabric retains color. Why not skin?' And so he set to work.

"But he could find nothing that would render his skin paintings indelible. One afternoon, very discouraged, he sat in the sun staring at the back of his own hand on which a firefly had alighted. He saw the blue veins in his skin and they seemed to resemble a tree. The veins were bluer and more prominent than he remembered, because, as time had passed while he worked on his skin pictures, his body aged. As he looked at the blue veins, a thought came to him. He thought, Perhaps it is possible to place the pigment beneath the skin. But how could that be done?

"Not long afterward, he happened to trip over a rock and he fell. The next day he had a great purple and blue bruise on his thigh, and when he contemplated it, he thought, The body knows how to do it! There is blood beneath the skin and it shows through as if it were paint. But how could he learn to paint beneath the skin? It seemed futile. He was so dejected that he did not even experiment.

"Then a savage from the north was brought down in a cart and people were invited to look in at the savage through the bars, and what should the skin painter see there but a savage painted all over with blue and red pictures. His excitement could not be contained. He persuaded the owner of the savage to lock the man in irons and he communicated with the savage through sign language. Could the man show him how to do it?

"Ultimately, he came to understand that the savage used a *hari,* a needle, or a sharp rectangular knife to thrust the inks he used into the skin.

"The man did not tire of his quest. He found some *hinin,* nonpeople, who agreed to be painted on if they could live with him afterward. In those days, the *hinin* had a great desire to live among normal people. Perhaps they still do. I don't know. Until I began my wandering, I had never even seen a farmer, and was not sure that people who lived in the fields were human. The *hinin* were looked down upon even by the farmers and fishermen, and so it was not difficult to persuade them.

"For several hours a day, each of them would have a design drawn on his back, and the man who wanted to paint on skin would try to inject dye beneath the skin. But nothing worked. The dye would spread out beyond the boundaries of the design, and even worse, it would eventually be erased by the body and it would be as if the painter had never attempted to paint on skin. There were other problems. After several weeks of injections, one of the *hinin* died of a high fever, and he was not the last. Some of the inks, as the painter was coming to learn, were poisonous. The painter was in despair.

"He set off to the northernmost prefecture in the land, determined to find the savages who knew how to paint on skin. To get there, he had to cross snow country, and because he was in a great rush, he calculated improperly, and found himself crossing in the dead of winter. One day, a blizzard blew in suddenly and the painter realized he was going to die. Then he saw an entrance to a cave, and although he feared a bear would be sleeping inside, he went in. He was lucky in this cave and this bear. The man curled himself beside the bear and so he kept himself warm. Even though he was warm and could lick water from the moisture on the cave walls, he had nothing to eat. Somehow, the bear knew there was trouble and roused herself. Bears in snow country store up ant paste and eat it through the winter. The bear smeared her paw with ant paste and offered it to the painter. The painter licked off the paste, and so he did not starve. When winter ended, he bowed low to the bear, and went on, going north.

"Finally, he came to the land of the savages. He found the man who had given the savage to him, and that man went to the chief of the tribe and explained what the painter wanted. The savages taught him how to paint on skin. As soon as he learned that, he began his trip back. This time, when he tried to paint on the *hinin*, they did not perish of dye poisoning, nor did the pictures he painted spread and dissolve under the skin. They remained where they were, and as time passed, he saw that they would remain permanently.

"The painter continued to perfect his art. His painting grew ever more luminous. People began to come to him and offer large sums if he would paint upon them, but most often, a man would bring his mistress and ask that something be painted on her. It was not long before the painter began to prefer painting on women. He became more and more selective and refused far more people than he accepted, and always, he painted on women. When he would turn down a particular woman, and the man who had brought her would grow angry, especially a samurai, he would say that he was looking for one particular woman, and after he found her and painted her, he would paint this woman he was then rejecting. All the men would ask the same thing. 'Are you looking for a perfect woman?' And he would say, with truth, that he was not.

"But what he was looking for was even stranger. He was looking for a woman whose entire body could be painted, a body whose skin would wrinkle in just such a way as to change his original painting as she aged, and as her skin wrinkled, the painting would change and become even more beautiful. That was the woman he was looking for. It had to do with her skin and little else. And since he could not find such a woman, he continued perfecting his skills on corpses that were stolen by others for him, and on living men.

"At last, a young woman was brought by her father to see him. 'I understand you are looking for a perfect woman,' said the father. 'Such is my daughter! Paint her!'

"Already the painter was running his fingers over her arm, which he had unceremoniously exposed by roughly pushing down her robe. 'If she will lie down so I may examine her back,' the painter said. The father hesitated for a moment, then ordered his daughter to lie down. It was the father who pushed her robe down to her waist.

"The painter continued running his fingers over the body. At last, he said, 'She will do.' He was tremendously excited, even agitated, but concealed his emotions.

" 'Then you will paint her skin?' asked the father, who had not dared to hope for such a resolution. 'Daughter!' he said. 'You will be famous throughout the land. There is no one who will not want you!'

" 'I do not want everyone to desire me,' she said. But the father was beside himself with joy and paid no attention to his daughter's words. 'When will you begin?' he asked the painter.

"The painter was an honest man. He told the father of the risks posed by the inks, and how painful it was to have the dye injected, but the father kept repeating, 'That's all right! That's all right!' The girl, as one would expect, was weeping, but when the painter asked her if she was willing to be painted, she nodded her head in assent. 'She will have to stay with me until it is done,' said the painter to the girl's father. 'You must leave while I am painting. Will you agree?'

" 'Of course, of course!' said the father.

" 'How odd,' murmured the painter under his breath, 'that such a remarkable girl would be produced by such a father.'

"And so the girl was left with him, and the painting began. When she lay on her stomach, he painted scenes of the four seasons. 'You will see,' he said to her. 'You will not tire of these scenes. They will constantly change.'

"When it came time for her to lie on her back and he began to paint the other side of her body, he drew lords and ladies of the palace. He spent an inordinate amount of time drawing the exquisite robes of the ladies.

"When he was finished, he inspected his work and found it perfect. He left her hands and her neck and her legs and her face unpainted. Thus, no one could see her paintings unless she herself offered to show them, so that, if she so desired, she could keep people she met by chance from seeing the paintings altogether.

"When her body healed and she stood up in front of him, he told her, 'Someone else would tell you, "Now you must keep your body perfect. You must not age." But I tell you no such thing. Eat, grow thinner, grow fatter, but above all, age!'

"The girl nodded. When the father came for her, he was transported by delight. 'Beauty heaped upon beauty!' he exclaimed! 'Truly this is perfection!' Then the girl cried and said he had made her into a curiosity, a monstrosity, and no one would love her. She said it was bad enough when she was loved for her body alone, but now how was she to know why anyone cared for her? 'How does any woman know why someone cares for her?' the father replied, and he turned to the painter, who agreed, saying, 'No one knows that. Your father has spoken the truth.'

"After that, the painter accepted far more women when they were presented to him, but always he wished for that particular woman. He wanted to see what her paintings looked like as she grew older. If she had children, how had she changed? He decided he would have to live a long time in order to see what his skin paintings became as she grew old. And he did live very long. People said of him that he intended to live forever.

"Years passed as the old painter continued painting and waiting to see how the girl had grown old. Often, he thought she was dead and that was why she had not come to see him. But one day, an old woman came down the narrow road. She was hobbling and using a stout wooden cane.

" 'I am the young girl on whom you painted,' she said.

"He was frantic with excitement. 'Take off your clothes!' he told her. Can you imagine such a scene? An ancient woman and an even more ancient man? But she took off her clothes and stood before him naked. He had even painted her private parts after having her shave her hair, and she continued to shave there.

" 'Let me see your back,' he demanded, and she obediently turned. The wrinkles on her skin changed the image of winter. The wrinkles made it appear as if the snow were driven more thickly. It resembled real snow, not painted flakes. The autumn scene had also changed. The bright leaves of the trees were no longer shiny and flat, but appeared to have dried out as the fall neared its end. The summer sun now seemed to shimmer in the heat, and there was a new haziness about the spring scene. When he saw this, the painter smiled and said, 'My work is over. I have lived to see perfection.' But then he thought to ask her to turn again so that he could see the pictures of the lords and ladies. She did turn. The people's robes were wrinkled, almost disheveled. Their faces were deeply scored with wrinkles and in the painting, which was no longer only a painting, there seemed to be only living antiquities in the palace. 'Ah!' he said. 'That is what I wanted!' He looked deeply into her face and said, 'You have given me what I wanted and all I wanted. Thank you.' He bowed deeply.

" 'May I go now?' the old woman said.

"'Of course,' said the painter, who continued bowing and smiling, smiling and bowing.

"And then a strange thing happened. Instead of gathering up her clothes, the woman rose up in the air, and her clothes rose up with her. As she rose, he saw she had no feet.

"'A ghost!' he said in horror.

"'Now I can rest,' said the old woman's voice, which seemed to come from nowhere.

"The old painter was extremely disturbed. He began to make inquiries. Finally, he found her family. 'Oh, yes, Kimiko,' said an old man. 'She died long ago.'

"'When?' asked the old painter.

"'Not long after she was painted. People said she was exhausted by guests coming to see her, but I do not believe that was the reason.'

"'What was the reason?' the painter asked.

"'I believe she died of perfection,' said the old man. 'You can have too much of anything. She was perfect before. Then she was made even more perfect, which made her more than human. She would cry and say, "I am even less human than the *hinin*." She grew inconsolable. In the end, she took poison and threw herself in the river. She wanted to die, who can doubt it?'

"The old painter was horrified. 'I thought she would be happy. I thought she would be pleased,' he said.

"'We are both old,' said the old man. 'Please let us not delude ourselves. There was nothing I could do to help her. You did what you did to her because you wanted to paint the perfect picture on skin. You never considered her happiness or her fate. Let us be honest, as death now sits like a vulture on our left shoulders.'

"'I will go now,' said the old painter. 'I am sorry.'

"'I am glad to hear it, but that changes nothing,' said the old man. 'Do you want some water for your trip back?'

"The painter nodded. The old man brought him a gourd full of cold water. The painter drank some immediately. 'It is good,' he said. 'Very cold.'

"'That water comes from the same river Kimiko threw herself in,' he said. 'Please enjoy it.'

"At that, the old painter fled the house and began walking down the road. Several evenings later, it is said, they found him dead behind a bush on the road, his own body dried up like a husk. He looked barely human, skin and bones and his skin rough and tanned like leather. Some people in the village said that was Kimiko's doing. She took her revenge. The old man disagreed, saying that Kimiko's nature would never have allowed her to avenge herself. 'He, too, died of an excess of perfection,' the old man said. 'We are not meant to rival the gods. We are not meant to grow more beautiful as we grow older.'

"But the village sage said that perhaps the gods wanted us to grow more beautiful the older we became, because were not the gods themselves ancient? I understand that the people in that village still argue about that. But there is no question the girl's fate was tragic."

"And her father?" asked the samurai. "What happened to him?"

"He went quietly and peacefully to his grave, respected by all," she said, her voice turning bitter. "Such are the destinies of fools."

"A terrifying story," the samurai said.

The woman lowered her eyes. He understood that when a woman lowered her eyes and looked down, there was something she wished to hide.

"Is it a true story?" he asked suddenly.

"Of course not," she said. "Whoever heard of such skin painting?"

"But someday, there may be."

She nodded.

"Is it an old story?"

"No," she said.

"Did you invent it?"

Now a cloud of confusion, almost palpable, emanated from the woman. "Yes," she said. "I make up many stories. I did not answer honestly when I spoke before. It is a true story, except, of course, for the skin painting."

"Except for that," the samurai said thoughtfully.

"I will not tell you stories if you interrogate me afterward," the woman said. She was not speaking playfully.

The samurai did not answer, but regarded her steadily.

"What is it you want?" she burst out.

"You are upset by your own story," he said. "I am not easily upset."

"'The tale is terrifying.' That is what you said!"

"The tale, yes, but I am not terrified," he answered.

"Nothing terrifies you?"

"Now we are back to an old question. If you are not afraid of losing your life, you are not easily terrified. You cannot be a good samurai if you fear death. But you can be terrified when you think of the deaths of others, although you are taught otherwise. I would be terrified in that way, if there were others I cared for or who cared for me."

"And no one does?"

"No one," he said. "Not any longer."

"Then we are alike in that," she said.

"Can that be true?" he asked. "When everything inside this hut testifies to someone's attentiveness to you?"

"Orders from someone who no longer lives," she said.

"Even my lord gave such orders, and those who survived him did their best to follow his wishes. Circumstances were against us."

The woman got up, broke some twigs and stirred them into the fire pit. Then she put on her long cloak. "It is getting colder," she said. "At night, it is almost intolerable."

"Yes," he said. "It is very cold at night."

"At least your fox sleeps with you," she said.

"It is true that she is warm," the samurai said.

"We have two mats, one on each side of the fire pit," she said. "We could move our mats together. We would be warmer. The fox might sleep between us."

Taken by surprise, the samurai did not answer. Once before, something like this had happened to him, but since then he had not encountered women for whom he might come to care. The boldness of the woman's suggestion stunned him. He knew that his men, whom he commanded, or the men who commanded him, were often rough with their women, their encounters sometimes approaching, perhaps even reaching, rape. Lord Norimasa did not approve of such doings, but neither did he actively object to such behavior when he heard about it. Still, the woman must have known many samurai during her life in a castle and heard of many such stories. They were completely alone. She was in his power. Such trust, or bravery, affected him.

"HE IS ALWAYS the gentleman," Lord Norimasa once said. "A noble-woman can begin to undress in front of him, and he will pretend that nothing unusual is happening. And yet he will busy himself with those women who sell themselves in the village."

"I do not like having ties," said Matsuhito.

"Who can avoid them?" the lord asked. "Even I have not managed."

"I lose enough men every time we ride out to battle. I do not want to lose any more to whom I have ties."

"But a woman will cling to you like a vine," said Lord Norimasa. "Such vine-women will strangle the house and grow larger and larger until they bring the habitation down. You don't have to worry about losing them."

"Nevertheless," Matsuhito said.

"You will see," Lord Norimasa had said. "There will be a little chink in your armor, and a little vine will worm its way in. It has always happened."

"WE COULD MOVE our mats together," the samurai said at last. "Shall we be like brother and sister?"

"I had no brother," she said. "Did you have a sister?"

He said he didn't think so.

"Then we would not know how to behave as brother and sister," she said.

PASSION LOOSENS the rougher passions, but after those are satisfied, the softer ones begin to grow toward the light. After some weeks, the samurai and the woman grew easy with one another. They were both alike in one way: neither of them feared asking the other questions. "It is very unusual," the samurai told her, "very bold, to continually question a man."

"I was born asking questions," she said with a sigh. "You ask a great many, do you not?"

"Long habit and strong inclination," he said.

"Do you mind?" the woman asked him.

"No. I like it. Between men and women, there are too many veils."

They were lying together beneath her long robe and the fox was lying on top of them. At first, Utsu objected to another person joining their sleeping arrangements, but the woman fed her and petted her, and the fox found they were warmer when they slept together.

"Is Utsu happy?" the woman asked.

"Very happy," the samurai said. "Except when you go for your secret walks. Then she goes wild. She wants to break down the door. She is very fond of you."

"They are very curious, foxes," the woman said. He saw that she lowered her eyes, as if she were falling asleep.

"I wonder if that's all it is," the samurai said.

"Who knows what goes on in the mind of a fox?" the woman said.

Just then, the fox reached up and licked her chin. "Good fox," the woman said. Something in the woman's timbre awakened a curiosity in him. He searched back for the first time he had heard such a voice, but he could get nowhere, and this made him uneasy, yet he was unwilling to believe he was wishing himself into a delusion. It was time to get up and bring in some firewood. Then he would clear the path between the hut and the stable and spend some time with the horse. Every day, pushing the door open was difficult. The woman, too, had her tasks. She had breakfast to make, and, of course, her secret walk after the samurai finished his chores. She watched him dress and go out the door. She saw him trudge to the stable, raising each leg high because of the snow. He suspects nothing, she told herself.

SINCE THE SAMURAI'S ARRIVAL, Lady Utsu found herself reliving parts of the past she had not thought about for some time.

"Strong passions and stronger habits," Lord Norimasa had said. "That's what binds a man to a woman, but don't assume the same is true for a woman." The lord frequently told this to his men, because, as he said, that was the one bit of wisdom he possessed. One day, during winter festivities intended to cheer up a gloomy palace during a gray season, the women came up with their own idea. They swarmed over him like wasps loosed from a nest until the lord had to ask if he ought to call his bodyguards. One of the women proposed a contest. Each man and woman was to write on the faithlessness of women.

"Whoever heard of such a theme for a contest? There are set themes and set rules, and we cannot deviate from them," Lord Norimasa said. He sounded uncomfortable. The truth was, although he could do as he liked in his own castle, if the Emperor and Empress disapproved of these doings, he would find himself in difficulties.

"I will tell you what," said Lady Utsu. "We will make this contest more traditional. We will use one theme, as we always do, and write poems which also reflect the seasons. I myself will concentrate on winter. But of course I will do the other seasons as well." Lady Utsu's dread, if not hatred, of hot weather was well known. "Nothing goes well in the summer," she was often heard to say. "Now it is a traditional contest," Lady Utsu said innocently.

"Poems on the faithlessness of women! Is that a theme we can allow? This theme is not permissible," said Lord Norimasa, turning to her, his eyes blazing. "And if the Empress hears of it?"

"I was in service to the Empress," Lady Utsu said. "I shall ask her to contribute a poem of her own, and if she does not care to do that, since she is busy with a sickly child, she might yet agree to help judge the contest. I understand she has three very quick women in her court now."

"Ask the Empress?" Lord Norimasa said, his lips white with rage. "Why not start a war and commence making banners?"

"Oh, I am not interested in banners," she said. "Banners are for wars."

"You are proposing a war!" the lord shouted at her. "Or hoping for one! Asking women to write poems that go against everything we believe is true!"

"Pretend is true," she corrected him.

"If trouble comes from this nonsense," he said, "I will send you, Lady Utsu, from the palace." Now the women began laughing. At least twice a week, Lord Norimasa threatened to send Lady Utsu from the palace. The lord now appealed to the laughing women. "If you will order an incense contest, I will give each of you two splendid robes."

"No, no," said Lady Kitsu, "we want to write about how faithless we are and how cruel we can be. It is not right that a lord as important as you should live in ignorance of the women who surround him." At that, the lord decided to beat a retreat, speeded by gales of laughter from the women, asking himself why he had not sought out duller women, and why he himself had somehow brought on a contest sure to bring him trouble.

The Empress was infuriated with her own husband, who had taken another wife while she was incapacitated by her pregnancy. She heard rumors of the contest and sent for Lady Utsu, whom she always missed.

"Now the trouble begins," Lord Norimasa said. "Do not say I neglected to warn you."

When Lady Utsu arrived at the Empress's palace, a palanquin was at the gate and carried her straight to the door of the Empress's chambers. When she finished telling Lady Utsu again and again how she missed her and how quiet and dull it was now in the palace, she said eagerly, "Tell me about this contest."

Lady Utsu told her. "Really, men are outrageous," the empress said. "Women should be unfaithful!"

"Perhaps you will judge it, Your Highness," Lady Utsu suggested.

"Such a sober tone you use when you say that!" the Empress said. "You have not changed. How I miss that mischievousness, the strange games you dreamed up, your silly bets about how long the snow would last before it melts."

"And Your Highness's tricks, telling the gardeners to remove the snow little by little at night. How late I had to stay up with my women while we replaced the snow after the gardeners were finished. Remember, Your Highness, how puzzled you were when our hems were always wet?"

"Ah, you were impossible," the Empress said. "How much fun it was!"

"It was, Your Highness, because you were there," Lady Utsu said.

"Now you are trying to have your way," the Empress said, sighing.

"No, Your Highness," said Lady Utsu, "I have missed you every minute of every day. To tell the truth, the women of the castle are not as high-spirited as you are, and I do not love any of them as much as I love you."

"There are not many occasions for high spirits in an Empress who lives in a palace," the Empress said. "You would always carry everything before you. On my own, I do not manage it."

"You must command, Your Highness," Lady Utsu said softly, stepping over the bounds of what could and could not be said.

"My training goes against it," the Empress said after a pause. "My will is strong, but not as strong as yours."

"Your Highness," Lady Utsu said, moving closer to her and speaking softly, "you are now the mother of the heir to the throne. You may do what you like and say what you like. If anyone opposes you, you need only hint that such a person will surely bring misfortune on your child. Can you not see it?"

"You are bold," said the Empress, "to speak to me in that way."

"Is it true?" whispered Lady Utsu.

The Empress nodded and said nothing. She sat on her mat deep in thought. "So many resentments," she said at last.

"Yours?" asked Lady Utsu.

"Who else's? What is there for the Emperor to resent? You are right, of course. I must change now that I have the child, or people will take him from me and use him as a pawn."

"If he is to be a pawn, that tiny Imperial Prince the wet nurse just took away, then he is, by nature, your pawn. Why not use him, Your Highness? You will use him better than anyone else because he is yours."

"The Emperor intends to raise him in another household until he is older."

"Oppose it," said Lady Utsu.

"Oppose it?" said the Empress thoughtfully.

"Who else can so easily oppose the Emperor?" she asked in a soft, almost inaudible voice.

"He is coming!" the Empress said. "I have ears like a fox! I have heard about your fox," the Empress said, speaking in an ordinary voice. "I can assure you I will want to know about that."

"Whatever Your Highness commands," Lady Utsu said meekly.

The Empress laughed aloud. "Tease him when he comes in. He tries to look annoyed when you do, but really, it gladdens him."

"Oh, I have not heard that laugh since the Lady Utsu left the palace," said the Emperor, appearing in the chamber. "Is it you, O Wrecker of Peace and Quiet?"

"It is I, Your Serene and Beloved and Most High Highness," said Lady Utsu.

"You have not changed," the Emperor said, sitting beside the Empress.

"But you have, Your Royal and August Highness," she said. "Now you are a father. And I hear you are so happy with fatherhood that you have taken another wife."

The Emperor was clearly displeased by this comment. The Empress said only, "He has," as if she had almost forgotten that event.

"What?" the Emperor said to his wife. "No ranting and raving in front of Lady Utsu? Or has Lady Utsu reconciled you to the idea?"

"It is no business of mine, Your Most Revered and All-Powerful Highness who commands the course of the wind and the rain and the sun."

"I see you are up to something, as usual," the Emperor said, biting his lip as he did when puzzled or frustrated.

"Only a contest, Your Most Beloved and Wise Highness," said Lady Utsu innocently.

"Tell me about your contest," the Emperor said. Lady Utsu explained it.

The Emperor roared with laughter. "And Lord Norimasa? Which is he most concerned about? That you women are staging a revolt, or that our august personages will be displeased?"

"Both," said Lady Utsu, "Your Most High and Renowned Ruler of People and Ruler of the Gods Who Watch from Above."

"Enough!" said the Emperor. "You have not changed. You will always go one step too far."

"But, Your Highness, who else will do it?" she asked.

"True," the Emperor said with some irritation. Then he smiled.

"What do you think of the contest?" the Empress said with down-cast eyes. "We should do something to commemorate the remarkable good fortune of having borne a male heir. If we begin with such a contest, people will say of you, 'He is indeed a wise and spirited man. We must not underestimate him and we must take care.'"

"Hmmmm," said the Emperor. "You may be right."

"Of course she is right, Most Noble and Beneficent Father of All the People of All the Land," said Lady Utsu.

"Did I not ask you to stop?" the Emperor said. "You are causing the Empress to giggle. When you are here, it is impossible to say one serious word."

"I am not giggling, I am laughing," the Empress said. "Girls giggle. Mothers of future Emperors laugh."

"What has come over you?" the Emperor asked her, astonished.

"I begin to feel my role," the Empress said. "It is only natural."

"Yes, I suppose it must be," the Emperor said. He appeared slightly uncomfortable. "And you are in favor of this scandalous contest when, in literature, we always portray women as meek, obedient and faithful?

Poems like that set a good example. I do not think the poems from this contest will have that effect."

"Oh," said Lady Utsu, "everyone knows that people are not affected by poetry."

"It will delight every woman in the land," the Empress said. "Women everywhere are tired of such submissiveness."

"You mean it will provide sermons for every priest in the land, and spontaneous sermons from every husband in the land."

"We are not free of our animal natures," the Empress said. "Even though we in the palace live in the clouds, we should extend our claws every now and then so we do not forget how to use them."

"A frightening thought," said the Emperor.

"The better to protect Your Beloved Emperor," said Lady Utsu.

"Not another word from you on this subject, O Lady of Chaos and Faithlessness," the Emperor said. "I will leave you two alone to plot against the shogun. I hope I didn't interrupt your plans for an insurrection when I came in as I did."

"No, Your Powerful and Grim and Strong-Willed Highness," said Lady Utsu. "We had concluded our plans and decided on the signal for the attack."

"Good," said the Emperor, rising. "It is best to think matters through thoroughly." As he reached the door of the chamber, he turned to the two women and addressed Lady Utsu. "Try not to cause too many disasters," he said.

"No, my lord," she said meekly.

He was not long in the corridor when he heard peals of laughter from the Empress's chamber. At least she has stopped the Empress's moping and weeping into her sleeve, he thought. Visiting one's wife should not be like visiting a rainstorm. Your Powerful and Grim and Strong-Willed Highness, he thought, smiling and remembering the lady's words. It was a pity to lose her, but it was easier to rule the palace without her. Another peal of laughter echoed through the corridor, and in spite of himself, he smiled again. An outrageous woman, he thought. She ought to have been born a man. Although, he reflected, as he had so often before, she had been entirely faithful to the Empress. Other of her ladies might agree to share his bed, but he always knew better than to dream of such a thing with her. She is like a faithful dog, he told himself sourly, but even as he thought this, he knew it was not true.

The things the women had said! In the end, the poems were more restrained than the commentaries.

Women hide a dagger in their hearts,
The best turn it against others.

The Emperor had reason to remember that poem. One night, incensed by his defection to his second wife, the Empress took her dagger, ripping and shredding a newly made silk screen bearing the image of a woman resembling his new wife. He had no doubt that she would have preferred ripping him to shreds. The Emperor decided that the contest was timely. All men should remember that those tiny creatures, their wives, were most capable of bringing the high ones to their knees.

People still spoke of Lord Norimasa's contest. In the end, Lord Norimasa was pleased. Yet there was one samurai who thought the women were creating fairy tales, each trying to outdo the other, when really, none of them were capable of feeling the violent and malevolent passions they expressed. Lady Utsu, who spoke with him, said from behind her screen, "I pity you. It is not wonderful to learn such things."

"If they are true," he had said, somewhat smugly.

CHAPTER TWENTY-NINE

THE WINTER WORE ON. The woman said, "Never have I seen such snow. It is trying to keep us where we are. How odd."

Only occasionally did the samurai think how unusual his life had become, and then he would see a certain color reflected on the snow and he would stop to ask himself, How did this come about?

"How does anything come about?" Lord Norimasa once asked, to which the samurai had no answer, then or now.

The samurai was happier than ever before. Before this, he never thought about happiness, only duty. Happiness was something one felt after accomplishing one's duty. This was strange, to experience happiness without first doing something difficult and dutiful.

They were both happy when night fell, and would often, without consulting one another, postpone going to bed until they felt a fierce desire for one another. When she mounted him, and her hair fell forward over him and he could see her face clearly, he experienced a joy he had never felt in battle. "People will tell you," Lord Norimasa once said, "and more would say the same thing if they were honest, that going to a battle is not as fearsome as going to a woman." The samurai, however, did not find this to be true. To do something so pleasurable that would not end in his losing his head: he could not imagine anything better than that. If the samurai feared that he was insatiable and the woman would tire of their nightly activities, he soon learned that she was equally voracious. In the beginning, he was constantly surprised and somewhat unnerved by her curiosity.

"But surely you have slept with men before," she said. "Did you enjoy it?"

"I could not have enjoyed what I didn't do," he answered. "Many of the younger men attached themselves to older samurai who protected and taught them. I was attached to Lord Norimasa."

"And do you mean to tell me that that perpetually humping dog did not make love to you?"

"Never," said the samurai. "Although I loved him, and I believed he loved me, but it was not a sexual love."

"That is astonishing," said the woman.

"After every battle, he had a second battle," said the samurai. "Always many women. I don't know where they came from."

"I can tell you," she said. "When he set fire to a village so they would have enough light, the samurai grabbed the attractive women when they ran out of their huts. If a woman was holding a child, they pulled the child from her and threw it away through the air. Lord Norimasa and his men were known for this. People said that was why no one dreamed of rising up against him. If he was so savage when all he needed was light, what would he do if he were bent on revenge? Did you never see such things?"

"Yes," he said.

"Why not pretend I am a man," she said, "and enter me as you would enter another samurai?"

"You are almost a samurai," he said, delaying such an experiment.

"Then it will be easier for you to imagine it," she said. She flopped down on her mat and rolled over so she lay on her stomach. She did not dread appearing ridiculous and so her spontaneous actions had a charm unlike any woman's he had ever seen. Sometimes she had the air of a child, he thought, yet certainly she was not.

The woman could see he was reluctant, but in the end, he would do what she asked. He was learning that what she asked him to do was always pleasurable.

"At our ages, to be discovering these things," he said, as they lay side by side on the mat, she on her stomach, he on his back, staring at the ceiling.

"And when we are together at night?" she asked him. "Do you feel old then?"

When they lay alone at night, he was once again a young boy and she was a young woman. The dimness of the light, even when a full moon shone on the snow and lit the room with odd patterns through the crisscrossed lattices, did not expose them harshly. She would spend what seemed hours tracing the lines of his face. "Such a beautiful face," she said. He would cup her face in his hands and look at her as if he were thirsty and she a cup of water he put off drinking. "It is your face that is beautiful," he said.

"It is the face of my old age." She said that there were hundreds of thousands of women who looked exactly like her. This made the samurai laugh and say, "I wonder where they were hiding all those years near the capital."

"In snow country," she said. "Every woman there resembles me exactly."

"You will say anything," said the samurai.

"That is true," she said.

Once their activities subsided, the fox, who always crept across the floor and lay down at the door, would come up to them tentatively, as if to ask permission.

They began to talk about everything. She spoke far more easily than he did, and she was usually the one to begin asking questions. One night, when they both were lying together happily, she suddenly asked, "In battle, what is the most exciting thing? Once, I thought to disguise myself and go to war as a soldier," she said, laughing. Her laugh was throaty. Every time he heard it, he was reminded of something, a faint sound heard far away.

"There are many exciting things," the samurai said. "It is hard to choose."

"Choose," the woman said.

The samurai thought.

"Have you fallen asleep?" she asked him accusingly.

"No, I am thinking," he said.

"Think faster," she said, "or I will fall asleep." She understood that he would not respond until he knew the true answer to the question she asked. He was precise and clear in that way.

"I think the most exciting thing in a battle happens immediately before it. Everyone is massed, waiting for the command. The cavalry always goes first, so the horses draw their excitement from the riders, and it is always hard to control them. This horse and that one will rear up, perhaps out of fright. They snort and whinny. Behind them, the infantry is waiting for the horses to begin running toward the enemy force, and behind them, the archers are waiting for the foot soldiers to pour over the hill, because there is almost always a hill. Lord Norimasa preferred high ground. So everyone is waiting, you understand. Lord Norimasa raises his war fan. In an instant, the lord will lower his war fan and the horses will pour down the hill and the battle will begin. But he does not. He is waiting for a specific moment in time and only he can determine what that will be. If the lord so much as moves, everyone begins to move, and there is a wave that goes through the army that takes time to subside.

"Everyone is staring at the lord and that war fan. No one breathes. Time stops. Nothing is more exciting than this, not even fighting for life. And then the fan is lowered, and everything is determined by the outcome of the battle. Once the battle begins, there is no longer any thinking. There is only instinct."

He remembered leaving the peasant village he and the other samurai had defended, and how the horse reared up against the dead sky, and how he leaped up to grab the horse's bridle, and later, he was told he was speaking to the horse from the moment he approached him. But he did not remember this as he remembered other things. It was as if he were watching someone else whom he did not know.

"You were protecting a village?" asked the woman. "Why?"

"There was a bandit troop. They were destroying the villagers. The villagers asked for our help. We had no food. They offered us rice. What they really offered us was a fight worth entering. The odds were against us. When we came to the village, the people there were capable only of beating a wounded man to death with a broom." He smiled, remembering.

"You have led an unusual life," the woman said.

"I told you, my life was ordinary," he said irritably.

"Why should it annoy you to hear that your life was unusual?"

"Because I was born base. I was a farmer from a farmer's village. How extraordinary could I have become?"

"How odd. To have achieved so much and not to understand the ways of your world," she said.

"I understood them," he said. He took up a hank of her hair and began winding it around his wrist. "Now," he said, "go to sleep and lie still or you will strain your hair against my arm and in the morning your head will hurt."

"The Empress and I used to play games with our hair," she said. "One day we got our hair so entwined that it took six ladies three hours to get us apart. She would take some of my hair and I would take some of hers and we would create little bridges, lattices, whatever came to mind. But of course one day we went too far. We both had headaches. You pulled my hair!" she suddenly exclaimed.

"No, you moved," said the samurai. "I told you so."

"Let me go," she said.

"No."

"Oh, that is not right when you have me bound."

"Only by the hair," he said.

"You will not let go of me?"

"No."

"I can sleep without moving until daylight. I was trained that way. If I did not keep both my legs together and straight, the nurse would straighten them out. How many times each night she must have done so! It is terrible, the life of servants."

"She was dedicated to you, and you gave her purpose."

"When I first came here, I spent many months sprawling in every position imaginable. Then I tired of it. So I am back to sleeping like the good child of a noble. You might as well release my hair."

He laughed. "No," he said. "I want to see how still you can be for an entire night."

"I will defer to you," she said. "This time."

THE SAMURAI FELL asleep immediately. But the woman remained awake. Her secret walks were becoming more and more of a burden. The footsteps in the attic above the stable made her lonely for the creature who lived up there. Sooner or later, the samurai would have to learn about him. She tried to imagine what his feelings would be, but could not. She was about to turn on her side when she remembered that she was tethered to the samurai's wrist. Probably he knows who I am, she thought, but is hiding it, as I am. We are afraid that this happiness will vanish if we admit we have found one another. She sighed, lay still and fell asleep.

CHAPTER THIRTY

"IF I HAD SOMETHING to tell you," she said the next morning, "something startling I have been keeping secret, what would you think of what I said?"

"I cannot predict my reaction to a cloud," he answered. He continued eating his rice and then stopped. The sun shone in and cast stripes over her face. She looked like a tiger. "What are you trying to tell me?" he asked gently.

"It is about my secret walks," she said. "It is about that."

The samurai nodded and was still, watching her.

"I would like to stop taking them in secret, but there has been a reason for such walks," she said.

"Does it have to do with the broom you take with you to erase your tracks when you return?"

"Yes," she said. "How do you know that?"

"You can lie all night without moving. I can begin to solve riddles."

She thought for some time. "I must tell you," she said. "It cannot go on. It is not fair to the beast."

The samurai's face remained expressionless.

"He is used to living in the house with me," she said.

"Is he a dog?" asked the samurai.

"Not a dog."

"A fox, then?"

Now the two of them stared at one another in silence.

"He is a fox," she said, her voice soft.

"And he lives above the stable ceiling, above my horse."

"Yes."

"So you are the woman I asked about, the woman who traveled with a fox."

"Yes."

"But you said you did not see such a person."

"I did not know why you wanted to find her."

"And now do you know?"

"Yes." She answered so softly he could scarcely hear her.

"Then you know who I am," the samurai said.

"Yes," she said. She was weeping silently.

"Why did you not tell me before?"

She waved her hand, her head bent, and did not answer.

"I will consider the things you have said." His answer must have sounded harsh to her, because she turned so that she was not facing him, and he could hear that her weeping grew less controllable. It tore at him to see how unhappy she was.

"Meanwhile," he said, "may I not see your fox? Once again?"

She turned back, and in spite of herself smiled, although the weeping continued.

"I will get him," she said.

His fox, named Lady Utsu, had heard her own second name, Fox, and lifted her head from the floor and now gazed at both of them

The woman, Lady Utsu, got up, put on her boots and her robe and went to the door. It opened with considerable difficulty, and then she was gone. The samurai remained sitting cross-legged on the mat. In the thatched roof, he could hear rats scurrying. For the rats, this was as good a way as any to spend the winter. He tried to understand what had happened, but he knew he would not have enough time before the woman—Utsu—returned. His attention was concentrated on her deception. Why hadn't she told him who she was? It was true that age had changed both of them greatly or they would have recognized one another immediately, but he did not believe she remained silent out of vanity. She never cared about her beauty and often enough wanted to be rid of it. And the story she told him, of the man who froze to death performing the task she had set him, that would not be enough to turn a samurai against her. Samurai respected both the challenge and the person who accepted it. Had she seen something in his eyes, something repellent? Her beautiful hair was now streaked with gray, but he thought little of that. He remembered thinking, Women, too, age, and he recalled the surprise he felt when he came to that realization.

"You must not be so innocent of domestic affairs," Lord Norimasa once said. "There are things going on in this palace that are far more complicated than problems we solve on the battlefield. One day you will be trapped in one of the hundreds of spider webs and then what will become of you?"

He had not realized that women age, because there had been only one woman he loved, and, like someone who dies young and whose image never fades for those who knew her, Lady Utsu was always as he had last seen her. As for the other women—they drifted by like thinning clouds and did not engage his attention. Except, perhaps, for Lady Tsukie, whose face changed horribly as she grew more and more mad. But she had changed, not aged, and he had watched her closely because he feared she might harm Lord Norimasa.

Why had Lady Utsu never let them know what became of her? She must have known how heartbroken the lord would have been to lose sight of her. If she had sent some word, any word, he would have been comforted. If she had asked him not to look for her, he probably would have obeyed her wishes. But perhaps he would not have. He might have wanted to see her one more time. And then Lord Norimasa had found the child, a replica of her mother. What became of the child? So many concealments, it was more than he could understand. Surely there were reasons for her decisions, there always were, at least men almost always had their reasons, but perhaps women were different. He didn't know. If Lord Norimasa were alive, he would ask him. Lord Norimasa studied two things: battle and the doings of women.

"They are both the same thing," Lord Norimasa had said. "Although a strategy for a war is simpler than seeing through the schemes of a woman. I read books on strategy, but I sharpen my mind trying to understand women."

And what would Lord Norimasa say about this state of affairs?

"AH, YOU ARE over your head here, Matsuhito," he said. "You must hope that she means you well. Easier to understand why, in the mountains, you shout and your echo returns. When it comes to women, you are always hearing the echo, not the real woman's voice. Only other women can hear that."

"But I must understand this," Matsuhito said.

"I am sorry for you," said Lord Norimasa. "Nevertheless, you must try. Do not struggle too much in the web. If she sees you flailing about, she will go after you like a spider. They cannot help it. But if you are quiet, you will have time to work things out. Step quietly. Her ears are sharp. You must know this. Otherwise, you would not have told her who you are. And, of course, you are afraid she will hurt you again— or disillusion you. In my experience, I found that samurai fear women and only women."

THE SAMURAI FELT that the world he knew was dissolving in water. This is temporary, he told himself. When my mind clears, I will again know the world as it is.

Someone was struggling with the door of the hut. Lady Utsu. He did not get up to help her, as he usually would have done, and she did not expect him to do so. She assumed he was stunned and disillusioned. She pushed against the door again, opening it wider, and her fox leaped into the hut. The animal stood still for a moment, his ears back, his teeth exposed, and then he seemed to accept, if not recognize the samurai. The fox looked from one to the other of the two people. So far he ignored the samurai's fox. She was standing, her own ears back, pressed against the wall. Suddenly the fox bounded toward the samurai and jumped up on him and licked at his cheek.

"You remember me," the samurai said. "You remember better than humans do." He was about to begin stroking the fox when his fox, deciding that the samurai was imperiled, flew across the room and landed on top of the woman's fox, trying for the new fox's throat. Lady Utsu's fox was taken by surprise. Both were growling and barking. The samurai forgot the woman and tried to control his fox, but the woman clearly believed that the other fox meant harm to the samurai. The samurai began shouting at her to stop. At the same time, Lady Utsu was calling her fox to her, and when he did not listen, she shouted louder and then louder again. Finally, they each had their own fox under control, but the two animals were straining at one another as if they intended to tear one another apart as soon as they were let loose.

"Well, this is a problem," said the samurai.

"Your fox is jealous," said Lady Utsu.

"And that is the difficulty?" the samurai asked. "They do not like one another."

"They are not accustomed to one another," she said. "That's all it is."

"And how are we to accustom them to one another when they intend to attack and kill each other when we let them loose?"

Lady Utsu looked at the samurai as if he were a simpleton. "We do not let them loose," she said. "Not yet."

Some time passed while both of them remained intent on staring at the floor. The samurai spoke first.

"You had a child," he said. "I believe that Lord Norimasa found her and brought her back to the palace. I hoped she was mine, but Lord Norimasa kept her to himself. Could you not have sent word?"

"Why didn't you try to find me?" she burst out.

"You forget. You were the one who was impossible to find. I was the one who stayed in one place."

"You could have died in the battle!"

"You could have found out easily enough," he said.

"It was winter! The roads were impassable."

"It was not winter," he said in a colorless voice. "It was autumn. Every year, when autumn arrived, I thought of you and thought of how to find you, but either my scheme didn't succeed or I was lucky and I forgot. But it was not winter. You are lying to me."

"I never lie!"

"Now you are being ridiculous," he said. "All women lie. All people lie. You must have a reason for lying, even after all this time."

"What reason could I have?"

"Out of the thousand possible motives, I cannot begin to guess."

"Perhaps I do not know myself," she said.

"You organize an escape—that is what it is—you determine to remain hidden and you succeed, you never contact anyone again, and yet you do not know why you did any of these things?"

"I don't know!" she said in exasperation. "I don't expect to get to the bottom of it now."

"Try."

She took a deep breath. "I was pregnant," she said. "I knew Lady Tsukie would think the child was Lord Norimasa's."

"Where is the child?" he asked.

"I don't know. I gave her away when she was a few days old."

"Gave her away?"

"Yes. I knew I could not provide a good life for her."

"You could have come back to me!"

"How? If you hadn't believed me, then what? And with Lady Tsukie set against me. She would have gone after you, too. I didn't see what else to do. I had left the palace. I didn't know where I would end. Or how."

"You ought to have told me. You ought to have given me a choice."

"I did not think so. Not at the time."

"And Aki? What did she say?"

"She was against it. So was my sister."

"And yet you insisted?"

"I thought it was best. She was taken in by a good family, I know that."

So it was true. He had a child! And yet, if she was not the girl Lord Norimasa had found, she was gone and he would never find her. How could such a thing have happened?

"I cannot understand," he said.

"No," she said. "Probably you cannot."

"This," he said, "is the worst thing you have done."

The samurai's fox barked once, sharply.

"You are upsetting the foxes," she said.

"Do not accuse me," he answered. "Of anything. I am not so easily distracted."

"I did think that somehow you would find me if you wanted to find me," she said in a small voice.

"Please do not say that again or I shall become angry," he said. "I know enough of life to know that if someone wants to be found, even under the most difficult circumstances, she will manage to leave a small trace."

"Perhaps I accomplished my purposes too well," she said.

"You accomplished them perfectly," he said, and then he rose and put on his straw hat, went to the door and was about to put on his fur boots. "I am going out. Utsu! You are coming with me." He went back for the fox, and she began leaping about him. Lady Utsu's fox barked, but the woman refused to look at him. "That is what men do," she said. "They go out the door."

The samurai looked at her, put on his boots just outside the door and dragged it shut.

His gratitude for the emptiness outside was immense. He had not realized how strong the pressure inside had become. Or the anger he now felt.

"Come, Utsu," he said, and he began to follow the path toward the woods. A little way across the clearing, he stopped and looked about him. The sky was lavender. The shadows cast by the trees were an ashy blue or a deeper purple than the sky. There must have been another flurry while they were speaking. Every twig and every needle and every bough was outlined by snow and stood out sharply against the sky.

"It cost her something to tell me about the child," he said aloud. "It was not easy for her to let me see her fox and to let me know who she was."

The fox barked softly as if in sympathy.

How beautiful it is in the snow, he thought. How many battles we lost because of the snow. But now it was beautiful. He had seen enough red snow once the blood began to flow. Out here, the snow was enchanted, a pure, clean world. Yet the woman inside the hut was not pure. And the world was not clean. How could he expect her to live in a world like theirs and remain clean and pure? He had not done it. He learned to intrigue and plan and he had killed more men than he could count. She does not reproach me for being a samurai, he thought, but he immediately understood that his deceptions arose from reasons entirely different from hers.

He continued walking. When he reached the wood, he went in far enough not to be seen, and, on an impulse, decided to lie down in the snow. The fox was disturbed by this and began barking. "Don't worry," he told her. "I don't intend to freeze out here. But how beautiful the sky looks coming through the white trees and how good it is to be cold. Cold is like water. It purifies."

The fox yelped more sharply. "Get up!" the fox was saying.
"In a minute," he told her.

"YOU ARE SURPRISED that she lied?" Lord Norimasa asked. "By the time they are four years old, they are already incapable of telling the truth. Perhaps it has to do with their larger imaginations. They are destined to spend most of their lives weaving stories and dreaming of whatever they are not doing. They lead double lives of the mind. Sometimes we do the same, but such dreaming is the result of ambition or failure. Usually ambition. She saw how you reacted and now she is thrown into confusion. Perhaps she has changed since she left our palace. Perhaps she really no longer knows why she did what she did. Once she spins a story for herself, she will find a speck of truth in it, and she will use that speck to make a very small hole in a frozen lake, and she will continue making it larger and larger until she can finally see her own face reflected in the water. When that occurs, she will either face up to what she sees or she will go under. You are asking too much. She cannot sort out the intentions behind what she did, and so she reacts with anger and accusations. You will get nowhere if you continue in this way. She will only tell you more foolish lies."

"But I am angry," said the samurai. "Never have I been so angry."

"Now you see what it was like all my life," he said. "You cannot win against them. I used to say the only thing I feared was a force of women bearing banners and beating a war drum. I had nightmares about such things. When I woke up, there was my wife staring at me with eyes like a snake. They are not like us. Do not think they are undisturbed by our differences from them. They have attendants and ladies-in-waiting and they understand one another perfectly, and so they grow to think that men ought to be able to know them in the same way that one woman knows another. It cannot be done. I tried. I know. I am sure that before she left the castle, she consulted with one of the women, one she trusted, and whoever that woman was, she agreed with Lady Utsu and understood her and could see no reason to oppose her stratagems. This is where most of the trouble begins. A woman feels wronged by her lover, but who does she consult? Another woman. They agree on everything. We think they are conspiring against us, but they are not conspiring. When two women are close and speak openly to one another, they are really talking to themselves. They can never speak so openly to us. Do you not yet understand that?"

"I understand nothing," said the samurai.

"Is there a man on this earth who has loved a woman and not felt as you do now?" Lord Norimasa asked.

CHAPTER THIRTY-ONE

"Get up! What are you thinking of?" the woman was demanding, shaking him by the shoulder. "Do you wish to die so much? Then leave it to me! I will go to the river!"

It was Lady Utsu, standing over him, wearing her cloak. "What were you thinking of, falling asleep in the snow?" she continued frantically.

"I was not sleeping in the snow. I was thinking," he said

"Now it is you who cannot tell the truth!" she said. "You were asleep, and sound asleep. I heard your fox barking and barking. When I heard that, I knew something was not right. Will you get up? Or must I go down to the river? The cloak will weigh me down. It will be over quickly in such cold. I shall not mind. If that is what you want most, I will happily go. I am an old woman and will not be missed."

"Stop speaking so wildly," the samurai said, struggling to his feet. "There is no need to throw yourself into a river. Someone would miss you."

"No one would. You cannot imagine how happy that makes me feel. To have become so entirely insignificant and useless. Before, I minded the idea of my own death, but I no longer dread it or fear it. I have no regrets at all."

"So you think now," the samurai said. "These states change with the weather."

"Will you come back?" she asked him.

"Utsu," he said, calling the fox, who had been staring wildly from one to the other of them. "Let's go."

He and the fox set off together.

"Can you not even wait for me?"

The samurai stopped, sighed, and waited for her to catch up to him.

They walked back to the hut in silence. Her anger was like heat in summer. He felt its waves beating about her.

When they entered the hut, she burst out, "You almost froze to death out there!"

He was affected by her concern and the intensity of the fright she had experienced. "All right, all right!" he said. "I did not die! I am not dead! We can stop considering it! All I did was lie down to look up at the sky and you are carrying on like a fishwife!"

"A fishwife!" she said in a fury. "Do you think the husbands of fishwives go out to sea in a storm hoping to drown themselves? And if one of them did, what do you think the fishwife would say? Probably she would beat her husband with a stick!"

"I am sure that is exactly what you would like to do to me," he said.

"And would it do any good? When you are so thickheaded?"

"Do not stay too long in an argument with a woman," said Lord Norimasa, "or you will find yourself in a maze from which you cannot escape. Run for your life!"

"I do not want to argue," the samurai said. "I am too tired."

"You are too tired?" she said, shouting. "You are too tired! I was the one who walked out there and found you lying on your back as if dead! You were the one who went out the door as if you never intended to return! You are tired!"

"Enough!" the samurai roared.

"You are just the same as the rest of them!" the woman said angrily. "You frighten me to death and then all you have to say is that you are tired. You will not die of exhaustion! You must explain to me what you intended. Was it your purpose to frighten me to death?"

"I do not know what I intended," he said, intentionally echoing her previous words.

"Oh, go ahead, mock me! It is not enough to make my heart thump and struggle in my chest like a dying fish. No, you must mock me as well. Should I now apologize because you went outside and tried to die in the snow? Is that what you want?"

"There is nothing I want except silence," he answered.

"Silence is the one thing you are not going to get! How could I have imagined you would ever be so foolish! It is a miracle you won a single battle. Lord Norimasa must have been out of his wits to make you his second in command! I wonder what he would have said if he found you trying to die in the snow!"

"Will you be quiet?" the samurai bellowed at her.

"That's right! Ask me to be quiet while you shout the house down! I suppose that makes perfect sense to you!"

"You are not going to win," Lord Norimasa said. "Give up the argument before she goes out the door and you have to pursue her."

"It is all over with," he said in a gentler voice. "I am back in the hut alive and so are you. Let us forget it."

"Forget it?" she asked, astonished. "After what I just suffered?"

"I am going to sleep in the stable with the horse," the samurai said. "This is intolerable." He put on his straw coat and looked down at the fastenings. When he looked up, Lady Utsu was holding a dagger to her throat.

"Go ahead, go to the stable," she said. "If that is all I mean to you," she said, and began weeping bitterly.

The samurai was stupefied. Her revelations were bad enough. The discussion before he left the hut was dreadful, falling asleep in the snow was shameful, but she was determined to make this into an event worthy of an elaborate tale, a *monogatari*. If this was what she wanted, he wanted no part of it.

"I'm going to the stable," he said.

"Go ahead! Kill me!" she shrieked.

"It's entirely up to you."

"Won't you be sorry?" she asked him. He saw that she pressed the dagger against her throat. A small rivulet of blood was running down one side of her neck.

"Not as sorry as you think I will be," he said, and went out the door.

She came flying out after him, coatless.

"Go back. You will freeze," he said.

"Can I have done so much wrong?" she asked. "Will you never forgive me?"

"I never said that," he said uneasily, aware that she might be maneuvering him into a corner.

"But is there any hope you will forgive me?"

"There is always hope," the samurai said.

"That is no answer!" the woman cried, stamping her foot in the snow.

"I cannot give you a better one," he said.

"I am not the same as I was then!" she said. She was crying so hard she was choking.

"Never be affected by a woman's tears," said Lord Norimasa. "Although sometimes those tears are genuine. When their mothers die, for example. Or when a close friend, also a woman, dies."

Still, he was not unaffected.

"If I come back into the hut," he said, aware that he was somehow surrendering, "will you calm yourself?"

"Yes! Yes, I will!" she said fervently.

"Then let us go in," he said.

The noise stopped. They began walking back to the door. When she stumbled, he grabbed for her arm and held it until they were inside. The two foxes were now frantic with worry. They had forgotten their enmity, if not their suspicion, of one another, and were watching the woman and the samurai with great concern.

"Come here, Utsu," said the samurai.

"Come here, Matsu," said the woman.

"Matsu?" the samurai repeated.

"I changed the fox's name after you went into battle," she said.

"I see."

"Yes," she said, sniffling, "after you left, I took to writing in a notebook. Mostly about waiting. I know I was the one who left, but still, I was waiting for you. Can you understand?"

"No," he said.

"I still have the notebook," she said. "I made it myself. It had to be beautiful. It is sewn with gold cord. On the cover, there is a beautiful phoenix scattered over with gold dust. I cannot remember how many hours it took me to get it right. Do you want to see it?"

"Yes, very much," the samurai said, "but not this moment."

He had never felt more exhausted, not after walking for twelve hours, not after waiting all night and listening for suspicious noises. This woman had worn him out more thoroughly than an entire army.

"I am sorry we quarreled," she said. "I dislike arguments."

"I have had few arguments," he said, and as he spoke, he realized that he had never had an argument of this sort before. When he was displeased with another samurai or with a soldier, he gave an order, and his attendants took the offending person away. An argument, as he knew it, consisted of expressing his dissatisfaction, and the object of that displeasure said at most, "But my lord, but my lord . . ." If someone he chastised said more, he was unceremoniously dragged from the place. The samurai he commanded could always see the execution grounds behind his words. But here! The woman would not obey. She refused to see reason. He found it incredible. No matter what he said, she produced another explanation, until he was entangled in vines bearing sharp thorns. And she was capable of going mad. He saw that himself with Lady Tsukie. But Lord Norimasa's mind had the ability to make his wife vanish into another dimension. He would have her dragged from his room by her attendants and taken to her own pavilion, and he would say, "I will deal with her later. It is a waste of time speaking to her now."

"Would you like something to eat?" the woman asked. "Are you falling asleep?" He could sense reproach in that last question. She was like the fox. She did not get enough attention. Yet he could not scratch her beneath the chin as he did the fox, who was always calmed by such attentions. But perhaps there was an equivalent?

"Your hair is disordered," he said. "Let me comb it for you."

She smiled, got up and got her comb. "Lord Norimasa gave it to me," she said, coming back. "It is very sturdy."

"It is beautiful," he said, taking care to examine the painting on its arch.

"It is, isn't it?" she asked, regarding him with what might perhaps be interpreted as a kind look. "The waves are so beautiful."

On the comb was a picture of cranes flying above a very stormy sea. Each wave was made up of many, many thin lines, so thin that it seemed impossible for a human being to make such a remarkable thing. The feathers of the cranes were made up of the same tiny lines which at first appeared as solid blocks of gold shaded by the artist. "What is that?" he asked, pointing at the picture.

"A red moon," she said. "It is a good omen. It means that whatever the people are doing on the sea, they will surely succeed."

"I see," said the samurai, who separated a hank of her hair and began combing it. It would take some time to comb her hair. He remembered her attendants doing it. By the time he was finished, order would be restored. On the other hand, by the time he was finished, he would not be able to keep his eyes open, and then she might think he was bored by combing. Life, he thought, was easier when he was attached to no one in the palace but Lord Norimasa.

"We never fought with each other before," she said. "This is the first time." She sounded content, even happy, that they had clashed, as if they now enjoyed a far greater intimacy. He stifled a sigh and continued combing her hair. After a while, he, too, grew calm.

Following the quarrel, a great peace descended on the hut. Both the samurai and the woman were unwilling to set sparks flying again, and each behaved as if nothing had happened. Lady Utsu did not mention the fact that Lord Matsuhito had not tried harder to find her and Lord Matsuhito did not again bring up the subject of her child—his child—who was given away.

Instead, Lady Utsu told Matsuhito stories when the light began to dim, and at night, before they lay down on their adjoining mats, she took out her journal and read parts of it to him.

"I will read you some of the parts I wrote about waiting," she told him. "Even though I was the one who had gone, I did believe I was waiting for you." This, she knew, was not the samurai's favorite topic of conversation, so she hurriedly opened the journal and began to read, but before she read two words, he pulled her toward him and she lay back against his chest. Lately, the two foxes had taken to sleeping together, each curled into a semicircle. But when it was quiet, the foxes would creep back to their own masters. Utsu, the samurai's fox, began to sleep above his head. He told the woman he did not mind. The fox kept his head warm.

"Is that pleasant?" he asked her as she leaned against him.

"Oh, that is very good," she said. "I am very comfortable."

"Let's hear about this journal," he said.

Lady Utsu said that it was not very good, but it was a testimony of sorts. Perhaps he should hear it.

"I am about to hear it, am I not?" he said. They were, as was their custom, warm beneath her heavy cloak.

"It is strange," she said, "but whenever I open that journal, I begin to remember things from my younger days."

"What do you remember?" he asked. "You are trying to keep from reading from that journal. Probably it is a book of empty pages."

"It is not!" she exclaimed, burrowing against him. "But I have been remembering my mother, who loved me so much. I remember how my mother used to clip off the chrysanthemum petals when they were about to fall, and then she put them in a thin netting, and I remember one of the servants suspending the petals in the attic of one of the servants' houses. My mother was too grand to go into the attic, of course, but I was allowed to go with my nurse, and there I saw the silkworms for the first time, all of them eating at mulberry leaves, and my nurse told me that these same silkworms would in turn create the cocoons out of which other servants would spin filaments which would be made into the silk from which we made our robes. A child cannot believe such a thing. But I remember," she said with a slight shudder, "the sound they made, hundreds and hundreds of them, chomping on those leaves, and a kind of humming. And there were buzzing, lazy wasps in the dusty air, and thin strips of light everywhere because the shutters had so many cracks. When I was still a child, I was unwilling to put on robes made of worms who ate mulberries. Old as I now am, a magnificent robe made of silk still reminds me of those worms. We are clad in the work of worms. Isn't it curious?"

"Your mother loved you very much," the samurai said.

"Yes, but in the house there was always something odd. I could never get to the bottom of it. Whisperings in corners, my attendants looking at me oddly from time to time, my mother and father conferring about something and watching me to be sure I couldn't hear them. I know there was some kind of secret. I thought they may not be my parents. I don't know why. Everyone remembered my mother giving birth to me. So I should have been hers.

"But then there was a child who was brought to play with me so that both of us would not be lonely, and we would learn dancing and singing, and she was meant to keep me busy while I studied. She said,

'You think that woman is your mother, but she isn't. They changed you for her real child. Her real child died.' I always believed that. I believed that to be true even before the other child said so. But why would someone have taken me from my parents?"

"Unless?" the samurai asked.

"Unless I was a hostage," Lady Utsu said uneasily. "Or they were hiding me because there were people who meant me harm. But who would have meant me harm?"

"In war," the samurai said, "the defeated clan often gave up their children as hostages to the victors. That way the winning clan was assured that the losing clan would not again try to attack them. It did not always work. Some clans had such determined leaders that they would sacrifice their own children. I remember one such lord saying that he could always have more children, but his clan's reputation could not be repaired."

"I was a hostage to prevent a clan uprising?" Lady Utsu said. "How improbable that sounds!"

"You might have been made a hostage, if you were the child of a defeated warlord."

Lady Utsu shuddered. "It is too much to think about," she said. "I prefer to believe that my parents were my real parents."

"Did you resemble them?"

"That was the trouble. That's why the rumors started. They were not ugly, but they were not handsome people. When I grew older, everyone said that they must have found me inside a turnip. I thought it amusing—for a while."

"The journal," the samurai reminded her again. She was becoming unhappy thinking about this part of her past.

"No laughing, no snorting, no scornful comments," Lady Utsu said. "Do you promise? The journal may be bad, but to me it is still important."

"I won't listen when you speak," he said.

"You are already laughing at me," she complained.

"I have never heard of such delaying tactics," the samurai said. "You would have been at home in a Council of War. Please start."

"All right," Lady Utsu said. "Remember, I wrote this right after I left the castle. I was not entirely in my right mind."

"Another delay," said the samurai.

She began to read, and when she did, she read in a higher, sweeter voice than she ordinarily did. This surprised him, just as it startled him to feel transported to the time they had spent together in the castle. How curious it was to become young again when you heard a particular voice.

"'Of all the kinds of waiting, this is best,'" she read. "'When you are sure of the outcome and what you wait for is certain; the waiting fills you as if you had eaten chestnuts wrapped in persimmon; it fills you with a persimmon-colored light, that color, the color of certainty. When it is only a matter of time. When time has become your ally and servant. When time itself has taken an oath.

"'You are smug, and try not to appear smug, but the certainty is there within you as you wait. People say, "How content you look," and you reply, "I am just as I always am. It is an ordinary day." You think, I could wait like this forever.

"'The weather is of no consequence. If the rain pours down, if it is an impenetrable curtain when it flows down from the eaves, if the grass begins to sink beneath the onslaught, still you are standing in the sun. If it is hot, the waiting cools you. If it is cold, the waiting heats you.

"'A sound. A shadow cast by a plum tree branch. A door sliding open, then shut. The light is dimming. Dark water. You are no longer certain. What can have happened? Accidents befall travelers on the roads. Your heart is not your heart. It beats oddly. And then the door slides open, and the dear one is here, and the waiting is over. This is the best. What can compare to this moment when the waiting comes to an end? As you knew it would.'

"Well, you are not laughing yet," said Lady Utsu.

"I am very moved," he said. "To have inspired such longing."

"Even when you came to the hut regularly," she said, "I spent part of every day longing in that way. It is harder, I think, than mourning."

"Yes," he agreed. "I think it is."

"There is more," she said. "Unless you are hungry."

"Please read," he said.

"'Of all the kinds of waiting,'" she read, "'this is the least beautiful. Time sneaks through the corridors like an assassin. Even in bright daylight, you cannot see it, that waiting to grow older. This kind of waiting has its tools, its chisels, its paint. The painter is like a person you do not know is there. You do not know you are waiting.

"'Yesterday, one of the women looked in the lid of her enameled box and cried out. "Look! What is happening to my face!" We ran to her. She discovered a small line between her brows, a crease, so faint, a shadow, the skin a little less bright, so small.

""Oh," I said. "It is nothing. You rested your head on your arm while you read." It was so hot. No breeze stirred the blinds. "It will be gone in an hour, that line," I said.

"'She grew wild. She began to cry, then shriek. She clawed at her face. One of the imperial guards called out to ask the cause of the disturbance. I thought, perhaps she fell asleep on the unlucky night when we must stay awake and a spirit possessed her. We could not hold on to her. We pushed her out through the blinds of the veranda so that the guard could grab hold of her.

""He will never come now," she cried again and again. "Never." Over and over.'"

"Was that Lady Kitsu?" the samurai asked.

"No, she remained in Lord Norimasa's palace. You are getting bored."

"No, go on."

"This was when I still lived in the Emperor's palace," she said. "I thought back to this when I was writing."

"'Later, the Empress called us to her. She said, "What happened today was terrible. It will come to all of us. Nothing escapes growing old. Remember that, when you neglect your books and care only for your faces reflected in the carp pond. Remember that, when you lean over the edge of the pleasure boats seeking to see your faces in the water." '

"I felt as if she were speaking directly to me. The Empress was a wonderful woman," she said, turning toward the samurai. "She had only to look at one of us and she knew what we were thinking. Did she really wait to grow old without fear? And so we asked her.

""You want to know if I fear growing old," she said. "All my life I have loved old people. I look forward to growing old. And when my husband is old, I shall not turn from him, either."

"'Waiting for your husband to grow old? I had never thought of it. Always it was myself I pictured, wrinkling and puckering like a wet sheet of paper left in the rain, forgotten, even more wrinkled after it dried in the sun.

"""When you grow older, you will understand many things," said the Empress. "Is this alone not a reason to grow old?" Her eyes flickered over us and stopped when they met mine. "You are not stupid girls," she said. "I do not surround myself with stupid girls. Go back to your rooms and think. Study those who have grown older. Engage them in conversation. Draw them out. Why live in such small worlds? The old often have worlds that are without boundary. Perhaps they will open their doors for you."

"'Nevertheless, I was uneasy: waiting to grow older.

"""The gift of beauty is not always a blessing," the Empress said. "Tonight, shall we play the shell-matching game?"

"'I loved the Empress. In her soul, she was older than I, although in years, she was younger. She was completely beautiful, and, I think, completely unaware of it.

"'I thought, I must become more like her.'"

"Is there more?" asked the samurai after a pause.

"No," said Lady Utsu. "It grew too painful for me to wait and write about waiting. And to know I was growing older while you were gone."

"So you stopped composing? Because of me?"

"No, I wrote poem after poem for the Emperor and Empress. How boring they were! Only after I left their palace for the last time did I begin to write the poems I am known for. For the Emperor and Empress, I wrote ones like these. You have heard thousands like it.

> The storied Moshino plain:
> Not even those blades of grass
> Outnumber the centuries of your reign.

> Crossing Shirakawa Pass:
> The red maples let fall their leaves.
> No matter how far we travel,
> It is your reign that dyes the sunset with its color.

Lady Utsu was weeping soundlessly. The samurai knew this from her breathing. "You are tired," he told her. "But when you are not tired, perhaps you will read more poems to me or tell me what things you remember when you were young. It nourishes me to hear those memories. It is like taking back lost time."

"I will do those things and I will be happy to do so," she said, turning to him. "And you will call me Utsu."

"Tears like drops of dew," he said. "For me, this is a new kind of happiness. I thank you for it."

She smiled, and softly recited a poem:

> The lotus leaves take root in the mud.
> I think they will last forever.
> Yet even Lord Kuronosuke's castle
> Has become a plain of grass.

"There are things we must discuss," she said.

"Later," he said.

The two foxes, sensing what was coming, got up and crept to the wall, twined themselves together and fell asleep.

There are times when life cooperates with human aspirations, and then, if that happens, a person can easily feel as if life on this earth is bliss. Once someone begins to feel this, he tends to forget the many times he has said, aloud or silently, This life is hell, or, We are truly in hell. Both the samurai and the woman had thought and said such things, but happiness can become more habitual than misery, and sometimes more attractive than food, and even more, can create an appetite for life. Now, what the samurai and Lady Utsu had was bliss and they would have, if they were asked, admitted they would try to do anything to keep it. In order to hold it, all they had to do was forget the revelations that had led to their quarrel, to erase what they had said and heard and continue as if those memories had gone up in smoke. They were completely happy, but memory is strong, and although they bound their memories with powerful ropes, they should have known those ropes would fray. But people in a state of bliss forget such things.

They lost all track of time. It stopped snowing, and often they saw crystal drops falling from the roof, which meant that the snow up above was melting. Winter must be nearing an end, they guessed, but spring was not yet there, because the leafless trees showed no sign of budding. They thought it was the fourth month, but they were not sure, and it did not seem important to know. They settled into a routine of their own. Lady Utsu cooked simple meals. The samurai continued shovel-ing the paths to keep them clear because Lady Utsu said that even after all the snow was gone, it was still possible to have a blizzard, so there was reason to be diligent. The samurai cared for his horse and rode it up and down what few paths he managed to clear. The foxes were let loose each morning, and would disappear into the woods until they called the foxes back. The samurai insisted on polishing the gleaming wood floor. Lady Utsu began to pay a great deal of attention to her appearance, and one day, as dusk began to fall, the samurai came back in and found her dressed in a splendid embroidered scarlet robe on which every possible symbol of longevity and good fortune was embroidered. When the samurai saw her in this robe, which trans-formed her utterly, his eyes filled.

"What has become of us?" he asked.

"We have become what we are meant to be," she said. "As we are now, so we are meant to be. Do you think that is such a poor thing? Come, lie down with me on the mat, as we did in the old days."

They were not under the robe long before the samurai began to feel uneasy. "Where did the robe come from?" he asked Lady Utsu.

"When I left, I brought a few with me," she said.

"And how did you hide it?" he asked. There was no place to keep a trailing robe out of sight in the hut.

"There are chambers beneath the floor," she said. "The robes are kept in some of them and food in others."

The samurai found this a sufficient answer, yet from the beginning, when he first opened his eyes in the hut, he had the uncomfortable feeling that there was someone else hovering about the place, someone else watching and waiting, dedicated to seeing that no harm came to this woman. He sensed this again, but now he lived in a special time. It was easy to dismiss his suspicions.

Lady Utsu again had begun to write in her journal, and occasion-ally she would write a poem and then read it to him. He grew accus-tomed to the way she abruptly stopped what she was doing, ground some of her ink stick, added water and wrote something on a sheet of paper. The paper was not stained or in any way smudged. It occurred to him to wonder about this, too, but again, he thought he was dream-ing together, or that both of them had died and they were dreaming, or that Lady Utsu was a witch, or that one of the two foxes had possessed them and caused them to live in this dream. It was a time of such happiness that the weightiest suspicions were swept aside as if by a feather.

The mat itself appeared to be magical. Time fell away from them when they lay down. They became playful and said ridiculous things to make one another laugh. They laughed easily and often and they were so secure and comfortable that they often fell asleep, their arms wrapped around one another.

One night, Lady Utsu had a dream. She had looked into one of the storage chambers beneath the floor and found the samurai's journal there, but when she opened it, she saw only page after page of blank sheets. The dream awakened her. Moonlight was pouring through the window. She could see again, as if it were still happening, the palanquin into which she had stepped when she left the palace. She remembered how beautifully it was fitted out, and how the palanquin swayed as the four men bearing it trotted down the road. She remembered how nauseated the swaying and jostling made her, and she grew aware that she was once more experiencing that feeling. How strange, she thought.

She went back to sleep, but in the morning she remembered the dream of the blank journal, and when the samurai was finished with his chores and she with hers, she said, "I have told you so much about myself, but really, I know little of your life before the palace. I should like to know what you were like when you were still small."

"I was never really small," he said. "Not in the way you mean. I was never young. If my mother once said, 'You were born old,' she said it a thousand times."

"But you were a good and devoted child," Lady Utsu said, as if she were certain she knew this to be true.

"No, I was an unruly child," the samurai said. "No one could control me. At one point, my parents sent me to my uncle's village so I would learn pottery. But I would get up early while it was still dark and steal out of the house and roam everywhere. I saw the most amazing things, bees the size of birds, and huge flowers. They are not describable. I climbed to the top of the mountain to watch the sun come up on the water and turn it gold, and the rocks were dark gray, and in the distance, a fainter gray. I prowled around the mountain all day. Until I was hungry. Naturally, my uncle got tired of me and sent me home."

"But after that, you were good," said Lady Utsu.

"After that, I was worse," said the samurai, laughing, "but all that is dead and gone. Why remember it?"

"Because you were not born in a peach. No one found you in the trumpet of a morning glory."

"Why, really, do you want to know these things?" the samurai asked. "Women always ask these questions. They are very persistent once they begin asking them. I don't understand why."

"When you love someone, you want to know everything about him," she said. "The more you know someone, the more you can please someone."

"And the more you can control him," the samurai said.

"That is true, too," said Lady Utsu. "Women will have their weapons, and words are usually their best tools. But it is untrue to say that they do not ask out of love."

"So you want to know in what way I was good?" the samurai asked. "What possible use can it do you?"

"I do not like to think I cannot understand the nature of the person I love," she said. "I also do not understand how someone who was not good became so."

"And how many times have you told a man you loved him?"

"Never," said Lady Utsu. "Many other things, flattering things, men I allowed to believe I loved them, but I never told any other man I loved him. Except you, when we were in the palace and the plague was raging."

"And did you conduct these inquisitions with other men?"

"Of course. You said it yourself. A woman must have some power. And as I said, words are the weapons of women."

"But now you are not doing that?"

"No. Still, it is a habit to make notes and remember."

The samurai considered and then nodded.

"I ran away, that was how I became worse," he said. "When my parents grew tired of my disappearances and my refusal to help with anything, I would go through the woods, which I knew very well, and come out on a road and start walking. You meet interesting people on the road. Then there were times when I met no one and was hungry and tired, so I would lie down near the edge of the road and go to sleep."

Lady Utsu recited a poem:

> The road is dusty and there is no rain.
> The path uncurls like a sash.
> I loosen my sash to sleep.
> I wonder where you sleep now.

"I never thought about my parents and if they worried," said the samurai. "I was having too good a time. The village was not an interesting place. I liked it better when I used to collect the other boys and stage battles with bamboo lances. I would sit up in a tree and play the general. But the parents put a stop to it. Too many children were injured. The other villagers said I was a monster. My mother stood up for me. She said I would become someone important and that no one else in the village would accomplish anything. After that, people said that she was proud and arrogant, and her attitudes had made me the demon I was. It is painful to think back and remember all the trouble I caused her."

"So," said Lady Utsu. "You were on the road. What interesting things happened? Women cannot behave like that, certainly not when they are young. A woman alone and young would be raped and killed almost at once. Not until you are old enough to wander on your own can you act as I did. At the time, I believed I was old enough."

"Best of all was the bandits," the samurai said.

"Bandits?" she asked incredulously.

"Yes. Bandits. One day it was very hot and I went beneath an arched stone bridge where it was cool. I fell asleep. Something woke me, and by that time it was dark. I knew from the sounds on the bridge that several people were up there, so I kept quiet. There were men talking about robbing a house. One of them said, 'You have to know how to break into a house. The house is always guarded.'

"They were going on and on about how to break into this house. So I suddenly said, 'There is no house you cannot break into.' It took them a few seconds, but they swarmed down the bank and found me under the bridge.

"One of them said, 'Now we will have to kill you.'

"I said, 'You can kill me if you like, but look how small I am. I will be good at breaking into houses. Take me with you.' The leader of the gang said, 'He's not afraid of anything and he's too young to be a spy. Let's take him.' So they took me with them to look at the house. I saw a way in right away. There was a hole in the roof for the smoke to escape. 'I can go down that,' I said. 'I am good at dropping from high places. No one is there, so the fire will be out. Then I can let you in. Of course, if there are guards, someone will have to kill them or tie them up. But it's one thing to break into a house and another to break out. How will you get out? The wall around the house is very tall. The horses cannot jump over it. Then what will you do?'

"They had not thought that far. 'I'll show you,' I said, and I scrambled up the wall and came down on the other side and opened the gate. I said, 'See? It was easy.'

" 'You have lived with bandits before?' the chief asked me.

" 'No,' I said.

" 'But I see you lead an interesting life.' The chief said, 'We have broken into a good one.' So I lived with them for a long time. I liked breaking into houses and seeing how other people lived. I particularly liked breaking into the storehouses to see what they thought was so important inside. But I was not interested in money. I wanted a good sword, and I found one in one of the storehouses. Everyone said not to take it. The sword maker's name was on the sword guard. Everyone said that he was famous for his swords, but his swords were unlucky. They were possessed by the sword maker's spirit and were hard to control. I took it anyway. It is here now, next to the mat."

"I have always been bold," Lady Utsu said, "but could I have been so daring? I don't think so."

"I think you have been quite daring enough," the samurai said. "You grew into your boldness. I had to grow out of much of mine. Lord Norimasa was my master. If both of us were to be impetuous and without control, it would have meant disaster for the clan. I was fortunate to attach myself to such a storm center. I used to think, I cannot be the worst person in this palace. That gave me great comfort. Once I no longer thought of myself as so bad and uncontrollable, I became quite well behaved, although everyone said my methods were unorthodox. They were."

"When I left the palace for the last time," she said, "I wrote this poem:

> As I rode though the red gate,
> The horse stopped
> As if
> His shadow had frightened him.
> Can you not see my fear and return?

But really, I was the one who was frightened."

"You had some sense," he said. "Everyone was in a hurry to tell me I had none. They said I would end up as a beggar on the side of one of my beloved roads. It could have ended that way if I had not met Lord Norimasa."

MATSUHITO'S HOME VILLAGE was a hamlet surrounded by hills that encircled it like a three-quarter moon. Steep mountains were at its back. He climbed up the hill and looked down at the village. From there, the small huts with their rounded thatched roofs looked tiny and the people like ants. He sought out his own house and watched his mother, who was traveling back and forth to the communal well. She would heat up the water in the tub, scrub her clothes and then she would bathe in the water, and so would her father when he returned for lunch.

In the summer, Matsuhito would go down the hill on the other side and stand beneath the waterfall. Then he would go back up the hill, cross the path and, while his clothes dried, watch the village again. From there, the village seemed like a simple toy, everyone the same, everyone going about the same business. He thought about what he wanted to do. He wanted to learn swordsmanship and use a good sword. He wanted to apprentice himself to the best warlord there was. Why waste time on an inferior one?

He looked down at the rice paddies in the spring, and was happy enjoying the sun when it shone on the water. At such times, the rice paddies were made of beaten silver. When night began to fall, the rice paddies turned red-gold. From up there, he loved the village, but he did not want to stay there. For as long as he could remember, he had believed that he belonged somewhere else.

"What are you thinking about?" Lady Utsu asked.

"My *furusato*, the village where I grew up."

"I used to think," she said, "that people who lived in such villages were not human. All of us thought that way. When we went on excursions from the palace, if we saw a farmer or a peddler on the road we stared at them as if they were exotic beasts. Rarely did we see their faces. They would prostrate themselves at the side of the road, their faces bent to the dirt, their hands out, and they did not rise until we had gone by. We knew that anyone who looked up at us or did not bow down or give way could easily be killed by one of the samurai escorting us. But a village appears to be a kinder place than a palace. So much intrigue in a palace!"

"It is kinder," the samurai said, "but it is not kind. People were killed if they stole a yam in times of famine. Then thieves were thrown into a pit and buried alive. Resentments buzzed like flies. Competitiveness among the women often grew unbearable. One mother insisted her son was smarter or stronger than another, and the other mother never forgave her. But in the end, they all stuck together. After all, they had only themselves to depend on."

"To me, it has its charms," she said. "The simplicity of it! There was no simplicity in the palace, except when we women were together and the men had gone to battle."

"I told you, it was not simple. No one would have approved of you. Mothers-in-law spied on their sons' wives and ruled over them day and night. How would you have liked that? If they had found you reading something, you would be beaten black and blue because you were not working in the fields or doing chores in the house. You would have spent your time in the rice paddies collecting leeches on your skin and removing them afterward with a burning stick. And when you grew old, you would have walked slowly and with a stick, and you would have been bent over at the waist so that you could only see the ground. You would not have been able to see the sky. It was a hard life."

"I might have been more fortunate, even so," Lady Utsu said.

"That is sentimentality," he said. "It is comical to think of you there. If you decided to keep a fox in the village, they would have brought exorcists and diviners, and if that hadn't rid you of the desire to have a fox, you would probably have been found somewhere dead and far from your hut. They would have thought you dangerous and ill-omened. The peasants can be more brutal than any samurai. It is only delusion that makes you think otherwise."

By now it was growing dark, and the two foxes were restless. The samurai took them out, and they disappeared into the woods while he cleared the path. He saw that the water had stopped dripping from the deep eaves, and realized it was colder. It might snow again.

When he came in, Lady Utsu was preparing their meal. Almost always, they had the same dishes, a clear broth and dried river fish boiled with radishes and onions. Occasionally they had rice balls, although now Lady Utsu had begun to ration the rice, saying that they would have no more until winter ended and the roads became passable. She seemed to have an unending stock of green tea, and both of them came to feel as if the meal had not ended until the tea was brewed and sipped.

They had just finished their meal when Lady Utsu abruptly got up, walked to the door, opened it and went outside. She had not put on her cloak, and her face appeared strange and strained. The samurai followed her. He found her in the snow, her arms wrapped around her breasts.

"What is wrong?" he asked her.

She did not answer, but only shook her head, and he saw her kneel down in front of the snow and place both of her hands in the snow in front of her. Then she began to retch.

"You are ill," he said in distress.

She started to say something, but began to retch again. This happened four or five times.

"The food must have been bad," the samurai said. "I will carry you back in," and he lifted her up and brought her back into the hut.

"I do not think the food was bad," she said.

"Then why should you become ill so suddenly?"

"It is not sudden," she said.

"Not sudden?"

"This has been happening every day for perhaps twenty days," she said.

"We must find a way to take you to a doctor," Matsuhito said.

"A doctor will not help."

"Is it beyond curing?"

"Yes and no," Lady Utsu said. "It is beyond curing right now, but it will be cured in perhaps eight months."

"Eight months is too long to be ill!" the samurai exclaimed.

"Have you never heard of morning sickness?" she said.

"Morning sickness?" he asked, puzzled.

"When Lady Tsukie began to be ill during the day, what was wrong with her?"

"She was pregnant," said the samurai. He looked at her in astonishment. "Is it possible?" he asked her.

"I thought my monthly pollutions had ceased," Lady Utsu said. "But two months ago, they returned. I thought nothing of it, assuming I was too old for such things."

"So, you are to have a child," the samurai said wonderingly. "And it is my child."

"But it is a disgrace to have a child at my age," she said. "Everyone would laugh at me and mock me. It is certainly inappropriate."

"And who is there to mock you and laugh at you?"

"I should . . ." She hesitated and then said, "I should make the baby leave my body."

"You mean kill it?" the samurai asked, horrified.

Lady Utsu said nothing.

"Say what you mean," the samurai told her.

"When the winter ends, you will want to resume your wandering," Lady Utsu said. "I will still be in this hut. How will I raise a child here?"

"I no longer have a desire to wander," said the samurai.

"You would like me to have this baby?" Lady Utsu asked.

"Of course. We are healthy. We might well live long enough to raise a child. We would teach the foxes to play with her."

"Her?"

"Or him."

"But the disgrace of it!" Lady Utsu burst out.

"In my village, this would not have been thought a disgrace. An older woman would have said that Kannon blessed her in her old age and the child would be a special child."

"I was not raised in a village!" said Lady Utsu. She sprang up and flew out the door. He followed her and found her in the snow, again retching violently.

"How often does this happen?" he asked her when she wiped her face with a handful of snow and stood up.

"Usually in the morning," she said irritably. "But it can happen anytime."

"This is terrible," the samurai said sincerely.

"It is natural. In a woman of the proper age."

"You make too much of your age. Perhaps you have been blessed by Kannon."

"I have been blessed by you," said Lady Utsu.

"I must know now," the samurai said. "Will you keep it?"

"I cannot answer yet," she said. "Perhaps I cannot answer at all. When a woman is as old as I am, many things go wrong. The baby often dies, and the mother, well, she is not as safe as she would be if she were younger."

"Then it is dangerous?"

"It is always dangerous, but when a woman is older, it is more so."

"Then you must decide," said the samurai. "It is you who would be risking your life."

"If I could be sure, it would make a great difference. If I could be sure the child would live and not be a monster."

"If you were sure you would live?" asked the samurai.

"My life is over, except for our time together," she said. "I should not mind dying. Where are the foxes?" she asked suddenly, looking around. If either of them spoke in a raised voice, the foxes immediately appeared.

"Still in the woods," the samurai said.

"They are spending longer and longer there," Lady Utsu said. "I don't like it."

"Call yours," the samurai said. Lady Utsu called her fox. Nothing. He called his, but his fox did not appear, either.

"Something else to worry about," Lady Utsu said. "Have you noticed that your fox is developing a round stomach?"

"It is cold outside," he said. "Let us go in. My fox looks exactly as she ever did."

"Yes, almost as I do," Lady Utsu said, going in through the door. "But I will not look the same for long."

Once back inside, Matsuhito and Lady Utsu continued discussing what should be done. "We are too old," she said. "The child will be left with no parents."

"Perhaps there is another way of thinking about it. Perhaps this child is meant to replace the one who was lost."

"I did not lose her, and you cannot replace one child with another," she said.

"Then perhaps she is the spirit of the man who froze to death on the ninety-ninth day," the samurai said. "Such things happen."

"No," Lady Utsu said. "They do not." But she fell silent, considering. He watched her and said nothing. "Do you think it is possible?" she asked.

"Yes," said the samurai.

"I thought you did not believe in such nonsense. Like Lord Norimasa, you defied taboos, unlucky directions, unlucky days, and neither of you stayed up all night when the dangerous spirits were about. Now you suddenly believe in reincarnation. You will say anything!"

"You would say the same thing if you had seen the young girl Lord Norimasa took into his house. It was a fairy tale for us having you back again."

"And was she intelligent?" asked Lady Utsu.

"Very."

"And did she write poems?"

"She painted. Everything she did came alive."

"I cannot paint," said Lady Utsu.

"Only because painting does not interest you."

"What did she paint?"

"She was particularly fond of painting the ten Chinese hells. But the castle was becoming too terrifying. Lord Norimasa would always put such a screen behind his platform when he summoned a person about whom he was angry. She also painted fans. All the women wanted her to paint a fan for them."

"What did she paint most often?"

"Most of the women asked for cherry blossoms. After some time, she said she would paint no more cherry blossoms. From now on, she would paint only screens. If there was nothing interesting to be painted, she would not do it. As I remember, she liked to paint the paradise across the Eastern Sea, Mount Horai. She was lovely and a delight. Everyone said so."

"Was she as beautiful as I was?"

The samurai laughed. "More," he said. "She had an uncomplicated heart."

"In other words, she was simpleminded," Lady Utsu said.

"She was not simpleminded," the samurai said sharply.

"And did you love her?"

"I loved the image of her and what she reminded me of."

"And she did quite well without me?"

"You gave her to a husband and wife when she was only weeks old. She had parents."

"So it does not matter who raises the child?" Lady Utsu said.

"I have seen the most cowardly man produce a child of great heroism," he said. "And the most malignant bandit produce a priest who changed the thinking of the country. Children are created by their parents, but they are not duplicates. They may seem to cast the same shadows as the parents, but in the end they are themselves. So perhaps it is true to say that it does not matter who raises them."

"Yes," said Lady Utsu, considering. "I have seen the same thing. A child of mine could be very unlike me. That is a comfort."

"Certainly."

"Am I so dreadful?" Lady Utsu asked.

"I think you should lie down on the mat and sleep."

"Already I am to be treated as an ordinary woman!"

"Stay up, then. Stay up for a week."

Lady Utsu glared at him, and lay down on her mat.

"And I suppose I must lie here alone?" she asked.

"I will lie there with you when I have called the foxes again," he said.

"I know what has happened to them. For weeks they have always been together. Now your fox is pregnant and they are building a den in a burrow or in a hollow tree or beneath this house. That is how pregnant foxes behave."

"I am sure my fox is not pregnant," said the samurai.

"You will believe it of me, but not of a fox," Lady Utsu said. "I have never understood men. Perhaps it is because I have listened to them."

He called the foxes. They did not return.

"They might have been killed," he said.

"Ridiculous," said Lady Utsu. "They will come back when they're hungry."

IN HER DREAM, Lady Utsu was once more living in the palace compound. The gate through which she passed was a brighter red than she remembered. It was midspring and the leaves were yellow-gold. Some red maples had already leafed out. As her palanquin took her through the streets of the palace compound, she saw many beautiful houses, their roofs elaborately tiled. At the corner of each roof was a dragon-fish meant to bring good luck. When she reached the innermost section of the compound where the Emperor and Empress lived, she stopped in front of a very tall strong gate built into a wall constructed of heavy stone blocks. "Lady Utsu has arrived!" one of the ministers called out, and a small window in the gate opened, someone made his inspection, there was a cavernous sound and the gate swung open.

She was carried by a minister through one beautiful garden after another. In the first garden, there were no plants at all, only shiny white sand combed into patterns. "That is the Garden of Longevity, where there are no seasons and nothing dies or falls. It is a place to contemplate eternity." She went on to the second garden, whose twin ponds were already reflecting white lilies and white flowers of every description. "That is the winter garden, where the flowers are the color of snow, and in the winter, when the snow falls and covers the trees, the garden looks the same as now, except, of course, the grass is missing. And next is the Garden of Utter Ruin, where you will live in that hut you see there."

"Must I live there?" she asked.

"Yes. There are good reasons and we know what they are."

Lady Utsu twisted this way and that, trying to see everything. Then she came to a fourth garden. In it was an artificial lake and many ducks floating on it among water lilies. Willows were planted at its edges and drooped down into the water, reflecting them. A beautiful bridge crossed a tiny stream and brought visitors to a small island. Willows hung down gracefully and were reflected in the stream. Workmen were busy painting and gilding two dragon boats soon to be set on the surface of the lake. Wisteria climbed several huts. Under one willow, a circular wooden platform had been built for outings. The paths were covered with white sand, and the workmen swept the paths with twig brooms and rakes, smoothing everything, removing tracks and footprints and any dead leaves that remained from the previous autumn. The wind had blown them. There was a small conservatory on the island in the artificial lake, and it could be reached by another bridge. Lady Utsu believed she had entered paradise. The usual faint smell of sewage mixed with fertilizer and perfumed flowers, and the smell of cut grass was purer here. The air smelled like perfume. Every so often, a hint of incense floated on the breeze. There were temple lions set everywhere. Every section of this garden was protected by them. Lady Utsu had never seen anything more beautiful.

"This is the Empress's garden," one of the ministers said.

A crow flew by. "It will not be beautiful for you," said the bird.

"There is no money in the treasury for Their Imperial Majesties, so Lord Norimasa pays what is necessary. He is a great man. You will meet him someday."

"I should like to meet him now and hear him tell me what to do," Lady Utsu said, her voice trembling.

"All in good time," said the minister. "Please act naturally before Their Majesties. They have brought you here to be their companion. They will be unhappy if you are stiff and off-putting."

Everywhere, tiled roofs swept downward from the roof ridge. Some were slate blue, others green and some yellow. Peacocks strolled through the gardens making raucous noises. "They were brought from China as a present to Their Majesties," the minister said. "One is about to spread his tail. Look!"

"It is not possible for anything alive to look like that!" Lady Utsu exclaimed.

"There are wonders upon wonders in the palace," said the minister. "Try and stay here. There is no place better in the land."

Lady Utsu was enchanted, and yet, when she was brought before Their Majesties and bowed down to the ground, she was weeping when she stood up.

"What is wrong?" asked Her Majesty, the Empress. "Do you want to go home?"

"Yes, Your Majesty," she said. "It is unfamiliar here and I will displease you."

The Empress smiled. "I would rather take in a young woman who had a low opinion of herself than the usual ones who arrive thinking they should be the Empress instead of me. We will try to comfort you, and if you are not happy, of course we will send you home. Come up here and see this monkey I am painting. A man from China taught me how to do it."

Lady Utsu crept up to the platform on which the Empress stood.

"Does it look like a monkey?" asked the Empress.

"Yes," said Lady Utsu dubiously.

"What is wrong with it?"

"Its face is not scrunched up enough, Your Majesty," Lady Utsu said. The Empress burst out laughing. "It looks more like a human baby, does it not?" asked the Empress. "Will you help me?"

Lady Utsu nodded eagerly, then remembered to speak. "Yes, Your Majesty," she said, and from that time, Lady Utsu knew she would indeed be happy there.

But then a strange thing happened in the dream. Time passed, and both she and Her Majesty were sitting on the imperial platform when the Empress suddenly stood up and said, "Who do you think I have been all this time? I killed the Empress and I am a fox impersonating her. I mean to kill you, too. For that reason, I had you summoned to the palace. Come with me to the lake so I may drown you in the water. But first you can see your reflection and what you have become." The Empress seized her with hands like iron and began to pull Lady Utsu out of the pavilion, through the roofed, open corridor, over the grass in the garden and toward the lake.

"Please, Your Majesty!" called Lady Utsu, but the Empress only replied, "I have never been the Empress you thought I was. I am going to drown you in the lake as I have drowned so many of the other girls. When you have stopped breathing, the others will swim up to you and take you down and tangle you in the lotus roots."

Lady Utsu screamed again and again, but no one responded. The area was free of any human sounds. And then she was at the edge, the Empress holding her by one hand, and with her other hand pushing her by the back of her neck, and she felt herself falling forward toward the water.

"I can't swim!" Lady Utsu cried, but the Empress only laughed, and her laugh was not human.

Lady Utsu awakened, shivering violently. It was terribly cold in their hut. As her eyes became accustomed to the darkness, she saw the foxes had pushed open the door and returned to their places against the wall. Her fox rose and lay down next to her. "I will have to get up and close the door," she whispered to the fox. "In the future, you must come back before we close the door for the night." She got up and closed the door, then went back to her mat. The fox nestled against her. How large he had become since she had first found him! She looked over at Matsuhito, and saw his fox pressed up against his side. All was as it should be, she thought. But why such a dream? It was almost like a story that had come alive. She had always loved the Empress. Had the Empress come back to tell her something about the baby? In the morning, she would discuss it with the samurai. Then in spite of herself her eyelids began closing and she was sound asleep, and this time, dreamless. But as she fell asleep, she thought, I miss the palace, I miss the Emperor and Empress and Lord Norimasa, I miss his palace. The world I knew is gone.

In the morning, she told the samurai of her dream.

"It is an auspicious dream," he said.

"You do not believe in auspicious dreams!"

"But this one is. The dream Empress wanted to harm you, and you left the palace because you were afraid harm would come to you and your baby. But now there is no Empress and you are safe. That is what the dream means. In the dream, you are frightened of the Empress, but when you awake, you see that there is nothing to be afraid of."

"As I was thrown into the water, I saw my image in it," Lady Utsu said. "And I saw the image of the man who froze to death. And the dead women from the pond did swim up to take me down. It was terrible! I wish Lord Norimasa were here!"

"And am I not enough to protect you?" the samurai asked.

"It's not that. But from the time I was a young girl, Lord Norimasa always comforted me and knew how to calm me. Even in the dream, I missed him. And I missed the palace as I first saw it when I arrived, before I knew there were dangers everywhere."

She hid her face with her sleeve.

"My father used to say, 'If your mother is weeping for no reason, you will soon have another brother or sister.' At such times, she, too, had terrible dreams," said the samurai.

"Is that true?"

"It is certainly true. She used to wake at night, screaming. She was not the only one. Many women in the village woke screaming when they were pregnant. And they ate strangely. One woman would eat only chestnuts and persimmons and when the child was born, it had an orange color, but it soon faded. There was another who would only eat eggs. Other families contributed their eggs, but people were beginning to grumble before she finally gave birth to her son."

"You are making up stories," said Lady Utsu, letting her arm drop so that Matsuhito could see her face.

"No, these are true," he said.

"Persimmons and chestnuts," she said, laughing. "What an idea! On the other hand," she said, thinking it over, "I would not mind eating persimmons and chestnuts. I have some of both dried."

"So that is to be our diet?" Matsuhito asked.

"I will set some to soak now," she said. "Of course, I will not expect you to eat the same thing."

"And if I told you that some woman ate only grass and plum blossoms, would you find that appealing, too?"

Lady Utsu considered. "No," she said.

"Then you will have this baby?" Matsuhito asked.

"If I said no, would you leave me?"

"No."

Lady Utsu considered. "Then I shall try and have the baby," she said. "And I will be happy if he is born."

Their arguments were beginning to seem familiar, powerful anguish and fear, followed by a kind of forgetting of what went before, a forgetting that allowed an intense and addictive happiness.

Now, when they lay on their mats, Matsuhito was fascinated by the doings of Lady Utsu's body. He would examine her belly and become puzzled if it had not grown, but if it had, he would become ecstatic and playful.

"I don't know," Lady Utsu said, "but I don't think other people behind their screens—"

Matsuhito interrupted her. "What have we to do with other people and what they do or do not do behind their screens? Do you see other people watching us?"

So time passed in that way. "It is like a dream," Lady Utsu said. "But still it seems disgraceful to be my age in this condition."

Matsuhito drew out a length of her hair and bound it around his wrist. "No more about your age," he said. "Or I shall have to consider my own."

They laughed and told stories, and Lady Utsu took out her notebook and recited poems. Meanwhile, the foxes were often gone most of the day, but returned late at night, and in the morning, when the couple watched them, they observed Matsuhito's fox and her swelling abdomen. "She will have her children before I have mine," Lady Utsu said. "If her time goes well, I will consider it a good sign."

"Let us not link unlike things," Matsuhito said.

"All the females in the hut in this condition," Lady Utsu said. "It cannot be coincidence."

"It is not coincidence. It is nature."

"Shall I read out this poem?" she asked. "I just wrote it. I am tired of writing according to custom. I have never liked it. I will stop obeying all rules. Here it is, such a preamble for such a short thing!

> Spring, and everywhere, new green shoots.
> It is frightening,
> As if, beneath the meadow,
> Thousands of bodies
> Began uncurling their hands.

"Thousands of bodies beneath the earth, uncurling their hands," Matsuhito said sadly. "If only the dead could come back."

"But if our friends could come back, so could our enemies," said Lady Utsu.

"That is true, too," he said, lost in thought.

"You never told me about Lord Norimasa's death."

"It was not pleasant," he said.

"Tell me."

He described the terrible heat of his body and how suddenly he had died.

"And Lady Tsukie?"

"I think she was already quite mad. After Lord Norimasa's death, she had to be taken away."

"People were afraid she would harm herself?"

"They were afraid for others."

"Oh," said Lady Utsu.

"What is this?" Matsuhito asked. "Your belly is leaping about as if there were a frog in it."

"It is natural," she said.

"Is the sensation strange?"

"Very," said Lady Utsu, whose face had gone white.

"He will soon go back to sleep," the samurai said.

"He is very busy in there," she said, "this poor frog in a well."

"He will get tired."

"He is tiring now," she said. "He has stopped! Something has happened to him!"

"He has only gone back to sleep."

And so they slept on in their happy new dream and both of them wished it could last forever.

CHAPTER THIRTY-TWO

SOME TIME LATER, when the snow was gone and the trees were leafing out, the two foxes disappeared into the woods and did not return that night. Both Lady Utsu and Matsuhito were worried, but in the morning both foxes trotted back to the hut, and Matsuhito's fox had something in her mouth.

"Another rat or a bird," said Matsuhito resignedly.

But it was no such thing. It was a tiny fox, still wet from its birthing. The fox dropped the kit gently in front of them and looked up expectantly. Both Lady Utsu and Matsuhito began praising the formless lump of fur. Then Utsu the Fox ran out the door and disappeared into the woods. She soon reappeared with yet another kit. This one was larger and redder than the first. Lady Utsu and Matsuhito could not bestow enough praise on the mother fox. Well pleased, the fox left the two kits and returned with a third, and then a fourth.

"That is well done!" exclaimed Lady Utsu. "May I pick one up?" she asked, reaching for the largest of the four. But the fox would not allow it. She yelped sharply, picked up the kit and moved it away from the mat. "Oh, I see," said Lady Utsu. "You trust only yourself."

Her own hand had gone to her stomach.

"Four fine foxes," Matsuhito said. "Is it not a good omen?"

"It is," she said.

Then the two foxes began carrying the kits back into the woods.

"They will keep them there until they are stronger," Matsuhito said.

"I will miss them," Lady Utsu said.

"They won't abandon us," Matsuhito said.

Lady Utsu didn't answer.

"You'll see. They'll be back." And that night, Lady Utsu's fox returned and took up his place next to his mistress. The next night, it was Matsu's turn. "They have worked out a schedule," Matsuhito said. "I told you they would return."

"I am grateful," said Lady Utsu. "I wrote this poem while you were outside. I don't know what it means," she said shyly. He had never heard her speak in such a way.

"Please read it," he said.

> In the summer, you brought back beautiful gifts.
> I wanted to give you some, but found only
> The drifting sky.
> Can you wear it?

"You have wrapped me in the sky," he said. "And soon I will have something to hold." Tears shone in his eyes.

"I am so happy," she said. "It is not normal."

"On the other hand, it is not strange, either," he said.

And so things went on peacefully, and there should have been nothing shadowing their pleasure, but at night, one or the other would wake, and it was as if everything they could see was outlined in brilliant white light. Perhaps it is foxfire, Lady Utsu thought uneasily. Perhaps it is the ghosts of our ancestors, blessing us, Matsuhito thought. Nevertheless, although neither of them spoke of it to each other, each was afraid, and at such times they felt a sensation of dread.

Time passed and spring began to give way to summer. In the clearing, wildflowers appeared, and Lady Utsu, who had begun picking some to keep in the hut, found it more and more difficult to bend down. For some time, her abdomen had appeared to remain the same size, but suddenly it seemed larger every day. Worse was the night, which often brought sudden, acute pains which both she and Matsuhito thought were the beginning of the child's delivery. "It is too soon! Too soon!" Lady Utsu would cry, writhing on the mat. At first Matsuhito was frightened, but they soon found this to be a regular occurrence, and Matsuhito remembered his grandmother being summoned every night to a woman of his village, and each time the husband who came for his grandmother would say, "This time it is certain!"

"These things happen," his grandmother used to say, shrugging on a straw raincoat and hat if it was raining. "Probably when it is not a false alarm, there will be no trouble with her," and this turned out to be true.

But these nightly attacks were tiring Lady Utsu, who now slept a great deal of the time during the day, and when she slept, it was difficult to wake her.

One day, early in the afternoon, there was the sound of an ox bellowing outside the door, and the answering whinny of Matsuhito's own horse. He went to the door to see who had stumbled upon their hut, and there he saw a beautiful wagon. As he watched, the driver climbed down from his seat and began to unload the first of many sacks. Matsuhito was about to call out and tell the man that he had come to the wrong place when Lady Utsu rushed past him, hissing that Matsuhito should remain where he was.

Matsuhito's two swords were thrust into his sash, and he watched from one of the small doors cut in the wall. He saw the driver bow to the ground, and then Lady Utsu, who was wearing her robe, apparently to disguise her condition, said something to him.

"After I have come all this way?" the man said. "I will not do it. My life would be forfeit!"

"Take everything back!" Lady Utsu said angrily. "I no longer want it."

"It is not you who decides," the driver said.

"You dare speak to me this way?" Lady Utsu said, her voice rising. "How dare you? It is because I am a woman alone."

"You have been gaining weight, I see," said the driver. "I will be sure to tell that to my lord."

"I have not gained so much weight," said Lady Utsu. "It has been a hard winter and there has been nothing to do but eat and write. I have a bundle of poems I will give them to you and then you will go. Take these things with you."

"I will not," the man said stubbornly.

"Leave!" Lady Utsu shouted, her hand unconsciously going to her stomach.

"If there is someone else there," said the driver, "come out!" His hand was on the hilt of his sword.

Matsuhito stepped through the door. "Did she not tell you to leave?" he told the driver.

"I will cut you down!" the driver said.

"Take care! Do not unsheathe that sword! If you have a sword, you know what will happen. Once a man unsheathes his sword, the other one must fight. I do not know you or why you are causing trouble. Therefore I should hate to kill you."

The driver hesitated. One inch of the sword had been drawn from its scabbard and glittered in the sun. "Lady Utsu!" Matsuhito said. "Go inside!"

"I will stay where I am!" Lady Utsu said.

"Should I kill him?" Matsuhito asked her.

"Not yet," she said.

"Who are you?" the driver demanded.

"Do not address me in that way," Matsuhito said. "I am Lord Norimasa of Omi. Must you be taught manners?"

"Lord Norimasa," the driver said, considering. "I heard he died."

"He adopted me and gave me his name," Matsuhito said. "I have had that name since the Battle of Sanomi."

"Sanomi?" the driver asked, taking two steps back. "What was your name then?"

"You ask too many questions, but my name then was Matsuhito."

"The Matsuhito of the Battle of Sanomi?" the man asked, his eyes widening. "The man who constructed a wall and destroyed the Minagas?"

"I constructed a wall," he said.

"And did you also kill a man while standing on a moving horse?"

"No, that was the late Lord Norimasa Yoshihide," Matushito said.

"I have no quarrel with you," said the driver. His hands were trembling visibly.

"Do you want these things?" Matsuhito asked Lady Utsu.

"It is all right," she said, her eyes averted, staring down at the ground.

"Unload them, you fool!" Matsuhito roared.

The man began flinging things from the wagon onto the ground.

"Shall I put everything into the stables?"

"Does he usually?" Matsuhito asked Lady Utsu.

"Yes," she said.

"Put them in the stables. Do not ask questions when you know the answer," he said.

"I apologize, my lord," said the driver, hurrying through his task.

When he brought everything into the stable, he took down a large lacquered wooden chest. "Here are the year's two robes," he said. "On one is a cherry tree in bloom. The second is dark blue with a pattern of butterflies and wagons in red and white and gold. If there is anything that needs mending, I am to take it back."

"There is nothing that needs mending," Lady Utsu said. Her face had flushed scarlet.

"Then am I free to go?" asked the driver.

"Yes," said Lady Utsu, almost inaudibly.

"If I hear rumors of a lady in a wood growing fat," said Matsuhito, "I will come for you. I, too, can fight from a horse's back while I am standing up."

"Yes, my lord, yes, my lord," the driver repeated, scrambling back onto his wagon. "I shall not say a word."

"If you say even one word, I shall hear of it through Yoshida."

"Yoshida the bandit?"

"He is my friend," Matsuhito said.

The driver turned his wagon and rode out of the clearing as quickly as possible.

Lady Utsu stood quite still and did not meet the samurai's eyes. "Come inside," he said. "Let me see you sit on the mat."

She obeyed him, but he saw that her face was wet.

"I am always unhappy when that man comes," she said. "It reminds me of what I have done."

"Sit down, and I will make some tea," he said, and set about making it. When he poured two cups, he sat down next to her.

"Drink!" he ordered her. She was shaking. He got up and returned with the saké bottle. He poured a little into her tea. "Now drink," he said, gently. "Drink it for me."

She looked up at him as a child would and drank the tea. Then she sat silently staring at the mat and would not raise her eyes. The samurai watched her. She was trembling, but not so violently. When the trembling stopped altogether, the samurai said in a soft voice, "Do you want to tell me who he was?"

"I must," she said.

"I am listening."

"He is a retainer of the family I wronged," she said. "The man who died in the snow and did not complete the hundred-day test, he came from this family."

"And yet the family contributes to your well-being and brings rich robes?"

"Two silk embroidered robes every year," Lady Utsu said.

"May I ask why?"

"The man who died asked his family to promise that, should he die, the family was to continue to care for me. He left very detailed instructions: what I was to be given in food and in clothing, combs and a mirror, several needles every year, spools of thread and two bolts of silk, a warm robe for the winter and bear boots. They were to outfit a place where I chose to live. All of these things were done, as you can see. The shame of it is intolerable! Every year when he comes, I think to myself, This is how you pay penance. Before you came, he called me a *obake-mono* and a *kitsune onna*, a fox woman, an evil spirit who bewitches men and kills them."

The samurai got up.

"Where are you going?" asked Lady Utsu.

"To hunt him down and kill him," the samurai said.

"No!" said Lady Utsu. "I want no more bloodshed. Sit down! Do you think another corpse to my credit will cheer me? I am humiliated enough!"

"All that happened long ago. The man took up your challenge. If he declined, no one would have thought badly of him. They would have said you were a selfish and willful woman and they would have asked him, 'Why should you obey her?' The fault was his."

"I cannot bear thinking of it. That face, covered in a white beard of ice. They say that in hell, there is a mountain of needles. People said then I should be placed on it. I was. I still am! I was so tired of having power over men I did not care for. I killed that man for no reason. He was a very kind man."

"You did not kill him. He killed himself. If he had stayed at home with his dying mother where he belonged, he would still be alive."

"Both of their spirits are restless. I know it," she said. "How many times I have recited the sutras in temples all over the countryside! How much money I have spent copying sutras in his honor! And they are restless yet."

"You have had a shock," said the samurai. "You must sleep."

"I cannot sleep," she said. "I am too afraid. And the baby inside is storming about. Even he is not happy."

"If I lie next to you, will you go to sleep?"

"I will try," she said.

Both of them fell asleep, and when they awakened, Lady Utsu seemed completely recovered and went about her chores cheerfully, going out to play with the foxes. Late that night, when she fell asleep, the samurai went to the stable and investigated what the driver had brought. There were ripe plums and dried ones, dried fruits of all description, dried beef and deer meat, pickled vegetables and saké, three heavy sacks of rice—the list seemed endless. When he came to the lacquered box, he hesitated as if he were opening another man's love letters, but in the end, his curiosity got the better of him. Inside of the box, wrapped in *washi* paper, was one robe. He unwrapped the robe and held it up. It was a deep crimson that shaded into a deeper and deeper color as it reached its hem. An enormous embroidered cherry tree shone with brilliant colors, one in the front and one on the back. Golden threads were used liberally. "I wish I had been the one to order that made for you," he said aloud.

"Do not say so," Lady Utsu said from the doorway, her eyes burning. "The design of the cherry tree is beautiful, but you see there are peacocks walking around its trunk. It reproaches me. I am the peacock who is so beautiful it dazzles, but its voice is ugly and reflects its spirit. Every year, he brings two robes, and the design on one is sure to reproach me."

"Things must be done with a good grace or not at all," the samurai said.

"There is no good grace left for me," she said. "Please fold it up and let us go back to bed."

That night, it seemed to them that they slept very well.

Days passed, and on a cool, blue day, the samurai said, "You should have some fresh meat. I will go hunt for some pheasants."

"Don't hunt for them, catch them," she said, laughing.

Ah, things are as they should be, he thought as he left the hut.

But when he came back at twilight, Lady Utsu did not come out to greet him as she always did. He put down the pheasants in their sack and went into the house, and once inside, he heard strange, strangled noises. "Utsu!" he called out. Then, as his eyes grew accustomed to the semidarkness, he saw a figure writhing on the floor. "Utsu! *Doshita! Doshita!* What happened!"

He tried to help her sit up.

"What happened?" he asked again.

"I am going to die," she said. "It is what I wanted."

"Is this your time?" he asked frantically. "Is it time for the baby?"

"No," she said, smiling strangely. "It is time for me. I am poisoned."

"By something the driver left you? What did you eat?"

"Nothing of his," she said, gasping for breath. "By things I went into the forest to eat."

"What things!" he shouted. "What things!"

"Mushrooms," she said. "Let me lie down."

"You ate poison mushrooms?"

"Yes. I cannot stand it, thinking that next year he may track us down and find you."

"Who?"

"The driver."

"I will kill the driver if we ever see him again!" He let go of Lady Utsu and went to the water jug. He remembered what Lord Norimasa used to do.

"Sit up!" he said roughly. "You are to drink water. If you do not drink, I will pour it down your throat."

He poured a cup of water and gave it to her. "Drink!" he said. "I mean business!"

She drank the water. "It feels worse," she said.

"I am sorry to hear it," he said, and put another full cup to her mouth. "Drink!" he commanded again.

This went on and on until she said, "I cannot drink any more. If I drink I will begin to vomit!"

"Drink! Don't talk!" he said.

She made a great attempt to swallow the cup of water, and just as she predicted, she began to vomit violently. She got up on her hands and knees like an animal and kept on vomiting. Finally, when she retched, only yellowish water poured from her throat and even her nose.

"Drink more!" he ordered, and he forced the water on her. She gagged on the water, but swallowed it. After two more cups, she began retching again. "Drink!" he ordered. She was doing her best to obey. After every two or three cups, she again began retching, and each time what she brought up grew clearer until it looked like the water in the cup.

He picked the exhausted woman up and lay her down on the mat. "You look as if you swallowed a full moon," he said, his hand resting on her stomach. "How much does it hurt now?"

"Not very much," she said.

"Tell me the truth!" he demanded.

"It is only a little sore," she said. "That is the truth."

"You are to go to sleep while I clean up," he told her.

Sapped of all energy, she fell sound asleep.

After he cleaned the floor, he sat cross-legged on the side of the mat, watching her. Was there no end to the torments she would devise for the men she ensnared? How could she have done this? Was it worth it to destroy his happiness because she felt humiliated? How important was humiliation?

"Twist off my head! Twist off my head!" he'd heard a wounded soldier beg once. "I do not want to come back alive! Think of the shame! My family! I would do it for you!"

Was domestic life also a battlefield? Why were they opposing one another? Had he won? He didn't know, and would not for a while. Probably he would know by morning. Tears coursed down his face and he used his sleeve to wipe them aside. "My sleeve wet with tears." The same image in five out of ten poems in the royal anthology. Now he understood that the annoying cliché was real and dreadful.

Was she still alive? He bent forward and stopped breathing to listen. He could hear her regular breathing, but, he thought, it was a little shallow. The two foxes crept in through the door and took up positions on either side of them. Eventually, the largest, reddest of the kits, who was now so big that she looked almost grown, came carefully through the door, looked about curiously and then lay down next to the samurai's fox. Well, well, thought the samurai, you are the brave one. He put out his hand to pat the new fox, but she drew back. She was still frightened of people, still wondering what people were for.

Some lives go on smoothly, he thought bitterly.

He bent forward to listen to the sound of her breathing. The same.

He must have fallen asleep. In the morning when he opened his eyes, he was still sitting cross-legged and Lady Utsu was sitting up on the mat.

"I am alive," she said. "I am surprised."

The samurai did not reply.

"Are you sorry? That I am alive?"

"No," he said. "Does your stomach hurt?"

"It is only sore."

"You said that last night."

"You are angry," she said. "If I promise it will not happen again?"

"Do not bother promising. I will watch over you."

"You no longer trust me."

"That is understood."

The two of them looked at each other. "The little fox is here," she said. "This is the first time she has ever come in."

The samurai said nothing. He was thinking, It is true that I do not trust her. If another samurai had done such a thing, I would have killed him for his betrayal, and when I thought of him thereafter, I would remember him as a person of no consequence. I do not trust her, and yet I feel love for her all the same. Lord Norimasa had been a far greater man than he had thought. He was able to move with equal understanding between the battlefield and the world of women.

"I am hungry," Lady Utsu said in a small voice.

"You are eating nothing," said the samurai. "Perhaps tomorrow morning. I will boil up some plum tea. The tea will soothe your stomach. The driver will have some use, after all."

"Please do not mention him," said Lady Utsu. Her big, round eyes were larger than ever, and in spite of the gray streaks in her hair, she looked like a child as she sat there on the mat.

"Why such a violent reaction?" the samurai asked. "He has evidently come many times before."

"He disgraced me in front of you. Before, when I told you the story of the frozen man, I knew that for you it was still a story, something remote, not quite believable. But to have that man come and make the story flesh! That I could not bear."

"And for that you were willing to kill yourself and the child?"

"There is more. I was afraid he would come back for me with more people, and you would be killed by them," she said. "That is the truth! I could not bear to cause another death!" She burst into tears.

"I cannot believe you would do such a thing. I am enough to protect you, and if I need more men, I can summon them. What utter nonsense! Will you now start trying to break my spirit? Or worse?"

"I see. Once again, I am a terrible woman," Lady Utsu said.

"Either you have a terrible streak in your nature or you are a very foolish woman, very credulous. I never took you to be the latter."

"I must not eat until tomorrow?" she asked.

"No," the samurai said emphatically.

"Have I poisoned the child?"

"I hope not. I think I arrived in time."

"Good," said Lady Utsu, who seemed to mean what she said. "But drinking the water was horrible!"

"Don't complain. Sometimes it works and sometimes it does not," the samurai said. Lady Utsu thought, and then recited:

> In the winter, I came to an empty hut.
> There was only a silver pail full of ashes.
> All the embers had gone out
> As had my life.

"I came close," she said.

"Too close," said the samurai.

"And you? If the men come, will you come too close? Because of me?"

"Do not worry about me," he said. "I will take extra precautions."

Suddenly there was a clap of thunder and then lightning flashed.

"Oh, now there is no going outside," said Lady Utsu, who was becoming restless in the hut.

"You are not going anywhere in any case," said the samurai.

"But this rain could go on for days!" she protested.

"If it stops raining and it is warm enough," he said, "I will carry you outside."

"I hate rain," she said, her voice sulky.

The heavy rain was pounding on the roof of the house and thick sheets of water fell from the eaves. "At least the roof doesn't leak," said the samurai.

"A leak would be of some interest," Lady Utsu said.

"You have your notebook and your *monogatari* scrolls," the samurai said. "Read or write. Or try to improve your painting."

"You are treating me like a child," she said.

"I told you. If the rain stops and it's warm enough," he said, "I'll carry you."

"Carry me?"

"You are still recovering," he said.

"My abdomen is very still," she said uneasily.

"Will you mind?" the samurai asked. "If there are no twanging bows, only my one bow twanging, no priests intoning sutras, no one burning incense, no attendants but me?"

"I will not mind anything," she said. "If we live."

He sensed that she meant more than what she intended to say.

"Is there something else? Some danger we should fear?"

Lady Utsu traced designs with her forefinger on the mat.

"The man who froze to death loved me beyond all reason," she said, "but his family did not love me."

"Tell me all you think," the samurai said. "I cannot come to any conclusions if you withhold information from me. There is more, isn't there?"

"It is what I said before. I am worried. When the driver returns to the family castle, he will tell the others I am living with a man and I am pregnant. When his family believed that I was living alone like a nun, they were angry and bitter, but not so angry that they would try to take revenge. Now they will hear that I am pregnant and think I have disgraced their son's memory, and I have no idea what they will do. They may well do something. And their anger, I think, will also be aimed at you. Because of that, it is best if you leave me here."

"You have lost your senses," the samurai said. "I am not going anywhere and I am not afraid of dying. But it is reasonable to be on the alert."

"If there were more people to protect us," she said. "But we are only two, and I am useless."

"Lord Norimasa used to say that I was worth one thousand men."

"Hyperbole," she said. "A figure of speech. He was expressing his respect. But he would not have expected you to supply the strength and work of one thousand men."

"I am giving this some thought," the samurai said.

"I am relieved," Lady Utsu said, smiling.

"They would not send many men against me," the samurai said, thinking. "A few of them might have forged papers to go through the barriers, but not a large force. The trick is to know when they are coming before they get here."

"Since you have decided to watch my every movement in this hut, how do you propose to keep guard?"

"I will think of something," the samurai said. "I always do."

"Ask the foxes to keep watch," Lady Utsu said.

The samurai smiled. "You speak more cleverly than you know."

"SEASONS CHANGE, and no one notices," Lady Utsu said later. "Until there is something, a small trembling in the air, and everything is different, nothing remaining as it was. We have gone through the winter and the summer and now it is beginning to rain and at night it is chillier. Autumn is coming and then winter again. I wonder if I will see winter one more time."

"Of course you will," the samurai said. "And you will be busy with the child. And I will be busy keeping the fire pit warm enough for the child. I am looking forward to winter."

"I have always liked winter. I thought it was the safe season. I know the samurai did not think that way."

"Snow often means trouble. Soldiers and horses leave tracks in the snow. A snowstorm extinguishes torches and puts an end to plots dependent on setting fire to a house or a castle. Provisions are not easily brought through. There may be no enemy, and no one may threaten you, but the snow is holding you siege. The snow can be a formidable enemy. Still, it is beautiful to see it."

"Yes, it is," Lady Utsu said. "I never dreamed that things would end as they did."

"Of course not. But you were young and reckless. You should not have been in a palace or a castle."

"I was happy enough in the palace with the Empress to protect me, but I could not outwit Lady Tsukie's tricks. Her writing master! He was my undoing, my siege in the snow."

"The writing master!" Matsuhito said.

"He could forge anything. Many times, Lord Norimasa intercepted letters from the heads of other clans and substituted other, quite different letters than the authors had intended. His writing master imitated the handwriting. Lord Norimasa caused other clan leaders to suspect that each was guilty of plotting against the other. When the ties were weakened, Lord Norimasa would come in, 'like a bird of prey,' he said."

"Then you think Lady Tsukie had the writing master forge letters with your handwriting?"

"I believe she caused others to believe that I was plotting against her so that I could have Lord Norimasa to myself. Or she intimated here and there that I myself was not loyal. I am quite certain she told some of the ladies she thought I was a spy for the Empress, and that I agreed with the Imperial Couple who thought Lord Norimasa was gaining too much power. The sight of me drove her to distraction. She was a terribly jealous woman."

"You must forget her and all other disturbing things," the samurai said. "The leaves are already showing a yellow tinge. Soon it will be autumn and I will take you outside and we will look at the mountain. Winter is not long after that.

"This man who died in the snow," the samurai continued. "Was his clan powerful?"

"He was a Fujiwara," she said softly. "They are very powerful."

The samurai nodded.

"Tell me," he asked, "do peddlers get as far as this cottage?"

"Very rarely," she said. "If one does come, it is in autumn, a little later than it is now. They know where everyone lives and they come to sell things or trade before the winter sets in. Usually I find something I don't need and trade it for saké. Otherwise, they become angry. They say things like, 'In the winter, when it is so silent and you begin to worry about bandits, you need a little saké.' Is there anything you need?"

"Yes," he said. "If I should be in the stable or if I have gone into the woods when they come, you must beat very hard on the large pot. I don't want to miss him."

"Such strange whims," said Lady Utsu, her eyes narrowing, but the samurai was lost in thought. "If anyone does come back from the Fujiwara, they will surely come before winter, which means they will come soon."

The samurai nodded. "But there is no need to worry," he said.

THERE WERE SHADOWS on their little hut, but time passed happily. Lady Utsu busied herself stringing together the dried persimmons and plums and the smoked deer meat. This year, there was even smoked wild boar. There were many dried mushrooms, and she strung all of those, although she shuddered when she saw them. She sat back on her heels and said, "It never occurred to me to wonder if any of the food they sent was poisoned. But I do not think they would do that. The man who died in the snow was a good man and ought not to have died in such a way."

"You go on about it," the samurai said. "He is dead and his spirit is at peace."

"I wish I believed that," she said.

"If he left such instructions about you, he knew something could happen and yet he was not angry. He thought it was worthwhile to carry out his task. A samurai would not become an angry spirit if he died trying to accomplish his task. I told you."

Lady Utsu nodded, and placed her hand on her belly. "The little one inside has awakened," she said. "He is very busy."

"You are a wobbly thing these days," the samurai said. "If your belly grows any larger, you will begin tipping forward. I can see you lying on top of your belly and when the wind comes in the door, you will begin spinning on that belly like an insect on a *temari* ball."

"I know how peculiar I look," said Lady Utsu, but she could not suppress a smile.

He began to notice that she often rubbed the small of her back with her hand. "When their back hurts," his grandmother used to say, "that may be the beginning." He watched her closely. He still refused to allow her to leave the hut unless he accompanied her. "Regard yourself as a hostage," he said. "You were always interested in war."

"And what war am I in?"

"The Great Mushroom War," he said.

The autumn leaves were beginning to blaze with color, and when the wind blew hard, some red leaves were blown into the clearing. "Truly," Lady Utsu said, "winter will not be long in coming." Yes, thought the samurai, and before it comes, the Fujiwaras will come, too.

He took to keeping the foxes in the hut more often. If he closed the door, Lady Utsu's fox would begin to whine and bark, and he would let him go. "I want you to stay here," he told his fox, who seemed to understand what he wanted and sat down next to Lady Utsu and looked at her and then at the samurai. "Yes, stay with her," said the samurai.

"Let the poor animal go," said Lady Utsu. "Why must everyone and everything be cooped up like this?"

"The door is open. If she wants to go out, she can," the samurai said.

A few nights later, the fox left the hut and seemed to disappear. The samurai, who was restless, sensed her going but did not awaken. A few moments later, there were two sharp yelps and then two sharp yelps again. The samurai listened. The barking appeared to be coming from beneath the floor. There was one more bark, and the fox was silent. Then the fox began scratching at the underside of the floor.

He gently woke Lady Utsu. "Someone is here," he said. "I want you to lie along the wall and put your dark cloak over you. Leave only enough room to breathe, but otherwise keep yourself hidden."

She obeyed at once.

For weeks now, the samurai had been sleeping with his sword thrust into his belt. Near his head, his bow was strung and his quiver was full of arrows. He considered what to do next. His fox had extremely sharp hearing. Probably there was a little time before whoever it was appeared. There was no moon and the only glimmer of light came from the banked coals in the fire pit. He was wearing his black robe, and had worn it for some time. He would be almost invisible in the dark.

He went out through the door and remained hidden in the deep shadows cast by the steep, low eaves. He went along the wall to the back of the house. He saw no one. Suddenly the fox appeared at his side. "Quiet," he told her. He began to climb the thatched roof until he had nearly reached the ridge pole. Then he raised up his head. He was able to see into the clearing. The fox, who climbed up with him, lay down, flattening herself, her ears up. "Now we will wait," he told the fox.

It often seemed to him that the fox understood what he said, or at least what he intended. Now, he felt that he had a companion who was helping him defend the hut.

Nothing happened. There was only the soft rustle of the trees, a different sound than earlier in the year; the trees were drier and more stiff. He grew sleepy and began to think that no one was coming and that this was only a false alarm. But the fox suddenly nudged his cheek and the samurai crept up a little higher and looked at the clearing. His eyes were accustomed to the dark, and he could see three figures emerge from the woods at the far end.

I will have to let them come closer, he thought, readying his bow and arrow. If I kill one now, the other two will have time to escape into the woods. The fox looked at the samurai as if she were waiting for instructions. He shook his head and she flattened herself out. They were close enough now, he thought. He let one arrow fly and one of the figures fell. He quickly let fly another and the second figure fell. But the third ran quickly to the hut, and in a moment he was inside.

"Let's go," the samurai said to the fox. He was on the ground immediately. Instead of going into the hut, he went beneath it. He had made several trapdoors that opened beneath the structure, and he opened one of them now. Inside the hut, he knew, the man would not see well. But the samurai saw him. He was approaching the fire pit. He saw the man put his hand to the fire, feel its warmth. The samurai quietly closed the lid of the first trapdoor and went to the second. This was larger and he had designed it so that he could stand and come up through it. He would be able to move his arms freely. He slid his dagger from his robe and held it tightly. At that moment, he became aware that the fox was no longer with him. Inside the hut, there was one sharp yelp. The intruder wheeled to see what had made the noise, and as he turned his back was to the samurai. Matsuhito let his dagger fly. He saw the man stagger as if he were about to fall, but he did not fall.

Matsuhito heaved himself up through the trapdoor and said, "I am Lord Norimasa Matsuhito. Speak your own name." The trespasser turned to face him. "I am Fujiwara Yoshihide," he said, "brother of Fujiwara Yasumoto, whom the woman killed. I have come for her. Are you a samurai who stabs men in the back?"

"You are one who comes with two men to kill a woman," Matsuhito answered. "You are cowardly and deserve no consideration." Matsuhito drew his sword. "Draw your sword!" he ordered the man.

"If I do, I will kill you," said the man.

"Go ahead. Kill me," said Matsuhito.

The man advanced on him suddenly, but Matsuhito moved aside at the last second and brought his sword down on the man's shoulder, severing his arm. It fell to the floor with a loud thump.

"You will not live more than a minute," the samurai said. "If you wish to say anything, say it quickly."

The man sank to his knees and was gasping for air. "Lady Utsu, you will roast in hell," he said. "More will come for you." Then he chanted something, probably a prayer to the Buddha, and fell forward on the floor.

"Can I get up?" Lady Utsu asked in a small voice. "Is it over?"

"Stay where you are until I have searched," he said. He went outside and his fox went with him. The fox was running ahead, as she often had in the past, meaning that she wanted the samurai to follow him. He moved quietly, following the fox. After some time in the woods, they came to a small stream where the foxes often came to drink. There was the sound of an animal pawing at the ground. Horses, thought the samurai. There might be more men. He approached cautiously, moving from tree to tree. One of the horses whinnied and the samurai knew he was not more than a few yards from them. Finally, he could see three horses, one horse for each man. So he had killed them all. At that moment, the clouds parted, and a crescent moon appeared in the sky. It did not shed much light, but just enough to give some definition to the trees and the horses.

The fox was agitated. She repeatedly looked up into the trees as if there were something dangerous there. Probably a mountain monkey, he thought. Then he saw a silvery glint. Someone was hidden in that tree. He stepped back behind a tree and readied his bow and arrow. I will have one chance, he thought. If I do not bring him down now, he will either kill me or he will escape. There was another flash in the tree. The samurai tried to imagine where the enemy was and exactly how he must be standing. The question was, had he extended his arm with the sword or the dagger, or had he raised it above his shoulder? Probably whatever he held was raised. Then the samurai could assume the man's head was near the glint. He continued to imagine the position of the man in the tree until he believed he could see him. This is my chance, Matsuhito thought, and he moved away from his tree and let the arrow fly. Nothing happened. I missed him, the samurai thought, going back behind the same tree.

The fox was growling deep in her throat. The samurai began to hear drops falling. It was going to rain, he thought, but there were not many clouds overhead. The fox was moving forward on her belly and stopped beneath a pine tree. Matsuhito heard her sniff and then heard her lapping at something.

"Come back!" he ordered her.

The fox flattened herself out and stayed where she was. There were many red maple leaves on the ground, and she was invisible as she lay there.

The fox waited. The samurai waited.

There was a sudden crashing, something falling through the branches of the tree. The fox was on her feet. Then the body hit. The samurai approached the man cautiously. He had fallen on his back and the samurai turned him over. His eyes were wide and staring. He was dead. But it was possible there were still more hidden in the trees.

His fox, however, began to prance about and jump up at him, yelping happily. The samurai went behind the tree and sat down. The fox tried to climb into his lap. "You great thing," he said to the fox. "How do you expect to sit in my lap?"

If the fox was happy and unconcerned, there was no one else there. It was time to go back to the hut. The fox came loping behind him. She was the first one in the hut, and immediately she began to howl. "Someone else is there!" the samurai said aloud. "I should not have left her alone!"

But when he entered the hut, he saw no one but the man's dead body, and in the corner, Lady Utsu, who, beneath her cloak, looked as if she were fighting with someone. He went up to her and pulled the cloak free. She was clutching her abdomen with both hands and rolling from side to side and panting. He knew she wanted to cry out, but she had been trained in a samurai family, and such things were not allowed.

"Stop that!" he said. "You will hurt yourself!"

He got up and lit the lantern. Now he could see clearly. He went back to Lady Utsu, who was continuing to thrash about. "I said stop!" he said. "I will sit down behind you and I will hold you up," he said. "It will not be long now."

He sat behind her, and as he pulled her onto his lap and raised her up by her arms, she seemed to relax, as if the pangs no longer hurt her so badly. "I thought you were dead," she said. "When you did not come back quickly."

"I am not so easy to kill," he said.

She began to push rhythmically backward against him and he had trouble steadying himself. Then she suddenly thrust her body upward and he almost fell backward. She thrust one more time and she said, "It is here."

It is here? Where was it?

He lay Lady Utsu down and got the lantern and set it near her. There on the floor was a tiny baby. He picked up the child, but the floor, which was slippery, caused him to fall, still holding the infant. He fell on his back, the baby clutched to his chest. The impact started the baby crying. It wailed and began flailing its arms.

"Do you know what to do?" Lady Utsu asked.

"Yes," he said.

When he had tied and cut the umbilical cord, Lady Utsu reached up her arms. He handed the baby to her. "She is alive," she said wonderingly.

"He is alive," he said.

"He?"

"He."

Lady Utsu began to weep silently. "I never thought such a thing could happen," she said. "We will keep him?"

"Of course," the samurai said.

"Good," said Lady Utsu.

He soon found some cloths in the storage compartment beneath the floor and had the child warmly wrapped. Then he handed the baby back to Lady Utsu and covered both of them with her cloak. "A good night's work," he said, lying down next to her, exhausted. "We can thank Lady Utsu the Fox for it," he said, and told her what had happened, but just as he was about to describe how the man had fallen from the tree, he realized that Lady Utsu had fallen asleep. He got up wearily and dragged the dead Fujiwara out of the hut. I will deal with him tomorrow, he thought, and went back in.

He himself was becoming drowsy. The excitement of the night had worn off, leaving him exhausted. He fell asleep, and his fox pressed up against him and also slept. Eventually, Lady Utsu's fox appeared with the kits and they fell asleep near him. In the morning, the door was still open and brilliant sun spilled into the room. The samurai propped himself up and watched Lady Utsu and the child. He thought, I could stay here like this forever. Then Lady Utsu opened her eyes and smiled, and the child, as if at a signal, began to cry until his face turned red.

"*Genki desu,*" said Lady Utsu. "He is healthy."

"*Yokatta,*" said the samurai, smiling broadly.

CHAPTER THIRTY-THREE

"I DON'T UNDERSTAND WHY," Lady Utsu said, "but it seems that lately I write such sad poems. And yet I am very happy."

"If you were unhappy, would you write happy poems?"

"It is not easy to write happy poems. Melancholy ones are dramatic and people pay attention. But to describe happiness! I should try to do it. Look at some of these!"

> *The spring wind makes the skeins*
> *Of dyed yarn sway on the bough.*
> *The wind is strong and blows my hair.*
> *I remember I am not yet a ghost.*

"That is a happy poem," the samurai said. "But you are still frightened by the Fujiwaras. That's why a ghost appeared in that poem."

"I don't like to think of them," she said.

"Then don't," said the samurai.

"Here are more," she said. "Tell me if they are happy or unhappy."

> *In the spring, I saw something strange:*
> *A wasp's nest, and inside it,*
> *The cheeping of birds.*
> *Shall I make myself a house wherever I find it?*
>
> . . .

The plums withered even as I wept
And at last, there were no tears to fall.
Yet in the morning, even the poor man's roof
was beaded silver with drops of dew.
I shall never be completely poor.

. . .

A gray rainy day in summer,
Yet outside the window
I see a giant poppy, blazing.
I think, I must widen my eyes more often.

. . .

In the long rain, the roof tiles shine.
Two black birds wait, stiff as iron.
I also wait, hoping only for you.

. . .

Autumn.
The wasp and its shadow climb the screen.
Cold winds shake the apple trees
Though the room is warm.
Winter comes closer.
Will you not do the same?

"What do you think?"

"They are about us and not about us at the same time."

"But are they happy or unhappy? I have always written melancholy poems. I was often criticized for it."

"I am no expert when it comes to poetry," the samurai said. "My own attempts were disastrous. But it seems to me these are happy poems."

"I hope so," she said, stretching languorously. "I am happy."

"And the child is happy and I am happy," said the samurai.

"It feels strange, this happiness. And frightening. As if we should not acknowledge it because if we do it will disappear. As if it were no more than a dream, and if we described it, it would vanish, the way dreams do."

"It is no dream. There are four dead bodies that paid for this happiness buried in the woods," the samurai said.

"What a way to think of it!" Lady Utsu exclaimed.

"Lord Norimasa used to say that it is important to know how much a human life costs. You do not decide to spend that sum unless it is on something very important. Because you may end up paying with your own life."

"I miss him," Lady Utsu said.

"It is strange that Lady Tsukie was so certain that he was the father of your child when she heard about it."

"Yes, it was strange," she said.

She lay back against the wall, the baby asleep on her chest. When she lay down, the baby slept on his stomach, and she kept one hand on his back.

"You will not let go of that child even for one instant," said the samurai. "I will show you how to bind him and carry him on your back."

"But then he will not see my face!" she said. "And I will not see his!"

"He will be very happy all the same. Most of the time he sleeps. You should follow his example. You stay up too long watching him. Nothing is going to happen to him."

"I hope not," she said uneasily. "Do you think a peddler will come soon?"

"You know the answer to that best."

"He should come soon," she said.

"HE IS NOT like a child," the samurai said one day. "He is like an army of children."

"Babies are a great deal of trouble," Lady Utsu said, her brow furrowing. "But what is worst about them is how much they make you worry. Every time he sneezes, I think the worst."

"He is strong, if not necessarily brave," the samurai said. "Yesterday, when I took him into the clearing, a crow came flapping down and he howled until his eyes bulged."

"He will be brave," said Lady Utsu.

They were both sitting in the clearing and watching the mountains beyond. In front of them was the grayish white pattern of leafless trees. The sun, beginning to set, cast odd shadows in the form of spindly tall men.

"There has been no rain for a while," Lady Utsu said. "We can spend a good deal of time outdoors."

The samurai was surprised at how Lady Utsu took to the baby. She told him, "I was sure I would not want a child, and now I see I was refusing an entire world."

"You are a natural mother," he said. "Like my fox."

"I suppose so," Lady Utsu said dreamily, looking down at the child.

"He will never learn to walk," the samurai said, "if you do not let his feet touch the ground."

"Then you will learn to fly, won't you?" she cooed at the baby, holding him and making him sail through the air.

"If I did that, you would hear him in the next province," the samurai said.

"It is wonderful," she said. "He has reduced us to simplicity."

"Or imbecility," said the samurai.

"No, he is teaching us simplicity," she said. "That is a great thing to teach. I think he is a little sage."

"You are always right," the samurai said.

"Since he came, what I write is far more simple," she said.

> It has not rained for days.
> The wind blows the long grass
> Like water.
> I think, I cannot drown in such water,
> And know myself safe at last.

"Even the grass is yellowing," the samurai said.

"I intend to stay this way forever," said Lady Utsu. Her comment caused a chill to steal over the samurai, as if the sun had gone behind a cloud.

More and more, he noticed, they each said what went through their heads rather than responding to what the other had said.

Mosquitoes were beginning to swarm, as were little black gnats. "Is it time to go in?" the samurai asked.

"Yes, I suppose we must," said Lady Utsu. "It is a pity to go in when there is no snow outside."

"I will make him a little sled for the winter," the samurai said.

No sooner had they gone in and begun to put the baby to sleep than they heard the tinkling and chiming of bells.

"The peddler!" said Lady Utsu.

"I will go talk to him," the samurai said.

"Have him come in," she said.

He thought a moment, then decided that the peddler might as well enter the house, because his plan required the peddler to know about the child's existence.

"Come in, come in!" the samurai said. "Welcome!"

"Such a warm welcome!" the peddler said. Obviously, Lady Utsu had not welcomed him warmly in the past.

"And what do you have for us this time?" Lady Utsu asked.

"Everything in the world and more!" the peddler said. "Hair combs and brushes, mirrors, gold thread to tie up your hair, a sparkling ball made from river stones, the child would like that, some dried fruit and some tonics against colic, very good for children."

"We will take the sparkly ball and the tonic," said Lady Utsu, "if you would like something I have in exchange."

Lady Utsu suddenly got up and opened the black wooden chest that always stood in the corner of the back room.

"I have some embroidered cloths," she said. "Perfect for wrapping gifts."

"Let me see," said the peddler. One was an orange silk square on which Lady Utsu had embroidered a dragon. It stood out from the fabric due to the lavish use of gold thread. Another was a square of pinkish silk embroidered with range after range of lavender mountains that receded into the distance.

"I should like the dragon," the peddler said.

"But then you should give us more for the dragon," the samurai said.

"What else do you want?" asked the peddler.

"A favor," said the samurai.

"What?" asked the peddler incredulously.

"Just because you cannot touch it does not mean that it has no value," the samurai said.

"I like things I can touch," said the peddler. "Other sorts of things bring danger."

"I am only asking for a favor, not demanding it," said the samurai.

"All right. What is it?" the peddler asked.

"Don't be so suspicious," said the samurai.

"A samurai in the middle of nowhere asking for a favor, and you tell me not to be on my guard? Do you think I have lasted this many years by being careless? Tell me the favor, and I will decide." His eyes kept darting back to the embroidered dragon on the cloth. Clearly he wanted it.

"Once there was a group of bandits," the samurai said. "They were led by a man named Yoshida. It is hard to remember how I came to know them, but in particular, I liked a man named Shinda. Have you come across such a man?"

"I come across many men in my travels," the peddler said. "But I have not heard of these people."

"Think harder. Yoshida said that some of his bandits went peddling through the countryside. He said that some of the *hinin* did the same. I know many of the *hinin*, too."

"You know some disreputable people," the peddler said uneasily. "Why should you want to find such people? Perhaps you are a spy for the palace trying to track those men down. It would not be worth my life to deliver up such a person—even if I knew one."

"I see you know the people I have mentioned," the samurai said.

"I never said that."

"Yoshida and Shinda are friends of mine. We fought together at the Battle of Sanomi. They would be unhappy to hear that you would not do a favor for me."

"The bandits are always on the move," said the peddler. "Even if I could find them, what would you want me to do?"

"I would want you to take a letter to the Fujiwara mansion outside of the capital, but before you got there, I would like Shinda to intercept it. Then he could bring it to the Fujiwaras for a reward. He could say he killed a thieving peddler, and in the peddler's purse he found this letter."

"I could deliver the letter myself," the peddler said.

"That is too simple for the Fujiwaras," the samurai said. "They will think we put you up to it and they will be right. I have known Shinda and Yoshida for a long time. I can trust them."

"What do you want me to do?"

"Contact Shinda. Have him meet you at a place you decide on in advance. Give him the letter. Tell him where to take it. If one of the Fujiwaras reads the letter aloud in his presence, he is to cry and say how sad life is. He is a good actor. Will you do it?"

"I may be able to contact him," the peddler said.

"If Yoshida hears you have not helped me, you will not be safe in the hills," the samurai said. "You understand?"

"*Wakatta,*" said the peddler. "I understand."

"Even worse, if Yoshida hears that you have not carried out my orders, but have done something else entirely, he will tell me, and then your life will be worth nothing. Understand?"

"*Wakatta,*" the peddler said with a sigh.

"You do not think he will be hard to find?"

"No," said the peddler. "He will know where I am. He also has his spies."

"Then it is time to write the letter," the samurai said to Lady Utsu. "Write that you can no longer bear living with the knowledge of having caused your lover's death. Say that you have taken poison and given poison to the child. Say you hope that now Lord Fujiwara's spirit will be at peace. Have you anything left that Lord Fujiwara gave you?"

"Only a mirror with cranes flying over mountains," she said.

"Give the mirror to the peddler. In your letter, write that you are returning the only thing you have left of Lord Fujiwara. Ask the family to bury the mirror to help release the dead man's spirit. Write, Utsu!" he said. "I will hold the baby!"

Lady Utsu returned to the box and came back with some thick *michinoku* paper. "That is good," said the samurai.

He went back to the chest. When he looked in it, he saw an odd image of a woman. He picked it up. "Is this the little statue I carved for you?" the samurai asked.

"Yes," said Lady Utsu, reddening.

"You kept it all this time," he said, holding it tight in his hand.

"It has gone with me wherever I have gone," she said. "It will go with me to my grave."

"Do not speak of graves!" the peddler exclaimed.

Lady Utsu and Matsuhito stared at one another in silence.

"Shall I write?" she asked finally. "Do you think they will believe I am sincere?"

"Such mirrors are worth a great deal. Women do not give them up easily. They believe their spirits have gone into the mirrors. Is it not so?"

"Yes, it is true," said Lady Utsu.

"Then write exactly as I told you," said the samurai.

The samurai and the peddler listened to the soft swish of the brush on the paper. Then Lady Utsu scattered some white sand on the sheet to hasten its drying. "I don't know if they will be taken in," said Lady Utsu. "Lord Fujiwara was beloved by everyone, but especially by his own family. That is only natural."

"At the least, it will buy us time. If we contact Yoshida and his band, we can enlist them as bodyguards. If they have expeditions in mind, I can go with them occasionally. They are not as skilled at strategy as I am. They know this."

"No tricks," the samurai told the peddler. "This is not a complicated task."

"Bandits, the Fujiwaras, it doesn't sound simple to me," the peddler said.

"You will not have to deal with the Fujiwaras, only with Shinda. Whoever receives a letter from Lady Utsu will be so upset he will not bother with you or whoever brings the letter. Leave as quickly as you can after you offer to show your wares. Will you do it?"

"I cannot refuse Yoshida and Shinda," said the peddler.

"You are right not to refuse them," the samurai said.

"WILL IT DO any good?" Lady Utsu asked.

"I think it will work. It will, at least for a while. By that time, we can move somewhere else."

"I have some money," Lady Utsu said. "In the stable under a plank of wood in the floor."

"If we need money, I can take a few trips with Yoshida."

"That is frightening to me," Lady Utsu said.

"We will worry when the time comes," said the samurai. "It may never come."

"I hope not," said Lady Utsu, putting away her writing utensils and then bending over the baby. "How peacefully he sleeps. I wonder what he will think of icicles when they come."

CHAPTER THIRTY-FOUR

THE SAMURAI WAS surprised and gratified to find that he was as content, far more content, caring for Lady Utsu and the child than he was when he commanded armies and was known throughout the land as a general. But always, he was haunted by the sense that nothing could last, especially anything as tenuous as happiness.

One afternoon, when Lady Utsu was asleep and the child, who had not yet been given a first name, slept as usual on his mother's stomach, he took Kuro from the stable and decided to look about and find a place that would give Lady Utsu pleasure. He discovered an old path through the woods beyond the clearing, probably beaten down by deer, and he wanted to see where it led. The path was just wide enough so that the trees did not brush up against him and snap back as he went by.

After a while, he heard the sound of running water close by. He got down, tethered the horse and followed the sound. He soon came upon a broad, shallow river. There had been no rain for several weeks, and the stones of the river bottom were clearly visible here and there. But someone or something had dammed the river, and the red maples and the yellow oak leaves of autumn carpeted the stream and gave the river the appearance of an enormous bolt of magnificent brocade. He had heard rivers described in that way before but had never seen one that displayed such beauty. Well satisfied with this sight, the samurai thought that this would be an excellent destination for Lady Utsu and the baby.

He noticed a persimmon tree on the other side of the river, and saw that the persimmons were only slightly wrinkled and still edible, so he took off his sandals and cotton socks, hiked up his *hakama* and began to wade across. Halfway there, he suddenly fell into deep water. Apparently there was a depression in the riverbed, and the samurai felt the shock of the cold water and began to swim. A few strokes brought him to the shallow part of the river, but he was soaked to the skin. Nevertheless, he was hungry and continued toward the persimmon tree.

Obviously, no one had tended it. Branches were growing up from the root while other, more venerable branches bent almost to the ground. The samurai plucked the fruit and ate until all thought of eating left him. Then he considered the river and began to cross it once more. He knew that riverbeds were always uneven, but the hole into which he had fallen was deep and did not appear to have been formed by nature. He went back into the water, looking for the deep hole, and soon found it. Rocks and twigs lined the walls of the hole. An animal might have attempted to shore up the hole with twigs, but it would hardly have placed rocks neatly along the walls. He let himself down into the water and decided to explore. At first he saw nothing, but when he resurfaced for air and then dove back down into the hole, he thought he saw a glimmer of something golden at the bottom. He came up for air and went down again.

He was looking at a clasp fastened by a lock. He resurfaced, looked for a sharp rock and found one in the shape of an arrow and went down once more. He began digging out the box. In the process, the water grew muddier, and his eyes stung. He found it hard to see, but continued excavating. Finally, the box came loose from the silt that had accumulated at the bottom of the hole and the samurai felt for the sides and found two handles and, grabbing them, pushed himself off from the river bottom.

The box was not heavy.

The samurai decided to take it back to Lady Utsu so that they could open it together. Just as he was back on the other side of the river and walking toward his horse, the two foxes burst out of the trees and ran up to him, barking happily. "What have you two been up to?" he asked them, and his fox jumped up on him and then seemed surprised to find the samurai's clothing wet. She barked and ran toward the path leading

back to the hut, and then back again to the samurai, waiting expectantly. "I'm coming," he said. The young foxes were nowhere to be seen.

Lady Utsu, holding the baby, was standing in the doorway as he
rode up. He dismounted and led the horse to the stable, removed his
saddle and wiped the horse down. When he looked up, Lady Utsu was
watching him. "You are wet," she said, "and the weather is growing
cold. Please change into dry things. I see the foxes found you." Then
she saw the box he was carrying. "What is that?" she asked.

"I found it in the river. Someone must have tried to hide it. He did
very well. I would never have found it if I hadn't fallen into a hole in
the riverbed."

"*Kappa* hide treasure in riverbeds," Lady Utsu said, frowning.

"Surely you don't believe in them," the samurai said.

"I do."

The samurai poured liquid from the big bucket of rainwater over
the box until it was almost clean. Then he picked up some fallen maple
leaves and scrubbed the box with them. After that, he again poured
water over the box. Now it was smooth, although because of its immer-
sion in the water, its sheen was gone.

"Let's open it inside. I'd like to know what a *kappa* decides to hide."

"I am not happy to see that box," Lady Utsu said.

"It takes me by surprise, every time, how superstitious you can be,"
the samurai said.

Inside the hut, the baby was put into the basket Lady Utsu had
woven for him. Then the two of them sat on the mat and contemplated
the chest.

"It has a strong lock," Lady Utsu said, her curiosity growing
stronger than her fear. "We will have to break it."

The samurai went outside, found a stone and came back in.

"I'll smash it now," he said. "Ready?"

Lady Utsu nodded.

It took five blows to break the lock. The two of them sat staring at
the box, reluctant to open it.

"Open it," Lady Utsu said finally.

As he pulled up the lid, the hinges of the box creaked and groaned.
"It was in the water a long time," Lady Utsu said. "Look how swollen
the lid is."

Now that the lid was open, the samurai began turning the box so that they could see the contents. He moved very slowly. He, too, dreaded what he would find.

Immediately they saw golden objects that glittered. Lady Utsu lifted one out. It was a beautiful comb, and on it was engraved a picture of wild, stormy water and a woman on the shore staring out to sea. She placed the comb on the floor. Next came several hair ornaments, also made of gold, encrusted with green stones. "Is that jade?" she asked herself, and placed those, too, on the floor.

"This is larger," said the samurai, lifting something out. It was heavy and covered in a cloth that was still dripping wet.

"Open it," Lady Utsu said.

"A mirror," the samurai said. "The surface of the mirror is a little pitted." He handed it to her.

"It is gold," she said. "Look at it." Again, the back of the picture was engraved with a stormy sea crashing against cliffs. The woman on the shore was staring out to sea and resembled the woman on the comb. Farther out in the water was a ship struggling to stay afloat. Waves half covered the deck of the boat and the sails were ripped in several places.

"What do you think?" asked the samurai.

"I think these things commemorate someone who died at sea, and the woman had them made to appease the drowned man's spirit."

"It might not have been a man. A woman might have died, or a child."

"But the woman is standing on the shore," Lady Utsu said.

"Perhaps it is another shore," the samurai said.

"You mean, she is the one who died?"

"It's possible."

She stared at the golden objects on the floor. "I hope none of them died," she said. "What is that globe at the bottom of the box?" It was also wrapped in a cloth. "Open it," Lady Utsu said.

The samurai unwrapped this object very slowly. The fabric covering it was bound by gold thread and it was difficult to unravel the knots that held it. When it was done, he proceeded slowly, not letting the cloth fall away from it immediately. "Ready?" he asked Lady Utsu.

She nodded.

He let the fabric fall.

Lady Utsu shrieked. The globe was a skull and inside it was filled with objects that must have belonged to the woman whose skull it was. In it, there was a small green jade bottle. Lady Utsu uncorked it. "Incense," she said, her voice trembling. "A wooden bear. A pot of makeup, rice powder and grease. A little pot of red grease for the lips and the cheeks. Two tiny teeth wrapped in an embroidered cloth. These are children's teeth," Lady Utsu said, dropping them and sitting back with a shudder.

"The end of a great love affair," said the samurai.

"Or a great hatred," Lady Utsu said. "Why assume that a man buried these things? The mother of the dead woman might have done it. Or her father. But why here? How did it get to this place?"

"Someone must have been fleeing, but fleeing what?"

"His own memories," she said. "Or hers."

"But why here?" the samurai insisted.

"Whoever it was must have thought this was pure, undisturbed water, and these things would be purified even if it took centuries for the purification to take place. Then the spirit of the woman in the skull would find rest."

"But two people may have died. The skull could belong to the man, and the woman's things were placed inside to keep the two together on their path to the next life."

"We have disturbed something holy," Lady Utsu said.

"You saw the peddler. I've known bandits. Possibly this is bounty and someone hid everything until he was sure he could retrieve it safely."

"Why hide a skull?"

"The skull is puzzling, and so are the teeth," admitted the samurai. "The gold objects, though, are worth a fortune. They would be worth hiding."

"It was not a bandit who did it, or a peddler," Lady Utsu said. "It frightens me, as if it were left here for us to discover the riddle. It was left there to remind me that I shall not live long, and neither will the child." She began to weep.

"Do not say such a thing!" the samurai said. "Anyone could have stumbled on that box!"

"But it was not anyone," she said. "It was you and me."

"I will put it back in the river," he said.

"It is too late," said Lady Utsu.

"Utsu," said the samurai, "you will make yourself sick. Stop thinking such dreadful things."

"I gave away Lord Fujiwara's mirror to keep us safe, and now we have a mirror back again."

"It is coincidence," Matsuhito said.

"I think not," she said.

"I will take the box back and hide it again and we will forget about it."

"It was meant for us," Lady Utsu said sadly. "We must keep it."

"You have strange whims. How can I understand them? How can I understand this one?"

"It is enough that one of us understands it," Lady Utsu said. "Please put the things into the box and put them in a compartment under the floor."

"I think we should bury the skull," the samurai said. "It is not right to have a skull preserved like a trinket."

"Whoever preserved it did not preserve it as a trinket," Lady Utsu said emphatically. "We are meant to care for it."

"That is wrong," the samurai said. "We will not be happy living above a skull. The skull will not be happy unless it is buried."

"It is meant for us," Lady Utsu said stubbornly.

"Will you overrule me on this?" he asked.

"Yes."

"This is courting evil," he said.

"The evil has already taken place," she said. "But perhaps it means something else altogether. Perhaps it is to remind us of two people who were very happy and are telling us now that we must struggle to be as happy as they were."

"You cannot win an argument with Lady Utsu," Lord Norimasa had said.

"If we are to keep it," the samurai said, "you should place the box in a compartment. You are the high priestess in charge of this box."

"I do not mind," Lady Utsu said.

"Please change your mind."

"I cannot. I know this is right," she said. "In a short time, you will forget it is there."

"I will not forget," he said.

Lady Utsu stood up, stooped to pick up the box and went to a compartment near the wall. She lowered the box into it.

"Now the skull will begin to find peace," she said.

Or wreak vengeance, the samurai thought.

But Lady Utsu was right about one thing. Within a week, the samurai forgot about the box and the skull, and only remembered it when he found himself standing above the compartment in which it had been placed. He noticed, too, that when his fox came in, she sat on the floor above the compartment as if she were guarding something. One day, when he found himself standing above the box, he felt Lady Utsu's eyes on him. When he turned to her, he saw she was reciting something to herself. "What are you saying?" he asked her.

"Only this," she said. "A poem I remembered. I'll read it for you."

> *Today, I said no more.*
> *Until I said it,*
> *I didn't know*
> *How much nothing was.*

The child began to howl and both of them set aside their thoughts.

Life continued as before, although both Matsuhito and Lady Utsu appeared more nervous. Matsuhito noticed that Lady Utsu watched the child even more carefully than previously. She could not sit still for five minutes before getting up and looking at him.

"How can he sleep if you are always popping up and down like that?" he asked her.

"He is a good sleeper," she said.

Early one morning, the rain awakened them. "It has been raining every day for three days," Lady Utsu said grumpily. "Everything we have is damp."

She turned on her side to look at the infant. "How red his cheeks look," she said. "He grows healthier and healthier." The child stirred in his sleep and waved his little hand and Lady Utsu caught it and held it. "His hand is hot!" she said.

"Because he is still asleep and the robe has been covering him," Matsuhito said.

"And there is a rash on his hand!"

"What?" said the samurai, sitting up.

"We've been feeding him new things," he said. "Probably something did not agree with him. When he wakes up, we will give him some water and beet sugar."

"But he never sleeps on like that!" Lady Utsu exclaimed.

"He is a person. He does not always do the same thing."

"And we have not even given him a name!"

"If I thought you would agree, I would name him Shinda. Shinda has always given me good luck."

"To name him after death! How can you even consider it?"

"Think of a name," the samurai said.

"We could name him Hiro," she suggested.

"Why not? At least for a while. If we don't like it, we'll change it when he reaches maturity."

"Hiro," she said. "A good name for him."

They lay quietly, listening to the rain and watching the rivulets falling in front of the window.

"I suppose he will never sleep in a palace," Matsuhito said. "Do you mind?"

"No. He will grow up to be his own man."

She nodded, and seemed to drift off to sleep. Suddenly she asked, "I meant to ask you this ten thousand times," she said. "How did you meet Lord Norimasa?"

"Because I was brazen when I was young," he said, "I decided he was the most worthy leader to follow. I went to his camp and began shouting, 'Let me speak to Lord Norimasa!' I got a good beating for my trouble. His guards said I had no right to expect to see such an important man when I was nothing but a scarecrow.

"But I kept it up, shouting that I needed to see him, and I had important information for him. I suppose Lord Norimasa was curious. He found strange people appealing. By the time I heard him call out, 'Send him to me!' I was black and blue. I told him he did not have one man in his army who would be as loyal to him as I, and that I could already see that the army needed some shaping up. How else would I have gotten this close to him?

"He considered what I had said and sent me off to be washed and fed. Then he brought me back. He asked me what I could do. I said I could do nothing as yet, but I could shoot a bow very well even though I was still young, and I could see into a stone when I set my mind to it.

He found me funny and began to keep me about. One night, I wandered off and heard two samurai talking about a plot they were hatching, and they mentioned a man who was a spy. I set a trap to catch him, and we got him. After that, Lord Norimasa and I were inseparable. It was destiny, I think."

"As soon as he saw me, he knew what he wanted," she said. "He was never wrong."

"Except when it came to his wife."

"That was an arranged marriage. In the beginning, she was so beautiful and so gentle. You would have understood it then."

She turned to look at the child once more. "He never sleeps this deeply," she said uneasily. "*Akachan! Akachan!* Baby! Baby! Wake up!"

The baby did not stir.

"Something is wrong with him!" Lady Utsu said.

Now Matsuhito picked him up. "He is too hot," he said, and began to soak squares of cloth in the water bucket and apply them to the child's forehead.

"He will die!" Lady Utsu cried out in agony.

"He is not going to die. He has a fever. All children have fever!"

Lady Utsu began pacing the floor, her hands clasped together so tightly that the knuckles were white. "Make him some plum tea," Matsuhito said. "We'll give it to him when it's cold."

She was weeping but did as he said.

The two of them watched the infant so intently that Matsuhito realized his eyes were burning. He had forgotten to blink.

By nightfall, the rain had stopped and the child was cooler. Lady Utsu picked him up and refused to put him down. "He is happier when he can feel my heart," she said. They gave him no further food, only plum tea. Finally, he fell into a peaceful sleep, and his body was again cool.

"We must not make ourselves sick every time he has a cold," Matsuhito said.

"He is the only child I will ever have," she said, "and I do not intend to take chances."

"We have not taken chances," he said. "The rain has stopped."

"It is so quiet," Lady Utsu said.

There was scratching at the door.

"The foxes are back," Matsuhito said, getting up to open the door.

His fox ran in, and he saw the first snow flurry of the winter. The fox circled back to the child, sniffing him. Then, satisfied that he was all right, she lay down behind the baby's head. Occasionally, she licked the top of his scalp. "She will keep him cool," he said. "Utsu," he said, "I meant to ask you something as well. Your fox cannot be the same fox you had when we were together in the palace?"

"No, he died of old age," Lady Utsu said. "Most of his teeth fell out. But this is the child of the first fox. Lord Norimasa arranged it for me."

"And how long did it take to recover from the first fox's death?"

"A long time," Lady Utsu said with a sigh. "I never thought I would have foxes as nurses to my child."

"It is snowing," the samurai said gently.

"It was bound to begin," she said.

CHAPTER THIRTY-FIVE

THEIR LIFE CONTINUED in its usual, by now well-worn path. Matsuhito would go out every three or four days and catch some fish in the same river where he had found the box, although he told Lady Utsu that he had discovered another, deeper river. But there were fish that tended to accumulate in the deep hole in which he had found the box, and because it was so unseasonably cold, he found it simpler to trap fish in that particular place.

As he was starting back on a brightly lit moonlight night, he inspected his four river trout, and thought how pleased Utsu would be to clean and roast them. But he was still some distance from the door when he heard Utsu's anguished screaming. "What happened?" he asked, bursting through the door.

"He won't wake up! He's still alive! I held the mirror up to him! But he won't wake up! He had a fit a little while ago! He was foaming at the mouth!"

The samurai dropped the fish he was holding and grabbed the child. He was much too hot. The samurai plunged him, clothing and all, into the water bucket.

"What are you doing?" Lady Utsu cried. "You are drowning him!"

"He will die unless he cools down," the samurai said. "I remember all this. Stop this screaming!"

She began sobbing softly.

"He will be better?" she asked, like a child afraid of the dark.

"Yes," he said shortly, although he was by no means sure.

"I am going to take the baby teeth out of the box under the floor and bury them. They may be enchanting him or harming him in some way. They may be envious because he is alive and the other child is dead."

"A good idea," the samurai said, paying no attention to what she was saying. He suspended the baby by the armpits and dipped him up and down in the cold water. A fever just like Lord Norimasa's, he thought, and he felt chilled to the bone.

Lady Utsu screamed. Matsuhito turned to her with terror.

"The teeth are gone! They're gone!" she screamed hysterically.

"They're there," the samurai said. "Look again."

"They're not there!"

"Hold the baby in the water and I'll look," he said. "Then I'll get some snow and throw it into the water. It's his only chance."

The baby teeth were gone.

"You see! You see!" Lady Utsu screeched. "They came out of the box and cast a spell on him!"

"No, they did not," the samurai said. "I took out the teeth and threw them away."

"Threw them away?" she asked, horrified. "How could you do such a thing? This is all your fault!"

"It is my fault," he said. He had not touched the teeth, but it was better that Lady Utsu thought he had done so instead of believing that the teeth were moving around the hut in an attempt to kill their child.

"We have to find them!" she cried. "Tell me where to look!"

"First give me the baby and get some snow to put in the water. Then I'll tell you where I threw the teeth," he said.

To his surprise, she did as she was told.

"Now where are they?" she demanded.

"I threw them behind the stable where the grass is always tallest."

She rushed out the door without putting on her robe.

She will be sick next, thought the samurai. He continued bobbing the child up and down in the cold water. The baby was beginning to hold his head up, although he had not yet awakened.

He did not know how long he spent doing this when Lady Utsu, her hair wild, appeared in the doorway. He looked at her and thought, She looks like a deranged ghost.

"I can't find them!" she said. "We are lost! Lost!"

"Look how he is holding up his head," the samurai said. "Surely that's a good sign."

"Now we are depending on signs!" Lady Utsu exclaimed, but she walked up to the pail and looked at the baby. "He does look stronger," she said.

"He is stronger," Matsuhito said. "When he is a little cooler, you can hold him."

"I will go out and look again for the teeth," she said.

"Look in the stable where the foxes hide their treasures," he suggested.

She disappeared silently. He had hoped she would be looking for some time, but she appeared very quickly. "He is still alive?" she asked, before daring to approach the pail.

"He is alive, and he is cool," said the samurai. "You can take him."

She snatched up the infant, lay him on the mat and sat up next to him. Her eyes were riveted to his chest and stomach, rising and falling. "He is alive," she said softly.

The samurai came and sat silently next to her. In the village, his grandmother had said children who suffered from such high fevers were never the same afterward. And the child was not waking up. His grandmother would have said that this was not a good omen. More than anything else, he was afraid of what would happen to Lady Utsu if the child died. She might go completely mad, he thought.

"We had better take turns sleeping," the samurai said. "If there is to be more trouble, at least one of us should be alert."

"You go to sleep first," Lady Utsu said. She noticed that the samurai was sitting as he used to sit when he presided over the Council of War. His hands were on his knees and he sat bolt upright. His face, she thought, was as ferocious now as it ever was. He will fight this and win, she thought, and immediately she felt a great sleepiness descend on her.

"You sleep first," Matsuhito said. "I am wide awake. Put him on your belly so he can feel you breathing." Meanwhile, his fox lay her head on his thigh. "Good fox," he said.

"Could one of the foxes have gotten the teeth?" Lady Utsu asked sleepily.

"Possibly," he said. "Anything is possible."

Lady Utsu fell asleep.

WHEN LADY UTSU again awakened, she saw Matsuhito sitting in the same position, watching them. She smiled at him and drew the baby higher up onto her breast. His head touched her chin and she felt something cold as a stone is cold in winter. Her eyes went wide and she could barely breathe. "Wake up!" she said, shaking the baby. "Wake up!" But the child did not move, and Lady Utsu picked up the baby and began shaking him violently.

"What are you doing? Stop that!" Matsuhito shouted, trying to take the baby from her, but she was holding on to the child as if she had nailed him to her by her own bones.

"Let go and I will fix him," he said, and Lady Utsu, her eyes still wide, let go of the child.

Matsuhito saw at once that the child had died.

"He is not very well," he told Lady Utsu. "Make him some hot plum tea."

"Hot plum tea?" Lady Utsu repeated, as if she had never before heard such words. "Hot plum tea?"

"We will give him some to wake him up. I'll walk about the room with him."

"It is your fault!" Lady Utsu burst out. "You threw out the baby teeth from the box. Before I fell asleep, I asked you if the foxes could have gotten them, and you said it was possible, but you knew it wasn't, because you said you threw them out behind the stable! Why have you been lying to me?"

"I did lie," Matsuhito said.

"What happened to the baby teeth?" Lady Utsu said, her voice rising to a scream.

"I don't know."

"You didn't take them from the box?"

"I haven't touched the box since we put it away."

"Could the foxes have gotten to them?"

"No. The box was untouched."

"Then spirits came for the baby," Lady Utsu said. "They wanted company, or they were jealous, so they took his spirit."

"Children die for no reason," Matsuhito said. He began to weep as he looked at her, her eyes like saucers, her pupils dilated. "He had a terrible fever, Utsu. Be reasonable. During the plague, did you think everyone who died was attacked by a spirit?"

"A plague may be an army of vengeful spirits who visit the living but no one can see them." Tears streamed from her eyes. "Can't you wake him up again?"

"No," said Matsuhito. "He does not want to wake up. But look how happy his expression is. Wherever he is now, I am sure he is happy." He continued weeping.

"Don't tell me silly stories!" she said. "Wherever he is, he is not here. Probably he is not anywhere! We will never see him again!"

Matsuhito's throat tightened and he could say nothing.

"We must bury him," Lady Utsu said.

"Or burn him," said Matsuhito.

"No, I want to bury him," Lady Utsu said. "Afterward, we can make an image of him and burn it and his spirit will go free with the smoke from the fire." She spoke coldly, as if she were giving orders to the palace cook.

"But we can keep him for a while," Matsuhito said. He sounded heartbroken.

"For how long can we keep him before he begins to smell? Before he begins to show purple marks everywhere? You know what happens. You've seen enough death."

"Death," Matsuhito repeated. "How can this be death?"

"Nevertheless, it is," Lady Utsu said, in the same cold voice.

"Death in a time of peace," he said. "Horrible!"

"If you had never found that box, we might have had a chance," she said.

"Don't go on about it," said Matsuhito, still weeping. "The box had nothing to do with anything."

"So you think the things in the box wanted you to discover them, and when you opened the box, the spirit of the dead woman would be liberated?"

"I don't know what I thought! I was curious!" he said. His voice was agonized.

"It is too late now. Too late to discover reasons," she said. Her voice was hard.

"You blame me!" Matsuhito said.

"No," she said. "I blame myself. I gave away a mirror, and I thought I gave away the Fujiwara curse, but the river restored a mirror to me, an even more expensive one, even more beautiful. I should have seen that the mirror meant that I would suffer more vengeance from the Fujiwaras. If I had thrown it out, things might have gone differently."

"This is wild talk," Matsuhito said, weeping. "You did not have anything to do with this, nor did the baby, nor did I. Something came to him and he was not strong enough to fight it off. That's all it was."

"All!" she exclaimed.

"You will make yourself ill," he said, and his voice broke. She seemed to take pity on Matsuhito and said, "I will be better once he is buried."

"Then let's do it now," he said. "The snow is not deep."

"No, let's wait until tomorrow," she said. "I have heard stories of the dead suddenly waking up."

"Whatever you say," said the samurai. They lit two candles and placed each one on a mat and then laid the baby on it. They sat on either side and watched. The child did not stir. After a while, the child's stomach gurgled, and Lady Utsu looked at Matsuhito as if he would tell her there was still hope. "It is only gas still left in the body," he said. "His stomach may swell, but it means nothing."

"Nothing," she repeated.

"Can we not comfort each other?" he asked. "Can we not sit next to each other?"

"Yes," she said. "I forgot. Now there are only two of us once more."

There was a scratching at the door. The foxes. "I will let them in," Matsuhito said.

"They will not eat the baby, now that he is dead?" Lady Utsu asked in a piteous voice.

"No. He still has his own smell. They know who he is."

Matsuhito's fox tried to climb into his lap as she had when she was small, and the samurai grabbed for her and held her tightly to him. He wept into the fox's fur. Lady Utsu's fox kept a slight distance, his ears pointed, as if poised for flight. "Even the foxes know something is wrong," Lady Utsu said.

After some time, Lady Utsu's fox moved closer to her. "You can come," Lady Utsu told him. The fox laid his head in her lap. "You are all I have left," she said, and burst into tears.

Matsuhito heard that, but said nothing. I still have Lady Utsu, he told himself. In time, she will stop speaking in that voice like metal and she will begin to be herself.

The silence in the hut was so profound that the foxes were uneasy and began whimpering softly. Matsuhito held his fox to him. Without thinking, Lady Utsu began to stroke her fox's head. The sound of her hand on the animal's head was suddenly very loud.

They remained in this way until the morning.

At noon, Lady Utsu said, "It is time to bury him." Matsuhito went out and dug a grave. "Wrap him in this cloth," Lady Utsu said, handing him the one embroidered cloth still left. "He deserves to sleep in something beautiful."

Matsuhito began to wrap the baby, but his hands suddenly refused to work. He looked up helplessly. "I will do it," Lady Utsu said. "I am accustomed to wrapping things."

"I will go and make the coffin," he said. He did not say, It is small. It will not take very long.

He went into the stable and went up the ladder into the storage compartment above it. There were some gray, wide, withered planks of wood. It did not take him long to saw six pieces to the right size. Then he hammered five together to make a box. He set the lid inside the box and, holding it under his arm, went down the ladder. Here is his new home, he thought.

"It is done," he told Lady Utsu.

Then they took the baby outside and laid him in the rough coffin Matsuhito had built for him. "Perhaps you should twang the string of your bow," Lady Utsu said, her voice softening. "And I will burn some incense."

They did those things.

"It is time to put the coffin in the ground," the samurai said. "Or the animals will get at him."

Lady Utsu shuddered and then nodded.

"Don't watch while I close the coffin," he said.

"No," she said. "I must watch. I must remember that he is really gone."

But with every strike of the hammer, she shook uncontrollably.

"It is done," he said finally. "Help me lay the coffin in the hole I have dug for him."

They did this.

"Tomorrow, we will burn his image, and soon it will be over," she said. Matsuhito did not like the way she said it.

"Yes, tomorrow," he said. He determined not to leave her alone, not for a moment, although, even then, she could awaken while he slept and find mushrooms that would end her life—perhaps she kept some in reserve.

The next day, they made a small pyre and the little image went up in smoke.

"Now there is nothing more we can do. Do not worry. I will not poison myself again. I cannot leave you here alone. Please do not let me drive you off. Last night, I dreamed you had left me and gone on your travels. In my sleep, I wrote down some notes. This morning, when I got up, I still remembered them and so I wrote them down. Shall I recite them to you?"

"Yes. Please say them out loud," he asked.

"You grew further and further away as I dreamed," she said. "Promise me you shall not leave me, no matter how dreadfully I behave."

"I promise," he said. "Read out the notes to me."

She began to read, her voice trembling. "They went on and on, you see," she said. "As if this were my last chance to write such things."

On the table, I saw an open book.
On the branches I saw half-opened leaves.
How can I bear to see the leaves open again?
 . . .

The lamp in the room lights the bird feeder
Where it sways outside in the dark
But the birds have gone and I think,
They will never come back.
 . . .

On the wall, a huge round pot.
It would make an excellent gong.
Will you come? I think you would come,
But you cannot find the way.
 . . .

Toward evening, some blue sky.
Soon, the dark will erase it
As you, too, were erased.
Why must I be left as I was?

. . .

The house:
One by one, its timbers rot, and are replaced.
When does it become another house?
Why can humans not go on forever in that way?

. . .

When rain poured down,
I cupped my hands and drank
The water and all the images in it.
Why did I not see your face was missing?

. . .

A small moon and cold.
The dead do not mind, their faces like moons.
Must they stay so far from us, so high?

. . .

Small burial mounds in the grass:
The mole tunnels are unseen openings in the earth.
The beetle vanishes.
I would go with him, I think.

. . .

It is only the clouds passing over,
Their shadows enormous.
I will walk the road with my stick forever,
Looking for you.

"Utsu," he said, "you will not lose me. We will live the rest of our lives together."

She regarded him steadily. He saw sorrow in her eyes. "Shall I continue?" she asked. "I think the rest are not cheerful."

"It is easier to write about sadness than happiness," Matsuhito said. "Didn't you say so?"

Lady Utsu nodded and began to recite.

When I left,
Snow fell through bare branches.
Now, as I think of you,
Snow falls
Through the plum blossoms.

On the horizon is the setting sun.
Again and again, I call you
But you walk into it and disappear.
This is what I most feared,
And so, I see, it must happen.
I should not dream so vividly.

"They end here," Lady Utsu said. "They are terrible poems."

"Yes," he said. "They are. You must promise not to leave me."

"I promise."

"I promise not to leave you."

She nodded. "But sometimes," she said in a low voice, "I think poems are premonitions, and you will leave."

"Never. Not while you are alive."

She read the rest of her poems:

After the rain,
Water dripping from branches
Like the beats of a heart.

"I forgot this one," she said. "There is so little time in a life."

"We must remember that," he said.

"I am not happy to have written this," she said.

"I know. Please read it."

Once more, the bright blue sky weighs heavily on me.
At the edge of the road are two black birds.
They are very still.
I think, I cannot cheer my heart.

"Sometimes," he said, "a heart is like my bow. You bend it, let it go, and it resumes its shape."

She nodded, her eyes bright with tears.

AFTER THAT, their life changed. There were times when Lady Utsu looked at Matsuhito as if she were remembering the box and once again blaming him. At other times, he looked at her and remembered the child and that he was gone, and tears sprang from his eyes. What had been bright was now clouded by shadows. Now, thought Matsuhito, we have finally become fully human. We are like everyone else who has ever lived. We have many things to regret, many from which we have yet to recover. Before, our regrets were of ours alone, but now we have created regrets together and we share them. We had a purity, but it has been lost.

Yet the death of the child made them both aware of the depth of their feelings for one other. Lady Utsu no longer asked herself if she could be steadfast in her love for a man, and the samurai no longer asked himself if he was capable of strong love. She expressed what they felt in her poems. At night the days rolled up like a scroll, and then unrolled again in the morning, and every day, there was less time left. And so, although it was the most difficult thing either of them had yet done, they began to make the most of their time.

They read to one another. They cooked together. They swept the floor together. When he went out to the stables, she went with him, and when he rode his horse, she climbed up with him. They discovered that they were more comfortable on horseback if they left the horse unsaddled. They stopped and looked at anything that caught the attention of either of them, and in time, they began to rediscover peace.

Then the snow started to fall and did not stop. Inside the house, they were happy together, their foxes coming and going as they pleased. The young ones now rarely appeared. "They will soon go off," Lady Utsu said. "They are young and have their own needs. But they will always return to their parents. That is the nature of a fox."

One day, Matsuhito was eating his rice and dried plums and said, "In spite of everything, we are lucky."

Lady Utsu hesitated, and then said, "We are. We might never have had him." They finished their meal and lay down on the mat. "I know I will never have another," she said. "It is just as well."

Matsuhito did not answer.

CHAPTER THIRTY-SIX

PEOPLE LOSE SIGHT of time in an unchanging snowy landscape. When the snow does not melt but is perpetually refreshed by another snow, the rhythms of the world outside seem to freeze along with the water that sometimes drips from the eaves. If it were not for night, it would be natural to look outside and think that the passage of time had ceased, and regardless of common sense, it would appear as if those who lived there were caught in one unending day. People who are happy often relish such a landscape. People who are not happy are tortured into a belief that their misery will never end.

Matsuhito and Lady Utsu, who had reached a fragile peace, were happy in the unchanging snow. It was only when Lady Utsu went outside and saw the icicles that her balance grew unstable and threatened to return her to her former state. She remembered saying that she wondered what the child would think of icicles, and tears stung in her eyes. If she thought Matsuhito could not see her, she would break off one of the smaller ones and say, "See, Hiro! This is an icicle!" And she would pretend to hold it to his mouth.

In truth, the icicles upset her, thick and wavy and pointed, like knives suspended from the eaves of the house. Matsuhito knocked down the icicles above the doorway, saying they were large and heavy enough to kill anyone they fell on. When he was finished, the icicles lay everywhere, the same color as the sky, as if the sky itself were too heavy and had let part of itself fall. She said nothing to him about the icicles.

Inside the house, the shadows of the icicles were clearly visible through the rice paper window. It was a very cold winter, and Matsuhito thought it might be best to replace the rice paper with oiled paper that was tougher and would keep out the snow. Lady Utsu eagerly agreed, thinking that the shadow of the icicles would no longer be visible, but even through the oiled paper they were there, more distorted and hazy than before, but there. Each time she saw them they reminded her of savage teeth, and those teeth in turn reminded her of the missing baby teeth, and she would feel the same rising panic she had experienced when she first felt the terrible cold of the baby's head. She learned to sit and to stand so that she could not see the window, and it was true to say that most of the time, they were content.

And so winter wore on.

"We have enough dried food for two years," Matsuhito said. "I will begin hunting in the spring." They no longer wanted to leave this place and go elsewhere.

"Wait until late spring when the animals fatten up on the new grass," she said, and he agreed.

Often he thought of the river in which he had discovered the box, and knew that animals would come to drink there. He would not tell Lady Utsu that he planned to revisit that river. He would climb a tree and wait with his bow and he would bring down many fat animals. He would take the foxes with him and he would ride Kuro, who suffered from the winter inactivity.

"The Fujiwara, the man who brought the things, has not come back," Lady Utsu said, thinking out loud.

"I am sure Yoshida or Shinda tricked them," he said. "Both of them can lie as easily as the wind blows. They can convince you the earth is not shaking even when the mountains are toppling around you."

"You like those men?"

"They are good men," Matsuhito said. "They live differently than we do, but they are as honorable as we are."

"Honorable bandits," she said.

"Not all bandits are like Yoshida," he said. "I was fortunate to come across him. At the time, of course, I did not think so."

"Good and bad fortune are like twins," Lady Utsu said. "In the beginning, it is impossible to tell which is which."

"You must wait to see what they bring," Matsuhito said, agreeing.

"Utsu," he said. "Why not begin embroidering? I love to see you at work on it."

"What should I make?"

"Our house in the snow," he said. "Or two red foxes curled together."

"I should like to make a picture of the foxes," she said, smiling.

They began looking for the material she needed, the needle and all her thread. "Strange," she said. "I thought I had put these in different compartments."

"You haven't thought of these things in some time," the samurai said.

She began her embroidery, and he watched her, sometimes for hours. Eventually she would sigh, put the sewing aside and begin to prepare dinner. Then he would stand, take up what she had been doing and examine her work. Soon the outline of the two foxes was stitched in and the heads of the foxes were finished. They looked alive. At such times, he often thought of the child and what he would now look like in the coffin. He is not our child anymore, he thought. Then he would make a great effort and turn his thoughts to other things.

Time passed, and at last there was the incessant dripping as the icicles melted. "Perhaps it is only a temporary thaw," Lady Utsu said. She was embroidering the paws of the foxes. "It is almost done," she said.

"I went out today and saw little flowers in the snow," he said. "It may be time to gather the new spring roots."

"I will come and look," Lady Utsu said, standing up and putting on her cloak. "Where are my boots?"

"Where they always are," he said. "In the box outside the door."

The box, she thought. That box. That skull. Those teeth.

The samurai put on his straw hat and they both left the hut. "You see?" he said. "The sweet roots are ready."

"Tomorrow we will come out and pick them," she said. "It will be delicious to eat things that were not first dried." She looked up at the sky. "Already the color is changing," she said. "It is softer and bluer. You are right. I do not think this is just a temporary thaw."

There was an enormous clap of thunder and almost immediately a great flash of lightning. "A storm," Matsuhito said. "Let's go back."

Rain began to pour down. Within seconds, huge chunks of snow were washed from the roof of the house. "Get in, get in!" Matsuhito said. Lady Utsu was standing still, watching the snow from the roof begin to slide and fall. She seemed to come awake when he shouted at her.

Outside, the rain continued to pour down. They began to hear the trees lashing in the wind outside.

"It is good that the rain is taking down the snow from the roof," Matsuhito said. "With so much snow, I was afraid the weight of it might bring down the roof."

"You pulled off most of the snow with your rake," she said absently.

"Even so," he said. "I could not reach everything, and you would not let me get up on the roof."

"This hut was built to be strong," she said. Matsuhito looked at her. She sounded as if she were talking in her sleep. "So spring is coming," she said, her voice exhausted.

"It always does," said Matsuhito.

She did not say, For some of us.

Inexorably, winter was turning into spring.

"Soon it will be hot," Lady Utsu said. "I dislike hot weather. It is so hard to move."

"I could begin a garden," he said.

"For that we need seeds," Lady Utsu said.

"The peddler may come again."

"I don't think he will return. He seemed to think we were dangerous people."

"But there are other peddlers," he said.

She said nothing. She was staring into space. "The icicles are gone," she said.

"Soon the rest of the snow will be gone. We can only see it now in shaded places and beneath the pine branches. Spring will be here sooner than we think. But winter still has some strength left in it."

"Heat," she said. "I do not want to live through another summer."

"Do not say such things. You promised!" the samurai said.

"I only meant—" she said, breaking off. "Already, now that the rain has stopped, the sun is beating down, and it feels hot in here."

"Hot? Here?"

"It is just the sun," she said.

He watched her closely. Her cheeks were flushed.

"You have caught cold," he said reproachfully.

"It is nothing," she said. "In the spring, I always catch cold."

"Is that true?" he asked.

"Yes," she said, and sneezed.

"I think you should spend more time in bed," he said.

"I think I should gather up the new roots," she said. "Activity is good for a cold."

"Only if you feel well enough."

"Of course," she said.

Winter disappeared, and spring exploded with its greens and golds. Wild poppies appeared at the edge of the woods, and Lady Utsu transplanted some so that they were closer to the house. "We will gather the seeds when they are ready and plant them," she said, but really, she dreaded putting things into the earth.

After the poppies were transplanted, Lady Utsu sat down next to them. She fingered one of the scarlet petals. "How soft they are, and how fragile. How thin their veins are. I prefer looking at them to the forsythia. Yellow things can never be as beautiful as scarlet ones."

The samurai was happy to see her busy. She took out her writing desk, ground her ink stick, mixed the gratings with water, washed her brushes and let them dry in the sun, and that morning she was absorbed, bent over her writing. Really, someone would expect no danger in her.

"How hot it gets, even in the spring," she said.

"Remember the huge umbrellas of the palace?" the samurai asked. "Regardless of how hot it grew, there was always shade."

"Often I dream of the fish-scale-shaped tiles of the palace, and how they glistened when it rained. I wonder why I remember that."

"And the dolphins at the end of the ridgepole in your pavilion," he said.

"And Lord Norimasa and Lady Kitsu and so many others," she said. "Lady Kitsu refuses to come to me in dreams, but Lord Norimasa often does. Even in death, he is kind."

"I dream of battles," he said. "Often I dream men are pounding the two-headed drum and then the other generals begin to ride up through the big gate. It always seemed to me that they arrived like avenging gods. I can see the old counselor now in his blood-red armor."

"And his blood-red cheeks," Lady Utsu said, smiling. "He drank more than was good for him."

"How could it have been bad for him if he lived to such an age and at last died in battle?" Matsuhito asked. He smiled, remembering.

"I'm going inside," she said. "The light hurts my eyes."

He stayed where he was. Did he imagine it, or did he hear the pounding of a galloping horse? He stood up and listened. Definitely it was a horse, and it was coming closer. From the woods, he could hear the foxes barking. He felt for his sword and his dagger, but he had no desire to go into the house for his bow. He moved back into the shadow of the barn and waited.

The sound of hooves was coming closer. At that moment, a large gray horse flew into the clearing and, suddenly reined in by its rider, reared up and then settled down again.

"It is me, Shinda!" the man shouted. "I came to see how you are."

Matsuhito was overjoyed. "Come in! Come in!" he said. The two men grabbed one another and pounded each other on the back.

"Before you go in," Matsuhito said in an urgent whisper, "you must know that the child died. Lady Utsu is still fragile. We try not to speak of it."

"Died?" Shinda repeated. "A natural death? Nothing to do with the Fujiwaras?"

"Nothing to do with anything on this earth," he said. "Come into the woods. I'll tell you what happened and what Lady Utsu thought killed the child."

He told Shinda about the box he had found in the river.

"A skull and some gold things," Shinda considered. "Either a thief who killed the woman he robbed, or a wife murdered by her husband."

He told Shinda about the baby teeth.

"That is strange," Shinda said. "It may have been revenge."

"I think so," said Matsuhito. "If Lady Utsu brings it up, say something comforting. She believes the box brought bad luck. Especially the baby teeth."

"She may be right," Shinda said.

"Don't say that to her!"

"Of course not," Shinda said. "I understand what you are telling me."

"Now she is dreading the heat of summer."

"I myself dread it," Shinda said. "You must not worry so much. She will sense it."

The two men entered the house.

Lady Utsu was sneezing again and again.

"Shinda!" she said when she stopped. "I recognize you from the way Matsuhito described you!"

Shinda smiled broadly. "Most women do not greet me so happily," he said.

"I don't know why not," Lady Utsu said, laughing. "Perhaps it is because you always arrive covered with dust. We will heat up a bath for you."

"Cold streams cleanse you, but they are not so nice," Shinda said.

Lady Utsu was putting out rice balls and pickled lotus roots. "We have fresh meat," she said. "Matsuhito killed a wild boar."

"Those are dangerous beasts," Shinda said.

"I killed him from high up in a tree," the samurai said.

"That is all right, then," Shinda said. He was eating wolfishly. Lady Utsu got up and brought more rice balls and sweetened red beans.

"Utsu wants seeds to begin a garden," Matsuhito said.

"Yoshida will take care of that," said Shinda. "And I will bring the seeds so I can come and eat more of your rice cakes."

"And my sweet root soup," she said.

"Sweet root soup!" he said, rubbing his belly. "When did I last eat such a thing?"

"Did the letter get to the Fujiwaras?" Matsuhito asked.

"Most assuredly," Shinda said. "They seemed pleased. They are stupid. They didn't suspect me."

"Who would?" the samurai asked. "Bandits and samurai are traditional enemies."

"Well, we fooled them," Shinda said happily, his stomach well full.

They gossiped throughout the night, and in the morning, Shinda left. "I will be back with seeds. And you," he said to Lady Utsu, "don't worry about the summer heat. It means autumn is coming."

"Another autumn," she said, sighing.

"That is nothing to sigh about! That is something to celebrate!" Shinda boomed. His good humor was contagious. Lady Utsu was smiling.

"You can always stay," she said, dumbfounding Matsuhito.

"Wh...? And let the people of my province begin to feel safe? Do you think life is exciting for a farmer or a loom user? Without us, they would die of boredom! *Abai yo!* he called. "Goodbye!"

"Well, so he is gone," Lady Utsu said. "Let's not go back in. Let's go for a walk in the woods before the mosquitoes begin to swarm."

It had been a long time since she had made such a suggestion. Even when he built her a sled, she avoided trips away from the house. "Does anyone really look forward to the summer?" Lady Utsu asked.

"Probably people in snow country."

"I wonder," she said.

SUMMER CAME, and with it, its moist oppressive heat and its inevitable thunder and lightning storms. "At least it is cold at night," Lady Utsu said. "Shinda will come soon with the seeds."

"He keeps his promises," the samurai said.

"We are turning into peasants," Lady Utsu said comfortably. "I like this."

Matsuhito handed her a wild plum. "No," she said. "I can't swallow it. My throat hurts."

He picked up her hand and held it. "It is warm," he said.

"My hands are always warm," she said.

"Drink some soup," he urged her.

"No. Even liquid hurts when I swallow."

"If only there was a doctor nearby," he said uneasily.

"It will pass in a day or two," she said carelessly.

"Your voice is hoarse."

"Only when I speak," she said, laughing. But she winced when she laughed.

Matsuhito noticed that his own throat was sore. "Tomorrow is hunting," he said. "We should sleep." He felt no shadows, no premonitions. They slept well and soundly.

The next day, he returned later than he had expected. The light outside was dimming, but he had three pheasants, enough to keep them for a while. "Utsu!" he called out happily as he opened the door.

The room was sunk in darkness. "Utsu! Where are you?" he asked.

"On my mat," she said in a terribly hoarse voice. "Come closer, but not too close."

He sat down on the edge of the mat.

"This is not just a sore throat," she said. "I am as hot as Hiro was. There are some things I want to tell you."

"Why? What things? Tell me later when you can speak without hurting yourself."

"I think there will not be a later for me," she said. "My soul is stained badly enough. I must not die without unburdening my heart."

"You will not die," the samurai said. How many times, in how many situations, had he said that before?

"It is about the first child, the one I gave to another family," she said.

"All that is over," he said. "Rest."

"I did not tell you the truth."

"It does not matter," the samurai said.

"It may not have been your child."

"You told me that. Then whose child was it?" he said.

"It might have been Lord Norimasa's."

Lord Norimasa's! He could not count the times she told him there was nothing between them. Or how often Lord Norimasa said the same thing.

"I see," said Matsuhito. "So there was a reason for Lady Tsukie's jealousy."

"Yes. The first time it happened, she tried to set fire to the palace. She burned down the stables. Three horses were killed. The grooms got the rest out. Afterward, it only happened infrequently. He was very drunk. Later, he couldn't remember."

"I don't care what you did!" the samurai burst out. "I want you to live!"

"How kind you are to say it," Lady Utsu said, beginning to cough. "And I would live, if I could."

"You can!"

"We will see," Lady Utsu said. "It is not always up to us."

"Don't you want to live?" he cried.

"I do," she said. "Believe that is true. Believe also that the young woman who lived with Lord Norimasa in the palace may have been his daughter. But she may also have been yours."

"He knew how loyal to him I was!" the samurai cried. "I loved him! I would never have done such a thing to him! He assured me he had no interest in you in that way! Otherwise, I would never have touched you! And yet he arranged it so that I would betray him!"

"He was drunk and he had help," Lady Utsu said. "I helped him."

"I should have been told the truth!" he said. "I should have been allowed to decide on such a grave matter!"

"All that is true. I told you many times that both Lord Norimasa and I were cruel. I would not do such a thing now. Hiro was taken from us to punish me, not you. It had nothing to do with the box, only with me. Once," she said in a whisper, "I ground up glass. I have been punished ever since."

"What?" asked Matsuhito. "Glass?"

"I swore never to speak of it. I cannot do it now," she said. "Did she do well? The young woman who looked like me?"

"I believe she married," said the samurai. "Her husband was sent to a post in the far north. Everyone expressed sympathy for her, but in truth, I think she was glad. She liked to be alone. Her husband and child were enough for her. Such a woman would find the palace too busy. It's so long ago," he said. "But I remember, or think I remember, how happy she was when she got in the carriage to begin traveling north."

"Probably she, too, was cursed by my cruelty," Lady Utsu said. "To punish me, she was punished."

"The young woman was young and happy. You are torturing yourself to no purpose! Why should you be cursed for grinding up glass? Please stop speaking and rest. I will bring you some water and cold cloths. You are so hot, but in the morning, you will be better."

"You said the same thing about Hiro," she said, smiling.

"Do not say that!" he cried.

"Perhaps I will recover after all," she said.

"Yes! You will!"

When he got up to find the cloth and the tea, tears stung her eyes. How would he manage without her? They had become each other's world. If she died, perhaps he would go back to the bandits. When Shinda came back, he could go then. She would suggest it; if she died, he should go back to Shinda.

She was finding it harder to breathe, and in her chest she suddenly felt a terrible stabbing. It began to run down her arm and she was afraid she would begin to vomit. But the pain died down and it was gone before Matsuhito was back. He began placing cool cloths on her head. "Say the prayer for the Buddha!" he said. "Say it!"

"*Namu amida butsu,*" she said.

"Again," he demanded.

She repeated it, but the pain was returning, and she found herself gasping for breath.

"I am afraid I cannot stay," she said, her voice weak and thready.

"Please do not say that," he said, pleading. "Please do not say it again."

In a hoarse voice, she recited:

> *Winter, and a sky of gray ice.*
> *Water pours over the falls.*
> *Will I also go over?*
> *I think, how like a leaf I am!*

"You are getting better!" he cried. "You are reciting a poem."

"There is a man standing on my chest!" she cried out. "He is heavy! Make him get off!"

"I am taking him off," Matsuhito said, weeping. "I have knocked him to the ground."

"There is another one. Can you not see him? Make him move!"

"He is gone," Matsuhito said, weeping.

"Yes, he is," Lady Utsu said. "He is gone. Thank you."

Her breathing was shallow, and she gasped for air.

"Norimasa!" she gasped. "Once I gave this to you, but it was never mine. I am giving it to him! Let him have it! Before, this was to be my death poem," she said, speaking now to Matsuhito. "But this is yours while you live," she said, and she recited a few words of the poem aloud.

> *The drifting sky.*
> *Can you wear it?*

"It is beautiful," Matsuhito said. He was choking with sobs.

"I have nothing else to give you. I should like to stop breathing now."

"Please!" he shouted.

"Let me go before the man stands on my chest again!" she begged.

"All right," said the samurai. "Take the peace you deserve."

Lady Utsu smiled and then her body relaxed. She no longer breathed.

The samurai picked her up and held her to him, weeping. He must have stayed that way throughout the night, because he was unaware of anything until the light began to seep in. The two foxes were on the floor, looking up at him sadly.

"I will have to build her a coffin," he said to the foxes. "First I must lay her arms at her side or they will stiffen and she will not fit into the box. Then I will wrap her in the cloth picture of the foxes." At that, Lady Utsu's fox yelped sharply. "No, that is not a good idea," the samurai agreed. "I will wrap her in one of her embroidered winter robes. She liked winter. Meanwhile," he said to the foxes, "let her rest here in the splendor she deserves."

He stumbled outside and went up into the stable's loft and came back down the ladder bearing long boards. She was so slender! He built the box and then went inside and lifted Lady Utsu and carried her outside. He placed her in the box, wrapped in her robe. "Now she looks as she always did," he told the foxes. The animals approached Lady Utsu's body. Her fox began to howl. Then his fox began. "You are the only Utsu left," he told his fox. "This place has brought us good luck and bad luck. It is time for me to leave it before anything else happens. I will leave the two of you here. I will tie you to ropes and I will be gone before you can gnaw through them. You will be happy here. Now there is no one I can make happy, not even a fox."

"It is easier to think that now," Lord Norimasa said, "than to think you will forget and once again be happy!"

"Only the dead are happy," the samurai said. "Lady Utsu told me the truth about the child."

"I do not think it was mine," Lord Norimasa said. "But think what you like. What difference does it make? Unless you want to find the girl. She is the image of Lady Utsu."

"I cannot think of anything more bitter," he said.

He began digging the grave. "This time," he told the foxes, "she will not jump when I bang the nails in. She jumped so when I made the baby's coffin." Tears streamed down his face. Finally, the coffin was sealed and he slid it toward the grave. He had to tip it in and let it slide into the opening, and in the end, he had to drop it so that it would enter the hole he had dug for her. When it was time to replace the heaped-up earth, he found it almost unbearable.

The foxes regarded him sadly. "Well, it is done," he said at last, "and tomorrow I will resume my wandering. I will go north, as usual. But you two will stay here and guard the graves. I know you will do it and do it well."

He went back into the hut for the last time, and for the last time there, he lay down on the mat and fell asleep.

BOOK FOUR

CHAPTER THIRTY-SEVEN

ONCE AGAIN, his wanderings were to begin. The sun had barely crept above the mountain when the samurai began dragging out sacks of dried food, his armor and his straw raincoat and hat. He took two earthenware jugs of water and a bag of food for his horse. Then he called the two foxes, who came flying to his side. He did what he said he would the day before, and walked to the woods, carrying two lengths of rope. Then he tied each fox to the trunk of a pine tree. It hurt him to see how trusting they were. "You will have a good time without me," he told them. "Chew through your ropes. Then you will be free."

He stayed awhile between the foxes, stroking each head. "Good foxes," he said, getting up and starting to walk back to his horse. The foxes barked loudly. The samurai wanted to take them, but he knew it would not be right. He could not say what was to become of him. Here, they were used to the woods and their offspring came and went frequently, like dutiful children.

"Well, Kuro," he told the horse, "it is time to go. Perhaps it is I who brought her bad luck."

He mounted his horse and looked at the hut. In the woods, he heard the urgent barking of the foxes. He dismounted, went up to the hut and opened the door. "They might as well live here as anywhere else," he said aloud. He was still in the habit of speaking to Lady Utsu. "And they will want food." He hesitated, wondering how long it would take them to open the compartments beneath the floor. They would accomplish it, but by the time they did, their paws would be raw and bloody. He opened two of the compartments and took out the food stored there. He knew the foxes would take the food and hide it in the woods. "So it is time to go," he said to the house itself. I should set fire to this hut, he thought, but the foxes may need it. They can open the door and drag it closed. Really, they are half human, half animal.

It pleased him to think that, some time from now, someone else would come upon this hut and be happy in it.

He went outside, looked around the clearing and saw a slight yellow haze on the trees. Summer. Again. He mounted the horse, and this time dug in his heels so that the horse flew down the path away from the hut and the clearing. Where was he going? he asked himself. Nowhere. North.

He rode until he needed to rest the horse and let him eat and drink. As was their custom, the horse immediately lay down on his side and the samurai pressed his back up against the horse's spine and went to sleep. When he awakened, the light was going. He tried to remember what he had seen as they rode, but he could remember nothing but the sun.

"Why is it so hard to find east?" Lord Norimasa once asked his men in frustration. "The sun rises in the east! How did you go west? Are you traitors?"

"I am sorry," said the head of the scouting party. "We are not traitors. We are only stupid."

"One more stupid mistake and I will crucify every one of you. Who ever heard of a clan leader looking for his lost samurai? It is disgraceful. You cannot be ashamed enough! What shall I do to them?" he asked Matsuhito.

"I will give them another lesson and give each of them a map," Matsuhito said.

"And if that does not work, and I am not there, order them to be crucified," Lord Norimasa said. He and Matsuhito rode off. When they had gone a sufficient distance, Lord Norimasa looked at Matsuhito and roared with laughter. "Have you ever seen such fools?" he asked. "Now we know why they are not generals."

"Once I found one of the samurai climbing a high tree in all his armor," Matsuhito said. "They couldn't find our camp. They knew it was south of them, but they couldn't find south, so the man climbed up and tried to see the camp. Of course he couldn't. We had hidden it well."

"We can't have this sort of thing going on," Lord Norimasa said. "One intelligent man must go with each contingent. Although I may be asking the impossible."

"Would you employ bandits if I vouched for them?"

"The same bandits who fought at Sanomi? How fast can you find them?"

"Very fast," Matsuhito had said.

The stars were very bright, and Matsuhito could not sleep now. He stared up at the stars and wondered if there were more stars than men killed in battle. Each of those men had families and probably each had several children. He had never truly considered the cost of a battle. He wondered if he could do it now after he had lived with Utsu and the child. Yes, he thought, he could. The desire to kill got in one's blood. No wonder so many masterless samurai turned murderous. If someone had harmed Utsu or the child, he would have killed that person without the slightest regret.

He felt the horse breathing in and out and the sensation brought him consolation. He was not completely alone. He missed his fox. Probably the horse did as well. He began to review his life. "Your will is too strong!" his mother had said. "You think only of battle! You are like a child playing at war games. There is more to a life than that!" She had been right.

Was that why Lady Utsu left the palace when she knew she was to have a child? Did she fear that he, Matsuhito, would not swerve away from Lord Norimasa and instead cleave to her, that Matsuhito would not find time or interest for her? How strange she and Matsuhito both were, each in love with the other, each unaware of how deep their feelings went. Yet, in the end, they found each other again. Few people are given such a chance. Faces began to appear before his eyes, faces he had never seen. They drifted by like bubbles on water and then were gone. Who were they all? Had he seen them or was he conjuring them up? He watched them floating by until he grew drowsy and eventually fell asleep.

It was morning and the early light awakened him. "And what shall we do today?" the samurai asked the horse in a bitter voice. "Of course we will go north and I will stop and weave some new straw shoes for you. Today we will go slowly."

Overhead, a hawk was circling and going lower. Something would die soon. "Probably today we will come to a barrier," he said, "but our papers will fool anyone. No one would be so arrogant as to forge papers from the shogun. On the other hand, we will stick to the lanes, so we may avoid such annoyances."

After several hours, the samurai heard the roar of a waterfall. He dismounted and went through the woods at the side of the road until the trees began to clear out and he found himself on gray rock. He was looking down at a gorge, its walls lined with trees thickly leafed out, and at its bottom ran a stream hidden every so often by the dense trees. The stream looked less like white water than like smoke. He thought of Hiro's little image on the small pyre. Even nature mourns, he thought. His thoughts returned to Lady Utsu, wrapped in her scarlet silk robe, embroidered all over with flowers and flower carts. "It will soon be warm even deep in the earth," he told her, "but you need not fear this summer's heat." Without warning, he saw her face vividly. She was smiling. Tears spilled from his eyes. "When I try to summon up your face, I cannot," he said. "I see you from the corner of my eye, but when I turn to look at you, you disappear. Why did you come back now? Tell me the trick." But there was only the sound of the waterfall far below. "If I come back to this place, will you come again?" he asked, but no one answered.

"You must stop this," said Lord Norimasa. "You are setting worms to eat at your spirit."

The samurai continued along the overgrown path. The rushes lining the path here were sharp and often he got down and cut them before the horse went ahead. Otherwise, the animal would be cut and would bleed, and flies and mosquitoes would begin to swarm around him. The trees were dark green. In secluded valleys, many of the trees still stood as they had in the spring.

He had a sharp desire to see Mount Fuji. Lord Norimasa had said, "I have taken many pilgrimages to see it. I would rather see Mount Fuji than a hundred temples. When you see Mount Fuji, it is always different. Each time, it gives you a premonition of what is to come, or it interprets what has already taken place. Yes, I will go to Mount Fuji again if I do not die."

But to see Mount Fuji he would have to go south. Still, he was in no hurry. He looked at the sun, and changed his path. On the way, he passed a small mountain, a volcano, black smoke rising into the air against the blue sky. The smoke appeared to balance on the top of the mountain like an enormous rock formation. He went on. He passed mountains and sometimes, when he looked down, he saw rice paddies far below in the distance. When the road began to climb, he stopped to look across at the mountains. It was a rough and wild scene. Mists still wreathed the mountains halfway up, and at the ridge, clouds rested on the rim. I have seen mountains before, he told himself. The smell of pine trees was particularly sharp.

After a while, he tired. It seemed to him that he made less and less distinction between his memories and what actually was occurring. He found a large cryptomeria tree and leaned back against it. Within instants he was asleep.

But the vibration of an approaching horse awakened him. His hand automatically made its way to his sword.

"*Baka,*" shouted a familiar voice. "It's me."

Shinda was standing before him.

He dismounted and they sat on the ground and talked. Then a silence fell. Shinda appeared to be pondering something.

"There's a strange story going about," he said. "Would you like to hear it?"

"Why not?" Matsuhito said.

"You may not like this story," said Shinda.

"Tell it," said Matsuhito.

And so Shinda told him this story:

"A MONK WAS making a pilgrimage and his goal was to visit every shrine in the country before he died. One day near twilight, he was in a particularly remote place. Up until that point, the terrain had been rocky, but now it was one grassy plain after another, so he thought, I will sleep here where the ground looks softer and there will be enough grass to make a pillow or I can cover myself with the grass I cut. While he was working, he heard a woman sobbing. How strange to find a woman in the middle of nowhere, he thought. But he decided that if the woman was crying, she might have come here to be alone, and he did not intend to disturb her. The sound of weeping went on and on. Finally, he heard a woman begin to scream, 'My eyes! My eyes!' and at that, he concluded he must find her and try to help her.

"He began to walk in the direction of her voice. But just when he thought he had almost found her, the voice would come from a different part of the plain. After several such attempts, he came to feel that he was not pursuing a person who still lived, but a spirit or a ghost. Finally, after searching persistently, he realized that the woman's voice was becoming louder and louder, and he knew he would come upon her very soon.

"'My eyes! My eyes!' the woman kept crying. But in fact what he saw was only a human skull, and from the eye sockets, the sharp blades of the grass had grown up toward the light.

"The monk was frightened enough to consider running away, but then he thought the skull was a woman whose spirit was still tied to a part of her body, and her spirit wanted to speak to someone. 'What is it?' he asked the voice, and the voice answered, 'I have done terrible things. I cannot rest until I make amends, but I cannot make amends because the people I harmed are already dead.' Now, this, thought the monk, was a problem. 'I will be tortured forever,' said the woman's voice.

"'But what can you have done?' asked the monk, and the woman replied that she had killed two men she loved, and she recited several poems. Then he was sure the spirit speaking was Lady Utsu, and that she was being punished for her past sins. He tried to comfort her, but he was overtaken by a sense of terror, and fled the spot. When he came upon a group of pilgrims on their way to the Grand Shrine at Ise, he told them what he had seen and heard. Since then, the story has been spreading, and a woman of the Emperor's court wrote a *Noh* play about the monk's story, and so the story is becoming well known."

Shinda's voice dropped to a whisper. "Can it have been Lady Utsu?" he asked.

"It was not Utsu!" Matsuhito shouted. "I buried her myself. Her soul is finally at peace."

"But if an animal had dug her up . . ." Shinda said. "A wolf, perhaps . . ."

"No one and nothing has touched her," Matsuhito said. "It was not Utsu's skull."

Shinda nodded, and seemed reassured. "Of course it could not be Lady Utsu," he said.

"No," said Matsuhito.

A damp, thick mist was rolling in and it was difficult to see Shinda clearly. Matsuhito must have fallen asleep, because when his eyes again opened, Shinda was gone.

He thought, I should like to have heard Utsu's voice once more, even if she is now a hungry spirit. But I will not hear her again. Then he thought about the story Shinda had told him, and it seemed to him that he would not have told the story in that way. His language was far more rude. Had he ever been here? Had Matsuhito dreamed the story? Or had Utsu herself come to tell it to him through Shinda?

I am living more and more in the land between spirits and living beings, he thought. I must not become too confused before I have finished my task. It is time to leave for Mount Fuji, and after that, there is only one task to accomplish.

IT TOOK HIM almost fifteen days to reach Mount Fuji and he arrived in the dark. The samurai took down the horse's bags and the horse flopped down on the ground, and once again he placed his spine against the horse's. "We will see it in the morning, and then we will go north," he told the horse. He missed his fox.

In the morning, mist covered the meadow where they had slept. Tall yellow flowers rose up out of the mist as if they floated there. When the horse stood up and moved off to graze, he had no legs and had lost half of his body. His neck and head looked as if they were drifting through the meadow. The sun continued to rise. The samurai chewed on a strip of dried deer meat. He watched as the mists began to lift and the scene came clear. The grass would be wet. The horse would like that. He must have drifted off, because when he next looked, there was Mount Fuji. It was a ghostly sight. Mists were still drifting past the mountain because Mount Fuji was dim and almost hazy. But what was most remarkable was the way the mountain floated in the sky. Between the earth and the mountain was a band of mist so thick that the mountain seemed anchored to nothing. This means something, the samurai thought.

"Do you see how the mountain is separated from the earth?" Lord

Norimasa asked. "That is an image of your soul. You are no longer tied to the earth. You must decide where you belong, in the air, like smoke, or on the ground, like other mortals. You see? Mount Fuji never fails to disappoint you."

He sat for so long staring at the mountain that Kuro came up and nudged him in the back with his muzzle. The mist that separated mountain from land was dissipating. Now it was only a mountain. "We will go on," he said to Kuro, but he believed he had seen a magical thing.

He set out again. He passed wonders. At times, he would stop in a secluded place and inspect the arrows he kept in his quiver. He had two whistling arrows and two that were meant to be ignited in order to set fire to an enemy structure. He adjusted them until he was well satisfied. "I could go into combat with these," he said. The horse snorted.

He found a path that led to the seashore, and, as night was falling, the ocean turned shades of gray, there was a dark gray sky and black rocks near the shore, and the ocean itself striped in every shade of silver. I will not see such a beautiful place again, he thought. The moonlight was so bright that they continued on, but finally it was time to stop.

He lay against the horse and thought. He had seen many wonderful things. He had experienced things even more wonderful. He had seen things he would like to forget. He had never liked seeing the severed heads when they were presented after a battle. Each head had been impaled on a stake and brought to Lord Norimasa.

"So many generals!" Lord Norimasa said. "A good job! Well done! You shall be rewarded!"

In Matsuhito's eyes, the dead men stared balefully.

"You do not like it?" Lord Norimasa asked. "It is the best part. Then you know you have won. You are too squeamish. Or perhaps you sympathize with the enemy?"

Matsuhito did not answer the question.

"Our tastes differ," Lord Norimasa said in a gentler tone. "Are there any more?" he asked his retainers.

"Two more," one of them answered.

"Only two?" Lord Norimasa said, disappointed. "Well, I must not complain. This is a very good crop. Wash them and clean them and put the most important generals in separate vessels and cover them with saké. Put as many of the others in as will fit. The fun is over until next time."

Matsuhito had always intended to learn the name of the village in which he had lived when it was set on fire by Lord Norimasa's troops. He had wanted to know the names of his real parents. He had never known if he was the real child of a farmer or the heir of the Kurono-suke clan. He had never known who he was. Neither had Yoshida's father, the man in the hut.

Neither had Utsu. She was one of the four children confused after the battle. Was she the child of a farmer, or was she the heiress? She herself never knew. They were hopelessly switched. In the end, did it matter whom you loved as long as you did love? And Lord Norimasa himself. There were rumors as long as he lived. People said he was not his father's son, but the child of an unknown samurai who had had an affair with Lord Norimasa's mother. Everyone whispered that he resembled a certain samurai who lived in the palace, a counselor of war. Could his father have been the old counselor?

All of them, not knowing who they were. And somewhere, someone who looked exactly like him, and a young woman who looked exactly like Lady Utsu. Perhaps she was Lady Utsu's daughter, but perhaps she was not. Neither of them knew who they were. The world was a riddle and a trap, and he had fallen into the same snare as everyone else.

"I am tired of this," he said, "and I think life has defeated me. I am a samurai and will not be held captive after a defeat. Kuro," he said, "let us look for a good place, but first I will fill my metal box with burning coals."

He set off again. He began to climb into the mountains. There had been no rain since he had set out, and the earth and trees were very dry, like tinder. This is how I want it, he said. At last, they followed a narrow path into the forest, and in time, he came to a large meadow. Tall grass carpeted it. He used his sword to cut a path into the center of it. Then he went back and led the horse a distance away and tethered the animal to a tree that seemed to grow out of solid rock. "You will be safe here," he told Kuro. "Someone will come for you and find you. And if they do not, you will begin to push and pull on the rope and it will let you go and you may go where you please."

Then he walked back to the center of the meadow. It was twenty times the size of the clearing around Lady Utsu's hut. He looked around him. He heard the horse whinny. The grass was dry and golden. When the wind blew softly, it swayed like waves.

Then he drew one of his arrows and let it fly. A little too close, he told himself. The arrows must reach the edge of the meadow. He opened his metal box filled with burning coals, and touched it to one of the arrows meant to set fire to villages and buildings. At once, the arrow was on fire. He drew back the bow and aimed. This time the shot was true. He saw smoke begin to rise from the grass at the edge of the meadow. At first, the smoke was almost misty, like thin clouds, but then black smoke began to drift up and orange and blue flames began to leap at the edge of the clearing. He had time to think of Utsu, the child and Lord Norimasa. He had time to ask himself if he would see any of them again. He thought not. He stood still and watched the fire begin to blaze. It was coming toward him like an amazing animal. He thought he heard the sharp yelp of a fox. There was nothing left to think or say. He was the still point. He stood absolutely still and waited. He waited until the fire took him.

EPILOGUE

OFTEN, I sit on the stump of a tree watching the mountains, thinking about the story I have just told. Today, everything is shrouded in mist and the colors are leached away by it.

It is peace.

My mother had little peace, nor did my father, nor did Lord Norimasa, but they were not the same people you meet when you are told the stories of the four children.

As accurately as I can, I have written down the story of Matsuhito, Lady Utsu and Lord Norimasa. The scrolls are safe in gold cases. Perhaps someone will find them or steal them.

Now I can rest.

I cannot say I am unhappy.

Were I not so superstitious, I would say I was content. In the end, Lady Utsu created a happy being. I hope she knows what she accomplished. And, of course, I pray for all of them. Yet I often find myself reciting this poem:

> *The color of the flowers*
> *has indeed faded.*
> *In vain have I passed through the world*
> *while gazing at the falling rains.*

It is impossible to be completely at peace at all times, but I have learned not to wish for that.

ACKNOWLEDGMENTS

I would like to thank Merrily Baird, who steered me in the right direction so many times, and whose book *Symbols of Japan* proved invaluable; Richard A. Cone, who first took me to see *The Seven Samurai* so many years ago; the remarkable filmmakers of Japan, with whom I became obsessed when I was sixteen; Olwyn Hughes, who first started giving me Japanese novels; the inestimable Yoshiko Miyakoshi, who taught me to speak Japanese; Mark McKinnon, who found the image of Lady Utsu when he sent me the perfect doll; Tomoaki Minaga, who could find anything; Yasu Umetani, who navigated us through Japan; Melissa and Anthony Berman's magic window; and the entire, amazing class of Advanced Fiction at the University of Chicago:

Erica Bleeg
Casey Carrington
Sangeetha Chandrasekharan
Catherine Chevaux
Robert Peter Cuthbert
Melissa Dean
Gina Di Ponio
Nefrette Halim
Jessica Riddle
Pete Uribe

I am grateful to all of you.

I will always owe a great deal to Sapphire, who first suggested that I return to teaching. She made sparks fly when she hit the nail on my head.

I want to thank everyone who helped me find Japanese dolls dressed in the costume of the period, and found robes, obis, prints and fabrics that let me start sliding inside the world of this novel.

I owe a debt of thanks to International House for its resources and hospitality when I was in Tokyo, and am deeply grateful to Robert McNeil, who helped make it possible for me to stay there. Donald Richie was a delight and gave me a strong sense of the kind of people I hoped to write about. Yoshio Wada, the Japanese theater director, was especially patient in explaining differences between Japanese and American attitudes and was in himself a remarkable resource as a person. I am fortunate to have known him.

And I especially want to thank my husband, who did not object (too much) to the myriad artifacts that made walking through our house nearly impossible.

Susan Fromberg Schaeffer
Chicago, 2003

THE
SNOW FOX
Susan Fromberg Schaeffer

DISCUSSION QUESTIONS

1. The structure of a novel—the events and characters—is the narrative plot. But there is also an emotional or intellectual "plot" in an imaginative work. What does the world of *The Snow Fox* say about the world in which its people live? What is the view of this world meant to communicate to the reader? Are there truths evident in that world that also rule the lives of people existing today? If so, which ones?

2. Matsuhito goes across a stream in search of persimmons, but on his way to pluck the fruit, he finds a box buried in the river. In the box are three things. What are the contents of this box meant to represent?

3. *The Snow Fox* begins with the story of the four children. Why is this important to the novel? Does this story have any importance in understanding what follows?

4. Lord Norimasa is, at times, very brutal. What motivates him? Is he an entirely savage person?

5. When Matsuhito and Lady Utsu meet, they do not recognize each other for some time. They have both aged, but is there another motive that explains their unwillingness to recognize each other? If so, what is it?

6. What significance do the two foxes have in this work?

7. Small narrative events often give a reader an opportunity to understand the major themes of a novel. Why does Susan Fromberg Schaeffer have Matushito discover the man in the cave? Is what he finds there important? The same question can be asked of Matsuhito's encounter with the eta or his encounter with the starving man in the old woman's hut. Why are these events important?

8. Some readers wished for a happier ending for this novel. Would you have preferred one or does the ending feel right?

9. If, at the end of their lives, Lady Utsu and Matsuhito had been asked whether they had led successful lives, what do you think they would have said?

10. A novel often has images that recur until they become themes. In *The Snow Fox*, one such image is fire. Another is snow. Are the two themes linked? Are there other such recurring images that build into themes?

11. Several authors have complained that many historical novels borrow a setting from the past, but have their characters behave as if they had contemporary concerns and customs. Do you find that a problem? How does *The Snow Fox* work toward or against this issue?

12. The events of *The Snow Fox* take place over eight hundred years ago when customs were very different and people's views of the world were very dissimilar. When you read a historical novel, do you hope to acquire information about another era or do you also read such a novel expecting to illuminate your own life, different as it may be? Did reading *The Snow Fox* cast any such light on your own view of the world?

13. Do you think that Schaeffer believes that there is such a thing as happiness? How do you think she would define happiness? If you think that she does not believe happiness exists, what in the novel shows that happiness cannot last?